With the exception of certain historical events and notable figures, the characters and events portrayed within are fictitious.
Any similarities to real persons, alive or dead, are coincidental and not intended by the author.

ISBN- 978-1-7376655-9-5

Cover Artist: Juan Padron

At the Mast

By Cal Clement

"No man will be a sailor who has contrivance enough to get himself into a jail; for being in a ship is being in a jail, with the chance of being drowned... A man in a jail has more room, better food, and commonly better company."

-Samuel Johnson

This book is dedicated to the man who first inspired my fascination with the sea. My grandfather.

Richard Calvin Clement

"Keep the bow pointed head on, straight into the waves."

Part One

H.M.S Allegiance
20 June 1770
Bermuda Harbor

"Hands to make sail!" a tinny edged voice rang over Allegiance's main deck and echoed up into her tops. "Set tops and gallants. Ready on the braces!"

A flurry of activity broke out aboard the British warship. Sailors hurried up the shrouds, while deckhands made ready at the mooring lines. A favorable wind had risen, and while Jack Horner had been curious to see the process of warping a ship out of the harbor, he had been warned that it was slow and cumbersome. From what he was told by his more experienced friend, a sailor affectionately referred to as Bowline Bob, it was also an extremely labor-intensive process. Allegiance angled her way out of the harbor before nosing around to take the wind off her larboard beam. The ship had undergone a massive transformation in the past six weeks. Teams of shipwrights and dozens of other craftsmen had joined their efforts to Allegiance's crew. Together they had repaired the damage done during their bout with a rogue French privateer. The extent of damage from the battle hadn't been known until they had made port in Barbados. Sections of bulwark had been shattered beyond recognition, the forward railing along the foc'sl had been all but blown away, but most concerning had been the damage to her foremast and bowsprit. Deep wounds had been discovered in the foremast, and rather than patchwork the job and reinforce with iron banding, the captain had elected to replace the mast altogether. The bowsprit had suffered a similar wound. Repair crews had actually discovered an eight-pounder cannonball lodged into the heavy wooden beam. It too, was replaced.

The work had taken weeks, with details running from before sunrise until after sunset. It was hard to reckon life on land being more strenuous than at sea, but within the first week, Jack had surmised that there would be no leisure afforded during their time in port. Captain Williams became a man hellbent on a singular purpose. He spent the first two weeks pleading his case with an admiral and netted six heavy twenty-four pounder guns for Allegiance's gun deck. The added weight to their broadside was a morale boost for the entire crew, but the task of loading them aboard was enough to erase the excitement. Their labor in Bermuda seemed to have no end.

As the ship rounded its way out of the harbor, Jack climbed the shrouds to the upper limits of the rigging. Bermuda fell away behind them and under the midday sun, the ocean opened up all around. Clear blue skies and calm seas stretched as far as Jack could see in all directions while a stout wind ferried them along on a southerly course. The watch bell pealed, gulls cawed, and the wind hissed as it filled Allegiance's canvas sails. Being back at sea felt somehow to Jack like going home. The time spent in Bermuda had been far more intense than he had imagined it would, but he had learned more about the craft of sailing than he had during the weeks spent at sea. While they had been hard at work, his friend Bowline Bob had spent many afternoons teaching him various knots and line splicing techniques. Lieutenant Sifton had rated him an Able Seaman, but it was Bowline Bob who made him so.

"Hey yo, aloft!" a voice called up from the shrouds leading to where Jack had perched on the cross of the topgallant. A whiff of rich pipe smoke announced Bowline Bob before Jack turned to look. "Watchin' land slip away with a heavy heart are ye?"

"Nay," Jack replied with a chuckle, "couldn't be rid of it soon enough."

"That's a lad," Bob said with a big puff of bluish smoke. "A sailorman through and through. I knew ye'd be Jack, I knew it from the minute I laid peepers on ye. A right hand to have when the weather turns foul, and a good mate ter have on yer's side in a scrap."

Jack felt his face flush with a streak of embarrassment. The crew had done a fair bit of talking about his exploits during their battle with the rogue French privateer ship. "I don't know what the fuss is, I did my job, nothing more, and Matsumoko was there too, he braved as much as I, if not more."

Bowline Bob hoisted himself up onto the cross of the topgallant mast and straddled the hefty wooden beam between his knees.

"Aye, Matsumoko was there, and doing his part, Jacky. But he was following yer lead, boy. That's what the tars down there on deck are in a fuss about. Ye's a greenhorn pressed man. Ordinary Seaman at the time just fer the facts that One Eyed Kenny smashed his foot under that gun carriage. But, ye's handled yerself like a regular salt. Taking fire at the bow chaser would have been more'n enough fer half the blokes aboard. But, not ye's. Ye went below and kept yer gun firin' right through the thick of it. Not many sailors have that kind of grit right from the beginnin' lad, not many at all."

Uncomfortable with the praise, Jack changed the subject. "Do you think the captain will find his rogue Frenchman?"

Bowline bit at his pipe stem and squinted hard at the horizon. He let a double cloud of smoke escape from his nose. "Aye, I imagine he will. But, it'll be weeks sailin' afore we find 'em. Laid up over two months settin' the old girl to rights, they could have sailed anywhere. May not even be anywhere near the Caribbean."

"But," Jack said to encouraged the old sea hand to continued his thought.

"Aye," Bowline replied. "But, they were sailing these waters to disturb the Brit's trade fer a profit. No place better in the world to do that. Too many hidey holes, too many leeward coves and plenty of shoals and reefs to run a pursuing warship afoul. I'd bet me left eye they're out there, just past the boundary of the triangle, if I had ter guess."

Jack gave that thought a few minutes to simmer. Their first encounter with the rogue privateer had dire consequences for both ship and crew. He wondered if the captain would employ some manner of strategy to their next brush, or if he was determined to beat them in the old naval fashion of drawing abreast, yardarm to yardarm and letting the guns slug it out until the last. He hoped not. His first, and so far, only, experience with ship-to-ship combat had been brutal, bloody, and gut wrenching. Even after months of repairing the damage in a shipyard, there were still grotesque stains on the planks of the gun deck. A visceral reminder of the losses Allegiance suffered on that horrid night.

"Haaaaands, ready for maneuvers!" a voice on the quarterdeck bellowed out with the tinny ring of a brass speaking trumpet. "Reef mains and headstay'sl, helm to come over larboard!"

A flutter entered Jack's heartbeat. All those long days ashore he had dreamed of the ship's return to the sea, and here they were. He relished the chance to ply his newfound craft and learn more about the tricks his experienced shipmates knew so well.

"Better make our way down to the maintop, Jacky," Bowline said while clapping the bowl of his pipe against the palm of his hand. "Wouldn't want the quarter to think we're up here to shirk our duties and all."

Jack shriveled his nose and frowned at Bowline Bob. "Well, Bob. I'm on watch. What exactly are you doing up here? Besides gabbing away the day?"

"Clap a stopper on it, ye scurvy wretch. I was up here ter sees after you!" Bob said with a grin. "We're havin' lines to haul and sail to tuck away, now after it whelp, afore the mate sees you and has yer tied ter the capstan!"

Both sailors laughed heartily and began their climb down to the maintop. Allegiance shifted in her course and the boatswain piped and called out for another sail change while the helm maneuvered the ship again. They came about from a course that had the wind at their starboard quarter and turned until the wind was as close to the bow as it could be without stalling the ship. Orders rang out from the quarterdeck and echoed across the ship and up into the rigging as sailors faithfully repeated the instruction with a lively cadence. The captain was putting Allegiance, and her crew, through paces to ensure seaworthiness. Any weakness in boom or sail would make itself known, and any friction among the crew would be fleshed out during the rigorous sequence of turns, tacks, and sail changes.

After coming as close to into the wind as any helmsman dared, Captain Williams ordered Allegiance to tack over and then back again. After a half dozen turns tacking over the wind, he ordered a course change to a southerly heading and the top men were afforded a break. Jack remained in the maintop with Bowline Bob and his friend Matsumoko.

"Show me that hitch you were using just there, Matsumoko. I don't think I know that one yet," Jack said with particular interest in his friend's rope work.

Matsumoko took up a bite of loose rope and walked Jack through the three steps of tying a midshipman's hitch. "It's easy, they named it so because even a fresh midshipman, still green at the gills can learn it, all while he is being sick over the side." He turned the length of line over to Jack and watched as he repeated the steps and produced the knot with ease.

"That one isn't so bad. Better than the mess I was trying to learn while we were ashore. One eye Kenny had me binding my arms up trying to figure his ropework," Jack said with a chuckle. He handed the finished knot back to Matsumoko and leaned against the mast. "South again, my friend. Off to find the captain's prize."

"If they don't find us first," Matsumoko grumbled as he undid the knot Jack tied and looped the length over a wooden pin on the railing surrounding the mainmast. "We're lucky they didn't blow a hole at the waterline last time. Who is to say it won't happen when we face them again?"

"Maybe Captain Williams has a plan," Jack said while he looked out to the west at the hazy blue horizon. "Bowline says there are all manner of coves and hiding spots among the islands of the Caribbean. The captain may have some clever scheme to give us an advantage over them. They are just a cut above common pirates after all."

A puff of smoke announced Bowline's attention into the matter. "Aye, don't be makin' the mistake of discountin' the sea skills of pirates now lad. Some of the sailorinest men in the world was labeled pirate by the crowns of one European monarchy or 'nother," said Bowline before he drew deep from his pipe and pointed toward the horizon with the stem. "Morgan was a nautical type. Straight from the ranks of some of the best navigators in history. I heard tell in an English pub that he demanded his crew be able bodied aloft to a man. No skirtin' the tops like so many 'o lads scared 'o heights nowadays. And he never failed a boarding action, in all his years, and with all those damn big Spaniard galleons he took, never once was he repelled." He cocked his head and looked at Jack with a wink. "Who's to say, lad. Someday it could be you, legend of the seas and all."

Jack fought the blush building in his face. Bowline knew he loathed undue praise and wasn't particularly fond of the due variety either. "Captain's about done with his maneuvers," he changed the subject. "Suppose he is going to call for close order training?"

Jack looked to Bowline, who was nodding as he drew at his pipe. "Of course he is. Close order, gun drills, maneuvers, all until this tub can do every one of them in our sleep, to a man. He lost his prize once, that won't happen again." Bowline motioned down toward the quarterdeck, where Captain Williams was standing along the weather rail. "He's on Admiralty orders, a prize like the one they have sent him after will net us all a tidy sum of prize pay, and probably give him his next step. He'll be commanding a flagship next, so they can groom him up for admiral rank. Lordship. That's what he is after, lad. Not just rank, real status."

A boatswain's whistle interrupted their idle chatter. "Hands, lay aft fer close order training!" a grizzled voice shouted over Allegiance.

Bowline plucked the pipe from his bite and grinned widely at Matsumoko and Jack. "What did I tell yers? Eh? Old Bowline Bob knows a thing er three, and the cap'n will 'ave his prize."

Jack, Matsumoko and Bowline Bob made their way down to the main deck, where the crew gathered at the waist of the ship. Pistols and muskets were the order of the day, and much of the afternoon was spent training with the use of each. Allegiance's marine contingent led instruction on firing and reloading of the pistol first and then the musket. After several iterations of demonstration, the crew formed two lines and weapons were passed man to man down the outboard formation. Each sailor had three turns to 'dry fire' and reload his weapon in the naval manner of rehearsed training, without powder or shot. At the culmination of these rehearsed rounds, the master-at-arms loudly announced that every man aboard would complete two shots with powder and ball from both a pistol and musket. Tension charged through Jack as excitement built in his blood. He had never actually fired a pistol, and the prospect seemed exhilarating. Loud reports thundered over the larboard beam of the frigate as her hands trained their peers for battle. Jack's turn at the firing line came and went. The loud report, the rigid recoil, the satisfaction of a solid splash a few hundred yards out to sea. Jack was hooked. He wanted to do more than fire a useless round out into the briny vastness. He wanted to fire at a target. As if he had read Jack's thoughts, Lieutenant Sifton stood on the fore of the quarterdeck and issued a challenge.

"I will have a barrel top hung from the extremity of the lee main yard. Whoever can hit it three times, consecutively, without a miss, will receive an extra tot for the evening's grog," said the lieutenant. He smiled as he issued the challenge and scanned the gathered crew for any takers. "But, there is a catch." He paused and smiled even broader. "I will meet the challenger for a single pistol shot. The winner takes the loser's evening grog. That's three tots, and no evening watch." He clapped his hands together and interlaced his fingers into one solid fist held just in front of his chest. "Do I have any takers?"

A few hands rose. Jack thought for a long moment. Three tots was enough to make him sick, and he wasn't overly fond of the rum in the first place, but the lieutenant said nothing about the winner sharing his spoils. He raised his hand.

"Hmmm. Only four challengers?" Lieutenant Sifton said. He furrowed his brow and dipped his head. "You men obviously don't share my affection for good, dark, navy rum." A ripple of laughter spread through the assembly of sailors and a couple more hands rose to meet the lieutenant's challenge. "All right, step up here." He faced the boatswain's mate on watch. "A barrel top from the main yard, if you please. Hang it low enough to be level with the rail."

An orderly shuffle took place on deck, and Jack found himself in line with a half dozen of his shipmates, all in contention for an extra share of rum in their grog and in hopes of winning the first lieutenant's tot of neat rum for the evening. The wind was lively, and the sea was keeping a consistent swell that Allegiance rolled through with a smooth rise and fall to her bow. Jack watched as the first sailor loaded the musket and prepared to fire. He was one of Allegiance's salty hands, a Scot, and a popular voice among the crew. When Jack had first come aboard the British man of war, he'd had a devil of a time understanding the man's dialect, but working in proximity to the Scot in Bermuda had forced him to learn the accent. The Scot spread his feet apart past shoulder width. In a deliberately slow movement, he raised the musket up and braced the stock into the pit of his shoulder just as the marines had instructed. A heartbeat elapsed. Jack looked at the hanging barrel lid as it swayed gently in the lee of the ship. A roar erupted from the musket and the Scot nearly toppled over backwards from the recoil. The barrel lid remained calm at the end of its suspending line, unscathed.

"Y'sonofabitch, its de damned weapon! I aimed fer her centers and squeezed off fair and true! Blimey, bloody, blunderin' bastard!" He knuckled his forehead to Lieutenant Sifton and returned the still smoking weapon over to the master-at-arms. "Beggin yer pardon, sir. Riled, that's all. I aimed fer her damned centers, held her true and didn't jerk on the trigger like the lobsterbacks was tellin' us."

Lieutenant Sifton grinned and nodded. "Aye, Scot, your aim was true enough, but you hefted the trigger so hard I thought you may just snap it off. Better luck next time sailor," He said and then turned to face the swinging target. "Next!"

The next two sailors struck their first shots. Jack recognized one of them as a pressed man from New York. He'd held the musket for so long, Jack thought he might have forgotten how to fire the piece, but the eventual thunderclap ripped through the wind and pushed a cloud of smoke out over the sea. The barrel top spun wildly at the impact of the shot, and a blossom of splinters sprouted from the back side of the wooden target. Cheers rose from the deck, and sailors shouted their congratulations to the pressed man as he calmly lowered the musket and began reloading.

"We got a sharpshooter on our hands, lads. Send the lobsterbacks home, we don't need 'em!" a cry came from the crowd of sailors.

Jack thought he could see the shooter flinch for a second when he raised the musket up to take aim again. A pause passed. The wind slipped through the rigging in its typical whisper and hiss. The barrel top settled to a steady pitch and twist before the musket thundered again with a belch of smoke. Another hit sent the target reeling in a violent spin, and a wild cheer rose from the crowd.

Lieutenant Sifton nodded with approval while the sailor from New York began reloading for his final shot. Jack clasped his hands together in a grip that squeezed the blood from his digits. He hoped for his colonial brethren to succeed at the lieutenant's challenge, if only for the small victory against the king's service. The sailor finished his reload and hoisted the musket up to his shoulder once more. A hush spread over the deck while he took aim. Long moments passed. Jack felt his heart throbbing in his throat. All at once, he realized he was holding his breath while the sailor drew out the pause of aiming far longer than the previous two shots. Allegiance rose with the action of a wave. The target swayed slightly and then drifted back like the slow swing of a pendulum. A roar sounded, and the sailor was momentarily obscured from Jack's view by a cloud of gun smoke. As the grayish white cloud vanished in the briny sea breeze, a scene of defeat became evident. Jack saw the sailor's shoulders slump forward, the target remained on its smooth pendulum swing, untouched.

"Three hits in a row, and then one with a pistol, that is what will win the day, along with no watch and extra rum," the lieutenant called out as the pressed sailor from New York departed the deck. "Who is next?"

Jack felt a nudge at his shoulder. His mouth went dry. It was his turn. A sudden fear of humiliation paralyzed him, but he fought through and forced his legs to move. "I am, sir, begging your pardon," Jack knuckled his forehead and approached the lieutenant and master-at-arms.

"Aim true, young man, your work on the chase guns and gun deck was fine enough, perhaps you are skilled with small arms as well," Lieutenant Sifton said with a slight grin.

Jack took the musket from the defeated sailor and felt the weight of the weapon. A slight tremble developed in his hands as he realized that every eye on the deck was solidly fixed on him. Inwardly, he cursed the swell of bravado that had prompted him to raise his hand. How could he possibly expect to do any better than the three men who had gone before him? They were all more experienced, smarter, stronger. He didn't stand a chance against the first lieutenant's challenge.

The musket weighed heavily in his grip. He took a paper cartridge from the master-at-arms and began loading.

"Have you spent much time with a gun in your hands, young man?" Lieutenant Sifton asked in a low voice so that none would hear outside of the two of them.

"No," Jack mumbled as he withdrew the thin ramrod and replaced it in the stock of the weapon.

Lieutenant Sifton took a deep breath and leaned forward over Jack's shoulder. "Then a word of advice, don't jerk the trigger. Pull it slow and smooth while you focus your eye on the end of the muzzle. Let the barrel top blur in your vision while you hold that weapon steady. Best to lead it a bit if your target is moving, as it is now," the lieutenant said.

Jack hoisted the musket and cocked the trap. He prepped the firing pan with a final bit of powder and steadied himself for the recoil. The wooden barrel top focused in his eye. He squeezed on the trigger, adding more pressure with every passing heartbeat. The lieutenant's advice came to the front of his mind and at the last moment, his eyes focused on the end of the long musket muzzle before a flash and cloud of smoke obscured his vision. The recoil hit Jack's shoulder like he had been kicked by a mule. It rocked his weight backward until he was reeling with steps that threatened to topple him over in front of the crew at large. He could feel a flush build in his face. A wave of embarrassment crashed over his mind as a ripple of laughter spread among the crew. Once he regained his footing, to his amazement, he looked up to find the suspended barrel top spinning furiously on its rope leash.

"A hit!" Lieutenant Sifton exclaimed. "A fine hit. Now, step back up here and give it another go."

Jack's heart raced at the realization that he had already bested the first challenger. He loaded the musket in a deliberately slow manner so he could recover the breath that had been forced from his lungs and calm his thundering pulse. When his hands felt steady, and the musket was loaded and primed, he lifted the weapon back up to his shoulder and cocked the firing mechanism back until it locked in place. He focused on the end of the barrel, just as he had the first time, and squeezed his finger until a roaring report boomed over the side of Allegiance. Pungent smoke flew away and revealed the target as it danced wildly from the impact. Jack had hit the barrel top almost in its middle and a new blossom of deadly splinters protruded from its iron rimmed boards.

"Another hit! He has tied the best so far!" Lieutenant Sifton called out to a roar of shouts and cheers that swelled from amidships.

Jack tried to calm his mind. He almost fumbled the paper wrapped powder charge when the master-at-arms handed it to him. A cautious glance upward confirmed that the crew was still staring at him, watching his every movement. Jack carefully poured in powder and then placed the paper wad. He rammed home the first set of essentials before loading a round shot into the muzzle and then used the ramrod to tamp it down to compaction. With the ramrod stowed, Jack let the weapon hang in his grip and took a deep breath that expanded his chest as large as he felt it could go. He hoisted the musket and settled the butt of the weapon into the crook of his shoulder. With the flat edge of his hand, he cocked the firing mechanism back into its locked position and began the process of aiming that he had used for the first two rounds. His head swam with thoughts. If he scored this hit, he would have surpassed all the prior challengers. His finger drew tight to the trigger, and he began to squeeze. The blurry form of circular wood took shape behind his sharp focus on the end of the musket's long barrel. He squeezed tighter. The striker collapsed into the musket's brass pan and sent a shower of sparks cascading into the primed breech. A flash and roar bellowed out and a cloud of smoke unfurled over Allegiance's side. Jack lowered the weapon and stared over the lee railing. He couldn't believe his eyes. As the grayish smoke cleared away, he was greeted by the happy sight of a barrel top dancing on the end of its rope. He had successfully hit the target, thrice over. A raucous round of cheers came from the crew. They shouted his name and called out for him to hit the last round of the challenge.

"Well done, my lad, well done indeed!" Lieutenant Sifton said. He clapped Jack on the shoulder. "Now, for our final round. Pistols!" He turned to the master-at-arms. "If you please?"

The master at arms unholstered a flintlock pistol and handed it to Jack. "The trigger is a bit light, just a breath on it, lad."

The weight of the pistol seemed heavier than the musket somehow. Jack knew it wasn't so, but as he lifted the weapon to aim, his arm felt like a cooked noodle. The sighting image he had achieved with the longer weapon became a fickle picture, as his arm trembled under the strain. He tried to calm his nerves with a deep breath. The barrel top shifted as Allegiance crested over a wave. The seas were growing stouter, Jack noticed. They had been since the lieutenant had issued his challenge. He released his breath in a long, slow exhale. A moment passed and the barrel of the pistol lined up with the circular wooden top. He squeezed the trigger with abandoned hope that his shot would find its mark. He had done better than any other challenger thus far. If it ended here, he could still hold his head high.

The cloud of smoke slipped away. Jack felt like his heart seized in his chest. His breath caught in his throat. The wooden barrel top tumbled from its suspension down to the waves. The rope that had held the target danced in the wind, its end frayed from a violent break.

"He shot the damned rope away!" the master-at-arms exclaimed.

"Three cheers for Jack, a dead eye if I've ever seen one!" shouted Bowline Bob. The crew roared with approval and cheers lifted from Allegiance's deck.

Sheer disbelief gripped Jack. He stared at the round wood target as it slipped away in the growing swells. A hand clapped onto his shoulder, and he looked over to find Lieutenant Sifton smiling down on him.

"A fine job, but I am aggrieved. You denied me my chance to defend my rum ration, you rascal," he said. "Perhaps a rematch on another occasion will be in order." His dark brows furrowed deep over his nose. "You prove to be a fine shot, young man. I suppose you must have experience. Did you learn to shoot from your father?"

Unsure of how to answer, and still stunned by the result of the final shot, Jack shrugged his shoulders. "Beggin your pardon, sir. But, my father was a blacksmith. We lived in Boston and owned no firearms. Closest I've ever been to one was through a glass display," He said with a breaking voice.

"Well, nevertheless, I'm sure he would be proud to see it. You will have to write him a letter and inform him of your newfound skill set. I'm sure he will be proud to hear it," the lieutenant replied. "Assuming you can write, and all. If you can't, I can assist you with such."

Jack swallowed at the thought. He felt the hot iron of old wounds burning in his belly. "No, sir. It's no use. He can't read my letters anyhow."

Lieutenant Sifton nodded brusquely. "You can tell him on your return to Boston, all the same." He patted Jack's shoulder and gingerly relieved him of the heavy pistol still clutched in his grasp. "I'll have that, lad. Why don't you rejoin your shipmates. Training is concluded for the day. We will pipe hands to supper soon."

Jack knuckled his forehead and turned to rejoin the rest of the crew amid a storm of shouts and cheers. Bowline Bob was standing alongside Matsumoko, both with broad grins on their faces.

"Sir," an approaching Petty Officer said to lieutenant Sifton. "Mr. Goodover's respects, and he wishes me to inform you that the weather glass has been dropping since we left port."

"Aye, that is common this time of year. How much has it dropped? Did he tell you?" Lieutenant Sifton asked casually.

"Fifteen points since we left Bermuda, sir," the Petty Officer reported. "Twelve of those in the last two hours."

Jack turned to the first lieutenant, curious to see his reaction to the news. The officer remained steadfast on the deck. His face betrayed no strong emotion, nor did his posture change perceptibly. "Twelve points in two hours, and nothing but clear skies as far as I can see. Nevertheless, we trust the glass. Have the Boatswain begin making her ready for weather, and see to it that the launch boats are put over in tow. That much of a drop in such a short time means a fast moving storm. Heavy canvas for the jibs and mains, if you please, and let's double the brace lines with Dutch preventers." He turned to another Petty Officer standing nearby. "Pipe the hands to supper and let the men fill their bellies. It could be a long night for us all."

H.M.S Allegiance
20 June 1770
31 Degrees 36′ N, 65 degrees 37′ W

Supper was a boisterous affair. Jack was cheered as a hero for his triumph against the first lieutenant's challenge. By the time he had collected his ration of grog and a plate of beans with pork bits, a piece of hard cheese and ship's biscuit, his shoulders were sore from a constant barrage of congratulatory pats and playful punches. He settled down to eat with his messmates and distributed the majority of his extra grog among them. One Eyed Kenny, Bowline Bob,

Matsumoko and a fellow from the press in New York who was new to their mess. Sailors shouted their approval and toasted his feat of marksmanship. Jack thought the flush of embarrassment would never leave his face.

"He's a dead eye, this one! Just wait until that Frenchy shows herself on the horizon, he'll be picking them off from a mile away he will!" a sailor cheered with his grog can raised high.

"Did you see the look on that l'tenant's face? He's baffled by 'im! Like ter make him a Petty Officer soon!" another roared before slamming his emptied vessel down in front of him. "He's a regular one fer up and over th' side, he is. A fellow yer want next ter ya when the guns start ter roarin' and there's blood on the decks!"

Jack felt his head spin as he settled in for his meal. The praises of his shipmates continued and made his meal of hard bread, beans and pork all the sweeter. Allegiance was pitching through increasing seas. The sway and flicker of lanterns below deck betrayed her heaving motions. Most of the sailors seemed oblivious, though Jack could see some faces beginning to turn a different shade as the meal continued.

"One of the mates addressed the first lieutenant as I was leaving, Bob," Jack said as he was tearing at a chunk of hard bread. He dipped the biscuit into his grog and swiped it through the pile of beans on his wooden plate. "He said the weather glass had been dropping since we left Bermuda. Does that mean anything to you?"

Bowline shrugged and spooned a mouthful of the meat and bean mixture. "Depends on how much. These waters are notorious for whipping up weather at a turn o' the watch, sometimes less." He wiped his mouth with a sleeve and took a slug of grog from his cup. "This time of year, could be a little bluster, no more'n a few hours 'o reduced sail and miserable rains. But, there's known to be frightful bad squalls down in these parts too, and hurricanes besides. Did the mate say how much the glass had dropped?"

Jack cleared his mouth of food and lowered his voice. "He said fifteen points, and twelve of those in the last couple hours. Is that bad?"

"I'm no expert," Bob said with a wince. "But, even I know that a drop in the weather glass means a storm. I can only imagine, if a Petty Officer addressed the l'tenant and rattled off the figures, it can't be good."

"Storm's a brewin'," One Eyed Kenny said with a rasp. "I don't need a weather glass ter tell ye that! Seas been risin' fer the last two hours. Don't take a damned weather glass. Clear skies and seas comin' up like they is. Even a green landsman ought to know there's a blow brewin'."

Jack felt his stomach tighten. He slogged down the last of his grog ration in a gulp and set his rough cut mug down just in time to hear the boatswain's whistle piping all hands.

"All hands! All hands, topside, tops aloft to make sail, jibs and stays fer a gale a' coming in!" a voice shouted down the main hatch. "Batten those gun ports and make ready on the brace lines, sharpish!"

Allegiance's gun deck boiled over into a hive of activity. Sailors hurried to stow their mess gear, each man making way toward his part of the ship through the frenzy. Gun captains began the work of sealing their individual gun's port, makeshift tables were stowed away, cups, plates and spoons were tucked neatly into sea chests and kit bags. As Jack made his way topside, the ship heaved with action from a wave. He kept his footing and barreled his way up the steep steps of the ladder well and up onto the main deck.

In the time the crew had been at supper, the winds had shifted from their starboard beam around to their stern. Allegiance was running before the wind with opposing seas that crested in foamy white caps. Jack scanned the skies and found that the wispy white tendrils of clouds were retreating southward from a northern advance of cumbersome dark rollers with an ominous shadow stretching from their front to obscure the northern horizon. The wind was strong, and much cooler than it had been since they were in the northern seas by Boston and New York.

"Captain! We aren't going to make it, she's going to catch us!" an officer shouted from amidships back to the quarterdeck. "I might say, we should shorten sail and get ready for the bluster."

"Nay, Mr. Dobson. We run for as long as we can, we'll reef our canvas only when we absolutely must. This will make for a boon to our journey southward," the captain replied as sailors flooded the deck from the main and fore hatches. He turned toward the helmsman. "Make your course south by west, put this wind at our starboard quarter and watch it drive us right to the doorstep of the Caribbean."

Jack made his way to the main shrouds while Allegiance sloughed down in between rolling waves and then pitched hard as she climbed the next set. He felt a hand slap onto his shoulder and squeeze as he reached for the thick shroud lines that would lead him aloft.

"Keep yer wits about ye, lad. This here's sailin' weather fer nautical types. Real sailorman work. Remember what I taught ye, one hand fer the ship, one hand fer yerself!" Bowline Bob said over his shoulder as the wind grew in intensity. "These are fixings fer a right howler. Best ter stick close ter yer mates and keep yer eyes on yer work."

As if on cue, a bluster of wind picked up and pressed Allegiance forward in a lurch. Jack seized the shrouds in hand and began his climb to the maintop. The wind pressed his loose fitting sailor's rig and for the first time in weeks he felt a chill creep across the skin of his arms and legs. Gone were the days when his hands were shredded by the biting grain of the shroud lines, the flesh of his palms and fingers was now guarded by thick callouses. He had grown accustomed to the pitch and sway of the ship, and while the crew was held over in Bermuda, he had come to miss the sense of constant motion. Also gone were the days when Jack would reach the maintop with the last of his strength. His arms, legs, and back were now conditioned to the rigors of sea life and the extended labor of climbing aloft and working the sails and rigging. He had seen foul weather before, but not since before the Royal Navy had boarded Salem Tide and pressed him into their service. The winds were growing in strength, and by the time Jack reached the maintop, a press of rain began to fall.

"They'll be calling to shorten sail any minute now," Mr. Skagg, captain of the maintop, said with a throaty growl. "I want ye's ready on the tops'l yard. In weather like this, they'll call fer the tops to reef first."

Jack followed Bowline Bob out along the tightrope of the topsail yard. Matsumoko followed behind them both, with another sailor close behind him. Mr. Skagg's prediction was correct. Within minutes of filing out along the yard in the heavy swell and driving rain, a shout from the quarterdeck came to reef and furl the topsail. Jack and his mates went to work in a quick fashion. They took in the rain sodden canvas hand over hand until it was bunched against the mass of the yard. Each man secured three points of cordage along the section of sail he had hoisted. The winds blustered even stronger, and Jack had to fight to keep his balance while he hunched over the yard to tie off his knots.

Allegiance shifted her course slightly and the predictable path of motion in the tops changed. Jack felt himself rise with the action of the ship taking a wave on the bow and then with no warning the mast changed direction. Bowline Bob shouted a warning to hold tight while the mast heaved over in a larboard pitch. Jack felt the yard fall with the rapid wave action. He hunched forward and wrapped his arms over the bulk of reefed sail and wooden beam. The pitch upward came as the ship recoiled from the wave action. It felt as though he would be flung from the stretches of the yard and fly through the air to a violent splash into the sea. He chanced a look forward and saw that Matsumoko had hunched down and was holding on for dear life to the yard in the same manner. Inboard from Matsumoko, another sailor had been caught off guard by the wave action. He hadn't braced himself for the recoil action. Jack tried to shout a warning, but his voice was lost in the bluster of wind that battered against the ship. The sailor lost a step from the tightrope as the yard pitched upward. A tremble shuddered through the line and reverberated into Jack's feet. He could feel the sailor's struggle to regain himself. The faltering sailor slipped again in the upward travel and fell in between the tightrope and the topsail yard. Jack felt his insides tighten as he watched the desperate struggle. Time seemed to slow as the sailor stretched his arms in a bid to arrest his fall. He managed a handful of bunched canvas from the sail they had just bound to

Jack kept his weight precariously balanced over the bulk of the topsail yard, his hands never far from a secure handhold and ready to brace himself against the wooden beam at any moment. Allegiance shifted again as a contrary wave washed into her starboard beam. The pitch and sway of the ship was just as intense as the storm he had experienced aboard Salem Tide. He remembered that fateful bluster, and the rogue wave which had nearly washed his now dear friend Matsumoko overboard to a frigid, watery death. Jack had saved Matsumoko that day, and earned himself the steadfast friendship of a young man who was fiercely loyal, and who had since returned the kindness at least once.

When Jack reached the mast, his relief was short-lived. Allegiance shuddered as the winds shifted again and the helmsman struggled to keep her course steady. Waves were irregular and slapping alongside her hull at odd angles. Jack looked over the side and out to sea, visibility had dropped to no more than a few hundred yards as a wall of gray haze and rain closed in around the ship. The movement high aloft in the rigging was wild and unpredictable, unlike anything Jack had experienced before. He kept Bowline Bob's advice in the front of his mind and held tight, only moving one limb at a time. Flashes tore through the darkened skies and an ear-splitting roll of thunder boomed through the storm. The winds were blowing even stronger when Jack began to descend the shrouds to the maintop. They battered his face, neck, and back with stinging drops of cold rain. His fingers ached from the tension of constant grip and his muscles shivered from the cold wind and driving rain. He wondered about the final moments of the sailor who had fallen and recalled the horrified look on his face the instant he had lost his grip on the sailcloth.

An exchange took place on the quarterdeck. Jack saw the captain standing a few paces behind the helm. At his side were a pair of officers who appeared to be pleading with him over something immensely important. Captain Williams stood resolute against the wind and rain. He looked impervious to the motion of the ship, one hand on the weather rail and the other tucked neatly away in his dark blue boat cloak. His hat had been surrendered to his cabin, for fear of the wind ripping it away, but it took none of the commanding presence away from the tall, dark-haired man. His face looked as hard as ever, unyielding to the storm, determined that it would not dissuade him from his course.

"They're begging 'im to reef up the last 'o these sails. Stubborn bugger. He'll get what he's after if'n he iddn't careful. The masts will crack up and then we'll all be a-tossin' in this storm with nothing but our hopes and dreams to keep us upright," Bob groaned as a fresh volley of winds battered Allegiance. Rainwater dripped from his face and his sodden clothes. Jack thought he looked rather like a drowned rat with the way he shriveled up his nose and frowned toward the quarterdeck. "The chase for this privateer is going to be the death of every one of us, Jacky. Watch an' mark my words. Better we be fer getting off 'o this tub."

A voice cried up from the quarterdeck fringed in a tinny ring and an edge of alarm. "Reef those mainsails aloft! Smartly, now men, look lively."

The battle on the quarterdeck had been won. Allegiance would reef in the last of her sail and ride out the worst of the storm before any damage was done to her fresh refit. From the maintop, it was a straight venture out on the main yard to haul in canvas. From the lower elevation, the ship's movements would not be nearly as drastic. The wind and driving rain ensured the task would be just as miserable and hazardous, but the shortened severity of height at least worked somewhat in their favor. Hands from the maintop shuffled their way into position along the yard while waves continued to batter and toss the ship in wild motions. Allegiance took a wave on her starboard bow which sent her reeling over a point or two before the helm recovered. Another wave crashed over the larboard bow, this one was tall enough to soak the foc'sl in its lap and sluiced the decks leading back to the quarter in a few inches of rushing seawater. Through it all, the captain stood as hard as iron, defiant to the effects of the storm, his face a dripping picture of steadfast resolve.

"Ready, now. Heave!" A shout from below signaled all hands to begin hauling in canvas while the clew lines were taken in from the main deck.

A gust of wind blasted Allegiance from her larboard quarter while she still reeled from the slamming impact of a wave. The ship tottered for a moment, all hands braced themselves against the contrary motion. Another wave rose up from the starboard side of the ship. Foam white capped its crest while a wall of greenish gray reached up and engulfed Allegiance in its fury. The sea seemed to have dark designs against them, for even as the wave washed over the deck of the ship and drained from her scuppers another howl of wind came from the north and hurried through the rigging. The wet canvas pulled taut, and Allegiance surged sideways as the force of the wind slammed the main yard at an opposing angle to the ship.

"Helm, hard over starboard! Right this ship or it will be the death of us!" the captain's voice thundered over the deck and rang high aloft.

On the tightrope, Jack and company held on with every ounce of tenacity they had. The sudden whip of the yard had thrown one sailor off the starboard side to a watery impact. Deckhands and Petty Officers cried out the alarm for a man overboard, but were silenced by the grave, unflinching stare of Captain Williams.

"Haul her over starboard, and reef that mains'l!" Captain Williams roared. "That canvas could have been hauled twice over by now! Look alive you top hands! Or I'll see every one of you with a holy stone in your hands until we make port!"

Jack felt a pang of resentful anger swell in his chest. The canvas would have been reefed if the captain had assented to the sailing master's plea when it was first given. That would have spared the soul now doomed to drown in the storm-tossed waves.

"Heave! Heave away fer yer lives, lads!" Bowline Bob shouted through the wind and rain.

The sodden canvas was coarse and heavy in Jack's hands. It fought against his grip and made every handful a fight to the finish. When the mainsail was finally reefed, and double secured with heavy cordage, the top hands were finally piped down to lay aft with the rest of the crew and ride out the storm. Allegiance would maintain her bearing against the brunt force of the seas with head sails, jib, and a half reefed spanker. They had tried their damnedest to outrun the weather, but failing that, the best they could do was keep her keel down and the waves on her bow.

Below deck, Allegiance seemed like a dismal cross between an infirmary and a funeral parlor. Sailors, even those seasoned to the toss and roll of a ship at sea, were being sick everywhere Jack turned. The slow weep of Allegiance's hull kept the berthing bay and gun deck in a state of cold, clammy, misery. The smell of regurgitations was inescapable. Wooden pails were inadequate to the task of containing wretched stomach contents as long as the violent motion of the ship continued. Jack paused at the base of the aft ladder well. He considered braving the storm on deck but was quickly hurried along by sailors eager to escape the blustering winds and rain. Supper was called, and while many hands abstained from food, the grog ration was doled out and consumed with eager thirst. Jack took up his typical spot by the larboard number seven gun carriage. He tipped a pair of wooden planks over the hulking iron weapon and settled them between gun seven and gun six. It was the spot where his messmates had gathered since he had first been pressed into the king's service aboard Allegiance. A streak of sorrow tugged on his mind as he noted the overturned half crate where his friend called Slop used to sit, and the notched initials of 'J.L' that his past messmate John Long had carved into their makeshift table. The ship rolled hard to its starboard side and the sound of water rushing over the hull wooshed and swished. Drips of seawater rained down from in between the overhead timbers. Allegiance was by any measure a tight ship, but no amount of pitch or daub could keep the storm out entirely. As the hull rolled back on the opposite sway, Jack leaned into the motion. He tipped his grog to keep from spilling the precious contents all over himself.

"That's a lad, Jack," Bowline Bob said with a toothy grin as he approached with plates of rations for them both in hand.

"Bob, I can't eat," Jack protested. "Not in this, not with the smell."

Bob shook his head and scrunched his nose. "I'd agree wit' ye, lad. Its ripe below deck. But, ye's goin' ter needs yer strength. We'll have sailorin work ter do before this is out, mark me words, and yer'll want yer strength about ye's. Eat something. Ship's biscuit at least. It's not bad, hardly any weevils and still soft enough ye might not break yer teeth on it."

Bob handed over a plate with two round pieces of cold salted pork and a pair of ship's biscuits. He squatted down and sat on an overturned bucket used to swab the cannon during firing and dug into his own meal in between hurried sips at his own grog.

"That sailor who fell from the tops'l yard," Jack said while pinching at his hard bread to break it into manageable chunks. "Did you know his name, Bob?"

Bowline Bob offered Matsumoko a smile and nod as he sat down with them for his supper before answering. "No, no, I didn't. That's a hard way of going though, a fall like that. I've seen it before, ship a tossin' in weather and hands out on the yard fer reefin' and such. That's why I tell ye's ter keeps one hand fer the ship and one fer yerself. Poor bastard didn't stand a chance as soon as he missed that step and alls he had was one hand ter grip with." Bob stared across the deck with his grog held just shy of his mouth like he was lost in thought. The thought passed, and he drank deep.

"And the sailor who fell overboard," Jack continued, but was cut short as Bob pulled his rough cut mug away from his mouth and swiped his lips with a sleeve.

"I know what yer thinking, lad. And, I'd say the same," Bob said. "But, its best we not talk too loose in mixed company. Too many ears fer hearin' here below deck, if yer know my meaning."

Jack ignored the seasoned sailor's warning. "If the captain had just relented the sails when the sailing master first said..."

"Aye," Bob interrupted in a raspy whisper. "He may not have lost the second man, eh? I says I agrees with yer, lad. No need ter go blabbing our yappers about it. Iff'n the wrong ears hear ye, it'll be a dozen at the capstan if yer lucky, and a short drop an' sudden stop from a yard iff'n yer not. Put a stopper in it fer now."

Jack pressed his lips together tightly. He felt his face flush with a mixture of anger and embarrassment. He could not let go of the fact that the captain's hesitation had resulted in such a tragic event. His mind gravitated outward through the thick hull timbers and lingered over the cold water of the Atlantic. In the waves and driving wind and rain, somewhere, was a sailor who had just within the last hour been climbing aloft a few men behind Jack in the shrouds. He had slept in the same berthing deck, drank the same grog, and heard the same songs for weeks. Jack wondered if the man was even still alive, still fighting against the waves in hopes of being rescued. He wondered if the fall had rendered him unconscious, or if he had already been swallowed by the depths and dragged below to Neptune's watery lair. The thought brought a chill up Jack's spine, and he shuddered involuntarily. He sipped at his grog and listened to the chorus of misery playing out all across the deck. Allegiance creaked and groaned under the strain of wind and wave, while her decks continued to weep salty seawater. Evening crept on, and little changed in terms of the sea state. The ship heaved and pitched while wind howled outside with an ominous hollow shriek. It would be a long night. Bowline Bob heaved himself to his feet with a grumble about having to relieving himself in the storm.

"The damned poop rail is going to be miserable," he growled. "And were I a lesser sailorman, I'd be a might skittish about fallin' overboard like the poor wretched soul earlier. But, rest easy my mates. Bowline Bob is the sailorinest sailor you've ever laid eyes on. I'll be back, mark me words. Wetter than a bilge rat and probably in a foul mood. But, I'll return."

A heave of the ship caused Bowline to hesitate slightly as he strode the deck aft for the rear hatch. Jack looked at Matsumoko, his friend's stony expression tinged ever so slightly green.

"Are you well, Matsumoko?" Jack asked as the ship rushed downward with the motion of carrying through a through between rolling waves.

"I'll be fine," Matsumoko replied with a dismissive shake of his head. "My supper won't be up to spoil the little bit of clean deck we have, if that's what you mean."

Jack chuckled and cracked a smile. Matsumoko was putting on a brave face in the midst of the ship's incessant motion. The smell below deck was enough to make most men sick, the smell and the never ending movement combined tested even the hardiest of seafarers.

"Are you not uneasy at all, Jack?" Matsumoko asked with a quick look from the corner of his eyes. "There are old salts stricken with green right now."

Jack shook his head. "I don't feel sick, if that's what you mean. The smell is horrid, but it always smells foul in this tub. I think my mind is occupied by other matters."

"The captain?" Matsumoko whispered low.

"Aye, the captain." Jack said with a slight nod. "He is so set against this rogue privateer that he will blatantly discard a human life? Abandon a man in his charge to a sure death in a storm at sea? What kind of monsters are these Brits?"

Matsumoko lowered his chin close to his chest, a long pause elapsed, and it looked to Jack as if his friend were fighting away the urge to be sick. He looked up at Jack after a long while. "The captain has a terrible burden of duty, Jack. He must weigh the common good of every man aboard against the life of one, in circumstances such as earlier. He must also weigh the lives of every man aboard against the duty of his tasking and the greater good of his nation. I do not envy him."

Jack could hardly believe what he was hearing. Was Matsumoko, his own dear friend, defending the ship's captain? "I don't understand, Matsumoko. If he had only relented to reefing sail when the sailing master first proposed it, that man would not have fallen."

"Who is to say that?" Matsumoko replied. "Perhaps the sailing master was not calling for the sails to be reefed after all. There is no way we could hear their conversation from up on the main yard, Jack. I know I couldn't. Maybe it was the captain who was more concerned with reefing sail? We don't know."

"You and I both know how set he is on finding the French ship," Jack said with a touch of frustration in his tone. "He is consumed by it. It is madness."

"It is his tasking, Jack. He has to pursue the privateer. The Articles of War apply as much to officers as to anyone. If he were to be found wanting in his pursuit of the enemy, he could be subject to court martial," Matsumoko said in a calm voice. "But, Bob is right, Jack. We shouldn't be discussing this, not down here where there are so many ears to overhear. We have already said too much."

The ship rolled hard to one side, pitching the deck at an angle that would be nearly impossible to traverse. Jack tensed his entire body and gripped at the gun carriage next to him to avoid sliding across the gun deck. His anger bit at his throat. He replayed the scene in his mind, the courtyard in Boston, the gathering of angry residents, the cloud of gun smoke that came after. He'd lost his parents to British musket fire, his freedom to the Royal Navy's practice of impressment, how much more would he lose?

As Jack stewed over the loop of thoughts that refused to let him free. He stared at his friend, disbelieving that he could feel so cold to the blatant disregard for a man's life. But, something else was off. Jack couldn't quite place it. Something gnawed at the back of his mind and wouldn't let go. He thought for a moment. His stare fixed on Matsumoko. Something was indeed wrong, but he couldn't place it.

Matsumoko turned and frowned. "Jack, don't be cross with me. I'm only telling you things as I see them."

Just over Matsumoko's shoulder, Jack saw a motion that wasn't right. Something in the ship was wrong. A movement, imperceptible at first, came from the area of the starboard gun number four. Jack sprang to his feet, the timber he and Matsumoko had used as a table toppled to the deck.

"On deck! That gun! That gun is coming loose!" Jack shouted. He ran in a ragged jaunt as the ship pitched bow up against a wave and then rolled larboard. "Help me!" he shouted as he skidded to a halt at the rear of the loosening gun carriage. "She's about to go!"

H.M.S Allegiance
20 June 1770
31 Degrees 36′ N, 65 degrees 37′ W

"Loose cannon!"

The piercing cry rang through Allegiance's gun deck and sent all hands into a frenzy of activity. Jack raced with everything he had to the site of the shifting gun carriage while a storm of sailors withdrew in fleeing panic. Without hesitation, Jack seized the gun's loosed side tackle and heaved against the weight with all of his strength. The slight shift of the great gun had grown as the rolling motion of the ship loosed the other line securing her. Instead of a barely perceptible shift, the cannon rolled inboard and her heavy iron barrel slammed down against her hardwood carriage frame. Jack held for dear life to the thick tackle line and the force of the shift nearly pulled him off his feet. He cried out in desperation and anger, "Help! Help me! We've got to secure her or she'll ram a hole in the hull!" His heart sank as Allegiance pitched forward again and began a larboard roll. The shift of the gun heaved against Jack's pull and dragged him to the deck. He felt the weight of her, she would never relent to his strength alone. He forced himself to his feet, battling against the tackle line again as Allegiance rolled to the opposite side and heaved forward. Hand over hand, Jack raced for every bight he could seize as the gun shifted back against the hull. One more, he knew, one more hard roll like that and there would be nothing he could do to stop it. In his mind he determined that if the starboard gun number four should go loose on the gun deck, it would have to go with him in tow, and freshly skinned from being hauled through the tackle block. He braced for the impact he knew was coming. Allegiance's bow surged upward. The roll to larboard was coming next. His fingers gripped the line so tight he felt fibers of the coarse rope embedding in his flesh.

A set of hands clamped their grip onto the side tackle line, right behind Jack's. Jack knew that even two wouldn't be enough. He turned to see what maddened soul had decided to join him in his desperate plight and nearly shouted as he found Matsumoko's determined stare focused right back at him.

"She's about to go on us, hold for everything we've got!" Jack said.

The ship groaned and pitched at an angle toward her larboard side. The weight of the gun pulled at the side tackle and Jack felt his grip already beginning to fail. He fought against the force, his arms crying out in desperate protest, the weight was too much. Jack and Matsumoko fought against the tackle line, their feet slid on the deck and inch by inch they lost their battle no matter how they heaved and fought.

"You sorry sacks of lubber scum! Help them! Come on boys, or it'll be the briny depths fer the ship and shark bait fer all of us!" the thundering voice of Bowline Bob filled the gun deck. Jack felt a sweep of relief come over him. Allegiance rolled back to her starboard side, and the gun slammed forward against the hull. The distinct crack of timbers split through the sound of waves washing along the outside of the ship. As he had before, Jack seized up every inch of the tackle line he could and braced himself for the next round.

"Grab that tackle line!" Bob shouted. "You there! Get a wedge behind one of her wheels! We'll get her secured boys, just hold her through this roll!"

A band of sailors joined the effort just as Allegiance began her leeward roll to the larboard side. The weight of the gun pitched, but with more hands to hold her, only a few inches were surrendered. Jack felt as if the storm had broke around him and sun was beaming in through the gun ports. It wasn't so, of course, Allegiance continued to be battered by a howling gale that brought driving sheets of rain and waves crashing over her decks. But, the gun had been saved from running away. A loose cannon in high seas could be the death of a ship, and all her occupants. Jack had heard tales on the dockside in Boston of how catastrophic a wild gun rolling free on deck could be.

"What in depths is going on down 'ere?" a raspy shout bellowed through the gun deck.

Jack turned and saw a pair of Petty Officers walking the length of the deck headed straight for the starboard gun four. He kept his grip on the tackle line while the sailors all around him finished securing the cannon and its carriage.

"High seas and a shabby knot, is my guess. Beggin' yer pardon, Mr. Blythe, but if it weren't fer young Jack here, we'd 'ave been stove in by our own gun. Jacky didn't hesitate none at all, he dove right in there and grabbed up that tackle line ter start a heaving like he was a-going ter cinch her all by hisself!" Bowline Bob crowed in his rasping voice.

Jack, doubled over and drawing ragged breaths from the effort, chanced an upward glance as Bob finished his bragging rant. His arms felt like they were on fire while his legs wobbled at the knees and refused to obey his command. He found the hard face of Petty Officer Blythe, a boatswain's mate with a particular penchant for use of his starter and as hard and foul a temper as any sailor aboard.

"Is that so, young man? A marksman and a hero is it?" the voice didn't belong to the foul tempered Petty Officer. Jack lowered his face and fought against an urge to vomit, the first he had since the outset of the storm.

"Well, the first l'tenant is speaking ter ye! Stand straight ye dog, and answer 'im!" Mr. Blythe hissed in a menacing growl.

"Easy, Mr. Blythe, easy now. Can't you see? He's spent. And for good reason. It takes a minimum of four men to manipulate those guns, and he hazarded himself to arrest a loose cannon on his own. That is action to be commended," Lieutenant Sifton chastised the Petty Officer before stepping forward through a cluster of sailors. "Make way, there, I want a look at him."

Jack forced himself upright. His head spun. Allegiance heaved forward and the gathering of men took a collective step to compensate. "Aye, sir, I caught the gun moving out of the corner of my eye. I knew if it got loose, it would wreak havoc with the way the ship is tossing about. So, I did what I could to set it to rights."

Lieutenant Sifton grinned in the swaying flicker of dim lantern light. "A marksman and a hero indeed. But, young man, I am cross with you. You won away my rum ration without the courtesy of allowing me to defend it. But, I suppose, such should be expected from a top rate sailor like yourself. We've already rated you Able Seaman. What more could you be aspiring to?"

Jack stumbled for words. He had no idea how to answer the lieutenant's question. "I, well, I just… ahhh. Sir, I just, well, I didn't want to let my shipmates down, is all."

Allegiance heaved forward as her bow stabbed into another rising swell. Lieutenant Sifton's smile grew twice over. "You'll make for a mate yet, Dead Eye Jack. Keep sharp. We are all well served by your tenacity."

Jack felt his chest swell. Not only had the ship's first lieutenant remembered who he was, he remembered his name. And he'd called him Dead Eye Jack for his display of skill at both musket and pistol on deck. The lieutenant made a sharp turn and gave Mr. Blythe a hard once -over. "Who is gun captain on that piece? I should like a word with him presently."

Jack's attention to the exchange faded. He felt the eyes of the crew on him. Stares that refused to relent. These weren't the angry despising stares he had endured for his first few weeks aboard Allegiance, these were very different. He had taken the lieutenant's challenge and won, and now proved himself with an act of raw courage recognized by all aboard. Lieutenant Sifton and Mr. Blythe made their way aft on the gun deck, looking for the Petty Officer in charge of starboard gun number four.

"A sailor's sailor ye are Jacky, knew it when I first laid eyes on ye," Bob growled with a devious smile. "He thumps away his gun at the privateer, and climbs the riggin' like he was damned born to it! He wrastles a loose gun fer sport and bests the first l'tenant at his own shooting match! Dead-eye Jack, he'll save us all! A sailorman if I ever seen!"

Bob opened the hatch on a wobbling oil lantern to steal a flame for his pipe. With a rush of bluish tobacco smoke he belted out, "What do ye say boys? Three cheers fer Dead-eye Jack!"

A chorus of sailors raised their voices as the ship tossed into another heaving lurch. "Hip hip, huzzah! Hip hip, huzzah! Hip hip, Huzzah!"

Jack's shoulders fell under a barrage of congratulatory slaps and playful luffs from nearby sailors. The ship pitched and heaved again, all aboard steadied themselves against whatever they could grasp. The cheers and merriment faded as reality turned back to the prospect of a long night spent being tossed by a storm.

The next day was much the same. Howling wind, driving rain, waves that slammed Allegiance back and forth, side to side, and caused her decks to endure a near constant deluge of seawater. Below deck, life was equally miserable as it was while exposed to the elements. The sea condition did not improve, and thus neither did the constant smell of sickness on Allegiance's gun deck. A constant rhythm of pitching and heaving mixed with the ship's natural motion of swaying side to side. The constant shifting of wind required frequent sail adjustments just to keep the bow oriented toward the breaking waves. A short stint on deck would result in hands being soaked through by rain and waves while simultaneously chilled through by the unrelenting gale. At times, the ship trembled under the opposing forces being exerted on her. Her decks creaked and groaned, her hull wept from the strain at her timbers and her overheads dripped from the never-ending deluge.

The watches passed with little variance in condition. Jack spent his morning watch amidships at the base of the main mast. He huddled close together with his messmates and prayed for no changes to be called for. Those prayers went unanswered though, as the winds tore at a loosened section of mainsail that fluttered and flapped dangerously in the gale.

"Mr. Skagg! Get a pair of hands aloft to secure that bit of sail before its tattered to shreds!"

Jack huddled close to Matsumoko. Rain dripped from the fore edge of his knit hat and ran in rivulets down his face. His tarpaulin jacket utterly failed to keep out the rain. Crowded close to the mast, he and

Matsumoko clustered together against the wind and rain, both hoping to avoid being called to go aloft.

"Jack, take yer friend and fetch up that sail afore it unravels itself ter shreds!" Mr. Skagg shouted through the howl of the wind. "Watch yerself out on that yard, she's going to be slick and the seas aren't calming fer anything."

Jack drew a slow breath through his ragged shivering. He gave Matsumoko a quick look as a pang of guilt struck his insides. But for his proximity to Jack, Matsumoko likely would have avoided being called upon for the hazardous assignment.

"Sorry, Matsumoko," Jack mumbled as they made their way to the main shrouds.

"Put a stopper in it," Matsumoko replied. "There's nobody aboard I'd rather go up with in a gale."

The vote of confidence filled Jack with a sense of resolution, and he hefted himself onto the starboard rail before taking to the shrouds one step at a time. The motion of the ship continued. The bow heaved upward with a pitch as it took on a new wave. A shudder of impact reverberated through the ship before the wave crested and broke along Allegiance's side. As the wave sloshed against the sides of the ship, her hull would pitch forward and slide down into a trough before the next swell would repeat the process.

Every step on the ratlines was a fight as the ship pitched and heaved. Rainwater sluiced down the thick shroud lines and chilled Jack's fingers until they ached with freezing pain. He hoisted himself step by step until he reached the maintop. Out of a sense of pride, Jack shunned the lubber hole and heaved himself up over the edge of the maintop platform despite the onslaught of rain and blustering gale force wind. The mainsail yard, and the tightrope that ran its length, was the next obstacle. Jack stepped onto the tightrope and began to shuffle his way out to where the mainsail was now fluttering with dangerous force. The section that had worked itself loose had grown in the time it had taken Jack and Matsumoko to ascend the shrouds and edge their way along the yard. What had started as three feet of canvas flapping in the wind had become a section almost seven feet across and extending for the full length of the sail.

"Watch yerselves lads! She's pullin' hard now! Don't let that canvas run away with yer grippin' on it!" Bob shouted from the main deck. "Haul her in with one hand while yer's holdin on with the other!"

Jack arrived at the extremity of the main yard completely soaked through. Shivers worked against his muscles and rattled every part of his body. Even his thoughts seemed jarred by the violent shaking. With one hand he held onto a lanyard line while with his other he collected a handful of sodden canvas and fought it back to the yard. Matsumoko arrived right after Jack and added his strength to the task. The two sailors took turns, one holding onto the canvas they had hauled while the other grabbed another fistful and brought in more. Arm length by arm length, they managed to reef in the loosed sail back to its intended place. Jack tied off the bundled canvas with three lengths of heavy cord doubled over and secured with a knot Bob had taught him, the 'New Englander Hitch'. With the sail secured, it was time for Jack and Matsumoko to retreat back to the safety of the deck. Allegiance pitched as she took another wave on her bow. Both sailors were sodden and shivering. It reminded Jack of the storm he had endured aboard Salem Tide, a storm that had very nearly seen both him and Matsumoko washed overboard. Jack had saved the sailor with quick action and a blatant disregard for his own safety and won himself the undying loyalty of a friend that had already proved his loyalty several times over.

"Hold fast, lads! Rogue wave!" a voice shouted up from the deck.

Jack and Matsumoko both clambered onto the main yard, wrapping their arms and legs around the timber beam to hold on for everything they were worth. The wave hit with savage force, Jack and Matsumoko had only a fraction of a second to brace themselves. It had come from the starboard beam and nearly enveloped the entirety of the main deck. Jack gripped at wood and sodden canvas. He flexed his arms and bound himself to the yard as the ship pitched and swayed with wild force beyond anything he had felt before. The recoil of the ship was almost as strong as the initial hit of the wave. Allegiance tipped side to side and sent her masts whipping through the dense weather. Jack felt like he would be thrown from the yard at any point. The motion continued, up and then down, side to side. It was enough to make him recall his breakfast from the depths of his stomach. Just as Jack thought he may be revisited by bits of ship's biscuit and small beer, the sway of the masts settled back to the steady pitch from waves on the bow. He recovered himself and lowered both feet down to the tightrope.

"Jacky!" Bob called up. "Jacky, are you two alright up there?"

Jack looked over at Matsumoko. He looked like a drowned bilge rat, his fists clung to the lanyard cinched that held the mainsail bound in place. His hat dripped streams of rainwater, and his arms trembled with violent shivers. His face was a picture of pure misery.

"We're fine, Bob. Have some water put on to boil and stoke a fire for us, will ya?" Jack shouted.

It was ludicrous. The galley had been cold since Allegiance left port. Jack started to laugh. He pictured the salty old sailor wearing an apron and tending a kettle of hot water for them as they retreated below deck from the weather. His laughs spread through his belly and into his chest. Soon, Matsumoko was laughing along with him, their cackles carrying through the gale as the storm raged all around them.

"Are you both mad? Get back down here. That wave carried a sailor straight off the quarterdeck!" Bob growled at them both. "Climb down so we can all tuck away below deck!"

Word spread quickly throughout the crew. The sailor who had been washed overboard by the rogue wave was Mr. Tullen, a quartermaster's mate, and one of the few Petty Officers who was hesitant to use his starter. For that, the crew lamented. It was rare in the Royal Navy for a sailor who achieved status as a Petty Officer to display restraint. Far rarer, was the display of compassion. Mr. Tullen was known for both and popular with the crew before the mast. His knowledge and cool head under dire circumstance also made him well received by the officers of the quarterdeck and the mates who freely roamed throughout the vessel. As morose as the gun deck had been before, the combination of unrelenting weather and the loss of such a staple to the crew plunged the men deeper into melancholy. Allegiance continued to be battered by the storm well into the evening and all through Jack's morning watch. Dawn brought a slacking of the wind. Hope was kindled as the gale blusters died to a manageable blow from the northeast, and a break in the clouds provided Jack with his first glimpse of the sun in two days. He hadn't realized how low his spirits had fallen, but the golden orange hues that mixed with rose red and pink caused a swell in his chest. As he and his messmates ascended the shrouds to make sail, he felt the first glimmers of sunshine lifting his spirit as high as the rain sodden pennant flying from the mainmast.

The first call from the quarterdeck came for half reef courses and topsails. Jack figured they were being cautious against the weather turning foul again as the skies hadn't cleared and only a thin ribbon of daylight was visible along the eastern horizon. The sun peeked its way up and lit the world with its brilliant glow before climbing behind a thick layer of dark gray clouds that still threatened a measure of fury. The rains tapered with the coming of dawn before finally lightening to a sporadic drizzle. Despite being soaked through to the bone, Jack felt the promise of clear skies and fair winds in their near future. He worked each task with renewed vigor as if the gods of wind and rain would look favorably on him and bring his hopes of sunshine and warmth to fruition.

With mainsails set at a half reef, and topsails filled with a strong wind, Allegiance began slugging her way against rolling seas that came from a southerly heading. The bow of the ship slowed in her rise and fall as the waves came at a more steady rate.

"Mr. Skagg!" a tinny shout came from the quarterdeck. "Remind the hands to be on the lookout for landfall, reefs and shoals. We have yet to get an accurate fix on our position!"

The words hit Jack like a dagger in the ribs. It was a strange and unsettling notion, that the collection of officers aboard hadn't the foggiest idea of where they were. Jack eased himself down the shrouds to the maintop and shot a glance aloft to where Matsumoko was making his way down. Bowline Bob was at ease leaning against the mast and fidgeting with his pipe. A dry scraping noise could be heard as he prepared the instrument for the first smoke aloft he had enjoyed since the outset of the storm.

"The officers don't know where we are?" Jack asked with a cocked brow.

Bob gave him a sideways grin. "We tossed about in a storm fer near two days, ye expect the officers ter just knows where we are as soon as she passes?" he said while scraping at the bowl of his pipe with the head of a deck nail.

Jack considered for a moment and looked out over the wash of gray seas bordered by gray skies of low-hanging clouds. "Well, I suppose not. But, I really don't know much about navigation. I was once told it requires mathematics."

"Aye, mathematics ter get where yer going, an ter figure out where ye are. Most important bit there is figurin' where ye is. Can't figure on going nowheres unless ye know where yer's startin' from, eh?" Bob said. He slapped the cup of his pipe bowl against one hand and blew into the wooden piece to force little bits of charred debris to fall out and wisp away in the wind. "They'll get their reckoning, mark me words. The sailing master jus' wants sharp eyes aloft ter ward us away from reefs and shoals and such. The triangle is known fer fingers 'o rock that can rip the old girl's keel right out from under us. Make us all shark food in a matter 'o minutes."

The bright peal of watch bells rang out from the quarterdeck. Four bells in the morning watch. It was time for the hands to change stations for their last two hours. Usually, Jack spent the last two hours of his watch amidships in the waist practicing knots and keeping the braces with Matsumoko. Occasionally, he would be summoned to the foc'sl where he would keep lines and tend the braces for adjustments being made aloft on the foremast. These familiar assignments weren't as exciting as being aloft, but they were a far cry from spending hours on hands and knees holy stoning the deck.

"Mr. Skagg," a tinny voice shouted aloft as the watch bells finished sounding. "Send that Able Seaman Horner to the quarterdeck for the last of his watch!"

Jack felt a trace of lightning hit his blood. The quarterdeck was one of the two places a sailor dreaded to be summoned, the other being the captain's cabin. With his heart in his throat, Jack mounted the shrouds and climbed his way down to the main deck just ahead of Bowline Bob and Matsumoko. His mind raced with questions as he descended step by step. Had he unwittingly done something to draw the ire of an officer? Was he being called to task for some misstep aloft? Mr. Skagg or Bob would surely have corrected him before the quarterdeck took note. His heart raced as he lowered himself from the shrouds and stepped off of the railing onto the main deck. His stomach twisted in knots as he imagined the horror that awaited him.

"Best not to linger, Jack," Bob said as he stepped down from the shrouds to the main deck amidships. "They called fer ye's. Better snap to and get going."

Jack chewed at his lower lip. "What do you think they want, Bob? Am I in some sort of trouble?" he asked with a shaking voice.

Bob furrowed his brows and cast a long glance aft toward the quarterdeck. "Reckon ye'd know it iff'n yer was about ter be flogged, Jacky. But, whatever the case, making them wait about fer ye won't help matters none. Hurry along. Might not be so bad. Might be yer in store fer a turn at the helm, or slingin' the lead line."

Jack hesitated for a heartbeat longer as Matsumoko followed Bob from the shrouds to the deck. His friend nodded for him to follow Bob's advice and hurry along.

"Able Seaman Horner, to the quarterdeck. Smartly, if you please," the tinny voice of the watch officer called out over the rush of wind and waves.

Jack's mind raced, but he forced his legs to engage for fear of compounding whatever situation he faced. He passed a crowd of sailors on their way forward from the mizzen tops, and then the mizzen mast. The quarterdeck stood in front of him, separated only by a short section of rail over a small step in the deck. It was hallowed ground aboard ship. One of the first things Bowline Bob had warned him of. The quarterdeck was reserved for officers of the ship, warrant officers, and mates who have specific business to be there. The only circumstances where sailors were called to the quarterdeck were to help man the helm or throw the lead line. Anything beyond that promised to have dire consequences. A failure aloft that caught the eye of a watchful officer, or dereliction to follow standing orders, would result in an invitation to the quarterdeck that would surely result in an unpleasant situation. Since putting to sea aboard Salem Tide, or being pressed to service aboard Allegiance, Jack had yet to be called to the quarterdeck. As was custom when addressing officers, Jack removed his hat.

"Able Seaman Horner, reporting as ordered, sir," Jack said to nobody in particular.

A pair of midshipmen turned and regarded him with cold looks. Jack remained motionless, his knit hat wadded into a ball in his grasp. The watch officer stared ahead, vigilantly staring over the deck and casting looks aloft.

"Horner, it's about damned time," a Petty Officer growled from beside the ship's wheel. "Castor here has to be aloft and he's waiting on relief. Now, get up here and take the wheel in hand. Ye's been called to learn helm duty by the first l'tenant hisself. We'll learn ye the ropes and see ye's right off the quarterdeck iff'n yer not cut fer it."

At hearing the Petty Officer's order, Jack guts unwound from the knot they had formed. A turn at the helm! He would be steering the vessel! His mouth went dry at the prospect and his hands began to fidget at his sides with excitement. He returned the knit cap onto his head and pulled it tight around his ears. Jack knuckled his forehead as he passed the watch officer and sailing master and crossed the quarterdeck to the helm. Able Seaman Castor stood with a rigid grip on the wooden handles that protruded from the wheel, his eyes were locked aloft as he gently handled the wheel in small movements.

"Yer next at the helm, eh?" Castor asked with a grunt.

"Aye, you stand relieved," Jack replied with a tense nod. He reached out and took the wheel's handle in his grip one for one as Castor released them and stepped away from the helm.

"It's not so bad once ye get used to her," Castor said in a low voice. "Jus' make damn sure ye's keep yer's trim slightly with the wind. Keeps the canvas filled and course steady." He paused for a second and let Jack come to grip with the feel of the sea playing against the rudder. "When the officers call fer it, ye do exactly as the watch officer says, iff'n he has the ship. If an order comes from the sailing master, or the first l'tenent or captain, then that's what goes. Savvy?" He paused again and waited for Jack's response.

"Aye, officer of the watch, sailing master, first lieutenant and captain," He replied.

"That's right. Mr. Brown isn't so bad, but, he won't hesitate wi' his starter iff'n ye gives him any reason fer it. Jus' keep her sails filled and don't wander from her course. She's a fair enough sea bird, handles quick and nimble under tops and t'gallants, an' just a bit more cumbersome wit' the courses flying full," Castor said with a gentle pat on Jack's shoulder. "They says L'tenant Sifton calls fer ye particular. Don't disappoint 'im now, sounds like he takes a shining fer ye's."

The wheel surged in Jack's grip. He muscled it back to its original position and looked aloft as he had seen Castor doing. The mainsail at half reef was filled and taut and the topsail was trim and arced from the force of the wind. The ship took on a different quality from his view behind the wheel. She edged over to lee as the sea played against her bow and the wind buffeted her sails, Jack corrected ever so slightly and the bow shifted back to windward.

"Easy does it, lad," said the Petty Officer that had called him up onto the quarterdeck. "Ye collapse that weather edge of the sail and yer'll feel me cordage on yer back, eh?"

"Aye, sir," Jack replied while easing back the helm just a breath.

The Petty Officer croaked his reply, "No need fer sir'in me, lad. I'm just a mate, Petty

Officer Lambden, Quartermaster's Mate." He leaned forward and put one hand one the wheel in between where Jack's hands were clamped onto the handles. "Ye have a fair touch fer her, specially considerin' the sea are a might rough fer a first trick at the helm. But, when the first l'tenant calls ye up, its not fer me ter says otherwise." He turned and growled over one shoulder. "Officer of the watch, Able Seaman Horner at the helm."

The watch officer drolled in a monotonous reply, as if bored by the report, "Aye, Able Seaman Horner, at the helm."

H.M.S Allegiance
23 June 1770
Devil's Triangle - Exact Position Unknown

A trick at the helm had sparked something inside of Jack Horner. The feel of the sea reverberating up through the rudder and into his arms transformed his perspective. He spent the afternoon hours awaiting his evening watch with eager anticipation only to feel sheer disappointment when he was tasked to go higher aloft as a lookout at the sound of bells in the middle of the watch. When the watch bells sounded again, Jack retreated below deck with his messmates, all eager for supper to be piped as the seas had calmed considerably. The galley fire was lit and a lingering smell of smoke held the promise of a warm supper accompanied by the daily ration of grog. Beans with pork, ship's biscuit and a small wedge of hard cheese, made for as enjoyable a meal at sea as Jack ever had. The fare which had at one time been enough to turn his stomach was now a bright spot in the evening as he gather with his messmates. The grog was strong and mixed with a good touch of lemon juice, it satisfied thirst and brought a relaxing warmth to the evening gathering.

"A trick at the helm, Jacky? What did ye think of it?" Bowline Bob asked with a broad grin.

Jack paused for a moment. The plate before him loaded with a hefty scoop of beans mixed with chunks of salted pork steamed and filled his nose with its aroma. "It was like nothing I have ever experienced before, Bob. Like the sea was alive and talking to me through the rudder and the wheel."

Bowline Bob stared off into the space of the gun deck as if recalling some fond memory of years past in his seafaring experience. He spooned a mouthful of beans and pork, as a slight smile crept across his face. "I knew it the moment I laid eyes on yer. Born fer it, ye is. A sailorman's sailor, right son of the sea."

Jack smiled at the compliment. "It wouldn't have been so if you hadn't talked with your Petty Officer friend, Bob. I really owe you thanks." He said before digging into his own supper.

"Say nothin' of it, lad. Tis me pleasure ter see ye come up in the ways of a sailorman," Bob said over a bite of beans. "Jus' remember yer old pal Bowline Bob when yer's a lofty l'tenant or a merchant captain commandin' yer own barky. Keep a hammock slung fer this old salt and we're square, eh?"

"Aye, Bowline. You'll have a place with me," Jack replied with a chuckle at the fanciful thought. He looked over at Matsumoko, who was wolfing down his supper with rapid, greedy bites. "As will you, my friend."

Matsumoko nodded and cleared his mouth with a drink from his grog. "Aye, Jack. Soon as you have yourself a ship, I'll be there."

The messmates had a chuckle to themselves and enjoyed the rest of their supper with toasts to the clearing weather and speculative conversation about their search for the rogue privateer ship.

Allegiance settled into a pattern of movement that was predictable and the evening wore on into the normal routine of sea life. Jack and his mates finished their supper, stowed their mess wares and reemerged onto the main deck to take in fresh air. To their pleasant surprise, they found that the deluge of the last two days had finally ceased. It was finally possible to dry themselves, and while the wind still held a chill, the prospect of drying out was too good to pass. Daylight had slipped from the world and Allegiance's deck was sparsely lit by the sooty glow of lanterns about her masts and by her hatches. Soon, the gathering on deck included all the hands from below as word spread of the ceasing precipitation. Pipe smoke invaded the sea air which was soon accompanied by the soft lyrics of a shanty being sung from aloft. Jack reveled in the lightened mood as the crew finally released tensions pent up from being bombarded by wind and waves over the course of two days. Jack leaned over the weather rail and peered down to the darkness of inky sea slipping by the hull. Little crests of frothy white capped the top edge of their bow wake and trailed away into sheer darkness.

"Do you suppose the sun will make it's appearance tomorrow, Bob?" Jack asked as he stared out into the black night surrounding them.

Bob fiddled with his pipe as he lit the bowl with a wick. He blew the little flame out with a stream of thick smoke before tucking the cotton cordage away and looking aloft. "Hard sayin' not knowin', Jack. That was a ripe gale with seas ter match. Could be a few days before we sees the clear skies again. But, I've been wrong in these tellings before. Might be we wake ter a bright clear morning with fair winds and a slight roll o' the brine ter match." He drew at his pipe and let a thick puff of smoke dribble out of his nostrils. A devious grin crossed his face. "Say, Jacky. Have yer ever had the pleasure of Virginia tobacco from a well seasoned pipe?"

Jack shook his head. "My father didn't smoke. He didn't have a taste for tobacco," he replied with a frown as he thought of his father. "And I've never tried it for myself."

"Aye," Bob rasped with another cloud of smoke. "Makes sense fer a blacksmith. He was always breathing the fumes and smoke from 'is forge anyways. That's like ter spoil it fer anyone." He leaned closer to Jack and held his pipe out stem first for Jack to take. "Iff'n yer interested, have a pull at her. See if yer likes it."

Jack took the wooden pipe and put the stem between his teeth. He drew in a small breath of the rich smoke. The aroma filled his nose and played on his tongue. It tasted bold and hot, with the flavors of spices. He handed the pipe back to Bob. The smoke settled and burned in his chest. He tried to casually blow out a cloud in the same manner Bob would, but his lungs betrayed him and spasmed into a fit of coughs. His eyes and nose began to water while at the same time his mouth went dry. His stomach tightened into a ball and he felt the remnants of his supper on its way to revisit him. His head spun and his vision blurred as tears welled in them to the point that they flowed freely down his face.

"Whoa, lad! That's a hearty cough!" Bob said through a deep rolling laugh. "That reminds me of the first time I had a pull at me old man's pipe! Thought I was going ter cough up me damned soul!"

Jack's breathing steadied. The flow of sweet, fresh sea air cooled his chest and set his chest back at ease. His head swam for a few moments as his heart slowed back to its normal pace. "I don't see the appeal, Bob."

Bowline Bob laughed all the harder. "Aye, I suppose not. But, neither did I the first time I tried it. It takes a bit, but yer'll learn ter love it. Nothing sets the soul ter comfort like a good smoke at sunset after a long day before the mast. Best companion ter yer grog and the surest way ter chase the smell 'o shipmates from yer honker!"

Jack laughed despite himself. The smell of pipe smoke had become a sweet aroma that hearkened the arrival of the old sea hand that had become his mentor, but he decided he would abstain from trying to acquire his taste for it for a time. A breath of sweet, fresh air chased the remnants of burning from his throat and chest. He leaned his back against the bulwark railing and took in the evening while the sound of more hands joined into song.

A fitful night of little sleep ended with the bright peal of watch bells. Without any coaxing from his shipmates, or the Petty Officer of the watch, Jack rolled from his hammock and stowed it away with an edge of expectation lining his every thought. Allegiance had passed the remains of the foul seas and the sunrise awaited. He pulled on his knit watch cap, which had dried in the night hours, and clambered his way up on deck. Without needing to be told, Jack hurried to the main shrouds and climbed aloft. The swells were easy, and the winds were warm and fair. Allegiance's bow lifted and fell away with a gentle rocking motion. Jack climbed the shrouds to the maintop, shunning the lubber hole as was his habit, and continued aloft to the topsail yard. No sail change had been ordered, and the winds seemed to be holding steady, so instead of making his perch there, Jack continued to climb higher before finally coming to a halt at the top-gallant masthead.

The sounds and light of the main deck had fallen away, Jack was left alone with only the whisper of wind to accompany his thoughts. Allegiance was surrounded by darkness, not even the silvery glow of the moon or a faint glimmer of starlight penetrated the layer of clouds Jack knew must be hanging overhead. Sitting at the cross of the top-gallant yard, he stared out in the murk of the wee morning hours. On his tongue, he could still taste the remnants of Bob's pipe smoke while he savored the fresh morning air. A glow began to lighten the eastern horizon as the first hour of watch wore on, and Jack could see that the day would be overcast. No brilliant orb would grace the skies, only light that failed to fully penetrate solid gray clouds. Bells pealed for the second hour, and Jack keenly scoured the seas ahead of Allegiance for any sign of shoal or reef.

Rolling gray waves stretched out as far as his eyes could see without so much as an irregular break or a calm spot signaling shallow water. His mind drifted as he stretched his eyes to the limit of what he could see. Thoughts of his father, and of his mother, the ship he had visited to have his forehead stitched, and the awful smell of burned gunpowder floating above King's Street while blood soaked into the accumulating snow. He choked back a bitter taste at the back of his throat. It was more acrid than the smoke from Bob's pipe, but the tears that accompanied it came slower. He tried to recall happier memories of his parents, days when they had picnicked along the seashore, church services when his father scowled at his fidgeting and his mother tried to soothe his energetic wiggles by holding his hand. But, try as he might, his thoughts drifted back to the cold night on King Street and the roar of British muskets that tore his parents from him so cruelly.

Four bells sounded, their peal was muffled through the wind, but Jack's spirit soared as he heard their sounding and he climbed down with his heart in his throat hoping to be sent to the quarterdeck for another trick at the helm. The winds held steady as he reached the topmast yard and started down the shrouds.

"Able Seaman Horner to the quarterdeck, Mr. Skagg." The tinny sound of Mr. Lambden's voice ringing through the brass speaking trumpet shouted. Jack's heart leapt in his chest. A broad smile spread across his face. By the time he reached the maintop, he could contain his excitement no longer. The main shrouds were not expedient enough to suit his haste. Jack took to the aft brace line on the weather side of the mast with both legs hooked over the thick rope, hand over hand he lowered himself to the main deck in half the time it would have taken him on the shroud lines.

Jack hurried across the deck and approached the fore rail of the quarterdeck.

"Able Seaman Horner, reporting," He said as he knuckled his forehead and awaited permission to cross onto the hallowed planks surrounding the helm.

"Aye, Horner," the watch officer said without enthusiasm. "L'tenant Sifton will be up shortly, and he has requested ye at the helm. It is to be your place of duty for the second trick of your watch from now on." He motioned toward the wheel where Castor stood ready to be relieved. "Mr. Lambden will see you squared shortly. Take over for Castor so he can make his way aloft."

Jack passed onto the quarterdeck and took the ship's wheel from Castor hand for hand.

"Might be a rough trick, friend," Castor muttered in a low voice. "My advice is keep yer mouth shut and do as yer told sharpish. The officers are a might skittish with the overcast. Not a good time fer ye te be sluggish on the wheel."

"Well, Castor," the watch officer snapped. "You've been relieved. Now, go aloft for your duties."

Castor knuckled his brow. "Aye, sir. Straight away," he said before hurrying forward to the foremast shrouds.

Jack puzzled at the cryptic warning for a moment as he gathered himself for his duty at the helm. Allegiance was riding easy with the wind at her starboard quarter. Her courses and topsails were trim and taut with wind, and her bow slipped pleasantly through gentle rises in the briny sea. The action of the sea on the rudder was smooth, not at all what it had felt like the day before. A slight vibration worked its way from the rudder, through the steerage lines and into the wheel. Jack could feel the tiny urges to leeward and held fast against them with a steady but gentle pressure. All seemed as fine as fine could be and he wondered at the watch officer's sharp tone and impatience with Castor for a beat before dismissing it as the officer's way of dealing with foremast sailors.

An odd quiet pervaded on the quarterdeck as Jack settled into his trick at the helm, supremely satisfied with the wind at his back and the ship's steady motion. The watch officer seemed ill at ease. He paced about the deck to the weather side of the helm issuing small mutters here and there as he clopped in a nervous circuit. Mr. Lambden was busy with the leadsman along the lee side of the quarterdeck, taking readings of their speed and depth soundings.

"Time, hold that line!" he called.

The leadsman clamped his hand onto the long line of wound cordage and called out his reading, "Nine knots."

"Very well, nine knots," Mr. Lambdin replied in a monotonous droll.

Lieutenant Sifton emerged from the aft hatch and pulled his fore-and-aft bicorne hat on before looking aloft for a long moment. He appeared to be taking in the trim of the sails as well as the weather. Jack fought the urge to grin at the sight of him. It had become apparent over the course of the last few weeks that the ship's first lieutenant favored him in some regards.

"Still overcast," the lieutenant observed as he crossed onto the quarterdeck and halted to the weather of the quarterdeck. "Our hopes of an accurate reckoning look as dismal as the day itself." He turned to the watch officer. "Has there been no sightings of land? A reef? A shoal? Anything?"

The watch officer replied with an exasperated rasp. "No, sir. I've doubled the lookouts aloft the foremast, and we are taking soundings in hopes of narrowing the possibilities."

Lieutenant Sifton shook his head. "Useful, but the charts we have of the triangle don't have enough depth markings to do us much good. Without a visible sun, or stars, we need some sort of landfall to orient ourselves. That storm wreaked havoc on our navigation and the captain is impatient for an accurate reckoning."

"Our southerly course should bring us to a sighting of land any hour now, sir. If we just maintain our course, I am confident of it," the watch officer said.

"We are a ship with a tasking, we cannot afford three days sailing in the wrong direction only to have to beat a course northward. There is no fix on how far south that storm pushed us, or if we drifted to the east. With seas contrary to the wind, our reading surely has wild variance. If we press on southward, we could miss sighting the leeward islands and end up off the coast of

Brazil before we make an accurate fix on our position. I do not want to explain such to the captain," he paused his explanation before continued. "Do you?"

"No, sir," the watch officer replied. He lowered his voice almost to a point beyond Jack's hearing. "How is the captain, sir?"

A long pause passed as wind whistled over the decks. "He is distressed, to say the least. It is quite possible that the French ship we have been tasked with taking could be anywhere by now. We must ensure the ship and crew are being kept to the highest order, if the captain notes any shortcoming, it will go hard on us all." He let another long beat pass before continuing, "As for our reckoning. We must do everything we can to hasten an accurate fix of our position. If that means sailing west to landfall, then that is what we must do."

Jack looked aloft to the mainmast and examined the trim of the sails. The sails were full and taut, but a glance at the compass showed him just slightly lee of his course. He held the wheel slightly to weather for a heartbeat before easing back with the wind. Silently, he hoped the officers present had not noticed the lapse.

"I was just about to correct you Horner. Well done," Lieutenant Sifton said over

Jack's shoulder. "Though, I would expect as much from a dead eye such as yourself."

Jack smiled at the praise. "Thank ye, sir." He held the wheel steady as a push from the sea flexed against the rudder.

"Do you find yourself well suited to duty at the helm?" the lieutenant asked. "It is not for everyone. Many foremast hands don't fancy being under the scrutiny that comes with duty on the quarterdeck."

Jack thought for a moment and furrowed his brow. "It suits me, sir. If I measure to the task."

"You most certainly do, young man. You possess the capacity and the temperament, if not all the knowledge and experience. But, that will come with time," the lieutenant said. "A steady hand, at the helm, is crucial. A firm, steady hand. Too often sailors are called to the quarterdeck to learn the helm only to be sent back before the mast for rash steerage that threatens both course and sail. Remember, bold when she needs it, slight when she doesn't. You seem to have a fair grasp already. Keep those words in mind and you will do fine, young Horner."

Jack felt his chest swell. For the briefest of moments he dared to imagine himself in the lieutenant's shoes, wearing a sharp officer's coat and fine hat, observing the hands at their duties with a keen eye for detail. The image faded as quickly as it formed. Jack chanced a look over to the first lieutenant.

"Thank ye, sir. Kindly," He said. "It was my dream as a boy, growing up in Boston, to be a sea going man."

The lieutenant stood silent for a moment before asked, "How is it that you found yourself at sea, Horner? You aren't old enough to be signed aboard a crew in proper manner. Not for a responsible captain, at least. Were you an orphan?"

Jack shook his head. The swelling of pride in his chest dissipated and was promptly replaced by a surge of grief. "I wasn't, well, ah, I am, so to speak, now. But, I wasn't. I had my mother and father. But, they were killed in Boston."

The lieutenant's face formed a deep frown as he stepped just ahead of Jack without obscuring his sight of the sails. "Killed? My condolences, young man. How did this come to pass?"

Jack swallowed hard. He fought at the tears that threatened the corners of his eyes as the image of blood running between cobblestones swept over his mind. "Redcoats, sir. We were passing through, by King's Street, that is, and the crowd blocked our way. My father thought we could make our way through without hazard. But, when we reached the head of the crowd, the soldiers, they opened fire."

"Yes," Lieutenant Sifton said before sucking at his teeth. "I read something about that in a bulletin at Bermuda. Awful business, just awful. That commander ought to be horse whipped through the streets, opening fire on unarmed civilians like that. Damned unfortunate. I grieve your hardships, Horner."

Jack drew a slow breath in through his nose. It was difficult to focus aloft while his vision blurred from a welling of tears. Fought as he tried, they came nonetheless. A hand clamped onto his shoulder and gave a tight squeeze. He dared not look over. He knew the hand belonged to Lieutenant Sifton. The officer's compassion touched his spirit. It shocked him, and after hearing the lieutenant rebuke his countrymen, Jack finally felt a sense of reckoning between the event that had ripped his family to shreds and his present situation. His inner turmoil eased, and with the passing of a rolling wave, his eyes cleared.

"I know it must be little consolation, young Horner," Lieutenant Sifton said in a low voice. "But, the hardships we face in life are going to be there. We cannot avoid them. It is up to you to decide. Will you allow your trials to destroy you? Or, like steel in a forge, will you temper yourself against further adversity? Those are the questions you should be asking. Your circumstances are unfortunate, to say the least. But, they have also presented you with an opportunity. What will you do with that opportunity?"

Jack pondered the first lieutenant's questions as Allegiance rose to the crest of another wave. Without a conscious thought of the motion, he corrected slightly for the action of the sea and then double checked sail trim and compass bearing. His thoughts drifted like the foaming froth brought up in Allegiance's bow wake. The lieutenant, in the course of a single conversation, had both offered his sincere condolences to Jack, while simultaneously throwing down another challenge. It was both comforting, and oddly inspiring. The ship met with another rise in the sea, and as it crested Jack felt a resolution inside himself. He would make use of these forced circumstances. To whatever end, he would take whatever benefit he could gain. So lost in these thoughts, and keeping Allegiance steady on course, that he hadn't noticed Lieutenant Sifton slip away from his shoulder.

"Watch officer, I have the ship," Lieutenant Sifton stated in the rigid naval manner.

The watch officer replied, "Aye, the First L'tenant has the ship."

"Mr. Lambden, hands to make sail. Give me a single reef on the courses and set heads'ls. Unfurl the gallants. Bring us about close reach on the starboard tack, make your course southwest by west," Lieutenant Sifton rattled his orders in the supreme confidence that could only come from years of experience aboard a man of war at sea.

Mr. Lambden raised the brass speaking trumpet to his mouth and bellowed the lieutenant's ordered sail changes. Without hesitation, or so much as drawing a new breath, he lowered the conical brass device and turned to Jack. "Bring her over starboard, four points. Close reach."

Jack understood making a starboard turn. The rest was beyond him. He knew the wind was at their starboard quarter, and the first lieutenant had ordered a westerly course. Allegiance could not sail dead on into the wind, but it could maintain speed and sail at an angle to the wind. He repeated the mate's orders in the fashion of the navy and brought the wheel over in the desired direction. Sailors scrambled aloft and sails were changed in all haste as the ship settled into her new course. The first lieutenant paced to the lee rail and then back to windward before pausing near the helm for a beat.

"That will do, Horner. Ease her back a point and keep a sharp eye on the t'gallants," He said flatly.

"Aye, sir," Jack replied.

Jack let the wheel rest over just a breath and the top gallants filled to a taut trim. Allegiance slipped along easy with the wind close reach and a lean to her larboard side. It required more effort and more concentration from Jack to maintain the delicate balance of keeping her on course while at the same time making sure her sails remained trim and full. The force against the rudder that played through the steerage ropes and into the wheel was the most intense he had felt. At times, it required him to put his full weight to the wheel to maintain direction. Jack split his focus between the compass and aloft while grappling with the helm every few seconds. Helm duty had gone from his boyhood dream job to a tasking that employed his full concentration while taxing his nerves. His focus tightened to the point that he failed to notice Captain Williams appear at the fore edge of the quarterdeck.

"Who is this at the helm?" the gaunt faced captain demanded. "Why are we steering a westerly course, sailor? Our enemy will be haunting the passages to the south of us!"

He stormed onto the quarterdeck, making himself large before the helm. "Heave her about, at once! We sail southward, for the straights east of Hispaniola."

Jack hesitated. He knew he should instantly follow the captain's orders, without question or delay, but Lieutenant Sifton had ordered a westerly course to raise a sighting of land and aid in the reckoning of Allegiance's position. Tremulously, Jack began to ease the helm over to larboard. He watched the sails aloft, their trim remained full and taut, but the ship leapt with the force of taking the wind at a more direct point of sail. The shrill of a boatswain's whistle squealed its high pitch and Mr. Lambdin raised the speaking trumpet to his mouth.

"Hands aloft to reef t'gallants," He shouted in a rapid order.

Captain Williams cut a glare across the quarterdeck sharper than a cutlass. "The hell you will. Belay that order Mr. Lambdin," he snapped.

Without delay, the Petty Officer lifted the brass speaking trumpet and recanted his last command. "Belay my last, stand fast, men. Belay last order."

Captain Williams crossed his arms in front of his chest. His glare was locked onto Mr. Lambdin with deadly, red hot fury painted plainly on his expression. "What on earth would give you the notion of reefing sails? We are in a desperate hunt, Mr. Lambdin, and we are weeks behind our enemy." He shook his head and drew a deep breath in through his flaring nostrils. "Must I remind you of the penalty for failing to confront our enemy?"

Mr. Lambdin snapped to a rigid posture at the captain's irate challenge. He knuckled the brim of his high topped hat and replied, "No, sir. I am aware. Lieutenant Sifton called for a course change, sir, to raise a land sighting ter reckon our position, sir."

The captain's gaunt features hardened further at the telling. He stared a hole straight through the mate in front of him and then shifted his gaze across the quarterdeck in search of his first lieutenant. "Is this true, Lieutenant Sifton? Did you order a course change?"

Lieutenant Sifton didn't shirk from the captain's glowering stare. "Aye, sir. I did. We need to make landfall to aid our reckoning. Without it, or aid from the sun, I fear our position could be off by scores of leagues."

The captain remained fast to his course. His gaze had locked onto the lieutenant and his arms remained tightly folded in front of his chest. "How so? Do we not trust our own readings? Were there not accurate logs being kept?" he asked with a pointed tone.

"No, sir. In a manner, they were. But, with the wind as it was, and opposing seas, our speed could have been miscalculated. Overhead cover does not allow for a noon reading to decipher our latitude with any measure of accuracy. I thought it best we triangulate our position by raising land. It would be detrimental to our mission if we were to misjudge our position and sail past the leeward islands," the lieutenant replied with a cool explanation.

It all seemed very reasonable to Jack, though even in his mind he recognized his partiality toward the first lieutenant. His own knowledge of reckonings at sea was a vague explanation he had gotten from Bowline Bob, secondhand from an officer who had once explained the matter to him in his younger years.

"I am very aware of the inherent dangers of misjudging our position, l'tenant. We sail southerly, in search of our prize. Is that understood?" said Captain Williams. A dangerous edge had crept into his voice, almost daring confrontation.

"Aye, sir," Lieutenant Sifton replied. "As you command."

The captain's hat tipped as he raised his chin with a triumphant glower down his nose at all within his sight. "Aye, l'tenant. You would do well to remember that. I am the captain, and this," he paused and extended a hand downward with all fingers extended, "is my ship."

H.M.S Allegiance
24 June 1770
Devil's Triangle - Exact Position Unknown

Allegiance's gun deck was dead calm in the stillness of night. Seawater washed against the hull while the action of wind caused a steady rock from side to side. Hammocks creaked, timbers groaned, and somewhere among the web of slung canvas and rope a sailor gently snored away the small hours of the first watch. Jack laid staring into the darkness that encompassed him as his thoughts drifted like flotsam in a storm. The exchange between Captain Williams and the first lieutenant refused to leave his mind. He had only stood for a trick at the helm at handful of times, but one of the things he had first noticed was the decorum observed between officers. They didn't snap at one another, their tones were typically pleasant with compliments being passed as they addressed one another. Deference to rank and seniority was always shown, but it was less rigid, less threatening than when a hand from before the mast was called to task on the quarterdeck. The terse exchange between Captain Williams and Lieutenant Sifton replayed in his mind, over and over. Moreover, Jack could not settle with the fact that the officers were in general disagreement over the ship's position. With the skies as overcast as they were, it was impossible for them to determine their exact location. But, as his last trick at the helm wore on, and he steered Allegiance westerly and then averted back to a southern heading, the officers began disagreeing about approximations of where they could be.

"Without celestial aid, or a firm sighting of land, this is all for naught," Lieutenant Sifton had stated for all to hear. "We could as well be fifteen leagues from the coast of Spanish Florida as we could from Bermuda. When the seas were tossing us about in that storm we could have drifted thirty or even fifty nautical miles off course. Not to mention the loss of our quartermaster's mate, and with him the log he had been using during his watch. That is four hours worth of reckoning we cannot take into consideration."

"With the winds in our favor, and the seas against, we were likely holding a somewhat steady position," one of the other lieutenants said. He pointed at a chart they had collectively unrolled onto a table behind the helm. "I would venture that we were within thirty miles of this last reckoning when the storm waned, and thus if we apply the speed and course we have taken since." He circled another area of the chart with his finger. "That would put us somewhere around here."

"Guesswork? A rough reckoning won't help us when we are fifteen or twenty days without raising land," Lieutenant Sifton had replied with a grumble.

The scene had dragged through Jack's hours at the helm. Disagreements continued. The captain grew more frustrated by the minute until he finally departed the quarterdeck for his cabin. As he left, he gave strict instruction for Allegiance to maintain a southerly course. He was to be sent for as soon as land was sighted or the skies were clear enough for celestial reckoning.

It all disturbed Jack in ways he didn't want to say aloud. The officers were supposed to be a united force, all knowing, in his mind. Lieutenant Sifton's fear that they had traversed east of their original reckoning was especially troubling. Jack recalled the scant lessons in geography he had attended at school in Boston. The Caribbean was one of the few places that had captured his interest. If Allegiance had drifted eastward during the storm, and they sailed south past the leeward isles, Brazil may be their next sighting. Worse yet, if the constant second guessing and disagreement continued, Jack feared they would be making course changes for days. The stories he had heard throughout the gun deck about the Devil's Triangle revisited him. Ships lost at sea, officers baffled by navigational anomalies, sea beasts dragging ships down into the briny, crushing depths.

The soft noise and sway of his hammock proved to be little comfort against the raging tempest in Jack's mind. Sleep eluded him. The sharp sound of watch bells pealed and Jack fought in vain to clear his thoughts and steal some rest. Each consecutive half hour a bell was added to the accumulation, their pure tones reminding Jack that his watch was drawing near. Eight bells sounded signaling four in the morning and Jack grudgingly rolled from his hammock without the aid of being awakened by his messmates. He stowed away the sling of canvas silently and emerged onto the deck. As he made his way toward the main shrouds, a coarse croak rose from the quarterdeck.

"Able Seaman Horner, to the helm, if you please. Castor is in sick bay, so you will be standing for him through the watch this morning," said Mr. Lambdin.

"Aye," Jack answered with a sigh. His chest tightened. Just a day ago he had anticipated his trick at the helm with the giddy manner of a young boy. Now, it seemed as dreadful to him as if the boatswain were waiting with his cat of nine tails ready to strike.

Jack took to the quarterdeck and relieved the sailor at the helm. He took stock of the sails aloft and gave the compass a careful study before testing the ship's responsiveness. Allegiance eased over a point and then backed with the wind as he played the helm over and then eased over to course. Slight swells matched their direction, and the wind traced smoothly from the northwest on their starboard quarter. The sky was dark, without a glimmer of starlight or the slight glow of early dawn. Jack surmised it would be another long watch spent in desperate search of something to aid their reckoning. Inwardly, he cursed the thick overcast and the torment it held over the ship. The sound of wind and wave dominated the early hours of his watch, and he was thankful for the tranquil quiet.

"Deck! Breakers off the starboard bow! Looks like rocks, and we're closing on them, fast!" a panicked shout came down from the foretop.

Jack didn't wait for orders. He heaved over the helm to larboard until the wheel was hard over as far as it could traverse.

"Hands! Brace for impact!" the officer of the watch shouted.

Tense moments passed. Jack waited to be jarred from his feet and hear the sickening crunch of timber as it split against rocks. His heartbeat pounded in his throat. Wind fluttered the courses and topsails filling them sporadically and then letting them droop as the ship reeled through her hard turn.

"Horner, come back about on the helm, damnit! Who told you to put her all the way over!" Mr. Lambdin shouted with his rough croak. "I'll have yer backside bloody fer that, ye lubberly whelp! Ye don't move that damned wheel unless yer told!"

The sting of Mr. Lambdin's starter lit across Jack's back from shoulder to shoulder.

He moved the wheel back in the direction it had been, but it was too little, too late.

"Mr. Lambdin, get the helm brought about and our sails filled! Now!" a voice from the darkness commanded.

Jack felt the sting of the starter three more times between his shoulder blades. He could feel red hot welts rising under his thin sailor's shirt.

"You put the helm too far over!" Mr. Lambdin slashed again with his knotted length of rope. "If the sails lose the wind, we lose control of the ship, you blundering idiot!"

Another stinging slash crossed Jack's back, this one was high along his shoulders. Hand over hand, he brought the wheel over starboard even while his back was being pummeled. Anger welled in his guts. Footfalls on the deck sounded and soon the quarterdeck was awash with officers.

"What is going on up here? I was nearly thrown from my hammock! Half the crew is below deck picking themselves up from that damned turn!" shouted Lieutenant Sifton.

"This one!" Mr. Lambdin howled with a finger pointed at Jack. "Horner, this sluggard, he threw the helm hard over larboard wi'out so much as a peep from me or the officers on deck!"

Lieutenant Sifton gave Jack a glowering stare. "Horner, is this true? Why would you take it upon yourself to throw the wheel over so suddenly?"

Jack hesitated for a moment, his back stung from the last slash of Mr. Lamdin's starter. His nose tingled, his stomach tied into knots or rage and his eyes were watering from the effort required to control himself.

"Aye, sir," Jack answered. "The foretop lookouts called out breakers along the starboard bow. I put the wheel over to bring her away from the threat and up into the wind."

A long moment of silent tension passed. Some of the midshipmen made their way up on deck to sate their curiosity. Jack felt a flush of embarrassment and anger burning his face and neck. Lieutenant Sifton paced to the weather rail and stared over the gloomy sea lit only by the pre-dawn glow. He cast a glare at Jack over one shoulder.

"You heard the call from the lookout, and took it upon yourself to make a course correction?" the first lieutenant demanded.

Jack nodded, trying to speak around the lump that had risen in his throat, "Aye, sir. That is exactly what I did."

Lieutenant Sifton nodded slowly, his eyes darted around in an accusatory glare between the officer on watch and Mr. Lambdin. "This young man took action to save the ship from an imminent danger. Why is it that he is being berated and senselessly beaten?"

Jack's mouth went dry. He returned his stare to the constant shift between compass and sails.

"Sir, he set the ship hard over. We very nearly lost the wind, which would leave us powerless to control her," Mr. Lambdin reasoned.

"Which is the point I would expect the quartermaster's mate to make a stern correction before praising the lad for his swift and decisive action. He acted, Mr. Lambdin, without orders or direction. Which begs the question, what exactly were you two doing while our helmsman was heaving the ship over to avoid danger? Eh?"

"Well, I, I was…" Mr. Lambdin began to protest but was coldly cut short.

"You were hauling up your starter to flog the young man responsible for saving the ship, the reputation of her crew and captain, along with mine! I won't have it, Mr. Lambdin. You ought to consider yourself fortunate that I am not taking your lack of action as dereliction of your duties. Young Horner here acted, albeit rashly, but he acted. That is more than I can say for the two of you!" He huffed in a breath and stared down both the Petty Officer and the ship's officer on watch. "Clear the damned quarterdeck before I have you both disrated, or hauled below to see the gunner's daughter. Now!"

Both men clomped off from the quarterdeck, thoroughly scorned. Jack heaved a sigh of relief while at the same time relaxing his grimace from the pain of the mate's starter. Wind filled Allegiance's courses and topsails, the bow dipped at the initial rush of motion and then trimmed as her hull slid through the sea.

"Mr. Lambdin, though entirely too enthusiastic with his starter, is correct. Heaving over the helm like that is reckless in all but the direst of circumstances. Your actions are worthy of praise today, but beware, there are officers and mates alike that would as soon flog a sailor for showing initiative as praise him," the lieutenant said. "I have shielded you from their wrath this day, but I won't always be around to put a stopper on their baser instincts. Keep a sharp eye, Horner."

Jack gripped the wheel tight. Wood grain bit into the wrinkles of flesh between his fingers and in his palms. His thoughts turned to the myriad ways that Mr. Lambdin could exact his revenge throughout daily life aboard the ship. The possibilities were too many to count, and being a Petty Officer, Mr. Lambdin would not have to be especially creative to find an opportunity. Lieutenant Sifton called for a chart to be brought up to the quarterdeck and spent the next several hours trying to decipher Allegiance's possible location. The rocky outcrop presented a handful of possibilities, but even these numbered over a half dozen spread out over many hundreds of miles. Disagreement, frustration and fear permeated the atmosphere on board. Jack longed to climb aloft and leave the noise and tension far below him.

"A point over larb'd, if you please, Horner," the lieutenant said with a glance toward the helm. "An easy point over, if you will."

Jack's face flushed a warm red. He moved the wheel slightly over in a smooth motion. Allegiance responded in kind with a swift correction as her hull slid through a low rise in the sea.

Chatter mixed through the space of Allegiance's gun deck. The smell of salt pork and peas mixed with a last lingering of gun powder from the afternoon gun drills. The grog issue flowed, the seas and winds were fair and spirits were high.

"Aye, Dead-eye Jack at the helm again tomorrow. Better tie yerselves inter yer hammocks tonight boys!" a sailor shouted in jest as Jack passed through the line with his plate of rations and filled tankard of double watered grog. "Ye know, Jack. The boatswain's mates don't take it lightly, stealing their joy and such. They wants ter be the ones rousin' the crew outta our hammocks in the morning!"

A roll of laughter spread through the crew and Jack felt a rush of red creep into his face and neck. He chuckled at the sailor's jest, though it was only the latest in a string of jokes that involved his rash steering as the punchline. All through close order training, sailors had made comments about making him the helmsman aboard an enemy ship. His shipmates insisted it would be the surest way to sap the rogue privateer's morale and hasten a quick strike of their colors. During the afternoon watch, all hands had been mustered to help hoist a top-gallant sail up the foremast. Jack suffered endless quips at how much harder the ship would heel over with the added sail when he next took the helm. Just when he thought his shipmates had lost their taste for the jokes, afternoon gun drills commenced, and the teasing started afresh.

The grog tasted slightly more potent than it had since Allegiance had been in port. It was accompanied by the sweet taste of citrus that lingered on Jack's tongue for a heartbeat after each sip. It wasn't long until the woes of his watch settled and the aches and pains of labor eased.

"A full watch spent at the helm, sorry fer yer luck, Jack," Bowline Bob grunted as he lowered himself to the makeshift mess table across from Jack and Matsumoko. "The quarterdeck can be the best place to spend a watch, but, it can be an insufferable menace too." He lifted his tankard and slugged a big drink of grog down before slapping the vessel onto the planks next to his meal. "I bet the mate of the watch had a few things ter say after ye put her over so damned hard."

Jack nodded. "Mostly he let his starter do the talking, Bob."

"Aye, I'll bet that bastard did," Bob replied over a mouthful of peas. "Mr. Lambdin was always a rough lead, and too damned eager with his starter by half. I knew him when I was a fresh pressed lad myself, aboard a King's Ship called Hunter. She was a third rate ship o' the line, a right powerful man 'o war. Sixty eight guns she had. Her broadside could lay waste to a ship in a single volley. It was a terrible sight."

Jack sipped at his grog and thought over Bob's comment. "Bob. Was Mr. Lambdin the fellow you were lobbying to have me sent aloft?"

Bob nodded. "Aye, Jacky. Unfortunately, he was. I didn't know they'd be fer taking ye ter the quarterdeck and slappin' the helm inter yer hands so damned quick. But, despite some lashing, yer better fer it, lad. I promise ye that," he said before leaning into his supper and grog.

Jack finished his meal in silent thought. He didn't hold Bob responsible for any of his problems. The old sailor had only tried to help Jack, and in many respects was the main reason Jack had been successful while at sea. He'd taken Jack under his tutelage, and kept a sharp eye after him in other respects. The sore spots on Jack's back were the sole responsibility of a quartermaster's mate named Lambdin, and Jack knew in his bones that he hadn't seen the end of it.

All around them, the chatter on deck seemed to revolve around the deep mysteries of the Devil's Triangle.

"This far south and no sun for three days, it's the triangle, lads. Mark m' words, there's evil afoot. It will be our undoing if the quarterdeck doesn't get it sorted, and soon," a sailor griped before slogging the last of his grog issue down in a thirsty gulp.

"The cap'n'll get it sorted," another sailor replied. "He's made a half dozen campaigns and sailed clear ter the East Indies twice over. I heard he sailed the south Pacific as a first luff and had ter look at the charts but once a day. Did the figurin' in his head, like. That's a cap'n I'll sail with, no matter what triangles are drawn on the map."

"That's all a bucket 'o hogwash," another sailor growled. Jack looked and found the hard scowl of Bitter End Bill's weathered face. "I been at sea since I was a boy. Can't even count the years now. An' I heard tell 'o tall tales 'o this cap'n and that. It's all bunk. They make their appearance on deck, sure, they does their figurin' and navigatin' in fronts of the crew like it's no task at'all. But, plenty 'o the king's cap'n's are hard figurin' in their cabins. Sweatin' every detail and praying ter the good Lord that they gets it right." He paused and set down his grog after a deep drink. "As fer the triangle. Yer'll see. It's befuddled better cap'n's than this'un."

A tense silence hung within the confines of the gun deck while several sailor's stares drifted off as dark imaginings took over their minds.

"They don't get their reckoning, it'll be us that bears the hardship," Bitter End Bill continued with a rasp. "The reckoning eludes 'em fer another day er so, and yers all watch an' see. They'll have some sorry soul bound ter the capstan fer a kiss from the cat. Sure as the tide, lads, ye mark me words. The officers gets tense like when they can't do their duty, an feel they 'ave ter keep order an discipline all the tighter fer it. Seen it a'fore, I 'ave."

A lump had grown in Jack's throat. He tried to chase it away with a drink from his grog, the bold flavor of rum and citrus flooded his senses but did little to quench the anxiety that had him stretched tighter than a topsail in a blow. He drew a breath in through his nose and shifted his attention back to the plate of food in front of him. His pork and peas had gone cold, but the staunch pangs of hunger prevented him from letting the meal go to waste. He ate a spoonful of peas and a bite of salt pork while reflecting on the conversation floating around the gun deck. Part of him wanted to share the tensions that had been escalating on the quarterdeck over the last few days. But, he thought better of it. Being assigned to the helm displayed a level of trust in him, he didn't want to betray that trust, and he was sure that no good would come from it. But, the urge to tell someone refused to leave.

"Eh," Bowline Bob muttered before gesturing toward Matsumoko's rations. "Don't worry about all that business, lads. The officer's will find their reckoning soon enough and we'll all be underway in right order." He narrowed his eyes and nodded at Matsumoko. "Are ye going to finish them peas?"

Matsumoko shook his head. "No, I've had enough."

Bob took the plate and scraped Matsumoko's pile of peas onto his own with a grin. "Never let it be said that Bowline Bob let a meal go to tossin', 'specially pork an' peas. It's one of me favorites."

Jack leaned in toward his messmates and lowered his voice. "Bob, it's just like Bill was saying, on the quarterdeck, that is. The officers, they're all a-tilt. They haven't made a proper reckoning and none of them agrees with the others about where they think we are."

Bob offered a knowing nod as he chewed a bite of peas. "It's a matter 'o time, lad. That's all. They is in a rush because the cap'n has a mad on ter find his prize ship. But, it could be days a'fore we're out from under this cloud cover." He thrust his chin out at Jack's grog cup. "How about a slog fer yer old mate, eh?" Jack held his tankard over Bob's and poured him the remains of his issue. Bob smiled and hoisted the vessel. "Thank ye, Jack. Thank ye." He drained the grog with one long gulp and wiped the corners of his mouth with the back of his hand. "I'm sure there's a mess of nerves aft of the mast. Things being what they is, and all. But, we keeps it together a'fore the mast. Keeps her sailin' and ship shape. The officer's will sort their lot out. Fer the time being, we carry on. Trust me, lad. Keep ter yer duties and do 'em as best ye can. Yer'll be just fine."

Jack shared a look with Matsumoko. "He wouldn't dare hit you with his starter, not after everyone saw you handle the marine sergeant at close order training."

Matsumoko didn't even crack a grin. "I'm not so sure of that, Jack. They don't fear one man."

Jack lifted his grog to wash the bitter taste of servitude from his mouth, only to remember that he had shared the last of it with Bowline Bob.

"It's not s' bad, Jack. Mr. Lambdin will come off his mad a touch after a few days. What he needs is ter find someone else ter draw 'is ire. It won't take long and he'll be twisted over someone else's folly. Yer'll see."

Jack rubbed at the still tender welts on his neck and shoulder. "I should hope so, Bob. I only regret that someone else will be subject to his wrath." He caught a glint pass through Matsumoko's eyes. His friend, quiet almost to a fault, had an unnerving look flash across his face. The difference was subtle, but, Jack could see that something was afoot in his mind.

"What troubles ye, Matsumoko?" he asked.

Matsumoko shook his head. "Not a talk for open company," Matsumoko replied quietly. "We'll talk later."

Supper carried on with the usual chatter of sailors. An old sailor retold of the troubles he and his shipmates encountered on a voyage around Cape Horn.

"Winds stronger'n any ye've ever seen. I swears, it felt like they was plumb picking the ship right off'n the seas as she crested a wave," the sailor said in a hollow croak of a voice. He paused and let the dramatic effect of his tale build. "The masts, they shuddered s' hard in the gale it took a twenty year hand right off'n his feet up on her tightropes. They's cracking and groaning all the while, and yer jus' a prayin' out there on the yardarms, prayin' she holds fer jus' a little while longer. All the while, the seas is so cold ice is buildin' up on the foc'sl. Sea spray clings ter the sails and freezes in sheets 'o ice. No fire in the galley, on account 'o the seas bein' s' rough. Swells near as high as the masts an' all." The gun deck had fallen silent to the somber recounting. All eyes were glued to the old sailor's weathered face, he glared around at the gathering and continued. "We lost near a dozen hands ter the sea. Right good men, washed clean off'n the deck, fell from the yards. We lost the mizzen topmast comin' about westerly, the winds were s' damned foul it carried the mast and three good hands right with it." The sailor scowled and let his gaze fall around the deck again. "Those winds were s' foul, angry like, ye could tell they wanted ter see the ship ter the bottom. The waves too, seas like nothin' I'd ever seen afore or since. Makes the storm we jus' had seem like nothin' but a blustery day. I has nightmares about the Horn ter this day. Jus' pray we don't wind up following cap'n's prize down ter them waters. Half-a ye's will swears off sailorin', mark me words."

Jack grimaced at the foreboding words. He couldn't imagine seas worse than the storms they had just endured. The waves had been as high as the yardarm for the mainsail, the winds had made climbing the shrouds an exercise in nerves and the rain had pelted them so hard at times it felt like stinging needles when it impacted with skin. He imagined the whole affair taking place in a clime so cold that sheets of ice were generated by sea spray collecting on the sails. It brought a chill into his blood.

Bells rang for the first dog watch and the gun deck dissolved into activity. Sailors stowed away their mess gear and took down the makeshift tables used for dining. The sailor's tale of woe hung heavy over Jack's mind while he was still processing the events of the day. He decided a tour up on deck with the wind in his face would do him well. He stowed his mess gear and climbed through the fore hatch into the evening. A boatswains whistle piped while hands swarmed the shrouds. The drab grayness of clouds had thinned to long trailing wisps laced with rose pink and traces of orange from the setting sun. Lively conversations struck up around the foremast. Whether it was the evening grog issue, or the clearing skies, spirits climbed to lofty heights along with the top men of the dog watch. Sunset blazed on for another hour and painted the western skies with glorious hues that stretched high before retreating with their fiery master to the horizon before finally submitting to the night. Stars emerged one by one, faint at first as the light of day died from the memory of the sky, and then bolder as darkness prevailed. Soon, the sky was alight with the twinkling brilliance of a million stars. All hands, whether on watch or not, made their way onto Alliance's main deck. More seasoned hands looked aloft with spyglass in hand or studied notes of constellations they had observed. Jack took in the glory of the night sky and followed the lee rail as far aft as he dared while searching out the constellations Bowline Bob had taught him to look for aboard Salem Tide. He heard snippets of a class Lieutenant Sifton was teaching the midshipmen, his subject; celestial navigation using the stars.

"Ursa Major, found in the northern hemisphere, is a useful means of finding Ursa Minor. This being the Big Dipper and Little Dipper respectively. When one finds Ursa Minor, he only needs follow the pattern of stars to the end of the Little Dipper's handle to find Polaris, the North Star," the lieutenant said in his gentle but authoritative voice. "These constellations are good indicators of north in the early evening." He paused and stared high into the night for a long beat before shifting his gaze down to the gathered midshipmen. "What are some good indicators of south we can find in the night sky?"

Jack listened intently as the class continued.

"Orion the hunter," a midshipman answered.

Lieutenant Sifton nodded and paced forward on the quarterdeck. "Aye, Orion the hunter is a good southern constellation. Handily enough, it is fairly easy to spot due to the straight line of three stars forming his belt. If you can find Orion, you should be able to find Taurus," he pointed high into the sky, "Taurus will be oriented high and west of Orion. The bull is visible fairly early in the evening, depending on relative latitude, while Orion will be visible slightly later."

The class continued, and Jack listened in as best he could while trying to absorb as much of the information as possible through the sound of wind and sea. He became so absorbed in trying to listen that he failed to notice Matsumoko approach over his shoulder.

"Aspiring to be a king's officer?" Matsumoko asked in jest.

Jack startled for a heartbeat before whipping around to find his friend with a rare grin displayed across his face. "Good lord, Matsumoko, you gave me a start!"

"I didn't mean to, Jack," Matsumoko said. "My apologies."

Jack caught his breath and slapped a palm onto Matsumoko's shoulder. "You're fine, mate. I just didn't hear you," Jack replied with a smile and then gestured toward the skies. "The clouds have cleared. That should improve the general mood aboard. Don't you think?" Jack suggested.

Matsumoko's grin faded, he shook his head. "One would think, but I doubt it, Jack. A fix on our location will just prompt the captain's urgency to his original haste. All the more since we have been so delayed."

H.M.S Allegiance
25 June 1770
Devil's Triangle - Exact Position Unknown

"A point over starboard, Horner," Lieutenant Sifton said. "The wind is easing."

Jack moved the ship's wheel in a smooth, gentle motion. Dawn had worn through the last wisps of cloud and revealed a bright sky of pale blue. Noon was hours away, and their reckoning along with it.

"Mr. Peele, extra lookouts to the fore top," the lieutenant said as he paced the windward rail. He had been on deck since before Jack arose from his hammock for the morning watch. Typically, Jack would not see the ship's first lieutenant until the half watch when hands changed stations, and he took up his place at the helm. There was a charged energy on deck, an anticipation of noon being called and the show of sextants on the quarterdeck. Allegiance's crew was hungry to know their position, from the lowest tar to the captain, it had been the main concern since the lapse of the storm.

"Deck! Land in sight, three points off starboard bow. Small island. Looks like sanded beach and a few trees is all," a sailor shouted down from high on the mainmast.

Lieutenant Sifton marched forward with a sharp call for a midshipman to fetch him a telescope. He halted next to the mainmast shrouds and leaned into the motion of the ship. When the midshipman arrived with his telescope, he extended the instrument and braced himself against the thick ropes used for climbing aloft. Allegiance lifted and slunk away with the action of a wave, and then another, while Lieutenant Sifton remained fixed in place staring through his telescope. For what seemed like an eternity to Jack, the officer peered through the cylindrical telescope without so much as relieving his eye from the eyepiece. Then, suddenly, he leaned away from the shrouds and collapsed the scope.

"Mr. Peele, notate the sighting in the ship's log. Be so good as to shoot an azimuth to the island's centerline, or nearabouts. It is about four miles distant, by my judgment," the lieutenant said as he paced back to the quarterdeck. "When noon is called and we make the reckoning, it could prove useful information to aid us with our longitude."

Allegiance slid over another set of waves, her bow rising easily before easing down and sending a gentle spray up from the bow. Jack held the wheel firm against the play of the sea and tried to loosely observe a pair of midshipmen as they worked through shooting an azimuth to the distant island. From his perspective behind the helm, it looked like a low-lying dark spot on the horizon amid the open vastness of the ocean. The midshipmen debated sharply for a few moments before settling on a figure to record into the log. Jack listened intently while they held their discussion and then finally came to an agreement. The intricacies of nautical navigation intrigued him. He remembered the conversation he had with the captain of a British man of war in Boston. The officer had gently encouraged him to stay at his studies and informed him of the importance of mathematics in navigation.

"Mr. Peele," Lieutenant Sifton called across the quarterdeck. "My respects to the captain, and please inform him of the sighting of land, if you will."

Mr. Peele, the midshipman on watch, saluted smartly in the naval fashion of touching his hat brim and departed to deliver the message to Captain Williams. Jack could sense a heightened tension fall on the quarterdeck like a cold wind. The chatter of the midshipmen ceased, and the general joviality from sighting land after their tribulations melted away. A look aloft prompted Jack to ease tension off the ship's wheel for a ponderous beat before edging back with the wind. Allegiance was dancing on her course while she took the wind bluff on her beam and he didn't want to be called to task by either the captain or Mr. Lambdin.

"Horner! Mind the helm and not the young gentlemen! Your task is course and sail, not the affairs of navigation," Mr. Lambdin said in his croak.

Jack drew a deep breath and fought the urge to say his piece to the ornery quartermaster's mate. His neck and shoulders were still sore from the last time he had found himself athwart the Petty Officer's hawse. He kept a loose eye on the compass and paid close attention to the top sails while Mr. Lambdin paced behind him muttering frustrated comments about new sailors and their lack of skill and discipline.

It boiled Jack's blood. He imagined Mr. Lambdin facing off against Matsumoko for close order training and it served to temper his mood.

When the watch bells finally rang, and Jack was relieved from his post at the helm, the crew had gathered on deck for the daily ritual of close order training. Captain Williams appeared from the aft hatch and stood rigid next to the windward rail while sailors and marines practiced with cutlasses, bayonets and boarding axes. As he usually did, Jack paired with Matsumoko for training. He was never in competition for his choice in training companions. Matsumoko had cast a long shadow for himself when he had stepped up to a marine sergeant's challenge and thoroughly defeated him in a match with cutlasses. While the rest of the crew drilled in regimented naval fashion, Matsumoko showed Jack the elegant movements he had learned while training as a child in Japan.

"Western fencing has all the grace of a battle of bludgeons," Matsumoko said as he took a training sword in hand and spread his feet into a broad fighting stance. "Try to picture water, how it moves and flows. You should be the same. Let your movements flow, advance where you can, retreat where you must, but always flow. Use your energy efficiently. Redirect your opponent into your attack, strike when he is extended and vulnerable."

Jack, trying hard to absorb his friend's wisdom, nodded with a deep frown. He tried to picture what Matsumoko was saying and how it applied to fighting with a sword in hand. There was no doubt in his mind, Matsumoko was lethal, with a blade as well as with his bare hands. He mimicked Matsumoko's movements as his friend demonstrated a series of three slicing attacks followed by a plunging thrust. Sailors on either side of them took little notice of their irregular training until Matsumoko instructed Jack to try and land an attack against him. At half speed, Jack tried overhand attacks, slanting attacks, and even a committed lunge. Just as Matsumoko had described, he redirected each attack with fluid parries that seemed to extend Jack just past his balance. It was masterful. Matsumoko looked completely at ease, even as Jack increased the speed and intensity of his attacks. Every sword stroke Jack mustered was brushed away in quick easy parries. Matsumoko was like an artist at work, the sword his brush. His feet were light and fast, his hands steady and precise. It wasn't long until Jack noticed the sailors and marines in their immediate vicinity had ceased their drills and were staring with mouths agape.

"You there! What's this all about?" croaked Mr. Lambdin. "All of you quit yer slack jawed lollying and get back ter yer drills! Next hand I sees idle will get a rap across his back he won't soon forget!" The red-faced quartermaster's mate barged into the midst of Jack and Matsumoko, his hat cocked forward and his chest barreled out in front of him. He smiled a grotesque grin at the pair as they ceased their match. "I shoulda known, our pressed lads from the whaling tender. Havin' a bit of fun while the rest of the crew is hard at drills, eh? I think an afternoon spent with a holystone in yers hands will set ye's to rights. Close order training isn't a free for all melee on deck, ye lubbers! It's training fer when we come across the rogue Frenchy, so's we can take her a'prize and haul in a fat purse!"

Jack couldn't hold his tongue any longer. "Mr. Lambdin, Matsumoko is especially skilled at swordplay. He was showing me a different technique is all," he said in as respectful a tone as he could muster.

The Petty Officer shook his head in disgust. "We all knows how good yer little Chinaman friend is with a sword," Mr. Lambdin sneered with a malicious glare toward Matsumoko. "But, I don't give a damn. Raises a hand ter me and I'll 'ave the skin off'n his back till we can sees his spine! Close order time is fer drills! The Navy way!"

A heartbeat of pure tension hung over the small crowd surrounding them. Jack chanced a look from the corner of his eye over to Matsumoko. He knew his friend despised being called a Chinaman, and he hoped it wouldn't elicit a foul reaction. But, Matsumoko's face bore only a stony expression betraying no emotion.

"Aye, Mr. Lambdin, drills it is," he said in a firm voice.

The Petty Officer stepped in close to the young Japanese man and beamed triumphantly. "That's what I thought, lubber. Back ter yer drills and yers two come see me after, there's holystones a-waitin' fer ye's."

After a final disdainful glare, Mr. Lambdin stormed aft through the crowd of sailors on deck. Jack clenched his jaw. He and Matsumoko had a long afternoon ahead of them, his knees, shoulders and back could already feel the ache that was coming.

"Deck, land-ho! A point larboard of the bow, on the horizon. Low island with sand and trees," the foremast lookout shouted down.

Jack waited for Lieutenant Sifton to respond, he held the wheel steady and minded Mr. Lambdin standing close over his shoulder. It was the second sighting of land during watch, and counting the small island spotted during Jack's morning trick at the helm, the third of the day.

"We are definitely further east than I had originally hoped for, damn my eyes," the lieutenant grumbled after acknowledging the sighting. "Our latitude should have us in the vicinity of sighting San Juan, but perhaps we are in fact approaching the leeward isles."

A look aloft prompted Jack to bring the wheel over just a fraction. They were holding a southward course with the wind drumming steadily from the east. With the wind on her beam, Allegiance danced between gusts as the steady struggle between sail and wave propelled them along. It was more laborious than Jack had grown accustomed to while sailing with the wind at close reach over their aft quarter, but Jack faced the challenge head on.

"Mr. Peele, an azimuth on that island, smartly, if you please," Lieutenant Sifton ordered. "If we are indeed making our passage into the leeward isles I would like to get a firm reckon on where we are entering. These seas are littered with reefs and shoals." He cast a cautious glare aloft and examined the top gallants. "Hands to shorten sail, Mr. Lambdin. Until we have a better fix on what lies ahead, I would rather not go plowing full speed into a reef or some such."

A sense of relief washed over Jack. Shortened top gallants would ease his battle with the wheel to keep Allegiance on her course. His hands and shoulders still ached from the strain of grinding at the deck for several hours with a holy stone.

"Sir, I agree that shortening sail is the proper decision," the voice of Allegiance's sailing master, Mr. Tillisby said quietly. "But, the captain won't be pleased. He is hell bent for Isla De Mona."

Lieutenant Sifton remained silent for a long beat before replying in a subdued voice. "We are significantly further east than his anticipated course, if my reckoning by these land sightings is at all accurate. I put us closer to the leeward isles, maybe as far east as Anguilla. We cannot afford to plow forward flying all sail, just look at the charts, Mr. Tillisby. We will run afoul of a reef or a shoal if we are not cautious in these stretches." Another long pause elapsed and Jack chanced a look out of the corner of his eye. "We can't even be certain that Saber is anywhere near Isla De Mona, she could be anywhere."

"Don't try to tell the captain that," Mr. Tillisby replied with a sigh. "I have debated with him in his cabin on the matter, to no end. He is convinced, and with fair reasoning, that Saber will be lurking between Hispaniola and San Juan to prey on merchant shipping."

"There is no guarantee of that," the first lieutenant replied. "But, even so, we are considerably east of that passage."

"Pass word for the captain, sir," Mr. Tillisby said with a hushed voice. "He needs to know."

Lieutenant Sifton drew a deep breath and released a sigh. "Yes, he does." A moment of silence passed before he spoke up with a louder voice, "Mr. Peele, my respects to the captain, and would you inform him duly of the new sighting of land. Please convey my opinion that we are considerably east of the passage between Hispaniola and San Juan, and that I recommend shortening sail in these waters."

"Aye, sir," the midshipman replied before plodding off to his task.

Jack held the ship's wheel steady as the sea played against the rudder. He felt his hopes of shortening sail slipping away as quick as the water beneath Allegiance's hull. The sun was bright and warm, it felt good on his face and neck while the sea breeze continued to bring gusts of fresh air tinged with salty ocean spray. Despite his struggles, his sore arms and back, and the lingering of welts across his shoulders, his spirits rose with the fair weather and moderate seas.

Captain Williams appeared at the aft hatch. His gaunt features tightened against the sun's shine as he made his way on deck and then to the windward rail where Lieutenant Sifton kept watch over sail and sea.

"You believe we are east of San Juan?" the captain asked his first lieutenant.

"Aye, sir," Lieutenant Sifton answered. "Given this newest sighting, I don't believe our earlier reckoning to be correct. The last land raised was to our lee, westward, that was several hours ago, and we've now left that in our wake. The new sighting is east, off our windward bow by a point." The two men looked over a chart that rested under a set of weights at a small table just behind the helm. Jack listened as they discussed their position, but kept his eyes locked forward, switching between sail and compass. "I believe we are approaching the leeward isles, here. If we shorten sail, and sail westward, we would know for sure on sighting San Juan. Alternately, we could beat a course for Anguilla and see if the harbor master there has any intelligence on our prize."

A long pause passed. Jack felt the tension of differing opinions fall heavily across the quarterdeck.

"I agree with your approximation of our position. We are further east than I had hoped, however, that bears little weight against the urgency of our mandate," Captain Williams replied. "Keep note of any more sightings, we should pass eighteen degrees latitude neigh on noon tomorrow. We will make our turn westward then, toward Isla De Mona and our prey."

"Shall we shorten sail until we pass into deeper waters, sir?" Lieutenant Sifton asked with heavy suggestion in his voice.

"No," replied the captain. "Double lookouts should be sufficient for the time being. If we mark readings of less than twenty fathoms, then you may take in sail."

"Very well, sir," Lieutenant Sifton replied.

As suddenly as he had appeared on deck, the captain retired back below to his cabin. He offered no further insight to the gathered officers on the quarterdeck, nor praise or correction to any sailor he happened across. Allegiance continued her steady gait over low rising seas while Jack wrestled with the helm at each fresh gust of wind. With a better understanding of their position, and the foul weather long behind them, the crew was settling into the routines of sea life. Top men re-reeved lines that had been damaged by the gale, heavy weather sails had been hauled down and lighter sails hoisted in their place. The galley had returned to providing hot meals twice daily, and during hours of darkness lanterns provided a wash of dim yellow glow to everything in their reach.

Eight bells sounded, and as Jack was relieved of duty he passed below deck at the fore hatch right after meeting with his messmates. He was greeted by a hearty roust on his shoulder from Bowline Bob and a slight grin and nod from Matsumoko. There would be only a few hours before evening gun drills commenced, and each man hoped to spend the time avoiding extra work details. The gun deck was crowded with all hands in anticipation of drills being called, and the din of chatter mixed thick within its wooden confines. Jack fell in behind Bowline Bob and the trio filtered their way in between small gatherings of sailors, each involved in their own matters of conversation. The talk ranged wildly and Jack heard snippets of every manner of sea life. Complaints about the food, lessons on line handling and operation of cannons, speculation as to where their enemy could be, all drifted in and out of Jack's hearing as he followed Bowline Bob aft.

"I heard th' cap'n when he comes on deck earlier, he means ter sail us right fer Barbados an' then its off ter the coasts of Brazil. Yeller Fever, wild natives, bad water, take yer pick, its all bad news," one sailor griped.

Jack turned at the blatant lie and regarded the scowling sailor with a stare. The man was one of the afterguard, sailors who attended the lines at the base of the main and mizzen masts while top men handled the work from aloft.

"That isn't what the captain said at all," Jack said with a deep frown.

The ranting sailor turned toward Jack and sneered. "What're ye getting at, cully? I hear it from his own mouth. Its Brazil fer us, the cap'n is sure of it. That rogue ship is down there hiding out, like."

Jack shook his head. "I was on the quarterdeck when he came up from his cabin. He said nothing of Brazil. We are to make westerly once we pass eighteen degrees latitude."

A quiet fell over the sailors immediately surrounding Jack and the griping deckhand. Jack felt their eyes lock onto him as if he had stumbled unwittingly into some type of trap.

"Yers sayin' I'm a liar?" the deckhand challenged in a growled tone.

Jack's breath caught in his throat. He had seen a pair of altercations take place aboard the warship already, one of which had resulted in a sailor being taken before the captain and then to the capstan shortly after. "I think you mistook what he said," Jack replied with a shrug. "That's all."

The deckhand stepped close to Jack with balled fists and a flush of rage building in his eyes. "Naw, yer takin' in sail now that yer know I won't let yers accusations go unanswered. Better clap a stopper on it, afore it gets yer arse in a sling, cully. I'll take ye over m' knee and teach yers a lesson yer papa probably should have."

The mention of his father sent a wild rush of white hot seething through Jack's blood. His chest tightened, his hands clenched into fists and his heart began to thrum through his ribs like it was trying to beat its way out.

"I said you were mistaken. I didn't say you were a liar," Jack replied while fire built inside his guts. "But, since you mention it. I think you were up at the main belaying rail for your watch. The captain never went forward of the mizzen. You couldn't have heard a thing he said."

Jack had been in his share of schoolyard dust ups, but this promised to be very different. The man standing in front of him was a grown man, twenty years old or older and fifty pounds heavier than Jack. He twisted his face in a grimace of rage and grabbed a fistful of Jack's thin sailor's shirt.

"That tears it, ye swab. I'll bloody yer nose fer that…"

Jack didn't hesitate. As the deckhand was drawing one fist back to wind up a powerful hit, he was caught by a lightning fast jab that Jack threw. The jab hit him in his throat, and he released Jack shirt without delivering his punch. A flurry of punches followed. Jack pounced on the deckhand as the man reeled from the first blow and fell onto his back. One after another, Jack rained furious punches on the recoiling deckhand hitting his face, throat, chest and forehead. His arms burned from the urgent pace while his mind raced with thoughts of mixed rage and fear. The deckhand was well out of his class, he was heavier, stronger, bigger and had longer arms. Jack knew the minute he let up his attack that the odds would tip out of his favor and he would take a pummeling, so he refused to relent. Punch after punch he continued until he felt a pair of rough hands lay a savage grip onto his shoulders.

"Jack! Lay off!" Bob's voice thundered through the gun deck. "They'll stripe yer back fer fighting! Lay off 'im!"

With a sudden pull, Jack was thrust away from the deckhand and plunged into the middle of a crowd of sailors who had gathered around the altercation. Their faces were long and eyes were wide, several mouths hung open in disbelief.

"Gangway! Make way, ye swine! What in the hells is goin' on down here?" the distinct croak of Mr. Lambdin broke through the crowd. "Ye bastards make way, I said! What is the damned racket abouts?"

Jack's heart seized in his throat. He knew it was all over for him. Mr. Lambdin would see the plain evidence of a gun deck scrap and he would be brought before the captain. Perhaps they would even string a noose around his neck and haul him up by the yards. Fear wracked every fiber of his body. The crowd of sailors parted and a clear line of sight to Mr. Lambdin and bared the ugly scene to his discerning glare.

"What's this?" he growled. "Horner in a gun deck scrap, eh?" He paced to the deckhand who was struggling to his feet. Blood dribbled from the deckhand's nose and mouth. "Ah, seems he did ye a fair turn.

No matter though, fighting aboard a man of war is a serious offense." He turned back to where Jack stood by his messmates and pulled the length of knotted rope from his thick leather belt. "I knew you'd be problems, Horner. I knew it the second I laid eyes on ye." With a flick of his wrist he sent the starter flying and caught Jack across the cheek. Pain sliced through Jack's flesh. He could feel the hot swelling of a welt already beginning to form.

Jack retreated beneath upraised arms. Another vicious swing of the starter caught him on the wrist, followed by a third which landed across his shoulders and neck.

"I'll beat yer bloody afore I take yer ter the cap'n, and another fer makin' me look a fool in front of first l'tenent!" Mr. Lambdin hissed as he wound his arm back for another swing.

Jack kept his arms raised. He tensed in anticipation of the coming pain. The starter fell along his arm and wrapped around his wrist. Mr. Lambdin immediately recoiled for another strike, but the rope bit on Jack's wrist and Mr. Lambdin's grip slipped free. Jack fell forward from the force and sprawled onto the hardwood deck.

"You impudent little son of a bitch!" Mr. Lambdin howled in a rage. "How dare you pull my starter out of my hand!" Jack looked up and found Mr. Lambdin's face a picture of fury itself. "Attempting to strike a Petty Officer, Horner? We'll see you hanged from a yardarm fer this!" He turned to the crowd of gawking sailors and pointed to a pair standing nearby. "You two, take him by the arms. He is going to stand before the cap'n fer this."

Jack's heart seized in his chest. He felt a streak of lightning run through his blood. Fear clamped his mind and stole away the breath from his lungs.

"But, Mr. Lambdin," Bowline Bob protested. "Yer starter wrapped his wrist. He wasn't trying ter strike yers!"

The irate Petty Officer turned on Bob with a scowl. "Shut yer mouth, less'n yer wants ter be right next ter yer messmate here, Bob. He pulled the starter right from me hand, and I won't hear tellin' otherwise!"

Two sailors seized Jack's arms and forced him up to his feet. His hands were still wet with sticky blood from the deckhand's nose. After a moment of jostling, they led him aft down the length of the gun deck with Mr. Lambdin clearing the way. His mind raced while his feet barely managed the pace set by the two burly sailors escorting him.

"Come on, lad," one of the sailors said. "Pick up yer feet. No use dragging them now. Best ter just get this over with, eh?"

Jack mumbled in a feeble voice. "I didn't grab his starter. You both saw."

"Makes no difference," the other sailor uttered low. "Best yer can hope fer is a mercy from the cap'n, lad."

Jack's guts knotted when he heard it. His situation was hopeless. He was about to fall victim to the heavy hand of the British crown, just as his parents had. At the aft hatchway, the sailors led Jack up the steep set of stairs and into the fresh open air of the main deck. Wind smack at his face and tugged at his loose-fitting shirt.

"Pardon, sir," Mr. Lambdin said to the officer on watch. "But, could I trouble ye fer the master-at-arms ter have this here lubbersome scally clapped inter irons below? He pulled me starter outta me hands and tried ter strike me with it when I interrupted a ruckus he was having with another sailor below deck."

The watch lieutenant scowled beneath his fore-and-aft bicorne hat. "Fighting and attempting to strike a Petty Officer?" He looked at Jack with a slight shake of his head. "Aren't you the young man pressed from the whaling tender?"

Jack nodded, somberly. "Aye, sir. I am."

The lieutenant's scowl deepened. He looked back at Mr. Lambdin. "Aye, I'll have him restrained and taken below. Lieutenant

Sifton will want to hear about this as well. He has taken special interest in this young man."

"Makes no difference ter me, sir," Mr. Lambdin said with a cocky jut of his chin. "First l'tenant or not, the cap'n won't have it, a common tar trying ter strike at a Petty Officer an such."

The lieutenant on watch shook his head. "No, I don't suppose he will." He gestured to a midshipman standing near the helm. When the young gentleman stepped forward, the lieutenant issued curt direction. "Pass compliments to the Master-At-Arms and do please inform him that there is a sailor on deck who needs to be restrained and confined below in the orlop. Then, if you will, pass my respects to Lieutenant Sifton and ask if he will come on deck, at his convenience. Do inform him of the sailor we have here who is to be restrained and confined, and the reason as to why, if you please."

The midshipman knuckled his hat brim smartly and acknowledged the order before disappearing down the aft hatchway. Jack felt his future slip away while the dark abyss of dreadful possibilities obscured his mind. His heart raced, thrumming through his chest and beating a panicked cadence into his ears. Everything seemed to spin while

Allegiance pitched over a slight swell and rolled from the force of wind on her beam. Seconds seemed to drag on forever. His stomach tightened into an impossible knot and he felt like retching. The Master-At-Arms appeared through the aft hatch with two marines under arms. In an unceremonious manner, iron manacles were clasped around Jack's wrists and ankles.

"Fer attempting ter strike a superior, Horner, ye are under arrest," the Master-At-Arms said before turning to the armed marines. "See the prisoner below deck ter the orlop, and make sure he is secured and placed under guard. I will make sure Sergeant Bremmer has supper brought to whoever is standing the first watch."

With rough grasps and pulls, Jack was transferred from the sailors who had brought him up on deck to the marines. Where the sailors had given Jack a sense of comradeship, and a slight sympathy to his plight, the marines held no such empathy. Without a word, they marched him below deck and into the bowels of the warship. As they passed down the aft stairs to the gun deck Jack looked for his messmates. Amidships, between the larboard gun seven and gun six, Matsumoko and Bowline Bob looked on with tightened expressions. For a heartbeat, Jack's stare lingered. He felt a wave of crushing guilt. He had let his friends down. Matsumoko's stare conveyed pure grief with a sense of emotion Jack had never gotten from him before. Bowline Bob's face was wracked with the pain of disappointment. A rough pull at his shoulder goaded him off of the gun deck and down the stairs to the gloomy confines of the orlop.

H.M.S Allegiance
28 June 1770
17 Degrees 55′ N, 65 Degrees 22′ W

A cold dampness ruled the deeper bowels of Allegiance. The orlop was removed from the hatch gratings by the height of the gun deck. Even if the gratings were hoisted away and the thick canvas covering peeled back, Jack would see no light down in his cramped confinement. The air was still and close, but it held none of the warmth he had been enjoying since the breaking of the storm. Down in the ship's lower decks, clammy cold seeped into everything. The iron shackles at his feet had been threaded through an iron bilboes bar attached to the deck. They radiated a chill through his skin and made the joints in his feet and ankles ache from their cold kiss. His wrists were similarly bound, though the chain in between his wrist shackles was long enough for him to sit up, it prevented him from laying down or even standing. He sat hunched in darkness, contemplating the miserable end that awaited him. In the stillness of night, he swore profane oaths of vengeance against Mr. Lambdin and any Brit who would stand in his way. He lamented the death of his parents and grieved the disappointment they would have felt at how he met his fate. He struggled to find any measure of comfort in the cramped space he occupied. His leg shackles were clamped just loose enough that any movement produced an uncomfortable rub of metal on skin, and his wrists were bound so tight that he could feel blood being constricted from their squeeze. Minutes dragged on while Allegiance pitched and rolled in her customary cycle of never ending motion. A bilge rat squealed, the marine sentry coughed, the swish and splash of seawater slipping past the ship's hull sounded. After what seemed like three lifetimes, but was probably only an hour, the bumping sound of footfalls on the gun deck above him pattered all around. Timbers creaked and groaned with strain and a muffled shout broke through the noise. More footfalls sounded followed by a thunderstorm of rumbles. They were conducting gun drills. The sounds of gun carriage wheels rolling on deck drowned away everything else. Jack longed to be with his messmates, sweating and working among them in hearty camaraderie.

The rumble and shouts of gun drills continued long into the evening. Jack wondered who had taken his place alongside the larboard gun number seven to help Matsumoko and Bowline Bob. His legs cramped in the awkward position his restraints forced him into. A pitch of the ship rolled him back until the restraints on his wrists were taut. The pain was compounded by the icy chill of the cold iron. Everything became a torment in the cramped darkness, the noise, the constant motion that denied him any manner of rest. Even in his thoughts, he anguished. Images of his mother came to him, her eyes filled with tears at his unjust treatment. He saw his father's shame at the state he had sunken to. Jack's eyes welled with hot tears and he admonished himself even at this. His father's words, "You have to be a man now," rang clear in his mind. He had failed. Streams formed at the corners of his eyes and made warm tracks down his cheeks. He had fought against it for as long as he could, he could fight no more. The wave of emotion he had been holding back broke through despite his efforts. His breathing quickened while his body trembled with sobs that racked through him in uncontrollable waves. He was overcome with a storm of grief, guilt, and sadness. His thoughts continued to drift in the darkness of his confinement. Memories of his early childhood in Boston, the smell of his father's forge, a mixture of smoke and searing hot metal. The softness of his mother's touch, her fragrance and her sweet voice. Jack felt lost in a never ending sea of despair. He had become so wrapped in his thoughts that he failed to notice when the racket of training had ceased on the deck above him. Allegiance slipped through the sea with naught but the creak and groan of timbers and the swish of seawater against the hull to mark the passage of time.

"Jack," a whisper came through the darkness. It was so faint he almost couldn't tell if it was real, but it came again. "Jack. Can you hear me?"

Jack tried to shift himself to see the source of the whisper. His constraints clinked and rattled in the dark. "Who is there?" he asked.

"It's me, Jack. Yer old mate Bob!" Bob whispered a little louder. "I slipped down 'ere with this."

In the darkness, Jack felt a warm touch on his shoulder. He extended a hand as far as his shackles would allow and found Bowline Bob's meaty hand holding a pair of ship's biscuits and a wedge of cheese.

"I figured these bastards probably didn't bring ye vittles fer yer supper. Can't ha ye goin' hungry, ye needs yer strength," Bob whispered as he handed over the small share of rations. "Biscuit is from me an' Bitter End Bill. Cheese is from yer Matsumoko, who is about stricken sideways worried fer ye."

Jack felt another stab of guilt, and then a slow resignation. "You shouldn't have. None of you. It makes no matter if my strength withers. I am a doomed man. But all of you need your rations," he said and handed the fistful of food back into Bob's palm.

"Ye aren't hanging, Jacky. Ye can't think that way," Bob said in a raspy whisper. He shoved the handful of food back into Jack's grasp. "Eat. Ye need yer strength. Yer goin' ter be standin' afore the cap'n tomorrow. Keep yer wits, Jack. He's the only thing a-standin' between yers and a noose round yer gullet. Jus' explains ter 'im how it all happened. He'll take a mercy on yer."

Jack tensed against his restraints. The pain against his ankles and wrists spiked to an intolerable throb and ache that penetrated all the way through flesh and into bone. It radiated from the tips of his fingers and toes, seized his joints in frigid pangs of pain and crept into each of his limbs. He nibbled at the ship's biscuit. It was hard as stone with no grog or ale to soften it, but Jack was grateful for his friend's kind gesture. The cheese was dry and hard, but it sufficed to quell his hunger. Jack ate as quickly as the tough bread and dry cheese would allow.

"You didn't think to bring a grog cup, did you Bob?" Jack asked.

A moment of silence passed, and Jack realized he had spoken too loud. Bob answered with an even lower whisper, "Aye, Jacky. I did, but havin' ter come down through the fore hatch and then crawl me way through the front part 'o the hold, I figured most would spill out anyway. I brought ye a skin 'o water. But, ye needs ter make 'er last. Cap'n will see yer at the mast tomorrow, and hope this all gets a-sorted. But, if'n yer stuck down here's fer a spell, I won't be able ter make me way down here whenever I fancy."

Jack took the leather canteen and uncorked the stopper. He raised it to his mouth and drank. Never before had water tasted so wonderful. Even though it was tinged with vinegar and citrus, it quenched Jack's ravenous thirst.

"Easy, there," Bob said. "It needs ter last yer. Like I says, I won't be able ter come a visit any old time I feels like." He checked over his shoulder and then looked toward the gangway where the dim glow of a lantern announced the presence of a marine sentry. "Ye keep yer nerve tomorrow when yer standin' afore the cap'n. Sea justice is harsh like, but it isn't altogether unfair. Ye tells it like it happened, and don't yer go bendin' the truth about yer duster with the deckhand. Mr. Lambdin is sure ter call 'im as a witness. Tells it true, Jacky, an' the cap'n, he'll do right by ye." He paused when a set of footsteps sounded out in the gangway. "I better get, iff'n I gets caught down here they'll clap me in irons right next ter ye." He gave Jack a feeble grin before disappearing into the shadows of the orlop.

Left alone in the darkness, Jack ate the food Bob had smuggled down to him with quick greedy bites. He hadn't realized just how hungry he had been until Bob thought to bring him food. He ate the last bite of ship's biscuit and devoured the cheese until not even a crumb was left. Against the caution from Bob, Jack unstoppered the leather canteen and upended it. His parched lips and throat savored ever drop of liquid and within a heartbeat, it was gone. A shuffle in the passageway caught Jack's attention just before the yellow glow of a lantern appeared.

"What is going on in here? I thought I heard a voice," the marine sentry challenged.

Jack shook his head and settled against his restraints. "Just me," he said in a morose tone.

The marine sneered, his lip shriveling in the warm yellow lantern light. "Right. Ye haven't a friend on board, I'm sure. None that'll come visit ye anyhow. Maybe the Chinaman. Just as well. I'm supposed ter turn away any of yer mess that comes a looking after ye anyway."

The words struck Jack, but their implication cut far deeper. Someone had given instructions for him not to receive any visits. His mind turned over the possibilities. He would stand before the captain and tell the truth, whatever comes from it.

"Haaaaands! All hands lay aft fer default!" a voice thundered through the wooden chasm of Allegiance. Footfalls sounded like drums beating above Jack's head and soon it was his heart thundering so loud he couldn't hear anything else. The moment had arrived. He would be escorted up on deck and then stand before the captain. Scant minutes after the shouted call, a pair of armed marines entered the orlop and unsecured his restraints from the bilboes. They took him with a rough hand each under his arms and hurried him topside. Every step was agony as the iron shackled rubbed his flesh raw. The stairs proved especially troublesome. His legs refused to obey him and after the first few steps the marines took to dragging him as much as leading him. On the main deck, Jack's eyes stung at the burning brilliance of daylight. He squinted to temper the glare, but even at that he could barely see in the shining brightness of day. His extended stay in dark quarters had taken an almost immediate toll on him.

Blurs faded to the clear stark image of Allegiance's crew all assembled on deck. Jack's guts twisted in knots while his heart continued to thunder inside of his chest. The marines led him to the fore edge of the quarterdeck where Captain Williams stood at the head of the assembled officers. The rush of wind and splash of seawater was all he could hear. Allegiance's crew was in a rare form of silence for the proceedings, a silence that spoke volumes to Jack.

"Able Seaman Jack Horner," Captain Williams began in a loud voice that did not match his gaunt frame. "Ye stand here before command and crew accused of fighting, and of attempting to strike Quartermaster's Mate Lambdin with his own starter. In clear violation of the articles of war, on both counts. The penalty for fighting is no more than a dozen lashes upon yer bare back. The penalty for attempting to strike a superior, aboard a man of war in service to the King's Royal Navy, is death." He paused and scowled beneath his ornate bicorne hat. "Have ye anything to say for yerself, young man?"

Jack felt the eyes of Allegiance's entire crew shift at once to him. His face flushed hot, and his breath seized in his throat. He swallowed hard and tried to speak, but the words refused to come. A second attempt finally yielded speech. "I admit to my part in fighting with one of my shipmates. It was foolish of me, and I recognize my error, sir. But, I did not try to strike at Petty Officer Lambdin. He was using his starter line, and it wrapped against my wrist. I did not take hold of it, nor did I raise it against him, sir," Jack said in a strong a voice as he could muster. As he finished speaking he felt the hot stare of Mr. Lambdin burning across the deck directly at him. Jack kept his eyes locked on the captain. He dared not avert them to anything or anyone. The gravity of what was being said was unbearable. He was in a desperate fight for his life.

"Ye say ye didn't attempt to strike the Petty Officer," Captain Williams said in a stern voice. "But, he reports to me a contradictory account." The captain paused and shifted his gaze between Jack and Mr. Lambdin. "These are serious accusations. On one account, striking, or attempting to strike a Petty Officer, warrants a death sentence. On the other, if a Petty Officer were to surrender his honor by rendering false testimony before me as commander of this vessel, it would be a most serious offense." He glared toward the leeward railing where Mr. Lambdin was standing and then looked back at Jack. "With that in mind, young Horner. Do you wish to amend your statement? I will give you this one opportunity."

Jack swallowed hard. His face burned. He drew a slow breath and remembered what Bowline Bob had told him. "No, sir. I told it true, sir," he said.

Captain Williams' face shriveled into a tight scowl. It was plain to Jack that he didn't like what he was hearing, or the ramifications it implied. "Have ye a witness to your account, Horner?" the captain asked in a hard tone.

"Aye, he does, beg yer pardon, sir," Bowline Bob's voice croaked out over the assembled sailors. "I saw fer myself, along with half the tars standin' here. Jacky lifted his hand, sure, but he was being flogged by the mate's starter. Its natural ter try and ward off a blow before it lands. But, he didn't take Mr. Lambdin's starter, and he didn't raise it ter strike him a-tall."

Jack felt a wave of emotion overcome him as Bob spoke on his behalf. His eyes flooded with the hot feeling of tears threatening to form while a chill ran up and then down his spine. Bumps formed on his skin as he watched Captain Williams reaction to what he was hearing.

"One voice in Horner's favor," the captain said. "Are there any others?"

Another sailor spoke out. "He didn't grab 'is starter, sir. Took 'is beatin' proper, didn't raise his hand ter strike, but ter keep from gettin' hit in the face again!"

"Aye!" another voice pitched in. "Any man would try ter ward off'n them strikes like he was gettin', head, neck, face."

Captain Williams raised his hand to cease the growing wave of shouts in Jack's favor. "Be that as it may. Able Seaman Horner, you stand here accused of fighting and of attempting to strike a superior. I hereby sentence you to one dozen lashes, to be carried out immediately. On the matter of the more serious offense, testimony has been given, and unless recanted or altered, cannot be stricken from the ship's log. Jack Horner, I sentence you to death by hanging. To be carried out at sunset tomorrow, lest the record reflect a withdrawal of the accusation."

A wave of shock seized Jack followed by the onset of a curious numbness that seemed to slow time. The crew on deck remained silent while Captain Williams said something that eluded his hearing. The marines that had hauled him up on deck took him under his arms and led him to the capstan. His wrists were freed of their shackles and tied with a coarse rope to the capstan bars. Mercilessly, one of the marines seized the collar of his thin sailor shirt and tore the back away in a downward swipe that bared the flesh of his back to the world. He braced himself as a drumbeat rattled with building intensity. He'd been a witness to Bitter End Bill's flogging, a sight that had turned his stomach for days, and now he was about to endure the same fate.

The drumming halted with a jarring stop. Jack felt the boatswain's first stoke land across his back in a fiery wave of searing pain. Breath was forced from his lungs. The pain flared through his flesh. "One!" shouted the boatswain. Jack tried to draw a breath but the second stroke landed just as he was recovering from the first. "Two!" Agony gripped his mind. He could not conceive enduring another stroke of the cat. His back felt as if it were on fire while simultaneously being torn. He tensed his arms. Tears welled in his eyes while his mouth went completely dry. Another slashing blow landed across his back. "Three!" Jack felt his knees trembling. His arms tensed and seized at the ropes biting into his wrists. Before he could think, the next blow landed. "Four!" His legs failed him, he dropped to hang by the restraint of his wrists over the capstan. The next slash hit, and then another. The boatswain, it seemed, was quickening his pace. Jack hung from the capstan, helpless to stop the onslaught of mind breaking pain searing across his back. He could feel blood oozing from openings in his flesh. A seventh stroke landed, then an eighth. He tried to scream, but his lungs failed to fill with air before a ninth lash fell across his back and all he could produce was an impotent whimpering squeal. The world seemed to spin around him. He could feel his stomach double over and tighten into a ball. Bile rushed up and invaded his throat. He coughed and tried to spit just as a ninth lash landed. For a heartbeat, he thought he would die. Then he realized that whether by the cat or by a noose, he was doomed. Blackness took him and the fall of the tenth lash found him unconscious to its effect.

A warm yellow light danced within tight wooden quarters. Jack felt a tug at his back and a fresh wave of white hot pain wracked through him. He groaned and tried to lift his head from where it lay against a hard wooden surface.

"Easy, now," a growling voice said. "I've almost got ye all wrapped up. Don't go ter shiftin' around, yer'll make a mess 'o everything."

The voice was not altogether unfamiliar, though Jack had a hard time in his foggy grasp on alertness in placing the owner. He relented back to the hard wood under his head. His mouth tasted sour, his head throbbed, he felt sick. He let his eyes close.

"None of these are very deep," the gruff voice spoke again. "I'd say ter keep them clean, but, I don't think it much matters, eh?"

Jack's heart sank as he recalled the events of the day. The assembled crew, the pronouncement of his sentence, the fiery kiss of the cat. He pried his eyes open and searched through the dimly lit confines of the cramped cabin. The wall he faced was lined with a collection of shelves and small cupboards. A variety of small glass bottles lined the shelves, each with a label written in messy scrawls of letting that Jack couldn't even begin to decipher. He was in the doctor's cabin. A deep breath revealed the pungent odor of alcohol.

"Alright. Yer all set, lad," the doctor said in a throaty rasp. "I'll give yer a hand up. The marines is waitin' out in the passageway. They'll help yer down ter yer quarters fer the night."

Jack accepted the doctor's assistance to sit upright. Flaming pangs of pain laced through his back and ribs. Strips of tightly wrapped linen around his torso restricted his breathing and his legs wobbled as he put his weight on them.

"Ye'll want ter have a tot afore ye go," the doctor said. "I'm sure the lobsterbacks won't be bringing yer ration to yer." He reached for a bottle tucked into the corner of a shelf. "I'll divvy out yer share here and now. But, don't tell anyone I let yer take it neat. I haven't water er lemon juice ter make a proper grog. Good navy rum will have ter do."

The doctor pulled a pewter mug from a cupboard and poured a healthy portion of rum into it. With a feeble grin, he handed the mug over and Jack took it gratefully.

"Thank you, kindly," he said before lifting the cup to his lips. The rum was strong and rich, thick flavors of cinnamon, vanilla, and other spices filled his mouth. It warmed him and helped to loosen his pain wracked body. He drank the cup empty and handed it back to the doctor. "I thank you, but, it's wasted on me. Keep your acts of kindness for my shipmates."

The doctor's face shriveled into a tight scowl. "An act of kindness is never wasted, young man. Be ye condemned to death or not, I won't have it said I refused a hospitality to anyone."

Jack nodded at the sentiment as the rum already started to work on his nerves. Perhaps, he thought, that was the doctor's true motivation. The cabin door creaked open and a marine sentry craned his neck inside.

"All finished, sir?" he asked.

The doctor rolled his eyes and removed his spectacles. "Aye, he is fitted. No labor for a week."

"No need fer that, sir," the marine said with a sharp look at Jack.

The doctor nodded and waved his hand at the sentry. "Ah, y-yes, of course. Foolish thoughts, force of habit and such."

The marines entered and seized Jack under his arms. Their movements were just a s rough and forceful as before, with no special attention given due to his wounds. They marched him out into the gangway and then down into the depths of the ship where he was again manacled into a set of bilboes in the orlop. Every movement elicited a streak of unbearable pain. By the time he was settled in the orlop, Jack's head was awash in agony. His back ached and stung in alternating bouts, his muscles trembled from the shock of his ordeal and his stomach spasmed in fits that brought him right to the edge of retching. The orlop was just as dark and miserable as it had been, but it seemed a stretch colder now that his fate had been laid before him. The splash and slop of seawater slipping by the hull was more of an annoyance than a comfort and the squeaking of bilge rats was a never ending torment. Hunched over the bilboes, Jack realized his idea of misery before this day had been a pale comparison to his current ordeal. In the depths of the ship, he took some solace in the fact that it would all soon be over. He would depart from the world and leave the cares and woes of it behind him. He wondered if he would see his mother and father on the other side of the obscure divide between living and death. It was a small comfort, but it was all Jack could cling to.

His sense of time had been distorted. Jack had no idea what watch currently stood, or if hands had already been piped to supper. He didn't know if he had mere minutes to wait until he was hauled on deck to face a noose, or hours. The last two lashes had hit after he had lost consciousness, and for how long he remained unaware to the world he was unsure. Creaking deck planks and footfalls told him that the crew was still active, so he had either slept through the night in the doctor's cabin, or it had only been a few hours. His eyes pried into the darkness of the orlop. A dim glow from out in the gangway failed to penetrate the gloom and Jack was left to wonder at the hour in near total darkness. He hoped for another visit from Bowline Bob, but the gloom dragged on as Allegiance rose and fell with the action of waves. He remained alone, unable to steal rest, awaiting his eventual doom. It seemed like an eternity, but could have been an hour or even less, the faint pitch of a boatswain's whistle sounded. Footfalls shuffled on the deck above and Jack surmised that the hands had either been piped to supper, or hammocks were piped down for the night.

The shuffling sounds of footfalls faded away, and Jack shifted to try and find some measure of comfort for his final night on earth. Allegiance settled to a steady rhythm of pitch and roll. The easy motion of the ship made Jack's eyes heavy, and he began to nod into fits of dreamless sleep. Timbers groaned with the soft motion of the ship, seawater swished past the hull, somewhere a rat squealed its displeasure. A stab of pain awoke Jack, and he opened his eyes with a groggy peer around the orlop. The typical sounds of nighttime at sea were all that met his ears. He shifted against his restraints and tried to settle back into a state of near sleep. The gentle rock of the ship continued and Jack tried to find a position to sit where he didn't strain against his wrists or put too much pressure on his back. He tried to lean forward, but the ache across his shoulder blades grew to a screaming, stabbing pain. He rocked back and stretched to try leaning against the bulkhead, but the iron shackles holding his wrists dug into his flesh and refused to let him find comfort. Nothing worked. Despair took him, and he submitted to a night spent in miserable agony awaiting his fate. Something felt off. Jack searched his mind to place what it was, but quickly dismissed the feeling on account of his exhaustion and anxiety. He wrestled against his chains and managed to lean one shoulder against the bulkhead. The bow climbed with a wave and the feeling hit Jack again, something was wrong.

It sounded like rolling thunder. At first Jack feared that Allegiance had come across more foul weather, but the sound continued steady where thunder would have died away. The sound grew louder, so loud it seemed to shake the deck above him. With each gentle rise and fall of the ship the sound thundered forward before just as suddenly rumbling back toward the aft end of the deck. Jack tried to think of what could cause such a commotion. It wasn't thunder, of that he was sure. Allegiance was pitching and rolling in a steady, gentle pattern. If there was weather, it would be the oddest storm he had ever heard of. The noise grew louder, rolling forward toward the bow and then away toward the stern. Jack held his breath for a moment. Shouts mixed into the rolling rumble noise. Had a cannon come loose in the night? He strained his hearing to make out what the voices were saying with no success. The rolling rumble was too loud. Outside the orlop in the gangway, the dim yellow light that accompanied his armed guards grew brighter. It penetrated into the recesses of the orlop and pierced at Jack's eyes.

"What in blazes is going on up there?" one of the sentries asked in a baffled tone.

A husky voice replied, "Has there been anyone down to visit the prisoner?"

"No. He isn't allowed visitors, 'cording to the l'tenant," the first voice replied. "What in the hells is that sound?"

A pause elapsed while the thunderous rolling noise rumbled its way across the deck again. "The hands, someone on the crew, or a group of someones, let loose a grip of twelve pounder shot balls. They're rolling free up there on the gun deck and none of the officers, nor the mates, have the stones on them to roust the crew and figure out the culprit. The mate of the watch said a voice in the dark shouted something about 'if the kid hangs, you'll all burn'. Or some such, I'm not quite sure. Everyone up there is on a knife edge."

Jack's blood lit with a trace of fire. His shipmates had drawn a line. They weren't going to surrender him without having their say.

H.M.S Allegiance
30 June 1770
17 Degrees 49′ N, 66 Degrees 30′ W

The heat in Captain Williams' cabin was stifling. Jack had been roused from his uneasy sleep before dawn by the marine sentries standing guard over him and shuffled aft to the waiting commander of Allegiance. His stomach dropped as he realized who it was who had summoned him, and as he looked at the captain's gaunt, hard features, he feared the worst. The captain stared at him for a long beat before motioning for the armed sentries to depart their company. He gave Jack a solemn look from under his furrowed brows and exhaled deep through his nose.

"Mr. Lambdin just departed my cabin," he said in a monotonous drone. "Would you care to know what we discussed?"

Jack was at a loss. "I wouldn't have the foggiest idea, sir."

The captain folded his hands behind his back and faced out of the fantail window array. "He admitted to me the truth of the matter, and in doing so, has resigned his position as quartermaster's mate." He paused and turned back toward Jack with a grim note in his eyes. "This is a serious matter, young man. Very serious. I almost sentenced you to death by hanging, and the crew is very near mutinous over the matter. You must be well liked among them, they rolled cannon shot on deck in the night, something I have sentenced men to two dozen for."

Jack grimaced as he thought of the agony that two dozen lashes would incur. His own back was in a miserable state, seeping blood, and sore to the point of near immobility. He hoped that he would never see the business end of the cat again, on his back, or anyone else's. "I have few friends, sir. If that is what you are asking." Jack said.

The captain shook his head. "No, I don't recall asking anything. I am not concerned over who tipped the shot rack. It is what it is. I could spend the rest of this voyage hunting the perpetrator and would very likely never come to any kind of real conclusion. I could pick one man and hold him responsible, but that would most likely only compound the problem. No, young Horner, I am not concerned with who it was. Only, that your shipmates value you so highly. An injustice was very nearly done, they spoke on your behalf knowing very well what it could cost them. Such is the way of sea life."

Unsure of how he was supposed to respond, Jack offered a feeble nod. "Yes, sir," he said.

Captain Williams gave a tight grimace. "You understand the precarious position this presents, Horner?"

"Sir?" Jack frowned as much from the pain of standing as his confusion of the question posed.

"Mr. Lambdin confessed his lie. He has been dis-rated, and he will face the cat himself. That will be the end of it. I will not have you or your messmates taking justice into your own hands. However grievous his crime would have been, it was averted." The captain's look was as hard as iron. "I need to know that you will not pursue vengeance, young man. Such as would see you standing before the boatswain with a bare back, again."

Jack shook his head. "No, sir. It is finished."

Captain Williams nodded. "Very well. I will hold you to it, though, I know things may go hard for Lambdin with the rest of the crew, he only needs see out this cruise. I will be sure he is transferred off the next time we make a friendly port."

"Aye, sir," Jack could hardly believe his fortune. He had been granted reprieve. His life, his future, had returned to him.

"That will be all for now, Able Seaman Horner. You may go attend the doctor. I'm sure he will order you laid up until you have healed enough for duty," the captain said with a dismissing wave. "Pass the word for Lieutenant Sifton, I have some matters to discuss with him."

Jack knuckled his brow, thankful, almost in shock at his near brush with a noose. "Aye, sir."

Supper mess was a particularly enjoyable experience for Jack. Matsumoko and

Bowline Bob both offered up a part of their grog to top Jack's cup, and a healthy serving of cooked peas and salted beef served to lift his spirits. Chatter throughout the gun deck focused on his near brush with the noose, and how lowly Lambdin could sink to condemn another man to death so coldly. For his part, Jack considered the matter well rested, with only an exchanged glance at the disgraced former Petty Officer as he passed with his cup and plate.

"He's a shite, Jacky. Don't worry yerself with 'im," Bowline Bob grumbled over his tankard of grog. "What he done will follow him the rest of his days. Maybe even get 'im drummed right out of the king's navy."

Jack winced as the pain in his back flared. "That could be a blessing."

Bob nodded as he swallowed the last of his grog. "Aye, it could be, but for a tar like Lambdin, He'd rather be dead than hauling sail on a merchant ship. Better pay, sure, but they sail to the bidding of their owner and not a chance fer prize. Not a life fer a man like Lambdin."

"Merchant sailing sounds like a life for me," Jack retorted. "Easier on the back, for sure."

Bob smiled at the sentiment. "Aye, easier, better paying, better grub. But, it's a different haul when a privateer comes in sight. Yer'll be wishin' fer those long nines at the bow and a twelve or eighteen-pounder when a hungry privateer crew comes along."

Jack drew at his grog and savored the bitter sting of watered rum. His belly felt full from just a small portion of his rations, but he kept at his plate, determined not to let any go to waste.

"What did the captain say to you in his cabin?" Matsumoko asked in a low voice.

Jack swallowed a mouthful of beef and peas before relaying what had been said. He tried to glean any reaction from Bob and Matsumoko as he told about the captain's veiled commentary on the crew being near mutinous. Bob nodded with a soft grin and squinted his glare at Jack.

"Best we don't bring it up again after tonight, boys," He said before lowering his voice to a near whisper. "But, I'd tip every shot rack on ship if I thought that's what it would have taken ter save yers from a noose, Jacky. I'd whip these lads inter such a frenzy, the marines would be jumping the side ter brave the sea on their own rather'n face the crew."

Jack's heart felt like it would leap from his chest. "So, it was you?"

Bob scowled a little at the question. "Aye, it was me. Did ye doubt it fer a second?"

"No," Jack replied. "I just, Bob, I'll never be able to thank you enough."

Bowline Bob leaned back and pulled out his pipe with an eye for a lantern hanging nearby. "I'll thank ye kindly not ter be thankin' me. Tippin' shot racks'll buy a hand a dozen on his bare back. Maybe two."

Jack was overwhelmed. His eyes tingled with the hot feeling of tears beginning to form. "And, who shouted that threat? If they hung me the whole crew would burn?" Jack asked.

Matsumoko leaned close. "You won't believe it, Jack. But, it wasn't me or Bob that shouted that threat. Best I could tell, it was Bitter End Bill."

Jack's heart fluttered in his chest. Bitter End Bill, the hardened salt of a sailor who had cussed him and scowled at every move he made since departing Boston on the Salem Tide. Bitter End Bill, who had taken three dozen lashes at his back when it was discovered he had previously deserted the Royal Navy. He had been the one to tell the officers and Petty Officers just how seriously the crew took Lambdin's dishonorable conduct.

"But," Jack said as he furrowed his brows tight over his eyes. "With all that, still. Why did Lambdin confess himself to the captain? He could have kept to his story."

"Aye," Bob answered as he lit his pipe. "He could have, but he'd have been a marked fer dead the minute yer feet stopped kicking." He drew a big breath of smoke and released it in a bluish cloud from his nostrils. "I agree, the slitherin snaky bastard would have let yer hang all the same. My guess is someone came ter him with a terse suggestion. Tell the cap'n er else ye gets it, sort 'o thing. Eh?"

Jack searched the busy chattering of the gun deck, wondering who would have had the nerve to pull a Petty Officer to the side and lay a cold threat at his feet. Such an act would have been taken seriously should Lambdin have run straight to the captain with it. Instead, he had caved and laid the truth bare, to his own detriment. Whoever had made a threat against Lambdin, one thing was true, it was someone he truly feared. Laughter mixed with animated accounts from adventures past and a swell of pride rose in Jack's chest as he realized he had become an accepted member of the crew. He was one of them. If only his friend Tom could see him now, he would choke! As if Bob had read his thoughts, he leaned forward with a rush of pipe smoke furling out of his nostrils.

"Yer a proper sailorman now, Jack. A regular tar. Aloft in the wind, taking sails in storms, and a striping across yer back. It's a hard life, but, there's nothing fer me but a life at sea," Bob said in his throaty growl.

The smoke was thick on his breath, and the rich aroma smelled good to Jack. He reached forward and took Bob's pipe in hand. "I suppose you're right Bob. It is a hard life, but it is the one I have chosen. Here's to the sea!" He clamped the pipe stem in between his teeth and drew a long pull of the sweet tobacco smoke into his chest. It burned, but unlike the last time he'd tried smoke, his chest didn't violently reject it. He let the rich aroma linger on his tongue as he released the smoke into a cloud the same way he had seen Bob do.

"Aye, lad," Bob said with an approving grin. "That's the way!"

"Hey ho, Bob!" a voice shouted aloft to Bowline Bob who was standing as the foremast lookout. "See anything from up there?"

Bob's voice drifted back down from his lofty perch in the rigging. "Nothin' but a wall 'o haze gray! Can't even see the deck from up here!"

At the helm, Jack waited anxiously for the watch officer to make a decision while the exchange between deck and lookout occurred. Allegiance had arrived at the latitude Captain Williams had decided would serve for their westerly approach to the island of San Juan. A day and a half of sailing had brought them to where they should have sighted the rocky coastline with the rising sun. But, as the morning watch pressed on into daylight, it had become apparent to all hands that they had sailed into a thick layer of fog. Daylight brought brightness to the world, but the fog stubbornly refused to depart and Allegiance was trapped inside of a sheer wall of gray haze that obscured everything around it from sight.

"Mr. Greaves, have us a point over starboard if you will. Ready to come up into the wind should we sight anything," Lieutenant Sifton said in a flat tone. He had been pacing the windward rail for the better part of the morning watch and exuding a quiet confidence amid the crews growing anxiety. "Steady now, Mr. Greaves. It's only a fog. We have navigated coastlines under worse conditions."

The officer on watch turned to Lieutenant Sifton and mumbled something Jack couldn't hear. It had been the pattern of the morning, both the sailors aloft and the watch on deck had grown weary of the tension. They expected a sighting of land at any moment, and the prevailing fear was that their sighting would be precluded by the horrid sound of scraping and buckling timbers as the ship ran aground on a rocky outcrop, shoal or obscured reef.

"Shadows in the gray! Looks like a finger of land!" Bob's voice shouted down with strain at its fringes.

Lieutenant Sifton immediately took post on the windward mizzen shrouds, his telescope in hand and a hard lean to the rigging so he had a steady sight picture.

"Ah, yes," the lieutenant said in a drolling, unimpressed tone. "Rocky finger off the starboard bow, not two miles distant." He withdrew his telescope and paced to the stand where the midshipmen filled their logs. For a long moment he stood hunched over the small wooden lectern and studied the chart. After examining the chart, Lieutenant Sifton stood tall a pace behind and windward of the helm. "Bring her over two points larboard. West by south, and lets take a reef on the tops'ls shall we?"

"Aye, sir," Mr. Greaves, the midshipman on watch replied. "West by south and taking in a reef on the tops'ls."

Jack eased the wheel over in a smooth motion to set the course as Lieutenant Sifton commanded. He was always surprised with how nimbly the ship answered, even in the light wind. The mist of the fog kept the morning cool and damp, it reminded Jack of the thick fogs that would roll in over Boston in the late of spring and early fall. So thick he wouldn't be able to make out the thin fingers of land that protruded out into the broad bay and provided shelter for so many seagoing vessels. Those same rocky protrusions had been known to ruin the hull of ships as well as provide the calm safety of the harbor. Jack recalled an incident from when he was younger and remembered the splintered mess of a two-masted brig. Her captain had unwittingly sailed to close to a rocky stretch and come under a change in the wind in fog as thick as darkness itself. For weeks the residents of Boston were finding bits of flotsam and timber washing ashore, some even discovered the remains of several sailors who didn't survive. The thought brought another chill into Jack's spine. He shook it away and focused on the sails. The dim outline of the topsails was barely visible through the fog.

"Deck! Deck!" Bowline Bob's voice cried through the mist. "Something in the water! Looks like it could be a man overboard!"

Jack tightened his grip on the wheel, ready for whatever command the lieutenant would issue next.

"Where away?" called up Mr. Greaves through the speaking trumpet.

A pause elapsed and then Bob's voice followed back, muffled by the dense wall of fog. "Starboard, passing by the bow now. Not even a ship's length away from the hull!"

Instinctively, Jack looked toward Lieutenant Sifton. The first lieutenant deferred for a moment and shot an expectant look over to Mr. Greaves. "Give your order, Mr. Greaves. The men are waiting."

Midshipman Greaves went as pale as the haze surrounding Allegiance. He looked toward the starboard gunwales and then back at the helm. "Come about starboard, bring us into the wind."

Jack hesitated for a heartbeat, his arms seizing before he could make the ordered turn. "Belay that, Horner. Bring her into the wind, but do it over larboard," Lieutenant Sifton gently interrupted before turning over to Mr. Greaves. "Don't forget, young man. There was a land sighting off our starboard beam. Now, have a launch lowered over the side and set get a crew together to investigate."

Jack eased the helm over to bring Allegiance to a crawl and spill the wind from her sails.

"Deck! Flotsam and riff raff ahead off the starboard bow!" Bob shouted down from the heights of the foremast.

A bolt of tension thrummed through the misty air. Lieutenant Sifton's face pulled into a hard frown and he paced to the starboard rail. He leaned forward with one hand holding onto the mizzen shrouds. "Something isn't right here," he grumbled while staring hard over the side of the ship. Urgency rose in his voice, "Mr. Greaves, beat to quarters. It looks like a ship has gone down here, and very recently."

Midshipman Greaves hurried to the aft hatchway and shouted down the general alarm. Within moments a marine appeared on deck and began the rattle of snaring drumbeats that signaled every hand to clear the ship for action. Allegiance thrummed with activity. Her launches were lowered over the side and brought along in tow, gun crews manned her cannons, marines lined her rails behind nets filled with hammocks to catch pistol and musket fire. In a matter of minutes she transformed from a relatively tranquil state into the pinnacle of combat readiness. The hard weeks of repetitive drills had honed her crew to a razor's edge.

Jack stood ready at the helm, waiting for the next turn of events. His mind raced with the possibilities of being caught in action while exposed on the quarterdeck. There were no thick walls of oak set around him to absorb the impact of shot. His heartbeat quickened as Allegiance settled into her state of readiness and Captain Williams appeared on deck.

"Lookouts spotted a body afloat, sir," Lieutenant Sifton reported sharply. "Before I could send a launch to investigate we came across this field of flotsam. It looks like a vessel has gone down somewhere very near here, sir, and recently."

The captain's face remained tight and unflinching. He paced to the starboard side of the ship and stared hard into the wall of fog surrounding them. A long beat passed with nothing but silence and creaking lines. Jack felt his chest burn and realized he had unwittingly been holding his breath.

"Get a complement of marines together and into a launch to investigate. Send Mr. Greaves here to coxswain for them with a few sailors to man the oars. Investigate the debris to find out what we can and recover the body," the captain said without averting his stare from the gray haze around them. "We remain at quarters until we know more, or visibility improves." He turned to

Lieutenant Sifton and offered a quick nod. "Good work sounding the alarm. This could be the work of our rogue Frenchman."

"My thoughts exactly, sir," Lieutenant Sifton replied.

"I want silence fore and aft, no calls, nor bells or whistles. We don't want to announce our position any more than we already have," the captain said. "Have both batteries run out to firing position, and extra lookouts stationed fore and aft."

"Aye, aye sir," Lieutenant Sifton replied with a touch of his hat. He turned and set to his orders, keeping his voice low as he delegated tasks to waiting midshipmen and the lower lieutenants who had all congregated on the quarterdeck. He gave a pause and then cast a long look in Jack's direction. "How is your back, Horner?"

Jack frowned at the question, confused. "Still raw, sir. But, I am able enough." He assumed the lieutenant was asked about his duty at the helm.

"Good. Gather your messmates. You will accompany Mr. Greaves and the marines on the launch. Our Dead Eye Jack, in case there is a waiting enemy out among the mist," Lieutenant Sifton said with a nod and a wink. "Keep a sharp eye, I'll want my midshipman back in one piece."

Stunned, Jack managed only a simple nod and a knuckle at his brow. He was relieved at the helm and began to pass the word to his messmates. Bowline Bob, Matsumoko, and their newest addition since the near mutiny, Bitter End Bill, all gathered on the leeward railing as arms were passed out. Each man took a hefty cutlass or a boarding axe, a pistol, and a musket. They climbed down a short rope ladder and piled into the launch boat. No mast or sails were rigged on the launch, but the marines had seen fit to mount a swivel gun on her bow. Jack took the oar immediately across from Matsumoko while aft of both of them, Bowline Bob and Bitter End Bill hoisted their own. Once the marines were all aboard, Mr. Greaves climbed into the stern and ordered them away from the ship. At first, Jack's back burned and stung in protest. The cat had left several lacerations in his skin and each stroke of the oar threatened to tear them open to bleed afresh. After the first few minutes of rowing, however, an almost pleasant numbness set in while he stretched and heaved in steady motion and timing with the others.

"Steady men, flotsam aplenty here, and I don't want to get too far out of sight with the ship," Mr. Greaves said in an uneven voice.

"Lay off the oars. Let's have a look over some of this wreckage."

Jack let his oar ease and drag in the calm water of the sea. Planks, bottles and a floating barrel clattered against the hull of the small launch boat. The sea was calm, the only motion on its surface a slight ripple of waves from the breeze. The launch rocked gently as Mr. Greaves fished some debris out of the water.

"Crates, barrels, scraps of sail. What can we decipher from something that is on every seagoing vessel the world over?" Mr. Greaves muttered to himself.

"The body," one of the marines suggested. "Have a look at the dead man. Maybe ye will find a clue with him."

The midshipman nodded and straightened his hat as he seemed to find some hidden well of resolve deep within himself. "Aye, the body, we will investigate the body of the drowned man. On the oars, men, he is floating but a few hundred feet away."

Jack and company resumed their rowing while Mr. Greaves remained at the tiller. The launch slid easily through low bobbling seas while odd pieces of debris clunked against the hull. Oars slipped in and out of sea in a steady rhythm as the launch made progress through the gray mist. Through the corner of his eyes, Jack surveyed the debris as they passed. Glass bottles, ale casks, shattered planks and bits of sail were all floating on the surface. His hands gripped onto the oar as he continued the repetitive motion in time with his messmates. Pull, recover, pull, recover. The mist slid around them, formless as it encompassed everything it touched.

"Hold here, men," Mr. Greaves announced with an outstretched arm. "There is the body."

Jack looked over one shoulder and saw the form floating still and calm in the low rise of the sea. A loose fitting white sailor's shirt, and rough hewn sailcloth trousers indicated that the drowned man was no stranger to life on the waves. The launch boat drew close to the floating body and Mr. Greaves ordered Jack and the other sailors to take him aboard.

"Its bad luck ter touch a dead man!" Bitter End Bill protested. "Ye'll be havin' us in another storm, or that French ship will get the drop on us again. Mark me words, don't touch 'im, ye'll rue ye ever did."

"Nonsense," Mr. Greaves interrupted with an annoyed edge in his voice. "Take the poor bastard into the boat and see what we can learn from him. Maybe he has something on his person, or in his pockets."

Bitter End Bill continued to growl his displeasure while Jack and Bowline Bob shipped their oars and grasped at the floating corpse's loose-fitting shirt. Jack felt a strange foreboding over the scene. The dead sailor's skin was an unearthly gray, his features shrunken and hollow. Bob hefted at the loose shirt and rolled the corpse over.

"There iddn't pockets on his shirt, nor trousers, sir. Ye still want us ter hoist 'im aboard?" He asked.

The young midshipman, visibly bothered at the sight of the dead sailor's face, shook his head almost imperceptibly. "Nay, let him lie where he is."

"Should 'ave let him alone from the start. Ev'rybody knows sailors don't 'ave any pockets on their trousers. Not like ye gentle officer folk. We aren't hauling back nothin' but foul luck," Bitter End Bill growled in an unrestrained display of contempt for the now thoroughly shaken midshipman.

"Silence," Mr. Greaves replied. "Back to the Allegiance."

"Wait," Bitter End Bill interrupted.

Mr. Greaves turned to the salty old hand. His nose flared, his eyes widened, and his jaw trembled at the brazen sailor's dismissal. "What do you mean, wait? I said back to Allegiance, now row damn you!"

Bill held up a single finger and cocked his head at an angle. "Wait, sir. Ye hear that?"

"I haven't time for your games, Bill. When we return to the ship, you can expect the bilboes and a visit to the captain," Mr. Greaves snarled.

Jack's heart sank. Bill had gone too far and Mr. Greaves was not going to let it go unanswered. He looked at Bill, a sinking feeling in his stomach as he realized the old sailor was destined for another encounter with the cat of nine tails. But, as he stared at the old sailor, Bill did something Jack had never seen from the salted old hand. He smiled. He smiled broad and defiant, his crooked, stained teeth bared for the gray light of the foggy world surrounding them. "Ye hear that, sir? Ye'd hear it if ye jus' shut yer yapper and listen," Bill said with a widening smile.

Jack sat in awe of Bill's defiance. It seemed the threat of a flogging had only set Bill to hold his course. It was an absurdity. He began to wonder if his messmate Bitter End Bill had lost his wits and was teetering on the brink of madness. But, then a sound wriggled its way into Jack's consciousness. It was slight at first, almost imperceptible. A swish. Easily enough lost to the steady sounds of floating debris and seawater lapping at the side of the launch, but, something set it apart. It became more distinct, a swish and then a slap of water.

"Ah," Bitter End Bill said with widened eyes, "Dead Eye Jack hears it! Go on, Dead Eye, tells 'im, the thick walled lubber still doesn't get it. Tell 'im!"

Mr. Greaves turned to Jack with a pressing glare. "Horner, do you hear something? Or, has your messmate here just bought himself a trip to the capstan for nothing?"

Jack frowned, unsure of how to answered the midshipman's prompt. His own back was still recovering, and he didn't want to bring a fresh wave of fury down on himself. But, there was something off about the noise. "I hear it. There is something out there, sir."

"What is it you hear?" Mr. Greaves asked with a deep frown. "I'll warn you not to play games with me. We ought to have already started our return to the ship."

Jack sat in motionless silence for a moment. The sound disappeared. His heart sank. Then the swish came again, followed by a slight slap on the water. A voice, almost a whisper, slipped through the dense fog. "I hear it! There is someone out there, sir. A survivor!"

All hands in the launch froze. Every ear trained to the gray air. The midshipman closed his eyes, Jack thought maybe to train his hearing to a greater sharpness.

"Help!" the weak voice drifted in off the sea swell. It was faint, barely more than a whisper. "Help!"

Jack turned outboard and searched the gray waste. The sea surface, almost glass calm, was dotted by flotsam and debris every few feet. The swish sounded again and a slight slap against the water followed. He stood up in the launch boat and scanned the debris field with every bit of intensity he could muster. At the edge of the mists, a ripple emerged. "There!" Jack said and extended his arm to point. "There! Man in the water!"

Midshipman Greaves set his brows into a deep frown and followed Jack's arm to the edge of the mist. He stared hard at the edge of visibility for a long beat before his features softened into an expression of pure disbelief. "Well, damn me back to land. Well done, Horner. Well done indeed," he mumbled.

Jack shrugged slightly and nodded toward Bitter End Bill. "I wouldn't have thought to be looking if it weren't for this old sea dog, sir. Pardon the phrase, but perhaps, he may have had a point."

The midshipman's glare hardened for a quick turn. He darted a look in between Jack and Bill and then to the rest of the occupants of the launch. "Let's fish this survivor out of the sea. My memory of recent events seems to be almost as foggy as out conditions of late. But, press me and it will regain its full clarity. Are we clear?"

All aboard, including the small complement of marines seemed to be of accord to spare Bill another encounter with the lash. Almost, it seemed, more than Bill himself.

"Already been twice pressed meself, sir," Bill said in his weathered voice. "Wouldn't dream of pressing you. Couldn't live with meself ter do that ter a God fearing young gennelman."

Jack's heart sank. It was almost like Bill wanted to be flogged!

Mr. Greaves stared hard at the crew of sailors as they sat behind their oars. A mixture of embarrassment and anger flashed over his eyes and his lips curled tight against his teeth. "Row!"

H.M.S Allegiance
30 June 1770
17 Degrees 52′ N, 67 Degrees 11′ W

"They came on us like a shadow in the night, they did. One minute it was calm seas and smooth sailing, next thing I knew we was takin' fire," the sailor said in a raspy voice. One of Allegiance's officers draped a wool blanket over the rescued man's shoulders as he recounted events at the forward edge of the quarterdeck. "They shot away our rudder, so the steerin' wouldn't answer none. Then another volley took our mainmast. Before we could make heads or tails of anythin' we was bein' boarded. Cutlass and musket. They kills the cap'n and 'is first mate, then makes us cross-load our wares off'n ter their hold."

"What was your cargo?" Captain Williams asked over the man's quivering shoulder. A large group of sailors and officers had gathered on Allegiance's main deck, glued to the sailor's every word.

"Mostly rum, sir. There was some furniture and other odds and ends. But the majority of the hold was rum," the sailor replied before breaking into a fit of wet coughs that made Jack's skin crawl. "The bastards had us load their hold, then cross back ter the ship. They fired another volley from their guns and sailed away as the old girl was going under. It was evil, sir, pure evil."

Solemn looks were exchanged between the Allegiance men on deck. The rogue privateer had found another victim. Jack took in the faces of his shipmates. Anger, disgust and fear were all prominently on display. But Captain Williams remained steadfast and stone faced among the throngs of reactions. He continued to press the weary survivor for more details.

"When they, the ship that fired on you, departed, what direction did they sail? Did you see?" The captain asked.

The sailor seemed confused for a moment, huddled under the blanket he had been given. He stared down at the deck with a lost look in his eyes before a spark ignited and he finally spoke. "They come on us at sundown, out of an inlet they were tucked away in. Wind was off our starb'd quarter, and we was sailing westw'd. If I had ter say which way it was, sir, I can't be sure. I was fightin' fer me own survival. But, iff'n yer must 'ave an answer, I'd say she sailed westw'd as the old girl was going down."

Captain Williams looked around at the gathered sailors. His gaunt features seemed even more hard set after hearing the harrowing tale. The rogue privateer he had been tasked with hunting and sinking, or taking as a prize, had struck again. There were souls lost to the sea that bore directly to Allegiance's failure to stop the French ship in their first encounter.

"Lieutenant Sifton," the captain said in a clear, firm voice. "Bring us to bear westerly. All hands to remain at quarters. I want the cannons left ready to fire at a moment's notice. They can't be far, and I have a solid notion of where this frog intends to bend his sails."

"Aye, sir, a westward heading," Lieutenant Sifton answered before making his way through the crowd to set the quarterdeck to the task.

The fog still surrounded Allegiance in a thick blanket of gray haze. It gave Jack an eerie chill despite the warmer climate they were in. Their enemy could be behind any part of the thick misty haze that encompassed their wooden world. Desperate battle could be days away, or as close as the next minute. Captain Williams stood next to the rescued sailor, to Jack he embodied the very image of strength while the quivering survivor showed pure defeat.

"Our enemy is in these waters, lads. Make no mistake, we will find them. Our paths will cross, and when they do, they will be ours!" said Captain Williams.

No triumphant cheers emerged from the mass of sailors on deck. Only hard looks and determined glares. The French privateer had struck again, they would be fat with wares from their recent prize, and Jack hoped they would be imbibing from their haul. A drunken enemy would make for a one sided fight, he hoped.

Mr. Greaves paced along the windward railing as the launch boats were hauled back to their stern tow positions. He gave Jack and his messmates a nod as he passed.

"Good work out there today, men, now to your stations," he said.

A moment passed, and a look was exchanged between Jack and his messmates. Every face had the same question painted across it. Did Mr. Greaves forget Bill's smart comments? As if he heard their thoughts, the midshipman turned and gave the sailors a sharp look.

"Men, because of the state of things, and our successful sortie today, I have decided to forget your shipmate's insolent tongue. See to it that he exercises more control in the future, eh?"

A wave of relief washed over Jack. He could see his messmates shared the sentiment, all that is, except for Bitter End Bill. Mr. Greaves departed hearing range, and Bill wasted no time.

"Stupid lout, he is, I isn't scared of 'is threats," he growled. "Wouldn't be the first time I had me back striped fer being smarter than these so-called gennelmen."

Bob shook his head. "Bill, it is a wonder ye've made it this long in life, eh? Ye don't have ter tempt fate."

Bill smiled a grin full of crooked yellow teeth. "There's a reason I barely feel it when they scratch me with the ol' kitty. Jus' can't help meself sometimes."

Allegiance's gun deck was a picture of silent tension. Long hours dragged on while the crew remained at quarters. Cold vittles were handed out, ship's biscuit and hard cheese, for the evening meal. No grog was distributed to aid in their jollity or comfort. Outside the gun ports, calm seas slipped past the hull in a steady flow that gently lapped against the ship. Jack sat at the number seven gun on the larboard battery and balanced his weight on an upturned half keg that once held powder. Matsumoko sat serenely on the opposite side of the gun, his legs folded into an uncomfortable-looking position. It was not a prospect Jack was entirely unfamiliar with, this drawn out pursuit of the enemy. During the last encounter with the rogue French ship, Jack had been stationed in the focs'l behind a chase gun. Hours had gone by without a change. The sea sluiced past the hull rhythmically, long faced stared up and down the gun deck, timbers creaked, ropes groaned. Outside the ship, the light of day faded from the silvery bright glow of the dense fog curtain to an ominous dark not even the most intense light could penetrate.

The ship slowed to a crawl for a while, and then finally the decision was made to drop anchor and wait out the night. Quarters stood down, the ship went to its typical sea routine of watches with one major change: there would be no bells, no whistles and all on deck must observe silence. Without a whistle, the word was passed to pipe down hammocks from gun crew to gun crew. Jack had never experienced such an unsettling event. It was anticlimactic to say the least. The enemy was out there, lurking somewhere in the shadows just beyond sight, and they were all going to turn in for the night. It seemed wrong somehow, but, he surmised, they couldn't very well go plundering ahead in the thick fog without risking the ship or exposing themselves to the enemy and handing them the advantage. He tried to imagine the turmoil and frustration Captain Williams must have felt.

With hammocks strung, and the gun deck lights doused, Allegiance settled for the evening at anchor. Jack heard grumbling from several of the experienced sailors that spanned the range of typical complaints. Bitter End Bill, who had slung his hammock next to where Jack and Matsumoko hung theirs, had a very particular set of worries.

"It's what they wants, it is," He said as he cinched the suspending cordage of his hammock and climbed in with expert ease. "They wants us ter lets our guard down, those slimy bastards. Mark me words, once everyone on this tub is sound asleep there'll be hell ter pay!"

Jack shriveled his face at the rant. "What do you mean, Bill?" he asked. "If they had any idea we were here, we would already be trading broadsides."

"Aye, that's what they wants yer ter think, lad. That's a demon ship, it is. They wants ter blow a hole in us and watch us blunder down ter the briny depths with all souls," he replied in his trademark rasp of a voice. "They is out there now, in the darkness. They is watching us and waiting for their moment. And this blunderin' cap'n is goin' ter lets his whole crew slumber right inter their trap!"

A lightning bolt hit Jack's blood. If an officer, or any of the mates heard Bill's rant, especially his criticism of the captain, he'd be clapped in irons to wait for his next horse whipping. "Put a stopper to it Bill, before someone hears you. You have already pressed your luck with the officers today."

"I gives a damn fer the officers," Bill growled from his hammock. "Ye wait, Jack. We'll be a-hearin' shot whistles a-fore the night is through."

Jack sat up in his hammock. His eyes cut through the darkness of the gun deck as a streak of clarity came to mind. "Bill, it may be. You may be right, it could be an elaborate trap. But, if it is, Matsumoko and Bob and I will need you to help man the damned gun. You can't very well do that if you are in bilboes below," Jack said in as strong a voice as he dared. He hoped the new tack with Bill would work.

"Aye, yer right, Jack," Bill said. "Yer three would make a shite gun crew without a stout hand like me, eh?"

Jack settled back into his hammock, satisfied that his messmate had ceased his tirade. The ship sat in near perfect stillness, just a slight rock from the action of the tide transferred from the hull and into his hammock. Darkness and warmth surrounded him, but Jack was unable to find sleep. His thoughts drifted over the sea and through the shadows. He imagined Saber standing off the shore just out of the lookout's sight, her crew ready at the guns. The image of mustachioed French privateers loading flintlocks and running cutlasses along whetstones sent an icy chill up his spine. They had bested Allegiance once, it was not far-fetched that they could do so again. A sway worked its way through the ship as the tide slipped beneath her hull.

With no bells, Jack had no way to gauge the time. He fidgeted within the confines of his hammock, shifting from one shoulder to the other. His damp wool coat served as a pillow, and he fussed over the fold to find some measure of comfort. He tried to convince himself that Allegiance's lookouts were sharp to their task, at any sign of the enemy ship, they would stealthily raise the alarm and all hands would spring into action. But, Jack knew better. The lookouts, high aloft, were most likely grumbling at the futility of their task while the sea was dark and covered in thick fog. Even on a clear night, the night watch was often cursed with heavy eyes. He shifted to his other shoulder and fussed at the wool coat pillow again. If the lookouts didn't spot the enemy, the watch officer, or the mate of the watch surely would. The thought lingered. Somewhere on the gun deck, a sailor snored softly, another coughed and the gentle lap of water against the hull bound it all together in the song of a ship at night. For a long while there was nothing but stillness and silence. In the space of this quiet comfort, Jack's mind finally relented, and he drifted into sleep.

"Bring her about with the wind as the anchor comes up," Captain Williams ordered, his voice stiff with tension. "Set topsails on the fore and main, then have the hands ready on the courses."

"Aye, sir," Lieutenant Sifton replied from the fore edge of the quarterdeck. Darkness still encompassed Allegiance, and the seas surrounding her, but the fog had lifted in the night and a golden glow from the east was rising, hearkening the dawn.

"Fourteen fathoms, bottom of sand and broken coral," the leadsman called from his station along the weather rail.

Captain Williams paced the quarterdeck from the windward rail across to the lee and then back again while crews at the capstan battled to raise the ship's anchor.

Jack stood ready at the helm, charged with excitement for a maneuver he had never completed before. Sailors climbed the shrouds and filed across the yards, readying to loose canvas on command. The eastern skies were growing bright with hues of gold and orange while striations of pink and light blue pierced upward through the deep field of night. A freshened breeze washed over them from the northeast and as soon as the anchor was freed from its overnight berth on the ocean floor Allegiance flew her sails and began to make headway to the west. Gulls cawed relentlessly while the steady wash of the warship's wake played out from her bow through calm seas.

"Anchor's up and secured!" a voice ranged back from the focs'l.

Jack squeezed his grip on the helm and felt the steady pressure of the sea plying against Allegiance's rudder. The sun edged over the eastern skyline and they were sailing again. It brought a mixture of fear and excitement into Jack's blood as the warship surged forward. The same feeling that had come over him when he had climbed the heights of Salem Tide's foremast all those weeks ago on his first seagoing voyage. The sails fluttered and snapped full of wind, a rush of motion built as the force propelled Allegiance on her course and Jack fought off the first surge of resistance against the rudder. It was a normal event to just about everyone on board, but to Jack it held the infinite possibilities of the world. Any given course, and any given circumstance could await them in the days to come. The villainous French privateer could be waiting around any spit of land or tucked away in any cove or inlet. At any moment, they could find themselves locked in a desperate battle for their lives. Alternatively, they could search the sea for days without a sighting and find themselves resupplying in port. Kingston, St. Kitts, Barbados, Nassau, the possibilities made his heart flutter. They could take on water from one of the remote islands that dotted the edge of the Caribbean, or find themselves hunting their prey along the long held Spanish trade lines to the south. Jack's mind raced with adventure and possibility while his arms held steady on the ship's wheel.

The debris field that had surrounded Allegiance during the night had washed away with the tide. To the south and the west the vastness of the Caribbean stood open, a broad field of gray blue that was changing in to a sapphire shade under the glory of the rising sun.

"A point over starboard on the helm if you please," Captain Williams said in a curt voice over one shoulder. He stood fast on the weather rail, just forward of the mizzen shrouds, with his bicorne hat cocked forward and a hard expression resolutely set on his face.

"A point over starboard, aye sir," Jack said repeating the order in the navy way.

The captain offered a grim nod in return and set his stare onto the coast Allegiance was skirting. Whatever good spirits the clear skies had generously spread on deck, Jack noticed, they missed Captain Williams. The hard set commander seemed no more at ease with broad visibility and fair wind than he had at a near standstill under a thick blanket of fog. Grumbling, the captain paced the quarterdeck for the better part of an hour while Allegiance slipped along the coastline. He hardly regarded the leadsman's soundings, nor the nautical happenings of the midshipmen and their constant dithering over the prime orientation of sails to the wind. Jack watched diligently from the corner of his eye and saw a man consumed with concern, almost to the point of anxiety. It gave him an uneasy feeling. Captain Williams was an experienced commander, and as far as Jack could tell, a superior mariner. The thought that he should be overwrought with tension was an ill omen.

"Lieutenant Sifton, stand us off further from the shore, for the love of all that is good. We needn't cling to shore. A point over larboard, if you please, and see to the heads'ls, they are a mite slack to my eye," the captain said.

"Aye, sir, standing further off from shore," Lieutenant Sifton replied. He gave Jack a quick nod indicating he should ease the helm over leeward before turning to address the captain. "If the charts are at all accurate, sir, we needn't fear a reef or a shoal until we reach the southeast point of Hispaniola."

"It isn't the depth that gives me pause, lieutenant. It is the shoreline," said the captain.

"Not a lee shore, sir," Lieutenant Sifton replied with a deep frown.

Captain Williams shook his head. "No, it is not a lee shore. But, I would stand off of it as if it were." He shot the ship's second in command a grim look and lowered his voice. "I have a feeling, in the pit of my stomach. I fear this shore more than any rocky stretch of leeward land I have ever gazed on." He pointed at a spot on the chart in front of his first lieutenant. "There are coves and inlets all along this stretch of San Juan. Some are charted, most are not, all are large enough to hide away our enemy without a trace. If he reveals himself, he already has the weather gauge. We will have no choice but to spread all sail and evade. I have no taste for it."

"Right, sir," Lieutenant Sifton offered in a mutter. "I have the helm over a point. We will stand further off shore on our course west."

"Very good," the captain said before turning back toward the shoreline. "As badly as I want this enemy to reveal himself. I fear this would be a loathsome circumstance to find ourselves within sight of him."

Jack imagined the sight of bare canvas flying out of a dark crevice in the rocky shore sheltered by its thick canopy of overhanging trees. He had no idea what the officers had meant when they were talking about a lee shore, it was obviously something they desired to avoid, but the thought of their enemy appearing from the northeast concerned the captain. Jack's stomach tightened further when the two highest ranking officers aboard the ship huddled close together and exchanged words he could not hear. Was the captain conveying some sort of post mortem directive to his second in command should he fall in battle? Was he expressing his darkest fears out of hearing from all but his closest officer?

After a tense exchange, the two officers parted slightly and Captain Williams returned to his dogged pacing and scouring the shoreline with naked eye and telescope. Lieutenant Sifton wandered back over by the helm, his face taut with some burden just laid on him by the ship's commander.

"Bear away another point there, Dead Eye Jack," the lieutenant said kindly. "The captain desires us to wear around with the wind once we are clear of San Juan and stand off in case we are stalked by our enemy."

Jack eased the helm over a point, mindful of the sails as he did so. Curiosity gnawed at him, and he though he tried to hold it at bay, he couldn't help himself.

"Sir?" Jack asked as the lieutenant looked over his shoulder at the captain.

"Yes, Horner?" Lieutenant Sifton replied.

"What is a lee shore?" Jack asked as he muscled the wheel against a surge against the rudder.

The lieutenant grinned and cast a look over to Jack. "Young man, it is grievously inconsiderate to eavesdrop on a conversation not meant for your ears. I ought to have you sent aloft."

Jack went rigid at the helm, his blood turning to ice water. "Very sorry, sir. It won't happen again, at least, I'll refrain from my questions, sir."

The lieutenant shook his head. "Quite alright, lad. It is bound to happen on the quarterdeck from time to time." He paused and cast a thoughtful glare aloft and then over the windward rail to the foreboding shoreline north of the ship. "A lee shore, being a shore in the ship's lee. That is to say that the wind would be driving from open seas in towards shore. It is a distasteful duty to navigate a lee shore. Any error, even the slightest, can be disastrous. There are many sea captains who misjudged a tack or failed in respect of heading and ran their ship aground sailing next to a lee shore. But, it is a challenge only, not something to be averted from at all cost."

Jack digested the information hungrily and eyed the shoreline as Allegiance slipped by it with the wind at her quarter. He decided to hazard another query. "Sir, earlier you mentioned wearing about with the wind to stand off. What is wearing?"

The lieutenant gave a knowing nod. "That is a good question, young man. Wearing is a method of coming around the wind to bring it close haul without ever having to cross the bow over the wind like when we tack. It is a more cumbersome method, but it is far surer and far more forgiving. But, the captain has decided against it. We will leave the San Juan coast and press on toward Isla De Mona, where our privateer is sure to be stalking around in search of a prize."

Jack tried to paint an image in his mind of the maneuver, but his imagination failed due to lack of reference. The world he had become engrossed in was loaded with nuance and skill beyond his comprehension. Sailors had their own language, a gait that was unique to their profession and a peculiar fondness for spirits. They prized the quality of line handling above all else, even the strength of a man's arm fell second to the skill tying a perfect hitch or knot. Ashore, men discussed politics or the activities of their neighbors. At sea, sailors talked of the weather and told the tales of their far ranging adventures. Jack couldn't absorb it all fast enough. He emulated their speech whenever he had the chance. He studied their line work and tried to learn new knots as frequently as Bowline Bob would show him. His life at sea was taking shape. But, it was not at all like he had envisioned it as a child in Boston. The days were long and arduous. The nights were spent crammed into tight quarters with grown men who smelled foul and snored. Jack lived for the moments when he was on deck, for the glories of mornings aloft, and for the warm camaraderie of his shipmates at supper.

Morning waned as the sun rose high. The San Juan coast slipped away and faded below the horizon behind Allegiance's wake. Clear blue skies and deep blue waters dominated everything in sight. When the watch bells sounded, and Jack was finally relieved from his post at the helm. He decided to climb aloft and take in the Caribbean sun. With a heave, he lifted himself into the shroud lines and began the long climb upward into the heights of the ship's rigging. Memories of his first climb aloft came to him as he reached the top of the shrouds and shunned the lubber hole. He greeted some of his shipmates and started up the next set of shrouds to the cross trees at the height of the topmast. The wind was steady and warm, and sunshine kissed his exposed skin as he climbed hand over hand to the highest point of sail Allegiance was currently flying.

The seas grew to a moderate swell as Allegiance plied her course away from the San Juan coast, and high atop the masts Jack could feel every inch of movement in the hull below. When he reached the topmast cross tree, Jack perched on the inner length of yard and craned his neck to take in the fullness of his surroundings. The open sea stretched out in every direction for as far as he could see. Waves of sapphire blue to the south mixed with shades of an aqua green north of the ship. Jack surmised that the change in color must correspond with the depth of the water below the surface. A haze of marine moisture blurred the horizons in every direction and the skies faded from a light blue to the most piercing deep blue he had ever seen. Jack lifted his face to the shining sun and took in its warmth. The sway of the ship changed slightly, and he studied the waves to find that sets of rollers were invading the lighter seas from the north.

"Crossing into the passage, we are," A familiar voice crackled from the shrouds just below him. Jack looked down and smiled as he saw Bowline Bob hoisting his way up the final approach to the topmast cross tree. "Those rollers coming in from the north mean we have left the lee of San Juan. We are pushing into the strait between that island and Hispaniola."

"The captain thinks we will find Saber prowling these waters," Jack said as he returned his gaze to the horizon.

Bob grunted as he hefted his weight up and swung one leg over the topsail yard. "And he is probably right. Secretly I would hope that we don't cross paths with them again, though I wouldn't recommend saying as much in front of our royal navy brethren."

Jack drew in a long breath of the fresh sea air. "He'll find them, Bob. I'd stake my wages on it."

"Its more than yer wages at stake, lad. Though I don't have ter remind ye of it." He paused and fidgeted over his pipe for a while before clamping the wooden stem into his bite and staring out at the horizon with Jack. "The best we can hope fer is ter catch the buggers off guard. Maybe right after they take a prize, or when their watch is changing. Something like that could even the odds fer us a bit."

Jack squinted his eyes at the horizon, hoping against all odds that somehow they would both be proved wrong. He remembered their first encounter with Saber. The horrid shudder of the ship as cannon fire ripped through Allegiance's hull, the deadly wooden shrapnel, the blood and smoke. A moment of quiet passed. Jack shuddered as he recalled the shrill sound of desperate screams as his shipmates were torn to pieces by jagged shards of wood and hot flying metal. The thunder of cannon fire, so loud it seemed to echo through time itself and reverberate into his ears.

"Did ye hear that?" Bowline Bob asked in a rasp.

Jack scrunched his brows and turned toward the old sailor. "Hear what?"

"A thud, like cannon fire in the distance," Bob replied while squinting hard at the horizon.

Jack turned northward to look in the same direction as Bob and scoured the hazy horizon. A faint noise met his ears, but just at the lower limit of his hearing. He could see nothing on the horizon but a slight distortion from sunshine on the naked sea. For a heartbeat, he held his breath and strained his ears. The effort yielded nothing but the sound of his own exhale.

"Do ye see anything, Jacky?" Bob asked.

Jack scanned the horizon again, staring hard at the hazy distortion where the sea met the sky. "No. Nothing. Are you sure you heard something, Bob? Maybe it a hand dropped something down on deck."

"Aye, could be true, Jacky. But, likes they calls ye Dead Eye Jack. Old Bowline Bob here has a sharp hearing. Leastwise in me right ear. I always makes sure ter plug 'em before we go to workin' the guns. It saves the ringing so I can hear sweet whispers from the gals ashore."

Jack grinned as he imagined the salty old sailor trying to woo a lady of society, he smiled full on when he realized that wasn't the type of woman Bob was referring to. "I can only imagine, Bob."

The pair of sailors chuckled from their perch high above the ship. Bob fetched out a length of cordage and began walking Jack through the steps of a new knot in the steady breeze and shining sun.

"Ye take yer bite, here, and wrap her around behind. Twice over, now and then feed her back through," the old sailor demonstrated with the length of well-used cordage. "When ye goes ter cinch her down, she grips against herself here and here," he said pointing to a pair of spots where the rope was binding. "That's how ye knows she's a good'un when ye ties it. If she slips after ye feed her through, it a'cause ye didn't feed her around twice over. See?" He passed Jack the finished knot and shot his brows up with an encouraged nod. "Try her…" His voice trailed away and his eyes drifted back to the horizon.

"What is it?" Jack asked.

Bob shook his head and squinted hard at the horizon. "That sound again, Jacky, I keep hearin' it ever' so often," he said.

Jack followed the line of Bob's nose toward the horizon and found nothing but a haze of open sea and bright sunshine. He squinted his eyes and lifted a hand to hide away the bright shine of the sun. Brilliant sparkles glimmered as direct sunshine fell on the sea surface. Jack focused on the horizon and scanned east and west in search of anything he could detect. Doubts about Bob's hearing were growing in the back of his mind. The old sailor had been through years of gun drills in the Royal Navy, his hearing couldn't be that sensitive. All doubts faded though, as a stark triangle of white protruded above the northern horizon. Jack swallowed hard and focused on the image, half unbelieving of what his eyes had found.

"Damn me back to land," Jack said in his best approximation of Bob's candor.

"What? What is it, Jacky? What do yer see, lad?" Bob rasped through a rising gust of wind.

"A sail," Jack answered. "And it looks like she's standing toward!"

H.M.S Allegiance
2 July 1770
17 Degrees 54′ N, 67 Degrees 37′ W

The rattle of a snare drum seemed to fill every void of the wooden warship. Jack and his shipmates raced from the main deck to their station at the larboard number seven cannon. While the gunner's mates crowed their orders, sailors set to readying their guns. Tompions were stripped from the cold snout of each deadly cannon. Sewn bags of powder were rammed into place, followed by a thick wad of leather and then a deadly iron projectile. A final wad was tamped into place before the gun was laboriously heaved out to its firing position. Each gun captain would then point his gun by making final adjustments to elevation or windage with the use of the gun carriage elevation mechanism or a crude set of wedges. When the gun was pointed, each gun captain primed the flash pan of his crew's weapon by penetrating the sewn shot back with a thin iron spike through the touch hole. A mixture of coarse powder from the shot bag, and fine priming powder from a small pouch issued to each gun captain was stirred together in the flash pan. The final step saw the gun captain cock the flint striker back before checking the travel path of the gun carriage. Any stray foot or leg in the gun's path would warrant a stern warning, but that was a far better fate than one instance Jack had already witnessed.

The flurry of activity that came from beating to quarters quickly settled as the last guns were run out to their firing positions. On the main deck, launch boats were lowered over the side and rigged for stern towing. Breathless from the effort of heaving out the gun, and sporting a thin sheen of sweat, Jack rested against the frame timber separating larboard gun number seven from gun number eight.

"All this, for the sight of a sail, it's a wonder the lookouts call out anything," He lamented as he drew heaving breaths.

Bowline Bob popped his head over the gleaming black cylinder of the twelve pounder cannon and beamed a broad smile of smoke stained teeth. "Aye, better we beats ter quarters than get 'erselves caught off guard by the schemes 'o the enemy, Jack!"

Jack thought on it for a long moment and recalled the pandemonium and carnage of their last encounter with Saber, the French privateer that had gone rogue and was currently wreaking havoc with British shipping in the new world. "Aye, better to be prepared."

Allegiance had turned northward and hauled the wind close to her sails immediately after Jack had called down his sighting of the small point of sail on the northern horizon. Lieutenant Sifton, the ship's first lieutenant, had called for all hands to beat to quarters and Allegiance cleared for action with a mixture of haste and anticipation. It seemed to Jack that everyone on board was eager for a fight. Even his fellow pressed men from the colonies threw everything they had into their labor. The ship sailed with purpose on a course to intercept while the slight popping of intermittent cannon fire grew that had first caught Bob's ear grew louder. It was not long from the point that Jack had first raised the alarm that Allegiance was ready for a fight. After all stations were cleared for action, the wait began. The ship pitched in a steady rhythm from the action of the sea while her decks rolled slightly from the counter force of her sails. Sailing close to the wind always gave the ship an extra roll in her motion, it wasn't long until the effects were fully felt by the newer hands that had been brought aboard in Bermuda.

"Fresh pressed and heaving, the old sailormen used ter say!" Bowline Bob said with a chuckle as a particularly young hand from the forward gun crews huddled over a wooden pail and lost his breakfast. "The sun is shining and fer not a cloud in the skies, lubber! Ye never sailed close haul 'afore?"

Jack felt a guilty pang as he chuckled at Bob's ridicule of the young sailor. It was not so long ago that he had been brand new to the ways of sea life. But, seasickness was not a malady he had suffered from. Bob had enthusiastically pointed out that it was because Jack was born to be a sailorman, though Jack wholeheartedly doubted this appraisal.

After a few hours of sailing north, news spread from the main deck; another sail had been spotted. The ship Jack had spotted appeared to have a pursuer. The news was welcomed with a rousing cheer from the gun deck. Sailors were eager for another shot at their French foe.

"They thinks they're going ter take themselves a prize! Allegiance has another plan fer 'em!" a shout echoed from one of the forward guns. "The cap'n will put us yardarm ter yardarm with her and it'll be over the side and prize money fer the purse, lads! Just keep yer guns boomin' as fast as ye can and don't quit 'er until the officers tells us!"

Jack's thoughts drifted to the last encounter with Saber. He and Matsumoko had kept their gun firing through the thick of battle while all around them cannon balls and jagged shards of wood sliced past them. Screams filled with pain and whimpers of agonizing defeat came into his mind. Allegiance had been soundly defeated. Her rigging had been shot all to pieces, her hull blown through with ragged holes. When the smoke cleared, and both vessels parted ways, Allegiance had a wounded mast, dozens of dead and wounded sailors, and yards hanging limply over her main deck. It had taken almost a month in Bermuda to refit the damage from the first meeting. Jack braced himself for the one to come.

Without warning, Allegiance's hull hauled over into a hard turn. All eyes shifted to the starboard gun ports where a vessel became visible. She was a Bermuda rigged cutter with a triangular sail. Everything about the small ship looked desperate as she crashed into a wave that washed over the forward point on her bow.

"She's flying English colors boys! Allegiance ter the rescue!" a voice from the starboard battery shouted. The cry was met with a chorus of cheers until Lieutenant Sifton came barreling down the aft companionway.

"Silence! Silence on deck!" the first lieutenant's voice thundered over the hearty cheers until all had died away. "Our countrymen are in distress. Starboard battery, ready on the guns!"

A wave of confusion washed over Jack. Were they about to fire on the poor unsuspecting vessel? Why? Shouldn't they be more concerned with coming alongside the small ship to render aid?

"There she is boys! That Frenchy is coming up fast!" another shout erupted from a forward gun on the starboard battery.

"Silence on deck, damn you rascals!" Lieutenant Sifton roared.

Jack huddled down and peered through the gun port opposite him. The Bermuda rigged cutter slipped through a wave and began a turn southward. Her decks showed evidence of her brush with the French privateer, a section of railing was shattered and her aft sail had several tears in it.

"Those damned frogs, they are all the same," Bowline Bob said with a croak. "They runs their elevation up near as high as they can an' try ter cripple their prey by blowing holes in their riggings."

Jack studied the cutter for the brief moment it was within sight of the gun ports he could see through. Their aft sail was torn, but she was still fit enough to sail. And sailing she was. Her bow cut through the waves and threw off a wake that trailed away at a broadening angle as she made her desperate turn. As suddenly as she had come into view, the cutter disappeared and all eyes were left searching the waves for the enemy. It did not take the gun crews long to spot her, however, with full square-rigged sails proudly racing with the wind coming into view on the northern horizon.

"Starboard battery, at the ready!" Lieutenant Sifton bellowed through the gun deck. "Raking fire fore to aft on my command!"

Jack braced for the bellowing thunder he knew was coming. The square sail to the north was in full view and Allegiance had her broadside exposed to the threat.

"Fire!" Lieutenant Sifton shouted. One by one the cannons erupted in turn. Each thundering report drowned out the last as smoke filled the tight space of the gun deck. Jack felt the concussion of each cannon shake his entire being. It stole the breath from his lungs and shook his core to the marrow. Allegiance's gun deck became a sooty haze of smoke while the sailors of the starboard battery didn't miss a beat in preparing their guns for another round of fire. Preparatory commands rang through the thickness of smoke and din of reloading. Jack felt the ship shift beneath his feet. They were coming about in a turn toward the enemy.

"Starb'd gun one, ready!" a gun captain from the front shouted.

Another called out, "Gun two ready!"

"Gun three ready!" a third voice announced.

Jack braced himself for the ship to complete her turn. In his mind he could see the captain ordering Allegiance over to unleash another broadside in the enemy's direction. It was more of a threat at this range, a warning to stand off and let the English cutter be on her way. But, if both ships held their course, there would be no more bold warning volleys. It would be a match of oak and iron. Steel blade and iron pistol ball, flesh and blood. Jack clenched his jaw as the sounds returned to him. The thundering crash of cannons, a sick splintering of wood, the mortifying cries of the dying.

"Lieutenant! Lieutenant Sifton!" a voice from aft cried. All eyes on the gun deck turned toward the ship's second in command as a fresh faced midshipman raced to him from the aft companionway. "Sir! The captain sends his compliments, sir. He wishes you attend him on the quarterdeck," the midshipman puffed for breath and doubled over as he reached Lieutenant Sifton. "It's Saber, sir. She is turning," he sucked in a ragged breath before continuing, "she is turning to make a run for it!"

A murmur of chatter broke across the gun deck as sailors began to celebrate the efficacy of their well threatening volley of cannon fire. A shout rose from the forward guns on the starboard side and voices began to lift along the entire battery.

"Silence! Silence on deck, damn you!" Lieutenant Sifton roared with a deep red flush crawling into his complexion. "She still has the wind on us, this isn't over! All hands stand by your guns." He gave a hard look over the gun deck and then turned aft to depart up the companionway.

"They isn't turning ter run," Bitter End Bill said in his trademark growl. "They's luring us north, don't ye see? They sails away ter spring a trap and blow holes in the old girl, stem ter stern. Watch and see if it isn't so, they isn't turning ter run away. Not from some piss pot broadside at twelve cables distant, no sir. An' this cap'n is gonna run headlong after 'em. Blunder right inter their teeth!"

Jack fought the urge to roll his eyes. Bitter End Bill was an experienced sea hand, a man who had been hefting sail and line before Jack was born. But, his constant grating against the captain and the rest of the officers rubbed Jack raw. It accomplished little, no matter how they felt, to constantly complain.

"Maybe the captain is taking that into account, Bill," Jack suggested.

The old sailor snorted his nose before spitting out of a gun port. "Aye, maybe. And maybe he's just a dumb sprite chasing his dreams of glory at the expense of yer own flesh. Ever think about that, Dead Eye Jack?"

Despite his irritation, Jack couldn't help but chuckle at Bill's stubborn rant. The man had a point, but he perpetually chose the worst ways to voice it. "Maybe we would all be better off with Bitter End Bill as a captain?"

The salty old curmudgeon shriveled his brows together. "Yer making jokes at me now, eh?"

"Aye," Jack said, "maybe you want to have it out with me in the middle of the gun deck? We can both add to our collection of stripes."

A wild grin cracked Bitter End Bill's face, and he shook his head. "Yer mad."

"Not near as mad as you are, Bill." Jack quipped with a wicked grin of his own.

"I didn't know about ye at first, Dead Eye Jack, but ye 'ave the makings of a decent sailorman about ye," Bill growled.

Allegiance's deck pitched with the action of a wave and rolled as the wind heeled her hull to a larboard cant. Open sea spread out for miles through the narrow gun port views to both sides and the gun crews settled in for a long pursuit. Dead stares, looks of trepidation and anxiety plagued the faces of Allegiance's crew. Their bravado had lost its luster. The hull of the ship slogged forward in repetitive, dogged heaves. Jack tried to peer through the gun port at an angle and steal a glance of their enemy only to see the vastness of empty sea. Minutes dragged into hours. The height of noon bled low into the western sky and Allegiance sailed on in what seemed like an eternity of the bow endlessly rising and falling. Watch bells sounded and hands from aloft came down to man the guns while gun crews were reorganized to spell their shipmates from the tops. A general shuffle took place on the gun deck while sailors settled into their new positions and a voice bellowed from the aft companionway.

"Able Seaman Horner to the quarterdeck!" the voice called. It was repeated by several of the aft gun crews and accompanied by long looks from Jack's messmates.

"They'll be wanting yer on the helm, Jacky," Bowline Bob rasped through a breath of pipe smoke. "I'd not delay. The cap'n'll be waitin' fer ye's while we're at quarters."

Jack swallowed hard. The thought of leaving his messmates below deck for the coming confrontation was almost as harrowing as the prospect of being exposed on the quarterdeck. He looked at Matsumoko only to find the same stony expression as always.

"Better go, Jack. You don't want to keep them waiting up there," Matsumoko urged.

Jack tried to flash a grin to his friend but failed and only managed an awkward smirk. "Aye, the officer's want their cannon fodder for the helm. Do you think they'll brace me up as a human shield?" The attempt at humor seemed to be lost on his messmates. Jack wondered if this would be the last they would see of him, or he of they.

"Able Seaman Horner, to the quarterdeck, now!" the voice rang through the gun deck, louder and more demanding than before. Jack hoisted himself to his feet and gave his messmates one last glance before parting from their company.

Evening painted the western skies into a glorious ballad of color as the sun entered its final stages of surrender to the horizon. Hues of blazing orange and red, pink and amber danced high into the heavens. Upon his arrival to the quarterdeck, Jack was hastened to the ship's wheel. Captain Williams stood along a windward bulwark, his face the picture of grim determination. At his side stood the ship's second in command, Lieutenant Sifton. The two appeared to be exchanging conversation in low tones and without making eye contact with one another, which Jack took as a black omen.

"Ready at the helm there, Horner," Lieutenant Sifton said in a tone slightly warmer than most officers would chance with a common sailor in front of the ship's commander. "I chance that you will be there until the sun rises, but tonight, young man, you will see some seamanship."

The vague promise intrigued Jack. Looking ahead, he could only see the faintest hint of Saber's outline on the eastern horizon. She had flown all sail and hastened north by east until Allegiance was hopelessly out of range. Nightfall would come and there wasn't a chance in hell they would catch her before the last light of day slipped from the world. Jack held the wheel steady. The seas were calm with low rolling waves that met Allegiance's bow and lifted the hull in a steady rhythmic pitch that produced only the slightest thrums of pressure against the rudder. Shifting his gaze between the sails and compass, Jack held their course just a few points east of north while Saber slipped further away with every passing heartbeat.

"Land ho!" called down a foremast lookout.

"Where away?" bellowed back a boatswain's mate near the ship's waist.

"Three points off the larboard bow, looks to be off Saber's beam," the lookout shouted.

Another low exchange took place between the ship's commander and his first lieutenant, but Jack couldn't hear what was being said, and did not want to appear as though he was trying.

"Looks like Saber is shifting course toward land!" the lookout cried out again. "She's hauling over to larboard!"

Jack gripped the wheel, his hands tight against the coarse grain of weathered wood in anticipation of command.

"Steady as she goes, Horner," Lieutenant Sifton said with a firm voice. "We'll not give up the game until daylight has faded."

Jack wondered at the cryptic comment, but held the wheel steady while the light of day failed in the western skies. Saber faded from a silhouette, to a shadow until it blended with the darkness of the night surrounding it. Stars glittered in the heavens while the last rays of amber hue slipped from the western horizon and left Allegiance plying forward into a world of darkness. It seemed like hours, every moment Jack waited for the command he felt was coming, until finally the first lieutenant turned to him with a smile.

"Alright, Horner. Bring her about, larboard," he said with a sly edge in his voice.

Jack turned the wheel and sent Allegiance's edging over toward the west. Her decks shifted and groaned while sailors aloft adjusted sail for the new heading. In the darkness, Jack's mind raced with questions. Were they trying to evade Saber? Had they come parallel to Saber's course and Jack didn't realize it? A quick glance over the starboard side of the ship confirmed to Jack that the island Saber had turned toward was still to the north of them. Why had they turned west? More low conversation took place between the captain and Lieutenant Sifton. They kept their voices low, but Jack was able to hear bits and pieces floating on the night air.

"… if the wind holds," Captain Williams said.

"With the dawn at our back…" Lieutenant Sifton's voice replied and faded into the dark. "But, we will still have to…"

"Right you are, lieutenant," the captain said. "It will be critical that we…"

Both officers continued their hushed conversation for the next several minutes. The exchange frustrated Jack to no end. He tried to piece together what snippets he heard and make sense of what was going on. From the sound of things, the captain and his second in command had no intention of sailing away from a confrontation with their enemy. But, Allegiance had diverted course and was now sailing west. Jack looked to the windlass and checked the compass direction.

He wasn't losing his mind, they were sailing almost due west.

Lieutenant Sifton stepped away from the weather rail and nodded toward Jack. "Steady as she goes, Horner. We will keep this westerly heading for the next hour, at least, as long as this wind holds. Then we will bear north up Isla De Mona's western coast for several hours. These waters are littered with shoals, though, so be ready at the helm. You just may be called upon to heave that wheel hard over, like we all know you are capable of," the lieutenant said with a slight smirk.

Jack smiled in the darkness as he pieced together the officer's plan. "We are sailing around the island, sir?"

Lieutenant Sifton gave Jack a look from the corner of his eyes. "As I said earlier, tonight, young man, you will be witness to some true seamanship and naval strategy. The captain plans to circumnavigate the island and approach out enemy from a direction he will not expect us. The sunrise will be at our back, while also in the face of our enemy." He leaned close to the helm and lowered his voice, "That isn't the only trick the captain has up his sleeve. He has knowledge of a reef from a previous cruise, it is unmarked on our charts, and thus most likely unknown to the frogs as well. We will sail into view, keeping north and east of our foe, if they make to meet with us, they will run their vessel afoul of the reef. We will have our run of them."

Jack smiled at the devilish cunning of the plan. "And the captain will have his prize, sir?"

Lieutenant Sifton smiled broad in the dark. "Aye, young Horner. Then we will all have our prize."

Allegiance pressed onward under easy sail. Just as Lieutenant Sifton had foretold, after a couple hours of sailing westward under the star strewn night sky, Captain Williams ordered their turn north. They paralleled the western shore of Isla De Mona for several hours with the wind crossing their starboard beam. The rise of the moon came and brought a cool, silvery glow over calm seas. Under the heavenly glow of night, Allegiance took on another form. Her decks seemed almost lonely under the pale light with all hands at quarters. Her sails glowed under the moonlight as they caught the steady breeze blowing from the island. Progress was steady, and no calls came from the lookouts as the ship slid her way northward. The moon rose high and Jack relished the peace of nighttime on deck.

Small waves brushed Allegiance's bow in repetitive succession. Jack noticed the ship slowing as the night progressed. With failing moonlight, the north coast of Isla De Mona came into view and another low conversation struck up between Captain Williams and Lieutenant Sifton.

"It is waning, but as long as the wind doesn't shift any more to the east, we should be able to make the cove by dawn," Lieutenant Sifton said with a quick look aloft at the higher sails. "If It does shift to an east wind, we could sail north and wear around onto a southerly course keeping it close on the larboard tack. But, that would likely put us at the cove closer to midday."

Captain Williams shook his head. "That will not do, Mr. Sifton. I want our foe to wake to the sight of our sails, with the dawn at our back. That will keep their eyes fixed on us, and make the reef at the north of the cove almost impossible to spot. Let's hope our wind holds steady, and maybe have the divisions broken for boat crews if it becomes necessary." The captain threw a glaring look at Jack as he stood dutifully behind the helm. "This is the notorious marksman, is it not?"

"Aye, sir, he is," the lieutenant replied.

"Is his best service to us at the helm? Or should he be loaded with a brace of pistol to board?" the captain asked with a cock of his head.

Lieutenant Sifton paused for a long beat and drew in a deep breath. "He would be of great service to us in either capacity, sir. But, he has been standing tricks at the helm for a few weeks now, and his handling of the ship has been superb, up until this point."

Captain Williams offered a solemn nod and narrowed his eyes. "Before we move to meet the Frenchman in battle, see that he is reassigned to a boarding party, or placed up in the tops with a musket. If what you have told me of the young man is true, and I don't doubt that it is, he will be of great use to us in either of those capacities. I will have my personal coxswain man the helm as we engage."

"Aye, aye sir," Lieutenant Sifton replied with rigid countenance before casting a grievous stare toward Jack at the helm. "He has shown prowess with both pistol and musket. During close order training, he sticks with his messmate, the young Japanese fellow who was pressed alongside him. I'm sure he will do the ship proud."

Captain Williams nodded and cast a glance towards the upper sails. "See to it that his messmate is rigged to cross deck as well, first wave. We will need all the help we can get," he said before a long pause. "Damn it all, if this wind slacks any more, we will be towing the old girl around the north of the island."

Part Two

H.M.S Allegiance
3 July 1770
18 Degrees 07′ N, 67 Degrees 58′ W

Isla De Mona's rough shoreline stood against the horizon like a murky black spot in the shadowy darkness of the night. Under the glitter of starlight, Jack struggled to make out the form of the island as Allegiance pressed northward under a light breeze. As midnight drew near, the winds became fleeting and backed to the east. Jack could feel the tension grow on the quarterdeck while the ship's officers discussed their options.

"We have no alternative, we must lower the launches and tow the ship east under bare masts," Lieutenant Sifton proposed.

The sailing master interjected, "Nay, we're better off sailing north under the light breeze until we can wear around and approach the island's eastern shore close hauled."

"Mr. Tillisby," Lieutenant Sifton retorted with an edge in his voice, "If we were set on making a passage to the other side of the island for watering or to take on stores, I would agree. But, we are closing with an enemy that is superior in both strength of numbers and armament. A mid morning approach simply will not do."

The quarterdeck fell silent as the last breath of a light breeze graced Allegiance's sails.

"Lower the launches and rig for towing," Lieutenant Sifton ordered in a stiff voice. "With all haste, if you please, gentlemen. Let's get about it."

With the lack of breeze to propel Allegiance, Jack and an assortment of other sailors were organized into two crews while the launch boats were lowered over the side of the ship. All at once, the gift of coolness given by the night had been rescinded. There was no blazing sun to beat down on them, but the stillness of the air left every man stifled as they labored over their oars. Two thick lines were lowered from Allegiance's bow and secured into the stern sheets of the smaller crafts. When the small boats made headway enough for the slack to come out of each line, the real labor began.

"Put your backs into it, men," said Mr. Smalley, the young gentleman in charge of Jack's boat. "If this doesn't work, they will surely order us to warp her across the breadth of the island."

Jack's thoughts drifted to this dreadful possibility. Bowline Bob had once explained the process of warping a ship in agonizing detail. Warping a ship involved lowering small craft over the side and attaching kedge anchors to each small boat. The small craft would then row ahead of the ship and drop their anchor. When the kedge found solid purchase on the sea floor, the ship's crew would haul on the capstan to draw the ship forward. Jack remembered the loathe tone of Bob's voice when he had described the process. Warping was a common necessity in ports with opposing wind and tight shores, or when a ship had to make progress directly against a wind. It was meant for a short distance, and typically a course the captain would order when the crew was fresh from port, rested, well fed and in good spirits. This was not one of those times. He imagined the repetitive agony of heaving his chest against the capstan bars while Petty Officers shouted threats and wheeled their starter lines. Pulling at the oars under the stars seemed like a nice alternative.

When the line astern of Jack boat drew taut, the crew hauled together on their oars. Jack second guessed his earlier assessment. It felt as if the launch boats were toiling against an immovable object. The dark outline of the island to the south of them remained static as Jack dipped his oar and heaved in time with his shipmates. He put all of his back into each stroke, pulling with every fiber of his strength. At the peak of effort, the crew lowered their oar handles and reset themselves for the next heave. There was precious little time in between each movement and no rest to be had from any of it. The force of labor continued while the stillness of the night wore on in what seemed like a never-ending pattern.

"Pull, men, pull for the ship, pull for the captain," Mr. Smalley encouraged.

A few grumbles rose from somewhere behind Jack as he heaves the handle of his wooden oar close to his chest.

"I'd pull for a fancy lass ashore, or a spot 'o grog," a familiar voice said in a weathered croak, "but, I ain't pulling fer the damned cap'n." A ripple of laughter broke out on the small craft and Jack winced as he recognized the voice as Bitter End Bill's.

"Silence, damn it," Mr. Smalley snapped. "Silence fore and aft. I'll have no mutinous talk from you lot! Now, pull you scoundrels!"

Night wore on under a muggy heat. Jack's head and neck became a constant fountain of perspiration. It flowed from his forehead and into his eyes, dripped from his chin and curled around the edges of his mouth. Each heave at his oar became a battle. His back was aflame from the exhaustive labor of repetitive pulling. He retreated into his mind. His eyes bore a hole into the back of the man ahead of him. Dip, push, raise, pull, dip, push, raise, pull. On and on they toiled. He thought of the bitter chill that gripped Boston during winter. What he would give for just a breath of that cold air. He remembered following his father in a frantic dash to the pier with a shoulder load of heavy harpoons. It seemed like child's play to him now. Burning fatigue crept into his arms and back. Every new effort seemed like a colossal undertaking. The pace of the entire crew lagged until it felt that progress had become as elusive as a breath of fresh air below deck.

"We're nearing the east channel, men, don't let up now." Mr. Smalley said in an exasperated rasp. "Keep going, put your backs into it!"

Jack stole a glance over his shoulder. The entirety of his world had collapsed into the tight confines of the small rowboat, but now as he looked out to the south, he could see that together with the other launch, they had towed Allegiance across the expanse of Isla De Mona's northern shore. The dark form of the island sloped down to meet the southern horizon and exposed the channel Captain Williams intended to sail.

The sighting proved to be a second wind for Jack and the rest of the rowing sailors. They plied their oars with renewed effort and found a steady rhythm that propelled their crafts and hauled the hulking man of war eastward. A low beat began to thump on the deck boards of Jack's row boat, and one of the sailors chanced a quiet shanty.

"Oh, a poor old man came riding by," he sang in a hushed tone.

The rest of the boat added their voices to the repose. "And we say so, and we know so."

"Oh, a poor old man came riding by, oh poor old man. Says I old man, your horse will die and we say so, and we know so, and if he dies we'll tan his hide, oh poor old man." The singer raised his voice from a near whisper to a more audible note that risked carrying across the water. "And if he don't, I'll ride him again,"

The crew replied with, "and we say so, and we know so."

"And I'll ride him until the Lord knows when, oh poor old man. He is dead as a nail in the gun room door."

"And we say so, and we know so," the reply sang.

"And he won't come worrying us no more, oh poor old man. We'll use the hair of his tail to sew our sails."

"And we say so, and we know so."

"And the iron of his shoes to make deck nails, oh poor old man. We'll drop him down, with a long long rope," the singer stretched his intonation and grew slightly louder.

"And we say so, and we know so," the reply sang back now from both boats of rowers.

"Where the sharks will have his body and the devil take his soul, oh poor old man!"

A pause elapsed with only the slopping sound of oars working against the sea. Jack felt a smile grow across his face as the shanty drew to a close. The end of their labor was drawing near, and every hand was pressing with vigor toward the culmination of their effort. A dull golden glow was gathering eastward. The first notes of dawn were forming, and with it, the promise for renewed wind. Almost as if an answer to silent, sweat soaked prayer, the sea rippled with a breath of cool breeze. Jack let his arms fall slack while a chill crept up his chest from the slight current of air meeting a layer of perspiration on his skin. Across the narrow sea gap separating them from the Allegiance, the sound of canvas filling with wind snapped across the water. To Jack, it was a beautiful crescendo, the culmination of a symphony of creaking oars and grunting sailors. Allegiance shifted and the tow lines went slack as the warship took up speed under her own power.

"Ship oars!" said Mr. Smalley. The sailors all shifted their oars inboard and prepared to climb a rope ladder extending up the side of the frigate.

"You men report to stations, we will be sighting Saber within two hours," Lieutenant Sifton ordered as the rowing crews made their way on deck. "Horner, you will go aloft with Mr. Smalley's watch. Into the foretop."

"Sir, my gun crew…" Jack spoke before he could stop himself.

Lieutenant Sifton's face hardened for a heartbeat before the flash of anger was replaced by a softer look of understanding. "Your gun crew will carry on, young Horner. The ship needs you aloft, to aid our marines and take up their places when we inevitably suffer casualties among their ranks. You will be reunited with your shipmates after we succeed in battle, God willing." He paused for a long beat while a smile broke across his face. "There will be glory enough for all, young man. But the first share goes to you brave lads in the tops. Once we come alongside, and the marines have swept the decks with swivel gun and musket fire, you will all come along to board the enemy in the first wave. Look to me, Horner. Stick close by, and you will fare fine."

The words settled into Jack's mind like blazing orange molten metal settling into a form in his father's shop. After the lieutenant turned to carry on with his duties, the words settled and cooled, as hard and unforgiving as freshly quenched steel. He drifted forward, as if in a fog, and began the long ascent up to the foretop. It was a familiar climb and Jack took odd comfort in the coarse bite of shroud lines on the flesh of his hands. Hand over hand he climbed higher until he reached the peak of the first set of shrouds and hoisted himself over the edge of the foretop. He drew curious looks from the marines, who gladly took the lubber hole. Rolled canvas sailcloth and a web of hammocks were strung around the extremity of the small deck and several braces of muskets were hoisted aloft with the aid of the head blocks. All around Allegiance, final preparations were being made for the deadly confrontation. Arms chest were carried up on deck and barrels of cutlasses were laid out next to the main and mizzen masts. Hammocks and rolled sails were piled into netting strung around both sides of the ship. The mizzen shrouds were covered with sailcloth to obscure the helmsman from view of enemy sharpshooters while more bundles of muskets were hoisted into the tops for the marines.

Dawn outstretched her arms and lightened the eastern horizon in a range of colors. Shades of pink, amber and golden yellow drove the night sky into full retreat and forced the stars to take cover from the radiance of the sun. Winds from the northeast had grown in strength and were now propelling Allegiance along at a respectable clip. Jack shifted nervously in the foretop as the eastern coast of Isla De Mona slipped by in the glow before direct sunlight.

The seas were calm, but Jack's stomach had tightened into a knot and rolled within his insides like a case of sea sickness he had never known. Every heartbeat seemed like an eternity. With every fresh glance at the shoreline he expected to find the enemy ship. His thoughts centered around the elusive enemy ship and the fight that lay ahead of them. He wondered if the rogues had anticipated Captain William's cunning and were setting their own trap. He thought of his friends far below on the gun deck and hoped for their survival through the chaos that would surely unfold in the coming hours.

"Deck, ho. Mast on the horizon. Three points off the starboard bow. Bare mast, no sails. Hull down!" a voice called the lookout station high on the fore topgallant mast.

Below, Jack could see Allegiance's deck erupt into a flurry of activity. Officers from the quarterdeck rushed forward for a better vantage. The bow gun crews made their final preparations, and sailors in the ship's waist armed themselves with boarding axes, pikes and cutlasses. Jack scanned the horizon in hopes of stealing a glimpse of the sighted mast. The shore of Isla De Mona stretched forward from north to south off of Allegiance's starboard beam. Thick vegetation and tall trees dominated the skyline while hazy tendrils of morning fog wisped skyward as the sun broke over the plane of the eastern horizon. Set against the lush surroundings, the lone mast was easy to spot once Jack focused in on the direction indicated by Allegiance's forward lookout. The enemy ship was obscured behind a curved outset of land that stood defiantly between opposing forces. Jack swallowed hard while the last hopes of averting confrontation dissipated like the misty wisps of fog inshore.

A musket was shoved into his hands by a stern faced marine with a curious scar extending from his starboard brow to the collar of his uniform coat.

"Steady aim wins the day, sailor," the marine said in a monotonous growl. "Don't waste our shot or we'll throw you from the top ourselves."

Jack's stomach drew tighter. He grasped the heavy weapon and made a silent prayer to hit his targets. A quick glance to the deck far below further ignited his blood. He hoped that the marines remained ignorant to his folly, should he miss a shot.

"Ready on those chase guns," Captain Williams bellowed from the quarterdeck. "We will have but once chance at this. We must not fail!"

Allegiance shifted her course as the closing distance seemed to open the small inlet saber had chosen for her shelter like a curtain drawing at the beginning of a play. A moment passed with both ships in plain view of each other. Jack marveled at the wit of the captain's plan came to fruition. The dawn had broken, and the sun was at Allegiance's back. Saber had been caught under the glaring scrutiny of direct sunshine. This was compounded by the sun's radiant rays catching the sea surface. Allegiance had the advantage of them with the light of day at their back, but also by virtue of position. Saber was effectively trapped into the confrontation Between Isla De Mona to her lee and Allegiance windward. Their only chance to maneuver would be to fly all sails and retreat under fire with the wind close hauled, a chancy proposition at best. But, even in this, Captain Williams had planned his advance so thoroughly that this last refuge of hope would prove futile for the rogues. From Jack's vantage point on the foretop he could see it; a lighter shade of blue in the sea. It stretched in a semi circle from waters too shallow for either vessel and extended out into the deeper blue of the main channel. Jack remembered the captain's tense conversation with Lieutenant Sifton the evening before. He had planned this out with the careful foresight of a master tactician and the cunning of a superb seaman.

"Fire!" a shouted command rose from Allegiance's bow. Almost simultaneously the two cannons mounted on Allegiance's bow roared in combined fury and spewed a thick cloud of acrid smoke laced with burning cinders. The cannon shots hissed through dense morning air and left slight trails of vapor in their wake. One of the shots sent a geyser of seawater spewing skyward while the other found its target and crashed into Saber's bow quarter.

"Bring her about starboard!" Captain Williams bellowed from the quarterdeck. "Larboard battery at the ready! We will draw her right onto that shoal, the scoundrels!"

Repeated commands echoed around Allegiance's deck. Jack gripped the musket in his hands and felt a cold thrum of tension pounding in his veins. His messmates below deck would be bared to the first volley from the enemy.

"Remember," the scarred marine said in his gruff voice. "Aim for the bastards on the quarterdeck, and any man holding a musket to return fire. The glory of the day goes to the man who brings down their helmsman!"

Across the narrowing gap of sea, Jack watched as a general panic took hold of Saber and her crew. Cannon ports opened, sails were hastily loosed without proper trimming, and a few wild musket shots were lobbed in the direction of the approaching British warship. Sailors moved in haste along the decks of the ship as they struggled to find purchase on the wind. It was plain to see for Jack and the rest aboard Allegiance, there would be no escaping battle on this day. But, to the men of Saber, a narrow band of open sea lay to their north, and through it, the chance of escape to fight on more favorable terms.

The rogue privateer ship settled after a few minutes of pandemonium aboard. Order in French echoed across the calm sea. Sails were sheeted home, and the helm went to work and brought the ship onto a northerly tack with the wind close hauled. A ripple of excitement fluttered through the foretop.

"They're taking the bait, just like the cap'n said they would. He'll have his prize today for sure. Stupid buggers will blunder right into that shoal and be sitting ducks!" The scarred marine said through a dry chuckle. "Get your muskets ready, boys. Cap'n is going ter be anxious to get this one over with, more'n likely he'll try to take her without too much damage to her hull."

Jack looked over at the scarred marine. "What do you mean?"

The scarred man cracked a smile and narrowed his eyes. "Ye aren't really that thick, are ye? I means, the cap'n will want ter take her without blowing her hull full of cannon shot. She'll be worth more whole, fer prize money an' such."

Jack squeezed his grip around the musket in his hands. Allegiance was closing with Saber, angling toward the north and west and driving her straight towards the bank of shoals off of her bow. More musket fire broke out and the sound of shot hissed and whined through the air.

"Time we earned our wages, lads! Remember, quarterdeck and marksmen first!" the scarred marine said. He rose braced his musket onto the web of netting around the foretop and took careful aim. Jack watched for a moment as the seasoned fighter primed and cocked his weapon before taking careful aim. A flash of smoke and a loud crack sounded amid a flurry of hisses from incoming shots. The marine turned to Jack and pinched his face into a frown of revulsion. "Well? Do ye think the first luff sent ye up here fer yer health?"

Jack hefted his musket. He primed the pan and braced its stock against the netting. A loud thud sounded from above and a piercing pain entered Jack's neck. Involuntarily, he winced and let out a howl. His hand drifted to the back of his neck and returned to his sight, covered in bright red blood. Another check revealed a small splinter of wood lodged just behind his right ear.

"Damn ye fer unlucky, dead eye," one of the marines growled, "but, I think ye'll live. Now, give those boys a taste of that dead eye we've all been hearing about!"

With his jaw clenched so tight he feared that his teeth would crumble, Jack returned his hands to the task of taking on the enemy. He cocked the striker of his musket and leaned into the foretop rigging. All around him the marines were finding targets and letting fly with their shots. He drew a breath and peered down the sights of the long weapon. Allegiance was still at a considerable distance, much farther than the barrel top used for musket training. But, the effect on the enemy ship was undeniable. The deck of Saber looked almost deserted. Her sailors had either taken cover, or were running full tilt from one task to another. Little puffs of bluish gun smoke erupted all around. More men hurried from one place on deck to another. Jack swept the muzzle of his weapon across the deck in search of a target worth aiming for. He found it curious that the marines had been so insistent on making their shots count, they were firing while he struggled to find anything to fire at. He traced from the bow, past the foremast and spotted a patch of striped shirt from a man taking cover behind an expanse of bulwark. He scanned aft, past the waist and the mainmast. More sailors hurried from the aft hatchway and found places of cover along the windward bulwarks.

Jack scoured the enemy deck in search of a viable target while the marines all around him continued to send a hail of fire toward Saber. Puffs of smoke stung his eyes while the crack of shots rang in his ears. The chaos all around him battered at his focus while he searched to find a target. As if summoned by the sea god himself, a shift in the wind caused Saber to alter course slightly inshore and reveal part of her quarterdeck that had been obscured by sail. Jack's heart rose into his throat. Down the barrel of his musket he spotted Saber's great wheel as it was manned by a broad-shouldered man wearing loose fitting sailor's rig. With frantic abandon, the helmsman desperately fought against the shift in the wind by turning the wheel hand over hand in the opposite direction. Jack lined his sights and closed one eye. The sailor struggled against the wooden apparatus until it would turn no further and then issued a loud shout forward. The cold metal of Jack's trigger met his finger. All sound faded from hearing. Allegiance trembled beneath him and a dark gray cloud of cannon smoke burst forth from the side of the ship. It felt like a dream. He was aware of everything, but singularly focused on the sailor at Saber's helm. His finger squeezed pressure onto the trigger. He slowly let a breath go as his finger continued to apply pressure onto the trigger.

The musket roared to life in an explosion of smoke and recoil that took Jack by surprise. He knew that was a good thing, but there was a sick feeling that accompanied the bitter smoke and harsh recoil. A heartbeat passed. Saber's cannons began returning fire on the Allegiance. Tremors shook the warship while thunderous reports from their own guns echoes over the sea. Jack lowered the musket stock from his shoulder just as a wave of cheers spread through the marines occupying the foretop all around him.

"By God! Dead Eye Jack, he is!"

"That'll show those frog eating bastards!"

It was a flurry of excitement, and Jack seemed detached from reality. He turned and faced the marines of the foretop to find that all eyes were on him.

"Ye did it lad!" the marine with the scarred face exclaimed. "Ye brought down their helmsman! What a shot!"

In a fog of disbelief and shock, Jack looked over the narrowing gap of sea at Saber. Her bow had drifted westward toward the shore of Isla De Mona. Without a hand to steady the helm, she was drifting at the mercy of the wind. Panic ensued on her deck once again. A sailor raced from cover to regain control, but the marines ceased their congratulations to Jack and resumed their firing. In a matter of moments, another round of cheers spread through the foretop while another casualty of their fire collapsed at the base of Saber's wheel.

"Keep it up lads!" a marine shouted. "It's working!"

The ships had drawn very near to each other. Shouts of terror and anger in French could be heard floating over the small inlet. More sailors had attempted to regain control of the ship by taking the wheel, but one by one they were cut down by the incessant volume of fire from Allegiance's fighting tops. A rumble growled in the morning air, and Jack could see that Saber's bow had crossed into the lighter colored section of water bordering the cove.

"She's run aground! Ready the grapple lines and prepare to board!" a shout drifted up from Allegiance's quarterdeck.

All around Jack, cheers rang through the smoke laden air while a fresh volley of cannon and musket fire began thundering out in ragged order. Voices shouted commands in English and French as the two ships drew within pistol range. Allegiance heeled over and crossed Saber's stern while the hands aloft backed topsails. Grapple lines were thrown in arcing lobs at the enemy ship. Swivel guns snarled their blasting reports and sent handfuls of grapeshot over the enemy deck. Agonized screams rose into the morning. Saber's deck was littered with dead sailors. The sight took Jack's mind and plunged it back in time, across leagues of sea and months of hard fought reconciliation. He saw the open courtyard in Boston. Splattered red bloodstains on fresh fallen snow. The ooze of his own father's life slipping between rounded cobblestones. Agonized moans. He could feel the cold invade his bones as he looked around him and saw the same red uniforms that had stolen his parents away on that frigid night.

"Boarding party! First wave, advance!" The shouted command drifted up to Jack's ears. He looked over the webbed rig of hammocks and sailcloth surrounding the foretop and saw a cluster of sailors and marines moving toward Allegiance's bow. Cutlasses, boarding pikes and axes, muskets, pistols, rail pins were wielded about in the hands of his shipmates while a broad boarding plank clattered down to bridge the gap between vessels. The first men across the plank moved in a frantic rush with their weapons held high. A screen of smoke and tattered sails obscured much of the deck from Jack's view, but it did not look like the boarders met much resistance. A few grunts and shouts signaled another casualty of the dying confrontation, but through breaks in the haze of smoke Jack could see that Saber's deck appeared barren of living enemies. Every breath seemed to last for an eternity. Time seemed frozen while the wind continued to trace gracefully over both vessels. The roar of combat died to a level of silence Jack had not experienced at sea. He could hear the men around him in the foretop breathe, and at one point thought he could hear his own heartbeat.

A blood-curdling scream broke the eerie calm. Every boarder from Allegiance froze in their tracks. The cry came from the bow of Saber and before the last of the harrowing voice died away, it was drowned by a simultaneous pair of thunderclap explosions. A hail of metal shot back over Saber's deck and tore into the pack of British boarders. Jack's stomach tightened. His breath was torn from his lungs. The shipmates he had just watched cross onto the enemy ship had been cut down almost to a man. Bodies writhed behind the thick screen of grimy smoke. Blood poured from a hundred wounds on the score of sailors and marines who had comprised the first wave. A rallying shout sounded from Saber's bow and her forward hatches flew open as her crew flooded onto the deck to defend their ship.

H.M.S Allegiance
4 July 1770
18 Degrees 4′ N, 67 Degrees 50′ W

"All hands! All hands! Take up arms and prepare to repel boarders!" the shouted command of Lieutenant Sifton reached high into the rigging where Jack and the surrounding marines were taking a hailstorm of incoming fire. Musket balls ripped into wood and canvas, sliced ropes and pierced flesh. Just moments after the rally aboard Saber, three of the marines manning the foretop with Jack had fallen to enemy fire. Within the span of a few heartbeats, two more were seriously wounded by splinters of wood Allegiance's own mast. The deck of the foretop suffered from the withering volume of fire. Jack could feel the impacts shuddering through his feet and legs. Planks cracked and splintered while the marines did their best to return fire.

"Up there in the tops! Come down and defend the ship!" the voice of Captain Williams shouted.

Musket shots roared amid a storm of shouts and screams. Jack could feel desperation broiling from Allegiance's main deck. The ship and her crew had lost their early advantage. What had started as an assault had quickly devolved into a desperate struggle for survival. Swords clattered together while pistols and muskets belched smoke and hot metal. The fight remained static at the gangplank for a moment until a group of fighters from the French vessel stormed forward with leveled bayonets and broke the line of British sailors.

Lightning traced through Jack's veins. His heart hammered inside of his chest so hard he thought it would burst through his ribs and fall to the deck. In front of him, a forestay running toward the bow swayed as the wind shifted against Allegiance's single reefed topsails. The foretop was littered with dead and dying marines. Spent muskets lay about where they had been discarded in anguish or haste. The battle had become a slaughter, and Jack feared for his friends on the deck below and in the ship's belly. An agonized scream drifted up from Allegiance's deck and solidified Jack's resolve. Fear gripped him, but he refused to sit idle while his shipmates struggled.

"Onward men! Don't give up the ship!" the unmistakable voice of Lieutenant Sifton bellowed. "Give them nothing!"

With a fire in his belly, Jack grasped onto the forestay line and heaved his weight forward. He hooked his legs around the thick rope and lowered himself hand over hand. The shrouds were safer in any other condition, but he knew that climbing down webbed lines would be too slow and make him an easy target. The forestay led straight to the base of the bowsprit. As he climbed downward, he could see discarded weapons laying on the deck. Some were still clasped in the hands of his fallen shipmates. Both ships had become an obscene display of blind violence. Blood pooled around slain men. Casualties moaned for divine relief, for God, for death, anything to end their suffering. When Jack's feet finally touched onto the deck, he was sick to his stomach. The air was thick with acrid smoke, the smell of burned flesh, hair, and the pungent stench of blood and bowels.

As if possessed by another spirit, it felt as if his actions were not his own. His hands found their way to a discarded cutlass, and then relieved a dead sailor of his boarding axe. Smoke stung his eyes, but he pressed onward toward Allegiance's waist. The mainmast towered overhead, but Jack's focus remained solely fixed on the threshold of the gangplank. A trio of enemy sailors had crossed onto Allegiance and were pressing their attack toward the aft hatch. The quarterdeck was left exposed, only a few officers and a handful of sailors and marines stood between the advancing enemies and the captain.

With cutlass a cutlass in one hand and a boarding axe gripped in the other, Jack began to cross the length of Allegiance. Amidships, more Frenchmen were crossing the gangplank. The tide of battle had shifted decisively against Allegiance.

"Hold the line, men!" Lieutenant Sifton shouted as he stood firm near the helm. He discharge a pistol into a nearby enemy with one hand and then engaged another with his officer's sword.

Jack forged forward through the chaos. Allegiance's main deck had become a deadly battlefield. As he passed the mainmast a musket ball impacted into the hardwood and sent splinters flying. The aft hatch opened and Allegiance's gun crews began pouring up the ladder well and into the general fray. Matsumoko appeared from the knot of sailors with a cutlass in doubled grip and a deadly look in his eye. Bowline Bob ran to the edge of the quarterdeck with a pistol in each hand and a boarding axe tucked into his waistline.

The advancing French sailors were met by this renewed attack and within the blink of an eye, Jack could no longer distinguish friend from foe. Cutlasses slashed and clattered together, pistols and muskets barked loud reports. Lieutenant Sifton held his sword extended at arms length and roared a victorious shout. The French sailors fell to blade and pistol shot. As Jack arrived to aid his friends, the pitch of battle shifted yet again. Lieutenant Sifton charged forward and stepped onto the gangplank.

"Forward, men!' He shouted while gesturing with his sword. "For king and country, and for the prize!"

The swell of sailors boiled from Allegiance's main deck and over the gangplank with Jack following close behind. His hands clenched onto the weapons he had armed himself with even while his mind raced with doubts about his efficacy in close combat. Battle cries broiled and the second wave of boarders crossed onto the Saber.

"Fan out and press forward!" Lieutenant Sifton ordered. "Do not stop until we have the ship!"

With weapons in hand, Jack followed close to the first lieutenant while the boarding party met another counter attack from Saber's crew. He saw Matsumoko smartly deal with a duo of attackers before moving on to carve another man from chin to navel with his sword. His movements were a mixture of fluid and furious, as if the sword held in his hands had become an extension of his body. He commanded it with precision and lightning quick speed. A flurry of movement broke out on Saber's bow, French sailors reloading their forward mounted swivel guns.

"Get to those guns!" Bowline Bob roared. "Or we'll all be fish food!"

Shock and fear tinged Jack's blood. His limbs felt as heavy as lead while he pressed forward. The small swivel mounted cannons were oriented aft to cover Saber's deck. If their gunners weren't stopped, the second boarding party would meet the same fate as the first. He passed Saber's mizzenmast, ignoring a struggle between two Allegiance sailors and a Frenchman trying to retain control of her helm. Both swivel guns were being reloaded with powder as he crossed next to the mainmast at a dead run. Unsure of what he would do when he reached them, Jack held his weapons tight as his feet drummed against the decks planks. The swivel guns were mounted on opposing sides of the foc'sl railing, and their gunners were loading shot as Jack passed the foremast. He hefted the boarding axe with one hand and wheeled it up over one shoulder. The larboard gunner finished his loading process and leveled his deadly weapon just as Jack let the boarding axe fly like a tomahawk. It narrowly missed the gunner and sailed inches from the stunned man's face, but it bought a moment of hesitation. Jack mounted the short steps onto Saber's foc'sl and drove his cutlass point into the swivel gunner's abdomen. The blade buried deep which took Jack by surprise. He'd never imagined taking life in close quarters before, and certainly not with a sword. The gunner's eyes went wide, and he looked down at the wound Jack had just inflicted. Jack looked as well. Blood stained the blade of the weapon and soaked into the fabric of the sailor's shirt. In the dying sailor's waistband, Jack spied a flintlock pistol. As the dying gunner collapsed, Jack relieved him of the weapon and cocked the striker. He turned and aimed for the starboard swivel gunner, who had just finished readying the deadly apparatus. A cloud of smoke burst forth from Jack's pistol. When it cleared, he found the second gunner had fallen to the deck while clutching a ragged wound in his chest.

Footfalls rumbled within Saber. Jack had no more than let the spent pistol fall from his hand when the forward hatch flew open and clattered onto the deck. Sailors from Saber's gun deck emerged wielding an assortment of weapons. The first of the men to make it on deck raced toward the stern where Allegiance's boarding party had taken control of the helm and were cutting away rigging to spill the wind from her sails. Jack realized that he was effectively unarmed until his caught on the abandoned swivel guns he had just prevented from being fired into his shipmates. A trace of panic crept into his veins as several of the sailors coming through the forward hatch sighted him on the foc'sl and recognized him as an enemy.

For a heartbeat, Jack stared at the nearest French sailor. He was holding a cutlass and the look in his eyes was one of a bear that had stumbled onto easy prey. A pause elapsed. The briefest of moments where Jack could feel as much as see what the sailor had in mind. With no weapon in hand, he was caught flat-footed on the foc'sl while the knot of counterattacking sailors swelled. Fear gripped his innards while the acrid bitterness of gun smoke choked his throat. The sailor stepped toward the forward ladder and Jack sprang into action. He had no weapon, but the swivel guns had been made ready. With his heart leaping into his throat, Jack sprinted toward the starboard gun and cocked the striker with a clumsy swipe of his hand. He grabbed a hold of the swivel gun's handle and turned the deadly apparatus inboard as far as he could. The French sailor advanced at a run. Jack was caught in the same race he had just won, but on the other end. He leveled the swivel gun and grabbed a short lanyard of spun cordage. With a tug on the firing lanyard, Jack sent a spewing cloud of smoke and embers over the span of deck between the foc'sl and the foremast. As the gray haze dissipated with the Caribbean breeze, it revealed a scene of complete carnage. There had been more than a half dozen sailors standing on deck when he fired the swivel gun. As the smoke drifted away, there were only bodies contorted into grotesque positions of agony. Some writhed in pain and torment while others lay motionless. Jack's blood was aflame in his veins. He felt as if his limbs were being commanded by some being of greater capacity than himself, a warrior spirit had taken control and was wreaking havoc against any who stood in his way.

The cheers of his shipmates did not even meet Jack's ears. He could only register the musket fire coming from Saber's maintop where a handful of defiant marksmen were continuing their stand against the British crew's assault. Jack crossed the bow at a sprint and took the larboard swivel gun by its handle. He rotated the weapon inboard and tilted the small cannon upward. Without a second of hesitation, Jack grabbed the firing lanyard and pulled. The swivel gun roared its report and spewed smoke and death upward into Saber's rigging. The chaos of battle quieted as the last tendrils of gun smoke dissipated into the breeze. Jack's heart continued to thunder in his chest, but as far as he could see on deck, the threat was gone.

"Cheers for Dead Eye Jack!" the familiar voice of Bowline Bill roared. A crescendo of lifted voices drowned his call for praise and Jack felt a hot flush build from his collar and envelope his face. He crossed from the foc'sl and walked toward the quarterdeck where Lieutenant Sifton stood victoriously near Saber's helm.

"It appears we have won the day, with no small help from our young mister Horner here," The lieutenant said with a broad smile. "All that is left is to clear the lower deck and locate the captain." He motioned toward the aft hatch. "I need a complement to go below with me, the rest will stay here and hold security." He turned and looked at Jack. "Find yourself an unspent pistol, two of them if you can. You are coming with me, and bring Matsumoko with you. He was quite impressive with that cutlass."

Thin columns of light pierced through Saber's hull from her open gun ports. The bright beams were accentuated by a stagnant haze of cannon smoke that had yet to be cleared away with the breeze. Everything seemed still, dead almost, as Jack descended the aft ladder to the gun deck. He held a pistol in each hand, both cocked and ready for any threat that may come his way. As his eyes adjusted to the contrast of light and shadows, his nostrils filled with the putrid smell of carnage and spent gun powder. The gun deck was a horrid scene of shattered hull timbers and shredded flesh. Blood pooled in low places along the deck and dripped from splattered spots along the overhead beams and bulkheads. Jack fought the urge to retch. He had seen more death in one day that a man could expect to see over a lifetime. His chest tightened as a realization dawned on him that a fair number of the dead on Saber's main deck had met their end by his own hand. A fleeting thought wondered what his father would think.

"This way, Horner," Lieutenant Sifton gestured with a nod of his head. "The wardroom and the captain's quarters should be our first order of business. My guess is we will find the captain there. If he isn't in there, then we will chance the orlop and the surgeon's bay."

Jack nodded and turned from the gun deck to a passageway barely wider than is shoulders. He grunted at the tight quarters. Months of heaving line and manning the helm had filled out his shoulders to a healthy sailor's build, broad and solid. The wooden framing barely left him room to face square, so he turned his body at an angle and tested the latch of the first cabin. The brass fitting twisted with little resistance and Jack pushed the cabin door open before stepping into the breach and squaring himself to the small room.

It was a small cabin. Likely that of the ship's sailing master or one of her lieutenants. Most of the deck space was dominated by the stance of an eighteen pounder cannon and the carriage it sat on. Small trickles of light could be seen filtering their way in through a still secured gun port. A hammock hung from the head timbers, and a small chest showed signs of hasty stowage with the sleeve of a well-worn uniform coat protruding from its closure. The air felt still. Tense. There was no sign of life in the small room, so Jack pressed onward through the passageway. The next cabin was bathed in the light of day pouring in through a ragged blast wound in the hull. Spindly splinters protruded from the maw of cracked and twisted timbers where one of Allegiance's newly acquired eighteen pounder cannons had found its target. Jack squeezed the pistols he held and peered into the glaring light of the cabin. The putrid smell of bowels hung heavy in the air. He looked down and found the reason why. At first he did not recognize the human form, just flesh hosting more than a dozen ragged shards of wood. But, as his eyes focused, Jack could see the face of the cabin's former occupant. His eyes were wide with shock and pain. His mouth was frozen in a breathless scream of agony, his hands gnarled and wrapped around a large chunk of oak that had impaled his torso a hand width beneath his collarbone. An involuntary shudder worked its way through Jack's legs and ran up his spine.

"Steady now, Horner," Lieutenant Sifton urged in a strong whisper. "Onward."

Closeness dominated the narrow passageway. The air was stifling and laced with the pungent sting of powder smoke and blood. At the end, a solitary door stood guard to the captain's quarters. With pistols in hand, Jack pressed forward at Lieutenant Sifton's urging. His palms felt slick and sweaty. His stomach was tied in knots of tension. The latch was simple brass. A ring that when lifted would allow the hatch to swing open freely to whatever awaited them in the space beyond. Jack forced in a deep breath. He held both pistols at arms length while the lieutenant leaned in and plied the latch.

With all the fury of a broadside, Jack plunged himself forward into the cabin with pistols raised and ready. It was much larger than the other cabins, and the fantail array of windows served to illuminate the space with a wash of sunlight. The span of a heartbeat elapsed. Jack forced himself to breathe. Nothing but stillness met his eyes. A hammock hung in the corner of the cabin, suspended just above a large sea chest. Along the opposing bulkhead sat a desk flanked by a large cabinet on one side and a wardrobe that appeared to be built into the ship's bulkhead. Displayed on the wall above the desk was a rack with multiple sets of ornate hooks. Each set of hooks delicately held a sword. Some were in elaborately decorated scabbards while others bared their steel on open display. Jack stepped further into the cabin with his heart pounding so hard he feared the lieutenant would hear it. For a moment, his senses relaxed. The cabin appeared empty.

"Damned French," Lieutenant Sifton said. "Their captain is either up on deck, dressed as an ordinary sailor, or hiding somewhere in the hold."

Jack relaxed his arms and let the aim of his weapons fall to the deck. His eyes gravitated to the rack of fine looking swords suspended above the captain's desk. One of the bare blades was engraved along its side with gold inlays. Allegiance's officers would all writhe in envy when Captain Williams claimed it as a personal trophy. It was his right, of course, as captain of the ship. Jack stepped toward the desk and admired the ornate blade. The writing was in French, and held no meaning to him, but the words were wreathed in flowery design of intricate detail that pulled Jack's attention like a moth to candle flame. Stacks of golden rose blooms flanked the foreign words. At the base of the blade, encompassing its full width, Jack recognized the Cross of Lorraine.

"Sir," Jack mumbled as he inspected the weapon, "the captain will want to see this."

Lieutenant Sifton stepped close to Jack's shoulder with narrowed eyes. "Aye, a fine weapon. The captain will be very pleased, indeed."

Jack's gaze drifted upward from the masterwork sword to the other weapons displayed on the rack. In comparison, they seemed rather plain, though there were others with engravings, they seemed a poor comparison to the centerpiece that was obviously the pride of the captain's collection. Each blade gleamed in the glare of sunlight streaming in through the fantail windows. Jack admired the collection in ascending inspection until his gaze reached empty hooks at the top of the rack. The wooden squeak was the only warning of danger. From the corner of his eye, Jack caught a glimpse of movement from the door of the cabin's imposing built-in wardrobe. On pure instinct, Jack raised the pistol clenched in his right hand and fired the weapon at the source of the movement. The thunderclap report roared and a cloud of smoke belched forth from Jack's pistol. The wardrobe door clattered open as the body of a would-be assailant collapsed onto the deck in a lifeless heap. In the same instant, an ear-piercing shriek filled the cabin as a man in an officer's coat erupted from behind the tall cabinet on the opposite side of the desk. He wielded a sword in a long slashing arc as he lunged himself at Lieutenant Sifton. Flatfooted, Jack was caught between the attacker and his lieutenant. He raised his left hand and discharged the pistol. Another cracking report flooded the space with gun smoke as a sharp pain split through Jack's brow and cheek. He toppled over backwards. Lieutenant Sifton fell under the weight of mass colliding with him as Jack and the attacking Frenchman both fell into a heap on the cabin deck.

Panic and pain flooded Jack mind. His thoughts raced in a circuit of fear and rage. How had they not noticed the missing sword until the last instant? Why had he not checked the wardrobe before he assumed the cabin to be empty? Had his shot found its mark? Why was the left side of his face burning with pain like he had never felt in his life? Movement interrupted the storm of questions. A weight shifted on top of him. Something foreign drifted into his hearing. A warmth crept down the side of his face and dripped from his jawline. He dropped both of his pistols and grabbed a hold of fabric attached to the weight of his attacker. His vision was blurred. He shoved the man off of him and scrambled to his feet.

"Horner! Dear God, are you alright?" Lieutenant Sifton asked.

Jack searched through the blurry mess of the cabin and stumbled into the desk. "I, I'm not sure, sir."

"Hold fast there, young man," the lieutenant said. "You've done admirably. Let me take it from here."

A shuffling noise filled Jack's hearing. The splitting pain in his head intensified, and he began to teeter on the brink of consciousness. His legs felt weak, and he stumbled while searching for something to grab a hold of.

"Here, young man, have a seat," the lieutenant said.

Jack could feel hands firmly guide him a few steps to the wooden chair in front of the cabin desk.

"My head," Jack mumbled. "What happened? I can't see."

"You did your duty, Horner. You did a fine job. I owe you my life," Lieutenant Sifton said in a hushed tone. "You stay right there." Footsteps sounded in the cabin and the lieutenant's voice took on an urgent tone. "Get the surgeon over here, now!"

Jack closed his eyes as a wave of stomach turning pain overtook him. He raised his left hand and felt along his cheek. It was wet with thick, sticky blood. His fingers traced upward until he felt the bottom edge of a deep wound. Gingerly, he traced his fingers along the split flesh until he realized he was feeling the spot where his eye should be.

"Sir? My eye. Is my eye still there?" Jack asked.

"Get your hands out of that damned wound, Horner! Are you trying to get an infection?" Lieutenant Sifton scolded. Footsteps sounded as he paced his way back in front of Jack. "Yes. Your eye is still there. But, I won't lie to you. It is a serious wound. You may well lose it, and be fortunate if that is all that is lost."

The tightness in Jack's stomach worked its way up into his chest. Dizziness overtook him. He opened his eyes and tried to see, willing himself with all of his might to focus his vision. Blurs of shadow and light were all he could see. His heart raced, and he suddenly felt out of breath. Jack's lungs cried out for air as he drew breath and exhaled at a maddened pace.

"Horner!" Lieutenant Sifton said in a stern voice. "Pull yourself together, lad. The surgeon is on his way. You need to calm yourself and breath slow and steady."

Jack fought against the panic racing through his mind. "Sir, I can't see anything."

"You took a sword stroke meant for me, lad. I doubt you will be able to see out of that eye ever again," the lieutenant replied.

"No, sir," Jack said, "not just my left eye. I can't see at all."

A gentle hand reached beneath Jack's chin and lifted it upward. He heard the lieutenant grumble something about the luck of his fate and then felt rough wool cloth rubbing against his right eye. "You have blood in your right eye is all, Horner. Try now."

Jack blinked in rapid succession before squinting to try and focus his vision. Out of a blurry mess, the lieutenant's concerned expression came into focus. "Yes, sir," he said, "Yes, I can see from my right eye."

"And damned lucky for that," the lieutenant quipped. "If that sword stroke had landed a hair further over, he would have caught you in the throat. We wouldn't be having this conversation, nor any other for that matter."

After what felt like an eternity, the sound of footsteps signaled the arrival of Allegiance's surgeon and a pair of rough hands elicited a wince as they prodded around Jack's wound.

"Hmmmm," the doctor grumbled, "it is doubtful that you will regain vision in the eye, if you retain it at all. The wound should stitch up easily enough, but as for the organ itself, very doubtful. The blade cut deep. But, with proper treatment, we should be able to avoid any subsequent infections." The doctor shifted Jack's head from one side to the other and clicked his tongue as he inspected the wound. "I fear the scar will be severe as well. But, you should feel fortunate to lose an eye, and not your life. Many of your shipmates did not fare quite so well."

"So I am told," Jack said through clenched teeth. His dream of becoming a seafaring mariner had not included a life changing wound, nor losing half of his vision to the blade of an enemy he would rather not have met with in the first place.

"See him to the wardroom, I will treat him there. It is a serious wound, but not deadly," the doctor said as he stood up. "My surgeon's mates have their work cut out for them aboard Allegiance. I will send one or two of them to help tend to the wounded over here once we have our men squared away."

"Very well, doctor," the lieutenant said with a brisk nod. "Please inform the captain that we have taken Saber, and that her captain is, well, he died at arms rather than surrender his ship. I will require a detachment of marines to secure her crew while we assess her damage."

The doctor helped Jack to his feet. "I will do that, sir." With one hand he guided Jack toward the cabin door while with the other he gestured to a nearby sailor from the boarding party. "If you would be so kind as to escort us up on deck. I would rather not meet with any disgruntled Frenchman without a strong show of force."

The boarder looked to Lieutenant Sifton, who nodded his approval. "Doctor, do not forget. I will require another detachment of marines."

"No, no, sir," the doctor replied as he and Jack exited the captain's cabin. "I will not forget."

H.M.S Allegiance
4 July 1770
18 Degrees 4′ N, 67 Degrees 50′ W

The close dark of Saber's innards gave way to brilliant sunlight as Jack was led up the aft ladder well and onto her weather deck. With one hand securing a folded linen bandage to his left eye he used the other to guide himself through the blurry mess his world had become. Flashes of clarity interrupted the chaos. He saw bodies laying in the final contortions of anguish, a mix of enemies and shipmates alike. It seemed insignificant to him, the struggle which had brought them to this state. Jack was sure, they were just short of the brink of hell. Saber's deck was slick with blood. Everywhere he looked, he could see the ragged wounds of battle to both ship and flesh. Twisted splinters, lacerations, broken railing, shot wounds, severed lines, mangled limbs. His thoughts were a cascade of misery as he observed the end result of the violence that had been done that morning.

Allegiance's surgeon guided Jack across the gang plank with a rough hand and a muttered curse. It seemed the aging practitioner was not looking forward to spending the next few days plying his trade.

"More'n a dozen with limbs that'll be fer cutting off, and most of 'em lost ter infection afterwards," he said in a grumble. "And o' course they wants me ter see ter the wounded Frenchies too. Like I haven't enough of my own woes."

Jack kept his thoughts to himself. He wondered what had become of his messmates, Matsumoko, Bowline Bob, and Bitter End Bill. A sense of dread enveloped him as his steps carried him from the gang plank onto Allegiance's deck. If they had won the battle, there was little evidence of it on deck. It seemed that Allegiance had suffered just as many casualties as Saber, as well as comparable damage to the ship.

"This way, lad, ter the wardroom," the surgeon said in a scolding tone. "Ye'll likely be getting some stern looks from her officers, but ye leave that ter me. Ye be there by my leave, as my patient." He pulled at Jack's shirt and faced him down the ladder well. "Trust me, it's a might preferable ter being down in the orlop about now. It smells of death down there, and it won't be long for quite a number of them."

Jack took each step of the ladder with searching placement of his bare feet. "Are there many from the larboard watch?"

"Aye, half of the damned battery took wounds," the surgeon replied in a rough sailorly way before softening his voice. "But, if it's yer messmates ye ask after, I believe their wounds are not so serious. The Chinaman…"

"Japanese," Jack interrupted. "Matsumoko is from Japan, Doctor."

"Aye," the surgeon said. "Your Japanese friend took some small splinters in his thigh. He'll fare well enough though, there's no need to worry yourself over him. His wound was minor considering the damage he did to the other crew."

Jack paused as they reached the door to the officer's wardroom. "How is that?"

The surgeon shrugged. "Ha carved his way through at least a dozen of those enemy sailors before he took those splinters. I didn't see it myself, but there isn't a soul down in that orlop that isn't talking about it. Well, when they aren't raving about your stunt." He pressed open the wardroom door and gestured to a wooden bench that spanned the gap between two twelve pound cannon carriages. "Have a seat."

Jack eased himself onto the bench and leaned against the rough hull timbers. "I was only trying to defend my shipmates. It was nothing to rave about. I am sure Matsumoko was far more valiant than I."

"He made a show of himself, for sure," the surgeon muttered as he pulled the linen dressing away from Jack's wound and inspected the cut. "But, everyone expected a fearsome display of swordsmanship from him. I am sure the first luff had expectations when he sent you aloft with the marines, given yer propensity fer marksmanship an such. But I doubt he expected ye ter slide down the stays, cross decks, and then single handedly pin down her entire bow section. As I said, I didn't see it m'self, but from the what the lads below deck were saying, I wouldn't be surprised ter see young Dead Eye Jack get hisself a step ter Petty Officer."

Jack shrugged at the mention. "I don't know about that, sir." He winced as the surgeon brushed at his wound with a bandage soaked in pungent alcohol. "I didn't fire those swivels to pin down the bow. I did it because those Frenchmen were going to run me through."

"Aye," the surgeon turned to a small wooden box resting next to him on the bench. "Why ye did what ye did matters not. The fact is, ye did pin down the bow. That let Lieutenant Sifton get more marines and sailors across deck. If it hadn't been for that, we may not have taken her, or spilled a lot more blood to do so." He produced a hooked needle and thread and then glared back at Jack over the top edge of his spectacles. "I am afraid that this is going to be quite painful for ye, son. And I can't spare laudanum for anything but the gravest of wounds, which this is not."

Jack braced himself by gripping tight to the rough wooden edge of the plank he sat on. The surgeon hovered for a moment and cocked an eyebrow before putting his needle to task. The pain in Jack's brow, eye and cheek flared. The piercing sting seemed to carry through his flesh and into his skull. Each new piercing was promptly followed by a long, slow tug at his wounded flesh. His vision was marred by white spots that persisted even when he closed both eyes. Jack felt the stabs continue from just below the middle of his forehead to just above his eyelid.

"The eye itself may heal, but I doubt you will ever have vision from the organ again," the surgeon said as he tied the final knot above Jack's eye. "You will have an unsightly scar, but, it could have been much worse."

The next stab of pain came at the crest of Jack's cheekbone. It was followed by another immediately below it. One painful gouge after another, the surgeon stitched Jack's wound shut. The sharp, stinging pain relented to a hot, throbbing ache that seemed to creep through his head and down his neck. Ha sat back and looked into the distorted reflection of a highly polished brass plate that served as a shared mirror for the officers who occupied the wardroom. The wound extended from above his brow, almost to his hairline, crossed through his left eye and well below the eye socket itself. The surgeon's stitch job looked sufficient, but his eye was mangled, and even the finest of doctors in New York or Boston would have been woefully unable to undo the damage caused by the French captain's blade.

"Ye will have quite an unsightly scar, I am afraid," the surgeon said in his rough voice. He was interrupted by a rasping wet cough that made Jack cringe as he heard it. "But, it is better than the outcome many of yer shipmates will be facing over the next few days. Missing limbs, hands, feet, some will be taken by infection no matter my efforts. It is the hidden toll of battle, the 'Butcher's Bill' a ship's captain so oft refers to doesn't include the souls lost after the fighting has ceased. But, that does not change the outcome of the poor lads who die under the knife, or from a resulting fever. The costs of battle, I suppose."

Gingerly, Jack traced his fingers on the flesh next to his stitches and stepped close to the brass plate in order to inspect his eye. "The eye is still in there?"

"Aye, it is," the surgeon replied. "But, I am afraid the surface of the organ was cleaved by the sword strike. It will heal, with time. But, you won't regain vision in that eye. The best you can hope for is blindness and discoloration in the affected eye. At worst, we may need to take the eye, should it become infected."

His fingers drifted from the stitches in his face and touched at the scarred edge of his left ear, a piece of it had been torn away in Allegiance's first confrontation with Saber. His forced term of service in the Royal Navy was certainly taking its toll on his flesh. The surgeon stood behind him and fitted his eye socket with a folded linen bandage secured by a thin strip wrapped around his head just above his ears.

"Rest at quarters for the remainder of the day," the surgeon said with a wave of his hand. "Then released to full duty. Will that suffice?"

Jack tried to frown, but the pain that shot through his forehead proved too much for the simple gesture. "My hands and feet are fine, doctor. Rest at quarters?"

The surgeon shook his head and gave a sharp wave toward the wardroom door. "Have it your way, then. Able Seaman Horner, you are fit for duty. Report to your watch and suffer through your stubbornness if that is the way you want it. Just don't have a fit when your wound becomes infected, or you drop from the tops because you are light headed from blood loss! Now, out with you! I have more agreeable patients that need my attention."

Clattering mallets chattered all around Allegiance's deck. Under the bright sunshine of day, the ship had become a buzzing hive of activity. Shattered timbers were being removed and replaced. Minor wounds to the vessel were being reinforced with planks nailed over the offending regions. Aloft, the top crews were busy replacing damaged rigging, while at the foc'sl the sailmaker and his mates were hard to task repairing holes in Allegiance's torn canvas. It took almost a full minute for Jack's newly impaired vision to adjust to the brilliant light, but once it did he searched the deck for his watch and mess.

"There's plenty to do aloft, Jacky," said a familiar voice.

Jack turned and found Bowline Bob with an armful of coiled line. "Aye, Bob! I was worried sick about you guys! But it looks like you fared well."

Bob nodded, but a slight grimace that crossed his face told Jack he was holding something back. "Fared well enough, for the most part. Mats got hisself some splinters in 'is thigh. Nothing too serious. Surgeon's mates had 'im patched up afore the boarding even began. But, there was others didn't fare all so well."

Jack frowned even though the expression brought a painful tension into his forehead. "Who? Bill?"

Bob shook his head. "Nay, that old codger couldn't do us the favor of parting. No, he's fine and fit for sailin'. Yer midshipman, the one who took yer turn out fer kedging last night."

"Mr. Smalley?" Jack asked as his stomach dropped. He had liked the young midshipman, and saw him as one of the fairer minded among the crop of officers to be.

"Aye, that be the one. He was on the gun deck when we first took fire. He did a fine job with the for'ard half of the larboard battery. But one of those damned eighteens hit just in front of gun three. I'm sure you felt it clear up in the top. It cut the poor sod near in half and stitched the living half with near a dozen shanks of wood as big as sword blades. He didn't stand a chance," Bob said. "Mats went near mad when he saw it. Boiled over right there on the gun deck. I never seen him get angry before, but I'll tell ye, he was livid. He pulled the young gentleman's sword from his scabbard and went topside afore they even called for boarders."

Jack nodded as the pieces fell together in his mind. "I saw part of it when I went over with the second wave. He cut his way through everything in sight. They didn't stand a chance."

"I heard he wasn't the only one givin' the Frenchies hell," Bob said as his eyes narrowed and a sly grin crossed his face. "Word around the ship is ye scurried down a stay line, which I know you hate. Then I hears that you went aboard Saber and lit off her swivel guns ter sweep the deck. Hearing the crew tell it, ye sent a score of Saber's sailors ter their maker, Jack. Not ter mention going below with the first luff, and saving his life afore killing their captain!"

The excited recognition brought a blush to Jack's face. He pictured his friend blazing through throngs of the enemy with sword in hand and that stone cold stare he always wore. "Can't say I could picture Matsumoko getting a mad on," he said to change the subject. "Say, Bob. Where is he?"

Bob smiled broad and pointed aloft. "Just as damned stubborn as ye are. He's up in the foretop helping to re-rig the stays."

Jack squinted upward and tried his best to pick out which form on the foremast belonged to his closest friend in the world. "I suppose I'll go aloft and lend a hand. Rigging will be trying with a wound in his leg."

"Won't be a Sunday stroll with one eye and half an ear, either. My guess is, ye two will make for a sailorman between ye," Bob said with a rasping laugh.

Tarred lines bit at Jack's hands as he ascended the foremast shrouds. What had once been a torturous nuisance now brought him a deal of comfort. He relished the course texture of the thick rope against his hardened palms and fingers as he hoisted himself hand over hand toward the foretop. Caribbean warmth carried on the breeze and the sun baked everything it touched. Climbing aloft was more than an ascension, it was transcendent. He left the world of the deck and bulkheads far below and lifted himself into the realm of birds, wind, clouds and sky. The horizon opened up for miles to the north and south with bright blue sea stretching out into eternity.

The song of wooden mallets became distant. Whistling wind, and the occasional exchange of shouts and commands between deck and rigging.

"Hands aloft," a voice echoed up from the deck, "make ready on the foretop yard! Prepare to haul the topsail and rig for replacement."

The bellowed order set a dozen sailors into motion. They climbed and scurried into position along the topsail yard just as Jack lifted himself over the edge of the foretop. He took position in between a pair of sailors who had climbed down from the higher rigging and filed out along the footrope to prepare for the work to commence. A half smile crossed his face as he realized that the sailor just in front of him, balancing himself between the topsail mast and oblivion, was his dear friend Matsumoko.

"You look a little worse for the wear, as they say," Matsumoko chimed as he expertly shuffled along the footrope.

Jack shook his head and grimaced at a wave of pain that laced through his cheeks and forehead. "I could say the same for you!"

Matsumoko shot a look over his shoulder and then down at the blood-stained bandage wound tight around his upper thigh. "I hadn't noticed until the battle was finished." He glared back again with a wry smile tugging at the corners of his mouth. "But, you. I had thought you were finished with reckless heroics after our last meeting with Saber. I guess I was wrong."

Jack began to frown, and then grimaced as a wave of pain wracked his neck and forehead. "I would hardly call any of it heroic, Matsumoko. It almost feels like it wasn't me at all. Like it was someone else. I half stumbled my way through the entire ordeal."

Matsumoko's grin grew. As he reached his place along the yard, he turned to Jack and offered a knowing nod. "I saw some of it,

Jack. You did some quick thinking. If you hadn't turned those swivel guns inboard, we wouldn't be having this conversation. Or, any other for that matter. You did what you had to in order to survive. But, I will say, we need to work on your sword handling."

Jack halted at his station on the yard and readied himself for the labor of hauling canvas. "I welcome the challenge, Matsumoko. But, I hope I never have to draw steel in battle again."

Work on both vessels lasted out the daylight and carried into the warm Caribbean evening. Sails were hauled and replaced, holes in the hull were mended or patched, and rigging lines were thoroughly inspected. The sound of mallets clattered away, saw strokes bit into planks with grating rasps and everywhere shouts and calls echoed back and forth as work the to repair the battle damage sustained to Allegiance continued. The sun dipped low over the horizon before beginning its long, slow surrender while painting the western skies in a range of orange and amber hues that faded into deepening violets. Lanterns were lit against the coming night and work continued as the heavens opened to reveal a tapestry of brilliant stars that flickered their majesty over calm seas. Work on the foremast finally drew to a halt. The after stays had been replaced and shored up, the damaged sails and a pair of wounded tackle blocks were all replaced. Jack and Matsumoko made their way down the shrouds amid a procession of exhausted sailors in search of their evening meal and a well-deserved issue of grog.

The mood aboard struck Jack even before his feet were planted firmly on the oaken planks of the weather deck. Sailors and marines alike were participating in a rare moment of jollity. Hot rations of beans, salt beef and ship's biscuit were being doled out near the mainmast while a musically inclined midshipman with a viola had taken the liberty of striking up a tune just forward of the quarterdeck. Laughter and relaxed chatter floated over Allegiance's deck within the warm glow provided by an abundance of lanterns. Jack and Matsumoko received their grog issue and hungrily took their rations before clustering together next to an open space of larboard railing that had yet to be repaired.

Jack savored each bite of his rations. The salted beef was a tough as leather, the beans were bland and overcooked to the point of being mush. But, to Jack, it was as sweet a victory feast as he could imagine. The grog ration has a distinct tang of lemon in it and every sip brought a new wave of warmth to his tired muscles. Sea stories were being born on deck all around him as his shipmates relived their shared experience of the battle. It seemed that since the conclusion of the fight, Matsumoko's crusade against the enemy had grown in its legend. Sailors could not settle on the number of enemies he dispatched. Some recounted that they had personally witnessed him slice through two men with one stroke, others insisted that it was three. It wasn't long until Jack heard his name, or rather, his newfound nickname.

"Dead eye Jack! I saw it m'self! He slid down a stay line and tore through those Frenchies one after 'nother. The whole length of the deck. Then he takes their own swivel gun and turns it against 'em! Must've killed him a score of those frogs!" a sailor remarked enthusiastically.

Another lifted his voice in testament, "A score! It was two dozen if it was one! He left those villains piled right where he found them. By cutlass, pistol, and swivel gun! One of the marines was just saying that he was the marksman to take down the man at their helm!"

"It's true! I heard 'im say it!"

Jack drew up a deep drink of his grog. He enjoyed the banter a lot more when it wasn't centered around him.

"He's a rippin' good shot with anythin' he wields, our Dead eye Jack! And that's afore ye mention he brought down their scoundrel captain!" a sailor said while lifting his cup high. "A toast to our Dead eye Jack!"

Jack took another drink from his grog. A pang of disappointment struck him when he found the bottom of his cup dry. He had never taken much liking to the grog issue, but on that evening it had been especially agreeable to him. The revelries continued as sailors finished the last of their rations. A song broke out among some of the men sitting up on the foc'sl.

"Come all ye bold, young thoughtless men, a warning take by me. And, never leave your happy homes to sail the raging sea. For I have plowed the raging main, this twenty years or more…"

More sailors joined and soon the rousing song was taken up by nearly every voice on the deck of the warship. Jack smiled despite the pain in his head and neck. He enjoyed watching his shipmates partake in a moment of hard won joy. On the heels of this victory, discipline relaxed, if only slightly, to allow them a chance to revel in victory.

The moment didn't last long. Voices died away in mid verse and the song halted progress before reaching its conclusion. The sailors turned their attention aft and seemed drawn by something at the quarterdeck. Jack searched to find the source of interruption and found Captain Williams and Lieutenant Sifton standing tall before the helm. Both men were looking sharp despite their uniforms showing signs of wear from the battle. A hesitant pause fell over the entire ship while the bosun's whistle pealed out the signal for all hands.

"A fine showing, by all!" Captain Williams announced when all eyes had settled on him. "We have taken Saber!"

A raucous cheer rose from Allegiance's deck and echoed through the rigging into the night sky. The captain allowed a moment of hearty revelry before calmly raising one hand to signal silence from the crew. When the cheers died away, he turned to Lieutenant Sifton and produced a rolled parchment from inside of his uniform coat.

"It gives me immense pleasure to announce that our fine first lieutenant is getting his step. I hold here orders for Captain Sifton to take command of Saber and guide her into the nearest friendly port for refit and supply before reporting to the North American station in Halifax," Captain

Williams said with a rare smile. He turned toward the new captain and addressed him directly as he handed over the rolled paper orders. "We will furnish a prize crew, and a complement of marines. St. Kitts is not far, and will be equipped to sufficiently refit your ship, though Nassau is nearly as close. I should think either station would do a satisfactory job, but the choice is entirely yours, Captain Sifton."

The newly minted captain smiled wide as he received his commission with one hand and exchanged an extended handshake with the other. His face was abeam with pride. Jack felt joy for him. He was a good officer. But, a pang of sorrow spread inside of his chest as he realized that the commissioning meant that he would no longer be serving aboard Allegiance. He had taken a shining toward Jack, and it was no secret either. With his impending departure, Jack felt his future aboard Allegiance grow a little more bleak.

"Three cheers for Captain Sifton!" a Petty Officer near the mainmast shouted.

"Hip, hip. Huzzah," the crew shouted their response in unison.

Cheer and revelry continued into the evening, though Jack struggled to share in the lively joy of his shipmates. Captain Sifton's promotion and new command brought the grim reality of his situation back into a stark focus. He was still a pressed man aboard a Royal Navy ship. Able Seaman or not, he had just under a year of service still to complete. In the short span of time he had been in the Royal Navy, he had several close calls. Who was to say that he would survive until the end of his term? Jack's mind slunk into an agitated state. The French sailors on the foc'sl of Saber, her captain's sword slash, Allegiance's battle had very nearly cost him his life. It had lost him the use of one eye. He sulked against the shattered remains of larboard railing amidships and listened while his shipmates enjoyed the extra ration of grog issued to celebrate their victory.

"Able Seaman Horner! To the quarterdeck, sharpish!" The abrasive shout of a bosun's mate cut through the chatter and song. It was soon echoed by others until Jack's companions all turned to face him with encouraging stares.

"Better go, lad," Bowline Bob said with his trademark growl. "The quarter don't like waitin' an they're callin' ye b'name."

Jack's stomach tightened. Something inside him screamed that he was being summoned to answer for some foul deed he had no knowledge of. Perhaps something of his conduct during the battle? Maybe that he had left his station aloft? Or the incident below deck, where he killed the Saber's captain? He hoisted himself to his feet. Even though the ship was at rest and anchored next to her prize in calm waters, the whole world seemed to list from side to side. His head and neck ached ferociously. Every step to the quarterdeck seemed to tack harder over than the previous. He knew something horrid awaited him. Another call to the grating? Was he to be striped again?

He was greeted at the threshold by the tight expression of Captain Williams standing shoulder to shoulder with the newly promoted Captain Sifton. Both men looked hard at him with penetrating stares that seemed to pierce Jack right down to his soul.

"Captain Sifton here was just telling me of your exploits in the boarding action against Saber," Captain Williams said, his speech sounded demanded and formal, as if he expected an explanation. "Not only did you bring down Saber's helmsman, but you then crossed deck and swept their decks with their own swivel guns."

Jack folded his hands behind his back. He was at the mercy of the officers now, he knew his only course was to face what was coming head on. "Aye, sir. I did."

"Marvelous showing, young man. You were pressed into Allegiance, were you not?" the captain continued his inquiry.

"Yes, sir," Jack said. He knew he should meet the captain's stare, but somehow, he couldn't force himself to do so.

"And, I believe you were flogged in recency, were you not? Fighting with a shipmate, wasn't it?" Captain Williams said.

Jack's heart sank. There it was. Surely he was about to be taken to task. All the wonder and marveling at his actions during the battle were a ruse. "Aye, sir. A dozen, for fighting."

Captain Williams exchanged a look with Captain Sifton. The two of them seemed to communicate something silently between themselves. "It isn't often that a sailor will take a striping and then prove himself so valiantly afterward. More often than not, his attitude and performance tend to degrade over time. Which makes you all the more prized." He paused and narrowed his eyes at Jack. "Which makes what I am about to do all the more difficult."

Jack bit his lip. His stomach churned. He inhaled slowly through his nose and steeled himself for what was coming.

"Captain Sifton has a problem," Captain Williams said with a softening tone. "As you have heard, he is to take Saber as his first command. Manning a prize is no easy task. There is no guarantee the Admiralty will purchase the ship into service, even if it is the plainest decision to all of us." He paused again and said something that made Jack ignore the pain in his head and frown deep. "But, it is harder still for me to release a young man such as yourself. One that has proved his mettle in the heat of battle. We thought it prudent to give you an choice in the matter."

Confusion wracked Jack mind. His insides were wound tight with the expectation of some horrid discovery or accusation. But, his ears were hearing things that sounded almost promising.

"Horner," Captain Sifton said, "I was discussing the particulars of whom I am to take aboard Saber with me, as my new command. Captain Williams informed me, that as an acting captain I do rate to name a coxswain for myself. I can think of none better than you, who has already spared me from death, and at your own expense no less. Would you serve as my coxswain?"

Jack's heart thundered in his chest. His tongue felt swollen and sluggish. He shifted his weight from one foot to the other and then back again. A coxswain. He had no idea the duties of a coxswain. It sounded important, but it was not one of the positions he was even remotely familiar with.

"Of course, it does not fit to have an Able Seaman serve in that capacity," Captain Williams interjected.

There it was. Jack knew it all along. They had called him to the quarterdeck to toy with him before dashing his hopes and sending him below to a life of toil and misery. His teeth bit into his lower lip until he was sure the taste of blood was not far removed.

"To serve as a coxswain demands the rate of Petty Officer," the captain said. "So, should you choose to accept this as your new assignment, we shall have to remedy this discrepancy."

A moment elapsed, and Jack became aware that both officers were staring at him expectantly. He fumbled for words in his mind, still reeling from the turmoil that had gripped his mind and body only moments past.

"Horner? Will you accompany me aboard Saber?" Captain Sifton asked.

Jack gripped his hands together behind his back. The officers wanted an answer, and they were not inclined to wait. "I'd be honored, sir," he said.

Saber
7 July 1770
18 Degrees 4′ N, 67 Degrees 50′ W

"The duties of a coxswain are fairly straightforward," Captain Sifton said while a flurry of activity continued on Saber's main deck. "Any time I assume direct control of the ship, you are to take the helm. You will man the tiller on any small craft carrying me, unless we are in the company of a senior officer, such as Captain Williams or perhaps a fleet admiral or some such."

Jack listened intently with his hands folded tight behind the small of his back. He nodded his head at the appropriate moments and tried to absorb the information as best he could.

"Most importantly, and this is why I chose you specifically for this duty, Mr. Horner. When we come into close order battle, you will act as a sort of, well, a personal guard so to speak," Captain Sifton spoke with an edge of distraction in his voice as a marine sentry approached the quarterdeck. "Excuse me, Mr. Horner."

The marine saluted smartly. "Sir, Captain Williams sends his compliments and requests that you meet with him in his cabin aboard Allegiance at your earliest convenience."

Captain Sifton gazed around the deck of Saber and exhaled a long sigh. "I have quite a few issues to attend here, sergeant. Do you know the substance behind this?"

The marine narrowed his eyes slightly while leaning back in an almost imperceptible slant. Jack could see that he did not want to answer the question for fear of being thought imprudent. He was trying to discern if he was being tested. But, after a moment's pause, the marine replied in a lowered voice. "Crewing, sir. I believe the captain wants to revise your prize crew to better suit your needs."

Captain Sifton stood unmoved for the span of a heartbeat. Jack thought for an instant that he could see the newly minted captain shake his head.

"More crewing revisions? He has already pared the prize crew down from sixty to forty five. If he holds back many more, I won't have enough men to hold alternating watches. The men will have to stand watch and watch as it is," the captain grumbled beneath his breath.

"Apologies for the nature of my message, sir," the marine replied. "I'd join your crew if'n I could. But-"

"Please return my respects, and tell Captain Williams that I will be over as soon as the foremast rigging is back in serviceable condition," Captain Sifton said in an even voice. It appeared on the surface that all was well and work was underway, but Jack could see from his interactions with Captain Sifton, that his former commander and his former ship were champing at the bit to fly sail and return to port. It was no secret that Captain Williams expected advancement shortly after news of his victory was delivered, and he had taken to summoning the junior captain several times a day, much to Captain Sifton's chagrin. He tried valiantly to hide it, but Jack could see

Captain Sifton become more and more vexed as each hour passed.

The afternoon had gone from hot to sweltering, without a whisper of breeze to cool or propel either ship or their crews. Similarly, work on Saber dragged to a grinding pace under the blistering sun and with the temperatures climbing by the hour, so did tempers. On the quarterdeck, Jack remained steadfast at his post despite the conditions. His head still thundered with waves of pounding pain, as if he were being bludgeoned all over again. Sweat collected on his brow and rolled down his neck, back and chest. When Captain Sifton was on deck, he dutifully took control of the helm. When he was not, Jack relegated himself to whatever duty seemed most prudent. He did not stray far from the quarterdeck, and kept a sharp ear for the peal of a bosun's whistle to signal Captain Sifton appearance on deck.

"Lower away the gig, and a mess worth of men to row," Captain Sifton ordered. "Whatever change in crewing is coming, I would rather meet it now."

When the ship's small boat was successfully lowered to the sea, Jack joined a crew of four sailors already aboard to take the captain over to Allegiance. At first, when he took hold of the tiller, Jack felt out of place. His shipmates were heaving at the oars, putting all their weight into propelling the small craft across a calm swath of open sea. Meanwhile, Jack's load was light. He moved the tiller over slightly one way or another and felt as the boat responded in kind. The water was a crystalline sort of blue, clean and clear enough that in shallower water the entire depth could be seen right to the sandy bottom. It was captivating.

"Straighten up on the helm and put us alongside amidships. You all will remain here and ready. This visit won't be long," Captain Sifton said in a flat voice.

Jack steered the small boat as he was instructed and slipped in close to Allegiance in line with her mainmast. He held the tiller over after the rowing party unshipped their oars and let the craft glide in next to the frigate with only a slight thump of wood on wood as their gig pulled alongside. A ladder of wooden steps suspended by thick lines was rolled over the side and Captain Sifton made his way up to the deck and out of sight while a bosun's whistle pealed out his arrival.

"It's a shame, really," a sailor in the rowing party commented as the captain disappeared over Allegiance's railing. "He's a good officer. As good as they can get. An' he's letting the old man push him evr'y which way. Ye watch, soon that flag chasin' bastr'd will 'ave us manning watch and watch, on half vittles, fer our entire cruise ter port. An' all the while he'll be slipping along in Allegiance wit' plenty 'o stores and extra hands ter man the ol' warhorse. Iddn't right."

Jack pondered on this thought for a moment and chewed at his lower lip. He wasn't sure if he was supposed to quell the salty talk from the rowers, but several of the older sea hands nodded their heads or grunted their agreement. It did seem that Captain Williams was holding back on Saber's prize crew. Thus far he had only allowed a scant few to come aboard. Even the working parties crossed deck with fewer men than were actually required to complete their tasks. Jack felt that the sailor was right, it did seem that the more experienced commander was trying to put off on his former second in command. But, such were the ways of the martial maritime service. What could any of them do about it? The boat crew waited in silence as the sea lapped against the side of the frigate. After a brief wait, Captain Sifton appeared over the ship's railing and descended the ladder down to his waiting gig.

"He means to shorten our prize crew even further," the captain grumbled as he slunk into the stern of the small craft. "Take us back to Saber. We need to get her in sailing shape, and quickly."

"Ship oars," Jack said in a strong a voice as he could muster. He thought he caught a distressed look on Captain Sifton's face, but he decided it would be best to keep his focus on the task at hand.

The sailors extended their oars and shoved their small boat out and away from Allegiance. In short order they were stretching out and Jack had the gig angled away and on course back toward Saber.

"I have some distressing news to share with you, Mr. Horner," the captain said with a deep frown under the brim of his three-cornered hat.

"Sir?" Jack replied while keeping his eye on their course back to the ship.

"I tried to negotiate with Captain Williams, to keep your old mess together. I know you and that young Japanese fellow are close, and the older man. What was his name?"

"Bowline Bob, sir," Jack answered as a knot formed in his stomach. He clenched his jaw against the news he was about to hear.

"Captain Williams assented to The older gentleman, Bowline, as you call him," Captain Sifton explained. "But, he will not part with the Japanese swordsman. I know he is a friend to you, and I did not want your duty as my coxswain to come at such a cost to you, but, alas, it appears that there is nothing for it."

Jack fought away the urge to shake his head in frustration. He had been watchmates and messmates with Matsumoko for months now. The two of them had become very close since the fateful day aboard Salem Tide when Jack had been all that stood between his friend and an icy cold death in the North Atlantic. He steeled himself and fought away the well of tears that threatened the vision of his remaining eye.

"Aye, sir," Jack said with as even a voice as he could muster.

"You and your friend are prisoners of your own success. You fought bravely, and saved me from what would have been a grisly death at the hand of our enemy. Matsumoko's skill with a sword is astonishing. I made you my coxswain, and Captain Williams refuses to part with your friend," Captain Sifton said. "I can't say that I blame him, Mr. Horner. I want him aboard Saber, selfishly, for the same reason. Though, I know he is a particular friend to you. I am sure your paths will cross again someday, should you both remain in the King's service."

Jack drew a slow breath while deliberating how he should respond. He decided that it was best for him to remain silent. Anything he had to say would not be to his new captain's liking. The gig glided through calm water and no sooner than it passed within arm's reach of Saber, Captain Sifton vaulted from the stern sheets and up the ladder to the main deck. Jack was left to his thoughts while the rowing party stood down and stowed away their oars. Tackle hooks secured the small craft to ready rigging and soon it was hoisted into its stowage forward of the main mast. It seemed like an impossible cascade of events were washing Jack overboard from the only refuge he had found since coming to sea, his friend. Since that fateful day aboard Salem Tide, Jack and Matsumoko had become nearly inseparable. They took their meals together, stood the same watch, and labored within arm's reach of one another. During close order training, Matsumoko had taken to pairing with Jack and ensuring that his skill with a sword would withstand the vigors of combat. Likewise, when the crew was granted any time for leisure, Jack made sure to stay close to Matsumoko. They spent whatever time they could visiting or skylarking high up in the ship's rigging. They discussed everything from fond memories of home and friends of their past lives, to their dreams of the future and their plans for life after their pressed service. But, all that changed with the stroke of Captain Williams quill. It brought a simmering anger into Jack's blood. He and his friend had swayed the course of an entire battle, and it felt as if they were being punished for it.

Work aboard Saber was rejoined with a renewed vigor once the ship was warped off of the shoal that prevented her flight from the small cove. Her hull was inspected and deemed seaworthy by a very hesitant carpenter's mate. The sun dropped low into the west and a breath of evening breeze graced both ships. Within minutes, Allegiance sent both of her launches across the placid gap of sea to deliver the remaining prize crew and fetch back all who would not be sailing aboard Saber. A roll call of sorts was initiated with Captain Sifton himself listing off the names.

"Watkins, Ordinary Seaman," the captain said, the heavy weight of his newfound authority seemed to drive his voice.

"Here, sir," Seaman Watkins called in response.

"Bowline Bob, Able Seaman," the captain continued without looking up from the creased, thick paper he held in both hands.

"Aye, sir, here fer duty," Bowline Bob grunted as he hooked his thumbs into the waist of his trousers. He glared around the deck and lit with a smile when he caught Jack in his vision. More names were called out and Bowline Bob discreetly wound his way through the crowd on deck to stand next to his young friend. He fetched up his pipe and began to press in a pinch of rich smelling tobacco while the captain continued rattling through the list of names.

"Seems our Japanese friend won't be joining us, Jack," Bowline said in a low, lamented growl.

Jack shook his head and replied, "The captain already told me."

More names were called out by the captain.

"Flynn, Ordinary Seaman."

"Here for duty, sir."

"Dempkins, Able Seaman."

"Here, sir."

"O'Reilly, Carpenter's Mate."

"Here, sir. Ready fer duty."

A pause passed, for a heartbeat the rapid list of names came to a halt and the beat of silence drew every ear.

"Lambdin, Ordinary Seaman."

A ripple thrummed through Jack's muscles. He couldn't believe what he was hearing. Matsumoko had to stay aboard

Allegiance, but Lambdin was sent to go with them?

"Isn't that the rawest damned blowhole ye ever heard?" Bowline grumbled low. "This traitorous bastard comes aboard the prize crew an' our own Mats has ter stay?"

Jack's vision locked onto the sailor that had falsely accused him of attempting to strike out at a Petty Officer, and very nearly got him sentenced to death. "It is, Bob." Jack narrowed his remaining eye and watched intently while the captain and Lambdin stared at one another.

"Once rated Quartermaster's Mate, sir. Respectfully, I'd ask yer consideration ter rate me as Boatswain's Mate," Lambdin said with an audacious volume in his voice.

Captain Sifton's gaze didn't wander in the slightest. He paused for a long moment, staring at the former Petty Officer who had very nearly gotten Jack hung from the yards, which simultaneously almost inspired a mutiny.

"No, Lambdin," Captain Sifton replied with an icy edge to his voice. "The circumstances of you being dis-rated are still a cause for concern in my mind. I will not have a Petty Officer whose word I cannot trust without question. You will remain rated as Ordinary Seaman and be grateful for that."

Lambdin didn't betray any reaction to his appeal being denied. He simply continued to stare at the captain as the more names were called out. When the roll was finished, three dozen sailors and eighteen marines had been called and accounted for. This would be the prize crew to man Saber for the voyage to the nearest friendly port. Captain Sifton folded the paper in his hands and tucked it away inside of his uniform coat. He surveyed the crew for an extended stretch that left nearly every hand fidgeting and shifting their weight in awkward silence.

"Allegiance sails with the tide," the captain said in a loud voice. "And while I wish to put to sea and get ourselves to a safe harbor, there is still work that needs to be done." He scanned over the crew, his eyes finally falling on Jack for an extended pause before he continued. "We are but a handful, and in a precarious situation. The prisoners aboard still outnumber us by more than two to one. We must remain vigilant, men. Vigilance will be our best guard against losing what we have gained. Not only for our prize, but for our very lives. Marines will set a double watch on the prisoners in the orlop, and on my cabin. Arms will remain strictly under lock and key." He paused hesitantly, almost considering what he was about to said one last time. "In addition, the grog issue will be restricted to once a day." Groans and muttering spread across the main deck and the captain lifted his hand for silence. "Now, listen. I have no interest in depriving you of your privilege at sea. But, until we are able to transfer our prisoners ashore, it is of utmost importance that we maintain the highest standards of discipline and readiness. I will allow the issue of two water grog, and suspend the officer and Petty Officer priviledge of taking rum neat, until we are rid of our prisoners. I recognize that this is a sacrifice, and I will reward the crew with extended shore leave when we reach a suitable port."

At the mention of extra shore leave, the last of the groans and sour looks of the crew faded. They were in the Caribbean, whatever port Saber sailed to would be a choice destination for sailors to let off some steam.

"Mr. Brusby has been named acting First Lieutenant. Mr. Hill has been given the step from Midshipman and he will serve as Second Lieutenant. I expect their commissions will be confirmed by the admiralty in due time. Please extend them both the congratulations and render due courtesies and respects as befits their new station," the captain said before turning to the newly promoted officers. "Gentlemen. Please conduct your affairs promptly and see the hands piped to supper. Work may resume thereafter, I want us in sailing shape as soon as possible."

Mr. Brusby, the former fourth officer aboard Allegiance, turned to the Royal Navy's newest lieutenant and nodded brusquely. "Watch and station roster, if you please." He held out a hand expectantly and took a rolled paper from the blank faced young officer. "Hands accounted for, and properly rated, your watch and stations are…"

Jack's eyes glazed while his shipmates all listened intently for their duty assignments. Many things aboard ship depended heavily on watch and station assignments. Who a sailor could choose as their mess mates, who they would stand watch with, and most importantly; where they would hang their hammock for the pipe down hours of rest. An unlucky berth could see a sailor swinging in his hammock next to a hard snorer, or smelling the result of particularly foul hygiene. A sailor's mess could either be his saving grace in a tight spot, or a constant torment. Every sailor was afforded the privilege of choosing his mess, but in order to change from one to another, he must find a willing participant to trade berths. Being assigned to an unfortunate spot could result make finding a willing trade difficult, sometimes impossible. Aboard Allegiance, Jack had witnessed the price of such trades. Finely crafted items of whale bone, portions of grog or tobacco rations, a coveted item of clothing or even the exchange of coin. Sailors put a high value on the mess of their choice, and to be messmates with the right type of sea hand often came with a steep price. But, that was only if a man were unlucky in his assignment.

A tug at Jack's shirt sleeve told him there was something he missed. He turned and found Bowline Bob with a crooked smile and his pipe clenched into his bite.

"Ah, Jacky. Can't get away from ol' Bowline Bob," Bob said with a crackle. "Same watch and mess. Yer a lucky lad, berthin' next to the sailorinest sailorman ter climb a mast or haul a line!" He puffed a cloud of bluish smoke skyward and shook Jack's shoulder. "See? Yer speechless. It's alright, Jacky boy! Yer old messmate will keep his eye on ya!"

Jack smiled halfheartedly at Bob being Bob. He loved the old sailor, not just for everything he had taught him, but for being the buoy to Jack's spirits when the seas seemed darkest. But, Jack's mind was not wholly centered on his friend's ranting. He heard Bob's words, but they didn't seem to penetrate. His vision focused over Bob's shoulder at the figure of a sailor wearing a ragged tarpaulin hat pulled low. There was something about the man that seemed off, but somehow vaguely familiar. Jack tried to place the name, but the sailor was careful not to reveal his face. As the watch and station bill was continued, Jack focused hard on the slender built sailor. He frowned and squinted his eye to try and focus his vision, but the flop of the mystery sailor's hat refused to reveal anything about his identity.

"Alright, lads," Lieutenant Brusby said. "Now yer watch and station is settled. Well have no dickering fer changes until the appointed day, which will be next Sunday. Until then, ye be fitted in yer places. Now, all hands fer supper and back ter work until pipe down."

The crowd dissolved into a mix of sailors and marines moving about the deck to find their messmates and take issue of their evening rations. In the warmth of the evening, and while the ship was still at anchor, the lion's share of the crew would elect to take their meal on deck in the embrace of the evening breeze. Jack tried to slip his way through the press of the crew without losing sight of the mysterious sailor. He passed several shipmates who congratulated him on becoming a Petty Officer with hearty handshakes and broad smiles.

"Dead eye Jack, our own pressed man gone and become a proper mate!" a sailor reveled. "Take it easy with the starter, if ye please mister Horner."

Jack smiled and nodded to the sentiment while he embraced the sailor's handshake. He tried to end the exchange quickly, but without giving offense. "Thank ye kindly," he said while searching the crowd. He had lost sight of the strangely familiar figure.

"So, they made ye a Petty Officer, eh?" said a voice with a menacing edge.

Jack turned and came face to face with Lambdin, who had an undisguised, disdainful sneer on his face. "Aye, Quartermaster's Mate, actually."

Lambdin shook his head while his lip curled up at one side. "This Royal Navy, isn't what it used to be. In days past, ye'd 'ave been strung from the yards three times over," he said while the sneer on his face tightened to an angry scowl. "But, I wish ye joy of yer step. Fer the time it lasts ye."

Jack redoubled his effort into showing no reaction to the snarling seaman. "Mind yer tongue, Mr. Lambdin. Or I'll have ye before the captain." He motioned amidships. "Now, if I'm not mistaken, yer station is at the waist, with the rest of the land fodder. See yerself there."

Lamdin's lip curled and revealed the fronts of his slightly crooked teeth. He drew breath and tensed in front of Jack, like a snake coiling to strike. For the flash of an instant, Jack thought the former mate would raise his fists. The irony was not lost on him and he shifted his weight onto the balls of his feet where he remained ready to move against the incensed sailor. But, the moment passed. Lambdin's shoulders slunk while a creeping red flush enveloped his face.

"Aye, Mr. Horner," He said with a nod of his brow. "Ter the waist fer duty. We'll talk more later."

Jack dismissed the veiled threat as Lambdin's last attempt at clinging to his superiority. He watched while Lambdin turned and departed for the ship's waist. After only a few paces, he cast a poisonous look over his shoulder and Jack's blood tinged with a streak of fear. Something told Jack that his troubles with the disgruntled sailor were far from over.

Work resumed and carried late into the night. Saber's prize crew made progress in the coolness of of the evening. Carpenters rigged the orlop into a secure cell. Top men replaced the last of Saber's battle worn rigging and the new captain made his late evening rounds while pointing out issues that needed to be addressed or giving nods of approval. While the work continued, Jack kept a sharp eye for the mysterious sailor he had tried to approach earlier. But, he was nowhere to be seen either on deck or below. The question burned at Jack's mind and vexed him further when his search yielded no sight of the sailor in the floppy tarpaulin hat.

When the boatswain's whistle sounded its call for pipe down, Jack studied each face remaining on deck for duty. There was no sight of the concealing tarpaulin hat, nor the slender built sailor who had been wearing it. Something about the man had struck Jack as off. He couldn't quite place a finger on it, but there was certainly something different, and Jack was determined to find out what it was.

When hammocks were strung and the lanterns below deck had finally been doused for the night, Jack lay awake in the darkness while Saber's slight rocking motion tugged at his consciousness. A cool breeze traced its way through the gun ports, which had been left open for just that purpose. The sound of the seawater lapped lazily against Saber's hull and the events of the recent past revisited Jack. It had been months since he had watched his parents die on that cold street in Boston, but the look in his mother's eyes would not leave his mind's eye. He wondered what she would think of him now. If only she could see him. He decided it was probably better that she couldn't, with his mangled ear and scarred face, he wouldn't be the son she had known. His thoughts turned to his father. Would the hard-nosed blacksmith who valued work ethic and craftsmanship above everything approve of his new life? Would he approve of Jack's newfound reputation? Or would he turn away from his son, disgraced by the violence he had committed? The questions tormented Jack long after the first snores began to rumble through the crowded gun deck. He was revisiting the memory of arriving home with his parents only to find a note from their landlord notifying the family of a vastly increased rent when a sudden presence caught his attention. He could feel it more than see it. The form of someone standing statue still next to his hammock. In the darkness below decks, the figure was as difficult to make out as a shadow in the night.

Jack tensed. He could hear heavy, halting breaths. Goosebumps rippled his skin. The hair on his arms and neck stood on end. His heart leapt from the tranquility of rest to a shock state. He shifted in his hammock and narrowed his eye in an attempt to pierce the darkness surrounding him.

"Justice of the lower decks, Horner," a voice said in a raspy whisper. "Ye robbed me of my post as a mate, an now yer rated the same. I won't have it!"

It was Lambdin! Jack's blood lit with a bolt of panic. He was completely vulnerable hanging in his hammock. In the dark he could see neither his assailant, nor a clear path of escape. A thousand thoughts raced through his mind. Did Lambdin have a weapon? Was he here to kill Jack, or just beat him mercilessly? Did he have companions complicit with his plan? Would they knock him unconscious and throw him overboard in the night? The rasp of a blade leaving its sheath filled Jack's ears.

Saber
8 July 1770
19 Degrees 7′ N, 68 Degrees 20′ W

Sheer terror gripped Jack as he lay helpless in his hammock. The shadow standing over him was poised to strike, ready to inflict a mortal wound at any moment. He had no time to react, no time to spring from his suspended bed and flee or mount any kind of hopeless defense. His vision could not penetrate the dark clutches of the gun deck. Everything faded from existence at the sound of cold steel leaving a rough leather sheath. His muscles froze in tension. Everything dragged to a painful crawl, as if the universe had conspired against him to amplify every agonizing misery of his end. His nerves hummed with panic, every instant they anticipated the piercing pain of the blade. Images of his parents came to him and departed as quick as the brilliant flash caused by lightning on a summer night. He raised his arms to shield himself, a last desperate bid for survival. But, just when he thought the imminence of his death could be postponed no longer, it passed. A grunt in the darkness. A hollow thunk sounded, followed by the unmistakable fall of a body onto the wooden deck.

With his heart racing, and his breath seized in his throat, Jack peered over the edge of his hammock. His eyesight adjusted to the gloom. There, next to his berth, stood a slender shadow crowned by a floppy tarpaulin hat.

"What in the blazes?" Bowline Bob's voice grunted in the darkness. "Jacky? Did ye fall from yer hammock again?"

Jack, overcome by confusion while simultaneously relieved from his mortal fear, reached out for the floppy hat. In a swift motion he plucked the article away in hopes of revealing the mystery sailor's face, but to no avail. The gun deck was too dark for any distinguishing features to be recognized.

"Jack? Are ye well?" Bob asked again with growing concern.

"No, Bob," Jack said. "Get a light. Any light. Something foul has happened."

The sound of creaking rope and shuffle of canvas was followed quickly by Bob's footfalls onto the deck. Steps pattered on the deck planks and after a moment that seemed to Jack like half of the dogwatch, Bob returned with the dim glow of a lantern swaying in one hand.

"Good God in heaven, Jacky! That's Lambdin on the deck!" Bob rasped in a throaty whisper. "He's supposed to be berthed forward in with his mess. What in blazes is he doing here?"

"He meant to skewer me with his knife," Jack said while climbing out of his hammock. His hands were shaking from the fire still lingering in his blood. "He said he would have his lower deck justice, and then I heard him draw his knife."

Bob smiled broad and nodded. "Then ye let 'im have it, eh?"

Jack shook his head and pulled his lips tight together. "That's the thing, Bob. I thought I was done for. I couldn't see him, I didn't have time to react. He had me dead to rights. I held up my arms to try and block the knife, but it never touched me." He held up the tarpaulin hat still clutched in his hand. "Someone who was wearing this hat put a thumping to this villain. I reached out and this was all I could grab hold of."

Bob's eyes were wide in the warm yellow glow. His face played out everything he was thinking to Jack as plain as if he said it aloud. "Wit' the history 'tween ye two, yer'll be flogged fer this 'un. No matter if'n the cap'n takes ter ye. He'll 'ave no choice in the matter, Jack. Fightin aboard ship is an offense on the king's articles of war. An' flogged all the harder fer'n it bein yer second offense. Least that's how it'll look."

The fire in Jack's blood rekindled. Bob was right. All it would take was a sentry to see Lambdin's unconscious body lying on the deck, and Jack standing over him to draw a fateful conclusion. He would be disrated, flogged and turned back before the mast. He looked to Bob. "What do we do?"

Bob rubbed at his beard and glared intensely down the gun deck full of softly swaying hammocks. "Reckon there be only one thing ter do about it. We hoist his sorry arse up inter his hammock an' make like nothing went amiss in the first place. But, we can't be fer waking up half the ship while we does it."

With his heartbeat thrumming. Jack stooped down and helped Bob hoist the unconscious Lambdin up off of the deck. Bob took hold of his arms while Jack hefted the failed assailant's legs. It squirmed in his thoughts, the struggle between following through with Bob's plan or dropping the cowardly cur to the deck and marching to Captain Sifton's cabin and baring the situation to him. On one hand, Bob had never led him astray. Jack owed much of his position aboard Saber to Bob's careful tutelage aloft. On the other hand, Jack felt that he was betraying the captain's trust to a measure. In the end, he knew Bowline Bob was right. With the history between him and Lambdin, there would be no denying the suspect circumstances, all the more damning that he had already been flogged for fighting. There was no other tack to take.

The ship was calm and quiet, which made every step a nerve-wracking evolution of slow progress. Every interrupted snore, and every shift inside of a hammock brought visions of he and Bob being discovered. He imagined how much more damning the situation would be were they caught in the act of hauling the unconscious sailor forward to his berth. A ripple of cool entered through the gun ports and Jack was grateful for the relief. His shirt soaked through with sweat from the warmth trapped below deck and the exertion of carrying the man who had tried to kill him. They passed between gun carriages and water barrels, shot racks, hammocks filled with sleeping shipmates, and avoided the last portion of the starboard battery where it was known that several men were exceptionally light sleepers. When they finally reached Lambdin's empty hammock, Jack was thoroughly exhausted. His hands felt weary from their efforts and his arms could no longer support Lambdin's full weight. He dragged the last few steps until finally lowering the menace to the deck.

"Let's do this smart, see," Bob said in a close whisper as he reached up to loosen Lambdin's hammock knots. "I'll not be liftin' his carcass up, when I can just lower 'is hammock down."

Jack followed suit and soon the hammock was lowered on its suspending rope to a mere few inches from the deck. He and Bob hoisted Lambdin into the sling of canvas and braided line before hauling the hammock hand over hand upward to a respectable height.

"There," Bob said in a hush interrupted by ragged breaths. "If the bugger falls out, that'll be his problem."

Jack examined Lambdin for a moment as he lay in the gentle rock of his hammock. He expected anger to take his thoughts as he looked onto the unconscious villain, but instead, Jack felt pity. Without the authority of position, this man had nothing. He hadn't even possessed the courage to challenge Jack face to face. He had chosen to kill Jack in his sleep, but he hadn't counted on the sailor in the floppy hat.

The remaining hours of night drifted by sleeplessly. No matter how Jack tossed in the slung canvas web of his hammock, he could not settle himself for rest. His thoughts resumed their spiral until the stoic peal of the watch bell sounded for the change of watch. He waited until his messmates began crawling from their respective lairs of comfort and tranquility before finally surrendering his feet to the deck and making his way topside. The mate of the watch approached him with a hard glare as he donned his new hat at the top of the forward ladder.

"Here's fine," the mate growled as he passed, eager to get below deck and get his turn at rest. "All is quiet, no sightings. Moon should be out in another hour or so. Cap'n ordered rovers on both sides to watch for prisoners attempting escape."

Jack paused for a moment, flabbergasted. The mate tipped the brim of his hat up and frowned deep at him, before shaking his head and going below deck.

"Yer's mate 'o the watch, laddy," Bob's voice grunted into his ear. "An' that was yer first watch change. He was bringing you up to snuff, so to speak, on the comings an' goings 'o the ship."

Jack took it in for a moment. Mate of the watch. At any given moment he could be responsible for carrying out the watch officer's orders. Or, if anything on the watch should go awry, he could face a different set of challenges entirely. He paced tenuously toward the quarterdeck and made his respects to Acting Lieutenant Hill.

"Sir," Jack said while knuckling his brow. "Men 'o the watch have all reported to their stations."

The young officer nodded. He was barely older than Jack, but by a year or two, and his face was plastered with the apprehensions of his sudden load of responsibility. "Very well, Mr. Horner. Se too the rovers on both sides of the ship, and lookouts fore and aft, if you will. The captain will not suffer anything from these prisoners."

"Aye, sir," Jack replied while rendering his respects again. He turned forward and faced Saber's dark decks. No lanterns were permitted on the main deck at night, at the captain's orders, so the ship took on a sinister menace under the dull silver of flecked starlight emanating from the heavens.

Unsure of exactly how to conduct himself, Jack mimicked the actions of Petty Officers he had seen in the past. He paced the length of the ship, inspecting knots and line lays as he went. When he reached the bowsprit, he cast a long glance aloft and longed for a moment to be in the far removed heights of the rigging. He yearned for the solitude of night watch high above the deck, and to watch as sunrise made her course above the horizon from those dizzying climbs. With each peal of the bell, dawn drew closer. The heat of day had long died away and settled to a muggy warmth that broke a few hours into watch as the finicky breeze grew in strength. As the eastern horizon betrayed the sun's movement to morning, Captain Sifton stepped up on deck. He looked every bit as tired as Jack felt and his movements seemed to relay a sort of heaviness that seemed out of place for the formerly lively officer.

"Coxswain to the helm, if you please," the captain said as Jack made his way across the ship. "Boatswain, sound dawn quarters and get hands aloft to get us underway."

"Aye, sir," replied the boatswain's mate before he disappeared below deck to roust the sleeping crew.

Jack crossed the quarterdeck and took hold of Saber's wheel. The moment he announced to the sailor he was relieving that he had control, it struck him that he had shot a man standing on the very spot on deck he now occupied. A chill ran up his spine while he shifted his feet slightly to the weather side of the ship's wheel. Footfalls followed the boatswain's raspy call to action and within a few minutes Saber's prize crew all hurried to their part of the ship. Top men heaved themselves up the long climb aloft before expertly moving along the yards. The waisters took up their positions at the base of the mainmast, ready to heave and pay out lines accordingly. The ship's officers took up leeward positions on the quarterdeck, something that Jack noticed didn't seem to ease Mr. Hill's anxieties.

Captain Sifton glared skyward, his eyes set toward the long streaming banner that flowed in the strengthening wind. It seemed like an eternity, but was in reality the span of a few heartbeats. All at once, his eyes flitted back to Saber's deck, and he called in a clear, calm voice, "All plain sail."

"Aye, sir. All plain sail," replied Lieutenant Brusby. He in turn called out a series of commands that set Petty Officers in motion with their raspy voices issuing the appropriate order of work.

Canvas flew loose and was drawn taught by the hands tending lines in the waist. Higher in the rigging, sailors made their way from one yard up to the next, while each level of the tops offered their full measure of canvas sail to the wind. Sheets were heaved tight and secured, stays groaned from the sudden strain while Saber's sails bowed in the force of the wind. The hull began to slip forward. Easy at first. But, as the ship built momentum, her deck began to move under Jack's feet and the familiar tug of the sea plying against her rudder thrummed through her steerage lines and into the wheel.

"Bring her over starboard, Mr. Horner," Captain Sifton commanded. Lay us into the fullness of the channel before we make our course northward.

Hand over hand, Jack turned the ship's wheel. "Aye, sir. Starboard into the channel and then northward."

Saber came alive as the wind propelled her out of the shallows of the cove and into the broad channel between Isla De Mona and San Juan. She built speed with the wind at her quarter, and Jack thought he caught the beginnings of a smile creeping at the corners of Captain Sifton's mouth.

"Three points over larboard, Horner, then steady as she goes," the captain said as Saber's hull sliced through the smooth seas of the morning. "Leadsman for readings, Mr. Hill, and see that the log is cast. I would like to know how she is getting along in these fair winds."

"Aye, captain," Lieutenant Hill replied. He snapped to his task and hurried a sailor forward to begin casting the lead line for depth readings before going to the starboard side and getting set to cast the log.

It was a fairly straightforward procedure, one that Jack had witnessed aboard both Salem Tide and Allegiance. A triangular block of wood, secured to a length of spun cordage with evenly spaced knots tied in its length, was tossed overboard. When the triangular wooden log touched the sea's surface, a sixty-second glass would be turned and the line would be paid out until the last of the sand passed through the waist of the glass. When the time was up, the sailor keeping time would call out, "Time!" Then the sailor tending the line would clamp his fist on the cordage and haul it in arm length over arm length. As he did so, he would count the knots in the line as it was hauled in and report his finding to the watch officer.

Saber surged forward in calm seas that increased to gentle rises that met the bow with a satisfying smoothness. The wind held steady while sunrise finally crested the eastern horizon and bathed everything in its brilliant shine.

"Nine knots and holding, sir!" called Lieutenant Brusby. "She's fast as a clipper, and we don't even know her strongest point of sail!"

"Indeed, Mr. Brusby. Nine knots without stuns'ls is impressive, but I have a feeling she can do more. A sea trial after her refit will be just the thing," Captain Sifton said with a mischievous grin tugging at the corners of his mouth. "I can still feel her picking up speed. Cast again before the hour is out."

As the ship stretched away from land and met the full openness of the sea channel, Jack brought the helm over to larboard slightly and watched while the bowsprit came in line with magnetic north. With the fullness of wind at her back, and flying all plain sail, Saber gained in speed to a rapid pace that saw looks of amazement from both the captain and his lieutenants. A northerly course could see them to any number of ports for refit, and many among the crew were already whispering about the possibilities. Nassau, Bermuda, or perhaps a circuitous route around the north coast of San Juan toward St. Kitts. Even while Jack handled the helm, he mulled the possible destinations that Captain Sifton could have in mind, but one in particular would not budge from the forefront of his thoughts; Boston.

It wasn't a logical hope. There were nearly a dozen ports capable of the refit that were closer, but for some reason he couldn't quite pin down, Jack's thoughts centered around the far-flung hope that their end destination would bring him home. He eyed the sails aloft and then glanced at the compass before holding the wheel over ever so slightly to adjust the fill of the uppermost sails. It filled him with a sense of exhilaration when his efforts were rewarded with a steady increase in the ship's already considerable speed. The log was cast again, and after the elapsed minute a reading of thirteen knots elicited a cheers from everyone within hearing. She was a fine ship, fast and quick to answer the helm.

"Captain," Lieutenant Brusby said from a few paces aft of the helm. "She is sailing great and handling well. The carpenter reports eight inches in her hold, and holding steady." He paused for a moment before continuing, "As far as our possible destinations for refit, sir. We have stores enough for a month, six weeks if we decrease rations to the prisoners. Or, eight weeks if the crew is put to half rations as well."

"No decrease in rations, Mr. Brusby. I won't have the crew suffer undo stresses on account of our chosen destination. Nor will we deprive the prisoners, unless it becomes absolutely necessary," the captain replied. "The obvious choice would be St.Kitts. Although there are other options that could serve. The question is, where is the best option to have the ship bought into service? There is no way to know for a certainty. We also need to keep in mind the prisoners, and choose a port where they can be secured without overburden to the local governor. That complicates matters slightly. I know that St.Kitts does not have a suitable facility for the number of prisoners we hold, nor does Bermuda. There is Jamaica, but at that rate, we might as well sail for Charleston."

"Nearest suitable friendly port leaves quite a berth for steerage, eh captain?" the lieutenant lamented with his commander. "Quite a few more considerations than I had thought of."

"Indeed, Mr. Brusby," Captain Sifton said. "And that is not even beginning to account for the state of the empire. Tensions in the colonies, and with France. That is before even considering Spain and the heartaches they have caused the monarch as of late. We must position ourselves where we can best serve our king and country, as well as accomplish the means we need to do so."

Jack listened intently while the two officers debated the merits of each destination. His heart skipped a beat when the possibility of Charleston was offered up only to be promptly dismissed. It seemed that the men were working through a much larger problem with far more facets than he had ever taken into account. He did not envy the captain or his burden.

"The refit would be best accomplished by a shipwright familiar with her build. Why not sail her back to the Massachusetts Colony. There is holding space for our prisoners there, and she would almost definitely be purchased into the service." Lieutenant Brusby offered.

Jack felt his heart leap within the bounds of his chest. The secret hope he had held close, and it had come from their own thoughts. He buried his joy deep, so as not to betray his feeling with any errant expressions, and listened with painstaking interest for the captain's response.

"There is merit to that, I will admit. But, I would surely be chastised for shunning the Caribbean without at least paying call to Bermuda first," Captain Sifton said. He paced the quarterdeck for a few moments and muttered something beneath his breath. "However, the Admiralty could surely use a ship like Saber in those waters for enforcement of the newest round of tariffs. I have heard it said that the colonials are quickly becoming better smugglers than the damned infernal Dutch."

Jack sunk the edge of his front teeth into his lower lip. No matter his respect for the captain, there would always be the diverging line between them regarding the standing of colonial subjects. Captain Sifton would do his duty to the crown without pause or reservation, and he would always see the colonials as lesser subjects. It grieved Jack to recognize these traits in a man he had come to respect and admire. He fought away the feelings that crept at the back of his mind, the image of his mother's face, his father's dying words.

"I may catch hell for it, but, I believe that is our best course of action. However, we will call on Nassau first. That being our closest port. I firmly believe my decision will be upheld as soon as the governor recognizes our need to offload prisoners. He will sign orders for us to sail north, and then there will be nothing to be said for any of it." Captain Sifton paced forward of the helm and shot a sideways glare toward Jack with a devilish gleam in his eye. "If memory serves, I believe you told me that you hail from Boston. How does a visit home sound?"

Jack grinned and nodded. "It serves, sir."

"Very well," the captain replied. "We will make our course for Boston, by way of Nassau and then New York. A refit from the very hands that originated her will do the girl wonders. Then she will be fit and trim for vigorous service."

"Stores won't be an issue, sir," Lieutenant Brusby added. "However, we will need to water, and soon. We have three days at most. Less, if any of the casks aboard are fouled."

Captain Sifton drew in a sharp breath and ran a hand over his chin. "Damned water. If only man could survive on seawater, eh? Do you have any suggestion for where to acquire said fresh water?"

The lieutenant folded his arms and rocked his weight back and forth. "That is touchy in the Caribbean, sir. I have heard that there is growing sentiment among physicians that the yellow fever is caused by foul water sources, and that has been a plague on every fleet to visit the Caribbean for decades. Nassau may have our best chance at water, but who is to say for sure?"

A long moment of silence passed, and Jack kept his focus toward the ship's heading as he waited to hear the captain's response.

"I shall consider the charts, and the previous captain's logs. He has been prowling these seas for some time, they had to water somewhere," the captain said. "I shall retire to my cabin for the time being." He turned to Jack. "Resume your regular station, Mr. Horner."

Saber continued running before the wind through the Caribbean on her northward course. The seas rose from gently rolling swells to small choppy waves that broke against the fair lines of Saber's bow and sent a refreshing spray along her decks. The routine of sea set in and Jack made his way aloft with the rest of his mess when a change of sail was ordered. As a Quartermaster's Mate, he was not expected to climb the fore or mainmast. His realm aloft was up the mizzen with the quarterdeck hands and the midshipmen. But the winds were fair, and the sun was shining, Jack's spirits soared with his knowledge of their eventual destination. He climbed the tarred shrouds with an extra measure of heart and took in the sight of the far stretching view from the foretop. The skies were clear but for a set of thin white wisps, the ship's pitch and sway was steady and gradual. Jack relished the sunshine and cooling wind while he took in the brilliant blue-green hue of the sea nearby Saber that blended to a deep blue in the distance.

The top men were in good spirits as Saber edged her way northward into the rollers of the open sea. They had crossed from the protection of the passage between Isla De Mona and San Juan with a fair wind at a good point of sail. Now the seas were rising and Saber rose to meet them in their fullness with all the grace and agility of a sloop, but also with the devastating broadside more like that of a proper battleship. Once she was refit, they would all be a serious force to consider. The kind of ship that captains and crews of other vessels would take note of in passing. Her movements would be asked about in port pubs and brothels from one end of the Americas to the other, and her presence in harbor would make any smuggler or hopeful hostile more than a little uneasy.

To add to Jack's rising spirit, the top men began to lift their voices and a rousing shanty echoed from the yards.

"Come all ye young sailormen, listen to me, I'll sing ye a song of the fish in the sea. And it's windy weather, boys, stormy weather, boys. When the wind blows we'll all haul together, boys. Blow ye winds westerly blow ye winds blow, jolly sou'wester, boys steady she goes.

Up jumps the eel with his slippery tail, climbs up aloft and he reefs the topsail, and it's windy weather, boys, stormy weather, boys. When the wind blows, we'll all haul together, boys. Blow ye winds westerly, blow ye winds blow, jolly sou'wester, boys steady she goes.

Then up jumps the shark with his nine rows of teeth, he says you eat the bread boys and I'll eat the beef! And its windy weather, boys stormy weather, boys. When the wind blows, we'll all haul together, boys. Blow ye winds westerly, blow ye winds blow, jolly sou'wester, boys steady she goes.

Up jumps the whale the largest of all, he says sing me a song and I'll blow ye's a squall and it's windy weather, boys. Stormy weather boys, when the wind blows we'll all haul together boys, blow ye winds westerly blow ye winds blow, jolly sou'wester boys, steady she goes!"

As if cued by the bidding of their song, the winds stiffened. Saber surged forward in renewed vigor and met the next wave. A slight cap of white was beginning to form on the crest of the seas, but the lovely lines of the frigate enabled her to slice forward with hardly a thought to the contrary. Her bow rose and dipped without the bracing impact Jack had come to expect from his time aboard Allegiance.

"She's a fine feathered seabird, lads! Fine as I've ever seen and I'm the sailorinest sailor you lot will ever climb a shroud next to!" Bowline Bob crowed from his perch in the foretops'l yard. "I reckon she'll do near fifteen knots under stuns'ls and runnin afore! I'd bet my pipe on it!"

Cheers followed the salty sailor's boasting and Jack felt his hear soar higher than the top-gallant mast. The motion of the ship had increased, but without the sudden jarring that typically accompanied waves meeting a ship's bow. It was like a dream. He was on a prime ship, with a hearty crew, and on course to go back to Boston. Jack raised his voice to meet with his shipmates as they struck up another round of song. Despite his restless night, he was beginning to once again feel at home among ship and crew.

Saber
13 July 1770
21 Degrees 8′ N, 72 Degrees 35′ W

"Deck! Breakers sighted," a shrill voice called down through the early hours of the morning watch.

"Where away?" called back Lieutenant Brusby in an impatient rasp.

A moment of calm passed before the response drifted down from the heights of the rigging, "Three points to larboard. About a mile distant, sir. Looks like a reef with no marker."

The lieutenant folded his arms and paced behind Jack at the helm. It made him nervous to be under such close inspection, and that the captain hadn't ordered him to alter course. The sun had not made its pass over the eastern horizon yet, but the growing light emanating behind gray streaks of nimbus glimmered over the tidal chop.

"Very well," Captain Sifton said after a prolonged silence. "Horner, bring us over two points to starboard. Two points, lad. No more."

The dawn had yet to fully reveal itself, but already Jack was exhausted. He had been roused from his slumber in the dead of night to man the helm when Captain Sifton had taken over control of the ship. All through the hours of darkness there had been sightings of shoals and reefs, some had markers while most did not. It gave Jack an uncomfortable ache in the pit of his stomach, a sense of dread that, try as he did, he just could not shake away. The first sighting had been a set of foaming breakers that revealed a shallow reef in proximity to the ship. That had prompted the watch officer to double the lookout. Next, a small spit of land was sighted in a stretch of sea the quarterdeck had not expected a land sighting. Then the moon had slipped behind clouds. The leadsman was roused in the dead of night, but his depth readings only gave the quarterdeck further anxiety when they did not coincide with known depths from their charts. At two bells, lookouts found the skeleton of a reef fouled vessel. Her hull was shattered, her sails were in ruins, and it looked as if she had been abandoned for an extended period. But, the reef she had run aground on was not on the charts, and a general anxiety formed on deck until Captain Sifton was summoned and subsequently took charge of the ship. Jack held the wheel over just as he was ordered.

"Sir, none of these sightings bear out against our reckoned position, it just doesn't make any sense," Lieutenant Brusby said in a hushed voice.

Captain Sifton stood firm to the weather side of the helm. Jack could hear him draw a slow breath before turning toward his second in command. "Perhaps, then, our reckoned position is incorrect."

"Not possible, sir, I did the figures myself," Lieutenant Brusy retorted with a huff. "I checked my calculations thrice, and Mr. Hill concurred. Our position cannot be off by more than a quarter mile or so."

The captain remained quiet for a long spell. He touched Jack on the shoulder and kept his voice low. "That is enough easting for now, Horner. Bring us about northerly again."

Jack let the wheel ease over without a response. He wished that he didn't have to hear the unfolding puzzlements of the quarterdeck the way he was, but with the billet he was holding, there was nothing for it but to do his duty and keep quiet.

"Sir, I recommend that we drop anchor, at least until we can figure ourselves properly. These infernal shallows and shoals will hull us if we aren't careful," Lieutenant Brusby said in an urgent whisper.

"These seas are notorious for this, Mr. Brusby. But, thankfully, our sailors are sharp on the watch. The age old process of the service seems to work. Let's let it work, shall we?"

"But, sir, the charts, they haven't indicated a single one of these sightings," the lieutenant rebutted insistently.

Jack felt a warm flush build in his face. He could almost sense Captain Sifton's growing irritation while a painful pause elapsed.

"Mr. Brusby, these seas are as inconsistent and ever changing as any in the world. If I were to order the anchor for every unknown sighting, we would not make Nassau before the year is out. Further, I suspect that we are significantly off of our reckoned position as far as longitude is concerned, I do not question your latitude reading, I compared it to my own calculations and found you to be within minutes. But, my order stands. We continue north with a sharp eye on the sea. Do I make myself clear? Or should I draw you a diagram?" The captain kept his voice low, not to shame his second in command to any but the closest of ears. But it was enough that Jack heard the exchange, and he was near paralysis from it. Never had he heard officers dicker about an order in such a manner. As a lieutenant, Sifton had followed the captain's orders to the letter. Any disagreement between them, Jack assumed, had been minor in nature, and kept from the hearing of the crew.

"Aye, sir," Lieutenant Brusby replied. "My apologies, captain. I meant no disrespect."

"In the future, I expect any dissent to be held for the confines of my cabin, lest you wind up confined to yours. Is that understood?" Captain Sifton said in a sharp whisper.

Jack felt a break of perspiration on the nape of his neck. He remained stock still at the helm, waiting until he was bid to move it. His mind raced while the surrounding tension hung in the air between the two officers. It lingered for the better part of the next hour, which was filled with agonizing silence from both the ship's commander and his second.

"I will retire to my cabin until the noon sighting," Captain Sifton announced. "Mr. Horner, resume your regular station. I believe we are through the thick of it. We will know more once we have a new fix on our position."

"Aye, sir," Jack knuckled his brow and relinquished control of the ship's wheel to the watch helmsman. He hurried away from the quarterdeck with a sense of relief and hoisted himself onto the fore shrouds. As he climbed the tarred lines up to the rigging, the woes of the quarterdeck seemed to fall away. The sea opened up in every direction and the world seemed to expand in his vision with every step he climbed. He was greeted at the foretop by Bowline Bob's signature grin and a puff of bluish smoke circling from the old sailor's nose.

"Had enough 'o the quarterdeck fer ye's?" he asked with a crackling laugh.

Jack returned his jolly friend's smile and shook his head. Daylight had spread over the sea and the breeze was warming with every passing minute. "I don't mind it much, when all is well down there. But the strife between the captain and first luff is enough to make me want to trade the helm for the capstan."

Bob raised a concerned brow and pulled at his pipe. "What ye mean, lad? Trouble brewin'?"

Jack shrugged, unsure of how much he should divulge. "The officers don't agree on some things, is all."

Bob scowled and shook his head. "Seems it gets forgot too often in the maritime world. The captain has the final say. He is the master of the ship, and that's the end of it. Too many times a lieutenant gets his step an' first thing he has ter deal with is a damned second challenging his every decision. I seen it afore, Jacky. It never ends well either. Cap'n will lock him in his quarters and put him off the ship first chance he gets, or, if'n he doesn't it could be the makings of a damned mutiny."

The thought of it gave Jack an uneasy feeling. He didn't like the idea of a power struggle within the ship.

"I knows what yer thinkin', lad. An ye have every reason ter be concerned. A mutiny from the lower deck is one thing, and rare enough. But, a mutiny from on the quarterdeck itself, it's a whole 'nother proposition. See, the crew is forced ter choose sides. An' it happens more often than ye's think. Bloody affairs, the lot of 'em. Bodes ill fer every mother's son aboard ship." Bob clamped his bite down onto the stem of his pipe and gestured for Jack to follow him aloft. "I know the cure fer ye though, Dead eye Jack. Climbing ter the top 'o the world and lettin' yer worries slip away with the waves. Mmm?"

Jack relented and followed his friend up the topmast shrouds to the highest point on the ship, the cross tree of the royal yard. It was a dizzying height, and Saber's motion was magnified what felt like ten times over. The ship seemed to be nothing more than a narrow spot of deck in the distance below them. Jack breathed in the warmth of the late Caribbean morning. Dawn had receded, and the skies were a piercing blue. The waves stretched out into the vastness of the world and seemed to carry Jack's woes away, just as Bob had predicted.

"The reefs and shoals," Jack said through the bustle of the wind. "The captain said that these seas change year over year. Is that true?"

Bob nodded. "Aye, Jacky. The Caribbean is notorious fer it. Some of the most treacherous seas in the world, maybe the most. But, it's not just year to year. The seasons, storms, tides, the seabed out here changes constantly. Ye'll have a shoal charted, knowin just where she lies and bein' careful ter avoid it an' all. A hurricane will blow through here and move it entirely. It's maddening."

Jack considered for a minute before replied. "Then, if the lookouts are sighting unknown shallows and shoals, wouldn't the first lieutenant be right? Wouldn't it have been safer to drop anchor and wait for the light of day to see the danger?"

Bob smiled a devilish grin and leaned against the bulk of the mast. "Aye, probably would be the safest course, Jacky, yer right. But, then, why do we make sail out of harbor in the first place, eh? The ship is safe at anchor, sure. But is that why we sets our sails and plot our courses? To heave to at any slight chance of mishap?"

Jack shook his head and fought away the urge to double over laughed. Here he was, hundreds, maybe thousands of miles from the school that had been the bane of his childhood, and still being plagued by philosophy and logic! "Aye, Bob. I suppose you are right. It just seems…"

"Like madness?" Bob interrupted. "That's acause it is, Jacky. Every last man of us is madder than a fox. But, a sailorman's logic is the soundest I've ever heard. Can ye believe there's poor sods on land that never ply the waves? Never seen the heavens away from the lights and trees and mountains?" Bob's face took a serious draw, almost as if the thought made him sad. "They toil their life away never knowing the kinship and brotherhood to be found with shipmates. Or the thrill of riding out a blustery storm and living to tell the tale. That's the real madness, Jacky. A lubber's life. I say no thank you."

Jack drew in the wide open expanse of the sea with a deep breath of the fresh air. The smell of salty spray was on the breeze and the vastness reached out to him. His worries of the morning watch were almost forgotten by the time he heard the final bell strike signaling the change of watch.

"Well, Jacky," Bob said in a rasp. "Let's see about some vittles and our noon grog. Eh?"

Jack took in one final scan of the horizon. "Yes. Let's..." He paused as something caught his eye. Far on the northern stretch of skyline. For a moment he returned his gaze to a spot that seemed to draw his gaze, although he couldn't tell why. The bluish gray of the sea met with hazy blue skyline while sets of crisp little caps of white repeated themselves like rows of crops in a farmer's field. But there was something his vision had picked up, something off about a particular spot on the horizon. When he examined the area, at first, all he could see were the small ripples of white that crowned the waves in the distance. He let his vision rest on the spot for a moment and recalled the time he had spotted whale spouts when he was aboard Salem Tide.

"What's yer holdup, lad? Grog 'n vittles!" Bob said in a grunt. "Let's go!"

"Hold on, Bob, damn ye," Jack said. "I see something."

A long silence elapsed with nothing but the creak of hempen rope and the whistle of the wind in their ears. Jack stared hard at the spot on the horizon. Something held his stare, and wouldn't allow his mind to dismiss it.

"Jacky, we linger much longer an' we're going to be drinking the dregs 'o the cask, and lucky fer gettin' that! Come on," Bob urged.

"Go then," Jack said with a wave. "I saw something, Bob. I know it."

"What did ye see? A wave? A whale plume? Nothing fer it. Only thing ter linger up here over would be the sight of a sail, an there isn't a soul fer a hundred miles in any direction," Bob grumbled and started his climb downward. "I'll hold yer share 'o grog, if there's any left by the time I get there. Don't be surprised if it's a hefty slurp short. Serves ye right fer holdin' me up here waitin' around..."

Jack cast a grin at Bob as the old sailor growled and grumbled while descending the shrouds. He knew that his old friend would ensure more than half of his grog issue found its way safely into his hands. He resumed his search when Bob was more than halfway down to the foretop. Blue gray waves and little ridges of white dominated everything around him. Was he losing his mind? Had he actually seen something, or was Bob right? He had but one eye. What business did he have being a lookout? Just as he was about to give up, his eye caught on a spot on the horizon. In the instant of a heartbeat he saw a glimpse of pure, plain white. It was a small spot, the corner of a triangle. He stared hard, willing the shape to appear again, waiting for confirmation that he wasn't mad. His patience was rewarded with a steady sighting. A white triangle that peeked over the horizon and lingered in place for more than a minute before disappearing behind the crest of a rolling wave.

"Deck there," Jack called down at the top of his lungs with one hand cupped around the side of his mouth. "Sail on the horizon!"

A voice called back through the distance. "Where away?"

Jack looked over the skyline again to where he had seen the spot of white before turning down to the deck and shouted. "Three points over starboard, off on the horizon. Hull down."

Jack turned back to where he had seen the corner of white sail. He could not find it again, but he was sure of what he had seen. Saber's deck turned to a bustle of activity. Sailors flooded to the starboard rail, in hopes of being the next to catch sight of the mysterious sail. Patches, one of the ship's powder monkeys, so named for the patched and tattered sailing rig he wore, climbed as far as the foretop to relay a message to Jack.

"Mr. Horner, Cap'n asks fer yer presence on the quarterdeck. He says to look lively!" the young boy shouted with great effort.

Jack nodded and began his climb down. "I'll be right along, Patches. Thank you." Hand over and step-by-step Jack descended the top-gallant mast to the topsail crosstree, he then swung himself over the shroud lines and climbed down to the foretop platform where Patches stood waiting with eyes as large as saucers.

"Is it a pirate, Mr. Horner?" he asked.

Jack shook his head. "Hard to say, Patches. I could only see just a piece of her sail. But, if she is a pirate, she'll be running from a ship like ours. Won't she?"

"Only if they're smart! We have Captain Sifton and Dead eye Jack!" Patches replied with a puffed chest.

Jack turned to start down the fore shrouds on his way to the main deck. "I'm not sure how much I count for, Patches. I only have the one eye left."

"All the better fer yer aiming Mr. Horner. You'll hit twice as easy!"

Jack grinned at the child's logic and admired his perspective. He had always wondered how the boys who served as powder monkeys managed such, given the things they were often witness to. "Follow me down, Patches. If it is an enemy sail and we beat to quarters, you don't want to be in the way as the top men are racing up to their part of ship."

The boy returned a mischievous look. "But, Mr. Horner. How am I going to be a top man if I'm never allowed up in the rigging?"

Jack motioned for him to follow. "Come on, Patches. Ye'll get yer step someday. But now is not the time. Let's get ye down to the deck before yer first lesson on sailoring has to be an introduction to the cat!" He descended the shrouds with the boy in tow and looked up to check after him every few steps. Patches seemed born to climb the shrouds, he lunged and stretched to put his weight on ratline steps that were spaced for full-grown men, without even a hint of fear in his heart. Jack recalled the paralyzing terror that had gripped him on his first ascent to the heights of the upper works. He had forced himself to shun the lubber hole in hopes of proving something to himself, and to Bowline Bob. It had worked. Now, he could climb the furthest extremities of the rigging without so much as a second thought. The heights were no less than they had been on that first climb, in fact, Saber's foremast stood at least thirty feet taller than Salem Tide's had. But, there was comfort in familiarity, and the tallest stretches of rigging had become a place of solace and comfort for Jack, somewhere the worries of the lower deck couldn't reach him.

"Horner to the quarterdeck!" the shout was repeated even as Jack's hands left the tarred shroud lines. His feet landed on deck and he rushed to the quarterdeck.

"Mr. Horner," Captain Sifton said. His face was hard and his eyes were narrowed, he stood along the weather rail with his hands folded neatly behind him. "Ye sighted sail, is that correct?"

Jack nodded and knuckled his brow. "Aye, sir. Just off the horizon, no hull yet. I couldn't tell which way she was standing."

The captain seemed unmoved. "Are ye certain of it?"

Jack frowned and repeated what he had seen. "Aye, sir. Certain as I can be. I didn't see her hull, she's too distant. But I know what I saw, sir."

The captain set his jaw and stared off into the distance. "Very well, Mr. Horner. Take the helm," he said before turning inboard toward Lieutenant Brusby. "I have the ship, Mr. Brusby."

"Aye, captain has the ship," Lieutenant Brusby repeated in earnest for all to hear.

Jack stepped to the ship's wheel and took a firm hold. Under all plain sail, and with the wind at their stern and slightly off of the larboard quarter, Saber was clipping along nicely over recurring sets of seas less than four feet high. The pattern of force that worked from sea to helm was like a song. It grew in intensity before slacking away and fading to almost nothing, then out of nowhere a crescendo would build and it would take Jack a considerable strength to maintain their course.

"Three points over starboard, Horner. On course to intercept," the captain ordered.

Jack dutifully turned the wheel while keeping a cautious eye on the tower of sails. "Aye, sir. Intercept course."

Saber's bow slid onto her new course with a sleek effortlessness. Her bow cut the waves and threw out a wake from her sleek profile. Jack admired how nimble she handled, and was settling into the joy he had once found manning the helm, when Lieutenant Brusby stepped forward to address the captain.

"Captain Sifton, sir. Do I understand your intention correctly? Are we to challenge this unknown vessel?" He asked.

A long silence followed, and Jack got the feeling that he had been sucked back into the same myriad of tension he earlier escaped.

"Mr. Brusby, it is my intention to intercept whatever vessel we cross paths with, identify it, and see that it poses no threat to British vessels or interests. If she be a common merchant ship, or a local fishing vessel, then so be it. But, by the articles of war, we are duty bound to investigate any sighting and ensure that the king's peace is enforced on the high seas." Captain Sifton said, as if rehearsed, while staring off to the distant horizon. "If she proves to be a smuggler, or a pirate, then we will have some decisions to make. Or, rather, I will have some decisions to make."

Lieutenant Brusby pursed his lips and followed the captain's gaze with his own. He stayed quiet for a spell before looking back toward the ship's commander and then at

Jack with narrowed eyes. "Sir, I feel I would be remiss if I did not remind you that we are but a skeleton of a crew. We barely have enough hands to sail her, let alone fight."

Jack fought through a surge of resistance in the ship's wheel. He tried to keep his focus, but the exchange between Saber's commander and his second had already resumed the tensions of the morning. His mind tried to balance the first lieutenant's reasoning against the strict adherence to the chain of command. What Lieutenant Brusby was saying made sense, Saber had a prize crew complement, not a full crew. They would be able to sail her, or man the guns, but certainly not at the same time. If they were to come in proximity of a hostile ship and be boarded, it would be over before the first exchange was fired. But the captain was right. His mandate was to protect the vessels and interests of the British crown. If they failed to pursue the mystery ship, they would not be fulfilling their duty. It was the same brand of tension that had held Jack in its unsteady grip earlier that day.

"Mr. Brusby, I am painfully aware of our precarious situation. However, orders are orders, lieutenant. We shall intercept her and see what she is made of. She cold quite possibly be a friendly vessel," the captain answered. His tone was softer than before, but somehow, Jack felt delicate sharpness, an edge that teetered on the brink of anger.

"Our orders are to take the prize into port and see her refitted, sir. Not chase down prizes of our own." Lieutenant Brusby muttered in a withering affront for only the captain's ears. Jack nearly lost his grip on the wheel. He fought away the urge to look over his shoulder where the two officers stood a half step apart.

Silence dominated the quarterdeck. Jack nervously kept his eye fixed aloft on the windward edge of the main topgallant. He could feel his heartbeat thrumming through his neck and into his jaw. The captain would not stand for this. Or, would he? As if to answer Jack's thoughts, the captain's voice rose strong and clear for the entire quarterdeck.

"Master at arms, see Mr. Brusby down to his quarters. Remove his sword and any other arms he may have in his personal effects, and see him placed under guard, not to leave his cabin under any circumstance. Am I understood?"

Jack's hands went cold despite the warmth of the day. He felt a prickle of lightning visit his bloodstream as the quarterdeck fell silent all around him. Nobody moved. It was as if the entire ship had fallen to shock. Sailors looked down from aloft. Men on deck stopped their work and gazed back at the scene.

"Master at arms! Escort Mr. Brusby down to his cabin, remove his sword and any other arms at his disposal and lock him there under guard! Do I make myself clear?" the captain shouted.

"Aye, sir," came the reply of the marine.

Footfalls clomped across the quarterdeck. Jack kept his eye locked aloft. He dared not divert his gaze anywhere. He didn't want to be sucked into whatever was going on. His conversation with Bob rang clear in his mind. He wasn't sure if the lieutenant's challenge constituted a mutiny, but he understood that what was unfolding bode ill for every man aboard. He rued the proposition of having to choose sides. Somewhere in his guts, he felt an abiding loyalty to Captain Sifton. The man he had crossed deck to the Saber with, the man who had given him a step and made him his coxswain. But, Lieutenant Brusby had a point. Saber was manned by the thinnest margin Jack thought conceivable. There was no way they would be effective at fighting the ship against a prepared enemy. The splitting pain that had wracked his head for days was beginning to return to him. His temples began to throb while his forehead welled with a fiery burning along the ragged wound that had not fully healed.

"Steady on the helm, Horner," the captain said in a flat voice. "We don't want to drift off our course."

"Aye, sir," Jack replied. With a quick look at the ship's compass, he realized he had let Saber fall off to the wind by a full point. He admonished himself quietly and brought the wheel windward until Saber was back on her heading. "Apologies, sir. I don't know what came over me."

Captain Sifton exhaled dryly. "It is an upsetting business, young man. But, hold her true to course. She will see us through to the end."

Lieutenant Brusby was marched off of the quarterdeck by the master at arms and a pair of marine sentries. It gave Jack a chill to watch. For a moment, it seemed the ship had come to a grinding halt. Work stopped. Men in the ship's waist ceased hauling on lines, top men in the rigging peered down from their lofty perches, and the quarterdeck became the center of attention. As the lieutenant departed the deck, Jack took note of the man's face. It was sunken, almost hollow looking. He didn't appear angry, which Jack found surprising. If anything, Saber's second in command seemed defeated, sad almost.

"Back to work, ye loafing lubbers," shouted a Petty Officer with a raspy voice near the base of the foremast. "Sheets need a haul and there's deck that could use a scour from holy stones. Any volunteers?"

Saber
13 July 1770
21 Degrees 49′ N, 72 Degrees 38′ W

Hours had passed since Jack had sighted the corner of white floating on the distant horizon. Hours without confirmation of another sighting. He held Saber on her course, faithfully watching the sails and her compass as he plied the rudder against the force of the sea. All around him, the quarterdeck seemed to fall into a state of suspended tension. He second guessed himself. Had he actually seen a sail? Had it been some kind of marine apparition? Or a trick his eye had played? Afternoon stretched on and the sun beat its course through the western skies, but still no sight of sail was made. Captain Sifton remained on deck, stern faced and quiet. He stared out into the far stretches of sea while Jack's internal distress seemed to compound with the passing of every hour. Watch bells rang, hands changed places on deck and moved aloft while others climbed down for their turn to take rations and get rest.

The northern horizon betrayed no sign of the white sail Jack had spotted. It tormented him with every passing hour. Occasional calls to the lookouts verified that there had indeed been no further sightings. Jack felt a flush of red build in his neck and face. He imagined the whisperings of his shipmates, and their doubts about a sail sighted by a one eyed sailor. The sun dropped low and began its descent from afternoon to evening. Radiant shades of amber and crimson invaded the skies and stretched high overhead while the northern horizons became abysmally darkened by a bank of thick clouds that seemed to hover low over the sea and tower high into the heavens. The tapestry of evening color reflected on the bluff front of clouds and painted a majestic scene for Saber's crew to take in, but it was lost on Jack. All he could think of was the nagging question of the sail that had disappeared.

Lieutenant Hill presented himself on the quarterdeck and paid his respects to the captain. "Sir, would you care for me to relieve you?" he said after offering a crisp salute.

"No, lieutenant. I will remain here with my coxswain until we locate the sail he spotted earlier. Thank you," the captain replied without averting his stare from the distant north.

"Aye, sir," Lieutenant Hill said with a nod. "Might I suggest, sir, that we take in sail before the weather?"

Jack chanced a look at Captain Sifton in hopes of catching his reaction. But, the commander's face remained unflinching, a stone expression of determination.

"Not now, lieutenant. We are in pursuit of an unknown vessel, shortening sail would be contrary to what we need to accomplish," he said without discernible inflection. "I see the weather, just as every other man on deck does. When it is time, I will give the order."

"Aye, sir," Lieutenant Hill said. "Would you like for me to have the hands stood up, in preparation?"

"That will not be necessary, lieutenant, thank you," Captain Sifton said with a brisk look inboard.

Jack squeezed his grip tighter on the wooden handles of the helm. The captain was making an all-out run in pursuit of his sighting. A sighting which had become dangerously elusive. The stakes couldn't be higher. They were sailing full tilt into a weather system of unknown strength, to chase an elusive ship of unknown size and origin. Jack wondered at the wisdom of it, and for an instant began to question whether he should have called out the sighting in the first place.

"I'll have a look at the charts, though, Mr. Hill, and the ship's log. We ought have an idea of what we are sailing into before the weather is upon us," said Captain Sifton. "Pipe the hands to supper, and have a plate brought up for my coxswain here, I fear it is going to be a long and trying evening for the lot of us."

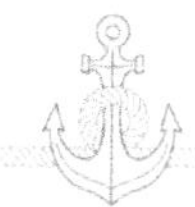

Saber's hull cut through the sea as she pressed onward in search of the vessel Jack had sighted. The night promised to be anything but peaceful. Flashes of bright lightning lit the darkened northern horizon beneath a towering wall of thick clouds. The crew took their vittles in silent tension as every man aboard collected himself for what was to come. The possibilities were many, and almost none of them brought any joy to the hearts of experienced sailors. Jack noted the stares and silent looks of his shipmates. He had been the only man to spot the sail on the horizon, and it had become apparent to Jack that popular sentiment was not fond of pursuing the vanishing ship into a storm.

As if passing over a threshold into another world, Saber sailed beneath the towering wall of cloud cover amid a flurry of terrifying flashes. It was like no storm Jack had ever seen. Lightning flashed all around the darkness surrounding the ship, but not a drop of rain was felt. The brilliant bolts of rampant vengeance from the heavens boiled through the clouds and occasionally touched at the sea's surface. Evening's glow faded to utter blackness and within the hour the only light visible was the intermittent instances of piercing white that exposed everything from the cover of darkness before disappearing. The wind built in strength and dropped in temperature. Jack felt its temperament degrade as the light of day faded from the world. Away from the cloud cover, the wind had been as welcoming as an old friend, warm and comforting. It now carried them with a ferocity that bordered on threatening. The call went up to the top men to shorten sail. Jack did not envy their plight as the sailors made their way up shrouds and across the yards. One misstep, one failed grasp, a single failure to anticipate the motion of the ship could result in a fatal plunge to the deck planking far below. These were always a threat to the brave souls who plied their trade more than fifty feet above the ship, but in foul weather the margin for error waned to razor thin.

Calls mixed in the howl of wind as top men battled to shorten the topsails. Jack looked on in horror, watching each scene play out in the varying illumination of lightning strikes.

"You there, mind that clew line! Do ye want to have a runaway spar?" a voice screamed over the wind. Jack saw the struggle unfold at the ship's waist. A crew of deckhands were fighting against wind and gravity to haul at the mainsail's windward side, and had begun losing ground when the spar was raised over half mast. A series of relentless flashes lit everything as bright as the noon sun. Jack could see genuine fear in his shipmates' expressions and then a stomach turning scream ripped through the night.

"Get down! Get back!"

The spar fell free under tremendous force from a gale strength gust that grabbed at the canvas and slammed against the ship. Seawater misted over the weather rail and blasted across Saber's deck. A flash of lightning revealed Jack's shipmates running for their lives behind a hazy fog of misted sea. Canvas tore, lines snapped, darkness covered everything and the sound of a spar crashing down to the deck eclipsed the wind and screams. Wood cracked and groaned. The whistle of a severed line recoiling from immense tension cut through the air. More screams rose from Saber's deck.

Jack battled the helm as the wind gust heeled the ship hard to one side. For him, the scene on deck was a singular frame of desperation as he struggled against the wheel. When the light disappeared, the sounds of wreckage and havoc were all that remained. In the aftermath, a lone voice cried out.

"Help! Oh, me leg! Dear God help me!"

Another flash of lightning revealed the shattered remains of the shredded mainsail and her spar. Canvas flapped violently while lines whipped wild just feet above the main deck. Orders to clear the wreckage and right the situation blistered through darkness. Another flash revealed sailors hurrying to aid their fallen shipmate. It appeared to Jack that he had been caught directly beneath the mass of falling timber and canvas.

A surge of force played against the helm. Jack struggled against it mightily. He felt the ship drift off course despite his best efforts. He summoned every ounce of strength he could muster, but the wooden wheel refused to relent it assault to the lee. He bent at the knees and redoubled his effort. The wheel heaved against him under pressure from the wind at her sails and the sea at her rudder, she wanted to break free and run eastward, but Jack fought to maintain her course. Try as he did, the bow slipped downwind. A point at first, then two. Just as he thought all hope was lost, and he was at the precipice of failing his task, the wheel ceased her incessant battering. As if by some miracle, the force against him seemed to cut in half.

"Stand tall at the helm, Horner," a familiar voice bellowed. Jack looked and found that Captain Sifton had taken the weather side of the wheel and was aiding him on righting Saber's course. "Heave together, Horner. Now!"

Together with his captain, Jack plied every fiber of strength he could muster. At first it was all both of them could do to stop the counter movement of the wheel. Then, inch by hard fought inch, both sailors righted the ship's course.

"Thank ye kindly, sir!" Jack shouted through the blustering gale. A streak if lightning split the skies and cast its ominous glow over everything. Captain Sifton wore a smile that belied a mix of joy and madness.

"Just like the shantyman sings, Horner. We'll haul together!" he said. "Now, can you hold her? I have to check on the waisters."

Jack nodded as a feeling of pride in his captain swelled though him. "Aye, sir. I'll hold her," he replied.

In a flash, the captain was off the quarterdeck. Jack had seen nothing like it before. Through the spasms of brilliant lightning, he watched as the captain aided the crew in recovering their fallen shipmate from under the shattered remains of mainsail. He witnessed the captain take direct command of the tops and instructed them to set double-reefed topsails and to bring in the top gallants entirely. He was as much a force of nature as the storm itself. The bedlam that had been unleashed was sharply set to order under his direct and confident command. Jack stood in awe. Captain Sifton was the very picture of competence and control. His shouts were pointed, but not aggressive. His direction was detailed but not in the lofty way of condescension. When the time came for the injured sailor to be carried below deck, Captain Sifton joined the deckhands and lifted the grievously battered man below deck. Jack found himself weighing the new captain against Allegiance's commander. Captain Williams would never have involved himself in such tasks.

No sooner had Saber's commander departed the main deck to evacuate the injured sailor than a call pierced through the night.

"Deck, there! Sail! Sail off the larboard bow, not a mile distant!" a lookout screamed.

Within the span of a heartbeat, Captain Sifton was back on deck. His uniform coat and trouser were stained with blood, but he strode to the weather rail with every bit of resolve and determination Jack had seen displayed in his time with the man.

"Mr. Hill, a glass, if you please," Captain Sifton called over his shoulder. "Horner, bring her into the wind by a point."

"A point into the wind, aye sir," Jack said while muscling at the helm to accomplish his task.

Lieutenant Hill arrived with a collapsed telescope which the captain promptly snatched from his grasp and extended. He lifted the instrument to one eye and held it there while flashes of lightning broiled across the night sky.

"Fore and aft rigged. A cutter by the look of her, most likely a merchantman or a smuggler. Alter course to intercept, fire one of the starboard battery, we will see what she is about," the captain said as he snapped the telescope to its collapsed state.

"Sir, should we perhaps hold course through the weather? We've already lost the mainsail, and the hands are struggling with the foretops'l as it is," Lieutenant Hill suggested. "We can shadow her course until dawn and then board her with the launch."

Captain Sifton turned inboard, he clasped the telescope in one hand while the other gripped a brace line. "I want to know her purpose, Mr. Hill. Alter course to intercept and see what she does in response."

The lieutenant snapped to a crisp salute. "Aye, sir."

"Horner, bring her over three points to larboard. Lay our bow on course to cross theirs. We will see what she is about," the captain ordered.

Jack brought the helm over to the captain's desired course. IT was a battle to manage the new heading, but not as difficult as it had been earlier. Saber's bow shifted in a sluggish lurch rather than the nimble handling he was used to. Lieutenant Hill had disappeared below deck to carry out the captain's wishes of a single gun firing. When the thunderclap of the cannon roar erupted, it caught Jack by surprise and sent a charge through his blood. He grit his teeth and refocused himself on the task of crossing the cutter's bow. It was a maneuver he had not yet executed at the helm, a delicate balance between steering too far forward and negating the deliberate message the captain wanted to send, or steering to close and risking an embarrassing and hazardous collision with the small vessel.

"She's coming about, standing away!" a voice shouted from the maintop. "They're running!"

Jack shot a look toward Captain Sifton. He knew the predicament they were facing, and he hoped the captain would make a wise decision.

"Hands aloft! Ready to make sail!" Captain Sifton bellowed over the deck.

Jack felt a drop in his stomach. Saber was sailing under double-reefed topsails, and that under protest from the sailing master. They had already suffered a mishap that proved devastating to one of their shipmates. But, for Saber's commander, there would be no relent.

"Gun crews at the ready, I want every cannon double shotted. Master at arms, swivel guns and muskets, marines to the weather rail and sharpshooters into the rigging, sharpish!" Captain Sifton paced away from the quarterdeck railing with an arm outstretched toward Jack and the helm. "Horner, point the bow straight at her fantail! If we can cut her stern and slip along the windward side we can steal her wind. A broadside should bring her captain to his senses."

With a tightening lump in his throat, Jack heeled the ship's helm over to larboard until the bowsprit was aimed at the diminutive fore and aft rigged ship. Saber's shroud lines filled with sailors. While the wind raged around them, the crew began working on baring more canvas. Shouted commands and responses rose and fell amid a constant howl of wind. The skies blistered with flashes of lightning, but had yet to offer any rain.

"Pass the word for Mr. O'Reilly," Captain Sifton said as Saber settled onto her new course. A streak of lightning tore through the heavens and blasted the sea surface on the far side of the cutter. Shouts of awe and terror riffled through the hands on deck until a rough shout from a boatswain's mate set them back to their task. Jack's vision went blank from the brightness of the flash, and the ensuing thunderclap brought a tremor through the ship that he could feel from his feet to his knees and his hands to his shoulders.

Mr. O'Reilly came on deck and approached the captain with hat in hand.

"Ye summoned me, sir?" he said with a knuckle to his brow.

Captain Sifton folded his hands behind his back and narrowed his eyes at the carpenter's mate. "Aye, Mr. O'Reilly, I did. I want to clap on every stitch of canvas we can. That cutter is running afore, and she means to lay us in her wake. I know Saber can catch her, I know it. But, with reefed topsails and no courses we are doomed to failure. Make it plain, man. Will she take the courses in this wind?"

The carpenters mate looked aloft and studied the masts and sails in a series of terrifying white flashes of lightning. He turned back to the captain, as pale as the canvas he had been studying. "Aye, sir. I reckon she will. A single reef on the courses, and she should hold them. That's not to say I would recommend it in this darkness, plowing ahead full tilt to the devil's door, but the masts will hold. Hard live oak, they are. Strongest wood I know of."

The captain clapped his hands together and rubbed his palms with a feverish intensity. "Very well, consult with the boatswain and see it done. I want every stitch she can carry. We'll have that cutter by her belt!"

It took a full turn of the glass, but eventually, Saber was flying reefed courses at both her main and foremast. A spare spar had to be rigged, and the boatswain's mates had double brace lines rigged with a preventer on each one, but when it was finished, the ship lurched through the sea with a renewed vigor. To Jack's dismay, the additional sail made steerage even more difficult. Every correction took a redoubled effort, and when the sea plied her strength against the rudder, it was all he could do to hold her steady. The cutter teetered at the edge of visibility all while the repairs were being made to Saber's rigging. Once the courses were flown and sheeted, Saber began to close the gap with them. It was a mad chase through pitch blackness interspersed by jagged plumes of lightning. Jack thought the pursuit was bold, almost reckless, but Captain Sifton seemed confident in the prize crew and their ability to manage the ship through the storm, so they pressed onward. Late in the night watch, with no sign of the storm or the pursuit ending, Jack was relieved of his post at the helm.

"It does me no good for my coxswain to be so exhausted, Horner. Stand to and get some rest. I will remain with the watch and summon you if necessary, but I want you sharp if we are to board her when daylight comes," the captain explained.

Jack was thankful. His arms had reached a state of fatigue he hadn't thought possible. In the last of his stand he had required help to course correct the ship and been promptly embarrassed when the relieving hand had taken the helm with ease.

"No shame in it, mate," the sailor had consoled. "Ye've been at it through this storm fer hours. I've got her fer now. Get yer rest."

Jack left the quarterdeck and headed for the aft ladder below deck. He cast a solemn glance toward the helm before he descended. Part of him felt that he had failed to fulfill his duty. The captain was still standing tall on the quarterdeck. He should be by his side, in case he was needed. But, he had been given specific instruction to pass below deck and get rested. Another series of lightning strikes tore the night sky. Their brilliant flashes left a purple blue haze that fogged Jack's vision as he clomped down each step to the gun deck. He could hear a shout from aloft as he crossed into the stuffy warmth of the deck below.

"Deck, she's coming about to larboard this time! And hard over!"

The gun deck was a display of the aftereffects of prolonged tension dying off during pursuit. There were far too few sailors to man all the guns, so the main cannons at the ship's waist had taken priority. Warm, yellow light emanated from the lanterns that lined the bulkheads and created a column of waving light that sloshed like waves with the motion of the ship. Toward the far end of the deck, where the meager crew could not afford to spare hands to man the guns, the cannons that lined each side of the ship were wreathed in shadow. The orlop was serving as Saber's makeshift cell, and the cable tier was packed to the brim with extra supplies cross loaded from Allegiance. Jack debated for a moment, the wisdom of hanging his hammock and trying to steal a few hours of sleep while the pursuit continued. Idle chatter and shouts from above would make the gun deck untenable for much of the night. He opted instead to search out the sail locker. Piles of folded canvas would make for a bed, and should he be needed, he would be a short run to the arms locker by the officer's ward. He regarded the sailors standing by their guns for a moment, looked to see if his friend Bowline Bob was among them, and retired below when he did not spot the old sea hand. Bob had most likely ascended the foremast. Jack smiled as he thought of it, the sailorinest sailor to ever climb a mast or heave a line wouldn't miss the chance to be aloft in such a bizarre storm. A symphony of lightning, without a drop of rain. His old friend would be telling tales of this night for years to come. It made Jack's smile grow as he realized that Bob would look to him in the future to vouch his story.

The sail locker was a small room along the starboard side of the ship. It rested just aft of the mainmast on the starboard side. Situated snugly in between the orlop and the officer's ward, Jack would be able to find some rest atop stacks of damp folded canvas. He let himself in and closed the door behind him. There was no light from the companionway, nor any that leaked down from the deck above. The hull played a repeating chorus of sloshing waves as seawater slipped past the outer shell of thick oak timbers. It would be the perfect respite from his labors at the helm. With both hands, he felt his way to a thick stack of heavy canvas meant to be flown in foul weather. He crouched his head down and climbed atop the makeshift mattress before stretching out for some desperately needed rest. The locker was warm and humid, the space was tight almost to the point of claustrophobic, but the sound of the waves sloshing by the hull soon had lulled him into a near dream state. Every trickle of of bubbling froth that cascaded past the hull timbers sang into his hearing and penetrated his subconscious. The rise and fall of the ship, tempered as it was down in the sail locker amidships, gently rocked him in a graceful ease that caused his entire body to ease and his mind to drift. He wondered how long he would enjoy this respite before Saber caught her quarry and he would need to spring into action at the captain's side. Images of the recent battle reanimated in his thoughts. The desperate dash to Saber's bow, his hasty retreat up the foc'sl and the roar of the swivel guns.

Jack's thoughts froze. His eyes opened to find himself still cocooned in darkness. Something twisted at his insides. He became acutely aware of another presence in the sail locker. It wasn't a noise that betrayed the other occupant, nor a smell, but another sense, he could feel it in his skin. He tried to hold his breath and listen, but the sound of waves sliding along the hull was all that met his hearing. In the tight confine he had wriggled himself into, he was as helpless as he had been in his hammock. Thoughts of Lambdin's attempted assault crossed his mind, and he cursed the folly that had led him to the sail locker.

"Who is there?" Jack said. His stern voice betraying far more fear than he intended. His challenge was met with only silence and darkness. "Damn you, who is there? Announce yourself before I run you through!" The threat was a bluff. Jack knew it, but hopefully the other party would not.

"You wouldn't dare," a familiar voice replied. "Besides, I know your skill with a blade. I am not concerned."

"Matsumoko?" Jack said. He lifted himself from the stack of heavy sail and struck his head on a crossbeam. The impact nearly stole him from consciousness, but he fought through. "How?"

"I stole away with the last longboat. Unfortunate for Saber that one of the water casks had a leak in it, but fortunate for me."

Jack slid out from the space he occupied and down to the floor of the sail locker. He reached out with one hand and felt the flimsy fabric of a damp shirt. "It is you. Why would you steal away, friend? Captain Williams will list you as a deserter."

Matsumoko embrace Jack's shoulder in a firm grip. "I owe you a debt, Jack. That isn't something that bends to the whims of the Royal Navy."

"Giri," Jack said somberly. He wondered if his friend really understood the gravity of what he had done.

"Giri," Matsumoko agreed. "I owe you, my friend. My very life. If it hadn't been for you that day, I would have died a miserable, freezing, watery death."

"Matsumoko, you could be flogged around the fleet. Five dozen, six dozen, maybe more. The kiss of the cat, my friend, it is not something to balk at. This is serious," Jack said with a low voice. "And the sentry guarding the orlop is right outside."

Matsumoko drew a slow breath. Jack could feel more than see his smile in the blackness of the locker. "Oh, Jack. I am not as worried about the sentry as I am about you. Lambdin had you dead to rights the other night. He obviously is not finished with his grudge."

Jack's blood lit with a trace of lightning. "You were there? It was you that saved me!"

Silence passed while Saber shifted in her course, her hull listed to the starboard side and Jack felt his weight shift with the movement of waves catching the bow at a different angle.

"It was, Jack. I believe you have my hat. I would like that back, if you are done with it," Matsumoko replied in a flat tone.

Jack couldn't help but grin in the pitch black of the sail locker. "You are as slippery as an eel. How in the world did you manage to stay undiscovered this long? How did you slip out of the locker and up to the gun deck?"

"I have my ways. British sentries are vigilant, my friend. But not quite so vigilant that I could not slip past them if I so desired. Especially in the small hours of the night," Matsumoko replied.

The ship lurched again, this time on a hard turn to the larboard tack. Jack paused for a moment. Hadn't they just corrected the other way? Something was wrong. The ship lurched harder still, and Jack had to brace himself against the bulkhead to keep his balance. "Something isn't right, Matsumoko. We shouldn't be making turns like this, not in this wind."

Darkness was all that met his comment. Darkness and the groaning of straining ship timbers and deck boards.

"Indeed, something foul is at work, but the ship is the least of it." Matsumoko growled in the pitch blackness.

Jack was struck by the odd comment. "What do you mean? How could you know what is going on? You have been hiding away in the sail locker."

Matsumoko's voice held an irritable edge as he replied, "Jack, you know well and good that I have not confined myself to this locker. This is merely where I come to sleep and to keep out of sight. And, as it happens, this bulkhead adjoins the officer's wardroom. I have been privy to several conversations over the course of the evening. Captain Sifton is pursuing a small vessel, a schooner or cutter."

"Aye, a fore and aft rigged cutter," Jack replied.

"Yes, well, he relieved Lieutenant Brusby of his post and ordered him confined to quarters?"

"Aye," Jack replied.

Matsumoko paused for a long beat as the ship settled onto a new heading. "Well, it hasn't settled well with him. Nor the warrant officers. Gathering from what I have heard, they mean to lock the captain in his quarters before the dawn breaks."

Jack breathed in a slow draft of humid warmth from the close quarters. "A m-mutiny?"

"It would seem so," Matsumoko replied.

Saber
14 July 1770
21 Degrees 45′ N, 72 Degrees 29′ W

Urgency flooded Jack's blood. He couldn't believe what he was hearing. From the moment he'd broached the topic with Bowline Bob, high up in the rigging, he had dreaded the outcome. A mutiny. But, Captain Sifton was a good officer! He was brave and decisive, he cared for the welfare of the crew! How could anyone want to depose a leader of his temperament?

"It's not a question of if, Jack. It is a question of when," Matsumoko said. "I could only make out part of the discussion through the bulkhead, and Lieutenant Brusby isn't alone in his desires. But, I could not venture to guess at the other party, or parties."

Jack bit his front teeth into his lower lip. He had heard the grumblings on the quarterdeck, the hushed conversations and awkward disagreements. He followed his thoughts through to their conclusion. If any of the officers were going to try to take command of the ship, they would have to do so when the captain was in his quarters. To avoid interference from the crew. Or, him.

"Damnit, Matsumoko," Jack said in disbelief. "Captain Sifton named me his coxswain! I can't let this happen."

Matsumoko's hand drifted to Jack's shoulder and gave it a firm reassured squeeze. "No, Jack. We won't let it happen."

Another shift of the ship's hull lurched. This time caught Jack off guard and he toppled sideways into the stack of heavy canvas sails.

"Why are we making these hard turns?" He grumbled as he clawed his way to his feet. "I must get armed and get on deck. The captain has to be warned."

"What will you tell him?" Matsumoko asked.

Jack halted as his hand grasped the latch of the sail locker hatch. He hadn't considered it. He couldn't very well approach the captain and tell him that his friend had absconded from Allegiance, and overheard a conversation while he was in hiding aboard Saber. Matsumoko would surely be dragged before the mast and flogged until the boatswain couldn't lift his arm. He hesitated before opening the locker's hatch. "I will think of something to tell the captain, but he must be warned. I cannot allow them to take the ship."

"If you are worried for my sake, Jack," Matsumoko replied as Jack pried open the timber hatch, "don't be. I will face the consequences of my actions."

"It won't be necessary, friend," Jack said. "I will find a way."

The passageway outside of the sail locker seemed like a double width road compared to the cramped space he had just occupied. Jack welcomed the dim glow of lanterns at either end of the corridor and hurried his way to the aft ladder. He had to warn the captain, and he had to find a way to do it without revealing how he had discovered the first Lieutenant's plot. As Jack stepped onto the first of the stairs leading aloft, he realized that he knew nothing of the specifics. He had his assumptions, but for all he knew the mutinous first lieutenant could already be rallying crew members to his cause. If he crossed onto the quarterdeck, the mutinous party would mark him as a loyal man and lock him away along with the captain without hesitation. Jack paused and looked forward to the sail locker hatch. He was frozen in a conundrum, mired by enemies on all sides and with no escape in sight. He needed a loyal friend, but the man best suited to the struggle at hand could not show himself on deck. He silently cursed his foul luck and lunged up the steps to the gun deck. Whatever he must face, he would face it head on.

The heavens had opened, and the rain was merciless. As Jack stepped from below deck, lightning tore across the sky and lit Saber in a flash of stark white light that revealed a grim scene. Captain Sifton remained at his place along the windward rail, one hand clutched to a brace line and the other holding his telescope. Water dripped from his three-cornered hat and sheeted off of his uniform coat.

"She's coming about again! Starboard this time, and hard over she is!" a voice from forward cried out.

Captain Sifton turned to the helm and barked, "Match her course! Hard 't starboard. She is trying to shake us, the devil!"

Another bolt of lightning shot a flash of white through the world and receded into a purple glow that faded as quick as it appeared. Jack looked forward and saw that the humble cutter had cut her course across Saber's bow. Her captain was maintaining an evasive course, and careful not to come within the purview of Saber's broadside. Jack wondered if the crew of the small ship were smugglers, or pirates. Whoever they were, their master was a capable sailor, and cunning.

"Deck, there! She's coming about again, still to starboard! Looks like she's making a run about to cross the wind!" a lookout screamed through the wind and rain.

Jack felt a pang of excitement and confusion. What were they up to? He bolted to the starboard rail where a glimmer of distant lightning revealed the menacing silhouette of the cutter as she bore off hard on the starboard tack. She was doubling back southward! Jack squinted against the wind and rain. He fought to catch another glimpse of the strange ship through a series of lightning flashes from varying distances. Her new course would take her directly through the field of Saber's broadside.

"Run out the starboard battery, on the double!" Captain Sifton's voice thundered. "We'll fire as she passes!"

Jack's mind snapped from the circumstance surrounding the ship. He sprung away from the starboard rail and crossed to the quarterdeck.

"Starboard battery, ready!" a shout from the aft weather hatch reported.

Jack crossed onto the quarterdeck. "Captain, may I speak with you, sir?"

Captain Sifton waved dismissively. "Not now, Horner." His stare was locked over Saber's starboard rail where the cutter was just beginning to pass abreast of the bow.

Jack swallowed hard. Even setting foot on the quarterdeck when he was not officially on duty was a punishable offense. But, there was nothing for it. "Sir! I have an urgent matter that requires your attention. Life and death, sir, if you mind."

Captain Sifton turned on Jack and glared with a look that struck him as if he'd been blasted by a pistol shot. "What is it, Horner? If you can't see, there is another life or death matter unfolding before us!"

Jack took a bold step toward the captain. He wasn't sure who to trust, and he dared not chance the wrong set of ears overhearing what he had to say.

"I set to rest in the sail locker, sir. But, I overheard a conversation between someone and the first luff, er, excuse me sir, Lieutenant Brusby," Jack said. "He means to lock you in your cabin and take control of the ship!"

Lightning flashed. Captain Sifton's face hardened into a menacing grimace. "Are you sure of what you heard, Horner? That is a serious accusation."

Jack replied without hesitation, "Yes, sir. That is exactly what I heard."

"Go below and arm yourself from my personal locker. There is a brace of pistols and a pair of swords. I believe there may be a boarding ax in there as well, I am not certain. Fetch them, and return here to the quarterdeck," Captain Sifton rasped through the wind and rain. "They'll not have us without a fight, eh Horner?"

Jack knuckled his brow. "Aye, sir. Not if I have anything to say about it."

"Off with you, and hurry back," the captain urged with a gentle slap onto Jack's shoulder.

He turned and found himself accosted with a sudden gust of the wind carrying a squall's worth of rain. Drops stung the flesh of his face like needles falling at an angle from the heavens. Jack wiped at his eye and made to leave the quarterdeck for the aft hatch when a pair of men in heavy boat cloaks blocked his path.

"Captain Sifton, sir," one of the men shouted through the wind. "If you would, come with us. There is a matter below deck needs yer fast attention."

Jack felt a strong hand grasp at the collar of his shirt.

"We'll be havin' ye come wi' us too, Dead eye Jack. Seems there is need fer ye below deck as well," the second man said.

Jack could not distinguish who these two sailors were. But, there was no doubt when a third party stepped in between the two cloaked men. His tri-cornered hat was dripping from the rain, but it framed Lieutenant Brusby's face as a flash of lightning lit Saber's deck as plain as noon for a fraction of an instant.

"This folly has gone on long enough, captain…"

The lieutenant's words were cut short by a deep rumbling growl that tore through Saber's hull. Her decks trembled and groaned while the blood curdling sound of cracking timber mixed with rolling thunder. Everyone on deck was thrown from their feet in a violent halt of the ship's momentum. Aloft, sailors braced themselves against the jarring halt. Brace lines snapped and hissed through the wind and rain as they recoiled from their tension while the masts swayed under enormous strain from both the wind and sudden stop of the ship.

"Reef! She's run aground!" a terrified scream rose from the bow of the ship.

Jack heaved himself from the deck and broke the grip of the burly sailor who had been holding his shirt collar. The deck was slick with rain, and he struggled to get to his feet. He could hear the captain similarly battling both gravity and poor footing.

"Mr. Hill, a damage report if you please!" he shouted.

The sailor who had arrested Jack's shirt collar grabbed his ankle. "Yer damned cap'n has gone and done it now, this isn't finished!"

Jack balled his fist and with a vicious downward punch, struck the sailor square along the side of his jaw. The man went limp for a moment, dazed by the blow. It was the break Jack needed, and he moved to take full advantage. In a series of short, unstable strides, he made his way to the aft hatch and headed below deck. Shouts of panic and screams of pain drifted through the night air. No sooner than Jack's feet touched onto the gun deck than a muffled thump rolled through the air. A shivering tremble beat through Saber's hull and a cry rose from the forward end of the batteries.

"It's the cutter! She's opened fire!"

Another muffled roar sounded, followed shortly by a gut wrenching crash into the hull. Timbers cracked and splintered. A sailor screamed out in pain. The ship heaved again as the force of a wave lifted her hull and receded. Jack turned for the companionway and forced the hatch to the captain's cabin open. The quarters were dark but for an occasional flash of lightning that bled through an array of windows spread across the fantail. In a spasm of bright light, Jack spotted the captain's arms rack. A brace of three pistols strung together on a broad leather strap hung from a brass hook beneath two swords in their scabbards. Jack raced to arm himself. He flung the leather strap holding the captain's brace of pistols over his neck and grabbed a sword in each hand. Another flash invaded the cabin, followed by a rumble of thunder that sent a crawling sensation through his skin and into his stomach. More cannon fire sounded, and Jack could feel the hits as they reverberated through the ship's timbers and up his shins into his knees. He left the cabin in a flight of near panic. Chaos enveloped the ship.

Another shaking impact of cannon fire sent a lantern falling from its hook. A swath of fire chased the fallen lantern and spread its way in a hungry crawl up the larboard bulkhead. One of the gun captains threw his crew's bucket of vinegar tinged water at the blaze while others scrambled to douse the fire with more buckets of the swab mixture. Jack took leaping steps up the ladderway until his feet touched onto the rain and sea soaked main deck. Raging wind and driving rain met him amid a torrent of shouts and calls. Above it all, Jack heard the authoritative voice of Captain Sifton.

"Ready the longboats for launch and heave in those sails, men!" He shouted without aid of the speaking trumpet. "Get the wounded below to see the surgeon!"

Jack hurried aft as a rolling wave crashed alongside. A spray of seawater sluiced the deck and threatened to steal his footing, but he braced himself against the windward rail and pressed his progress aft.

"Sir!" he shouted, "I have the arms you requested from your cabin." Jack held out the scabbarded officer's sword to his commander.

"Very good," the captain replied. "You keep that brace of pistols and tuck that sword into your belt, young man. We aren't out of trouble yet, by a long shot." His face showed the strain of the situation in a blistering series of lightning flashes that chased one after another for several seconds. "I sent Lieutenant Hill after a damage report and have not seen him since. Horner, I need to know the state of the ship below deck. Can you retrieve him for me?"

Jack knuckled his brow. "Aye, sir. I know there is fire on the gun deck, the crew is fighting the fire currently."

Captain Sifton's face tightened into a grimace as if he had been kicked in the chest. "Damn the luck," he said before encouraged Jack on with a quick nod. "Go find Mr. Hill and get him on deck smartly. We needs get our feet under us or this night will be the end of us all."

"I need more hands aft to man the bilge pumps, and the carpenter's mates below to seal the hold!" Lieutenant Hill shouted through a cacophony of mayhem. Orders were shouted and repeated, men ran past each other in a hurry from one task to the next all while the ship heaved and slammed from the beating she was absorbing. Cannon fire from the cutter continued as Saber continued to be battered against the reef she had slammed into. Jack arrived in the depths of the hold to find Lieutenant Hill passing orders and surveying the damage in the deepest bowels of the ship.

"Sir!" Jack cried over the litany of noises surrounding them. "The captain passes his compliments and has requested you to report to the quarterdeck with a summary of the damage Saber has sustained."

The lieutenant's face was drawn and fearful. He tore his focus from the hold for a moment to regard Jack with a brief expression of hopelessness. "I will be up presently, Mr. Horner. But, our situation is dire. The hull is breached along our keel. There is a starter up in the bow big enough to put Noah's old tub at the bottom! I fear if we do not get her sealed and get ourselves off of the reef, we will go down with all hands."

Jack's stomach tightened into a painful knot. More shots rumbled and shook Saber. His thoughts snapped to Matsumoko. His friend would not know the peril they were facing.

"Horner, take my report to the captain. Let him know of the breach in our hull and please relay my most insistent recommendation that we ready the launches and prepare to abandon the prize," the lieutenant said with a wave of deflation spreading through his face and chest. "I fear at this point, she is already lost and we are going to battle only to lose her in the end."

Jack nodded and knuckled his brow. He opened his mouth to reply, but found himself lacking words. Lieutenant Hill turned and continued directing hands in their efforts to save the ship. The water level was rising, and with it all manner of dry goods had been ruined and set adrift within the confines of the lower hold. He departed after a moment of hesitation as several of his shipmates waded their way through waist deep seawater toward the bow.

The gun deck was still a scene of pandemonium. Gun crews had managed to contain the blaze from the spilled lantern, but a section of the larboard battery spanning two guns was still aflame. Several men lay dead on the deck and several more looked to be severely wounded. Jack took in the struggle for a heartbeat before continuing topside. It pained him not to aid his shipmates in their battle, but his duty to the captain called him onward. The main deck somehow seemed even more grim than the struggle below. Lines blew free in the wind, fallen and wounded sailors littered the deck, and the state of the ship seemed to be in grievous disrepair. On the quarterdeck, Captain Sifton had bared the blade of his officer's sword as he continued to rattle off orders in an uphill battle to set the ship aright.

"Cast off that shattered spar and set her adrift," he shouted through the howling wind. "Prepare the main haul and heave out those longboats."

Jack approached and knuckled his brow. "Sir, Lieutenant Hill sends his respects and ordered me to pass along his report. The hull is breached in the bow, and he stringently recommends that we prepare all souls to abandon ship, sir."

Captain Sifton halted in his tracks. He glared at Jack as if the young man had offered him grievous insult for the span of a breath before his face softened in the recognition of defeat. "That blasted cutter and her infernal commander, he knew exactly what he was doing and I blundered straight into it. Right into the lion's teeth," he said. "Very well, the longboats are being hoisted presently. See to it that you find yourself into one of them, Horner. I will remain here until the very last."

Jack's heart sank. He glanced toward the bow. The sound of groaning timbers was now louder and the teetering motion of the foremast signaled what soon would become the warship's undoing. Impaled on a reef, her hull was taking on water. The rigging and deck was in shambles, and she had been battered by raking fire from the cutter as it passed. His thoughts turned from the captain to his messmates. Bowline Bob, Matsumoko, and the others. Jack felt an overwhelming rush of urgent need to ensure they made it safely into the longboats and away from the dying ship.

A familiar voice cried out from the bow of the ship, "Clear away! She's going to go!"

Jack searched desperately for the caller. He would know Bowline Bob's hoarse crackle anywhere, but he was not to be seen. A thunderous crack sounded, lightning flashed, and in the blistering brightness of light Jack saw the foremast begin its toppling sideways descent. Saber heaved from the counteracting forces of wind and wave while her foremast wrenched the wooden structure in yet another direction. Deck planks buckled and cracked. Splinters and twisted timber split into Jack's hearing. The ship groaned again like a behemoth of the deep that had been harpooned and was succumbing to its wounds. Matsumoko! Jack's blood lit with determination and fear. He had to retrieve his friend.

Saber was listing onto her larboard beam as Jack faced the aft ladderway to brave the depths of the ship. Each step had become a struggle to maintain his footing as the ship began to move in unnatural ways. The steps of the ladderway were canted from Saber's growing lean to one side.

"Abandon ship!" the scream echoed through Saber's gun deck just as Jack's footfalls found purchase at the base of the ladder. A press of sailors crowded aft to fight their way topside and Jack barely escaped the mob as he pressed his way down to the next level.

"Matsumoko!" he shouted as he reached the bottom of the ladder well and entered the lower corridor between the officer's wardroom and the orlop. "We have to go!" Jack wrenched open the sail locker and plunged himself into the abysmal dark beyond its hatch. "Matsumoko, where are ye? She's heeling over and about to go down, we have to go!"

"J-Jack…" a weak reply came from the near corner forward of the hatch.

"Where in blazes are ye Mats? We can't be fer lingering, friend," Jack shouted in a half panic.

Silence passed while Jack's heart pounded in his chest so hard that he could barely hear his friend's voice. "Jack, I'm pinned into the corner. The heavy canvas shifted…" Matsumoko's voice was weak and trailed away as if he were struggling for breath.

Jack reached toward the sound of Matsumoko's voice in the blackness of the sail locker. His fingertips found the coarse grit of heavy canvas in compressed folds, one on top of another. He stretched himself to find the edge of the stack, but only found more folds pressed together. A wall of stacked heavy sails was separating him from his friend.

"Jack, go. Get out of here with your life intact, if you still can," Matsumoko urged in a breathless rasp.

Jack snorted. "Be damned with that. Its like you don't know me at all," he paused and tried to climb the pile of sail, but only managed to ram his head into a timber crossbeam. "I'll be right back, Matsumoko. I can't see anything in this infernal hole."

In the companionway, Jack found that the marine sentry had abandoned his post outside of the orlop. All that was left to mark his flight was a swinging lantern, and a dropped musket. A trembling groan sounded through Saber's hull and sent Jack's mind racing with the possibility of the ship breaking up with him and Matsumoko trapped in its bowels. He drew a determined breath and scrambled for the swaying lantern. He seized the lantern with one hand and started to make his way back to the sail locker's open hatch when a panicked voice caught his ear.

"Help! Help us! Please, don't leave us to drown like rats in here!"

His stomach turned. The voice carried a heavy French accent and accompanied a series of desperate pounding impacts on the inside of the orlop hatch. Jack hesitated. Just days ago he had been in a dire battle against these same men. They were responsible for the deaths of a handful of his shipmates, and their captain had stolen the vision of one eye from his for the rest of his life. But, nonetheless, they were mariners, and human beings. An image of his mother's face flashed like the lightning outside through his mind. His father's dying words, "You have to be a man now, Jacky." Before he had left the sail locker, Jack had no idea how he was going to free his friend. But, an idea sprung forth like the first gust of a storm. He hooked the lantern's thin metal handle into his elbow and hauled up the musket left by the sentry who had deserted his charges to a watery death.

"Stand back from the hatch! Now!" Jack shouted as he cocked the flint of the musket. He braced the muzzle of the weapon against the thick metal padlock that secured the orlop hatch and pulled the trigger. A flash of powder and smoke erupted in a roar that sent the musket's ball into the lock. The swaying yellow glow of Jack's lantern revealed that the lock had not entirely released its clasp. Cursing his luck, Jack reversed his grip on the musket and slammed the butt of the weapon against the lock's metal body. After several hard strikes, to Jack's significant relief, the mangled metal finally gave way. He dropped the musket to the deck and drew a pistol from the brace he wore across his shoulder before he flung open the orlop hatch. The yellow glow emanating from his sooty lantern revealed a crowd of gaunt, pale faces painted with a mixture of gross fear and grudging relief. Jack cocked the striker of his pistol and wielded it in front of himself for all to see.

"I'll not see you all drown helpless in the hold, but you will do exactly as I say, or we will all die here in the belly of this ship," he said in his most authoritative voice.

Brows tightened. There were confused looks exchanged among the Frenchmen. Hesitantly several of the sailors stepped forward and Jack raised his flintlock pistol to assert his control.

"My friend is trapped in the sail locker," he said while fighting away a quiver from his voice. "And you will help me free him, or we will all die in the trying." More doubtful glares were exchanged among the French sailors and for a moment Jack began to fear that they would rush him all at once in an overwhelming wave to escape. He swallowed hard and aimed his pistol at the nearest Frenchman. "Test me, and I promise you that we will all die down here tonight. You have my word that you will be freed, but first, I need your help to save my friend."

The closest of the French sailors slowly raised his hands with opened palms. "Monsieur, if you will allow me to translate. My English is fair, my shipmates, not so much."

Jack motioned toward the huddled mass of Frenchmen with his pistol. "Be quick about it."

The French sailor turned inboard to face his fellow captives and prattled in his native tongue for what seemed to Jack like longer than it should have taken. Assent seemed to spread among the fearful faces as the translator finished his speech. He turned back to face Jack with a feeble grin and a nod. "Monsieur, it seems that we 'ave no choice. Lead on and we will help you to free your trapped friend. I only ask that if we do this, that you will not mistreat us. If I am saying this correctly."

Jack drew a slow breath through his nostrils. He allowed his pistol arm to ease ever so slightly. "My friend is caught behind a stack of heavy canvas in the sail locker. I need you men to remove the sails in order to free him and save his life. Once that is done, I will let you all flee the ship with us. You have my word."

The translator offered a slight bow to Jack. "A very generous offer, mon ami. Your sense of honor is evident. Lead on."

CHAPTER 19

Saber
14 July 1770
Exact Position Unknown

"Hold on, friend! We're coming!" Jack shouted into the narrow space of the sail locker as the French sailors heaved heavy canvas from the shifted stack out into the companionway. He held the sooty lantern overhead while the Frenchmen worked in a fury to accomplish their bargained task. "Come on, put yer backs into it! Time isn't our friend today!" he urged the freshly freed sailors before their translator repeated his point in an animated bout of French.

Saber's hull groaned and listed with a dangerously oblique cant. Jack could hear the ship sing out her impending death with the same urgency of a man who knew his end was near. His heartbeat thrummed through every fiber of his body and soul. He stared at the diminishing pile of sail in near panicked anticipation to see Matsumoko's face. The French sailors worked with fervent urgency until their brows were dripping with sweat from the mixture of labor and oppressive tension.

Fold by fold, the stacks of coarse, heavy canvas were stripped away while Saber groaned her protest against the circumstance of her inevitable demise. Jack forced himself to maintain a sense of calm. He was surrounded by more than a dozen men, all of which he had very recently been locked into a mortal struggle for survival against. If they were to conspire against him, it would be a swift and violent end. The sooty globe of his lantern emitted a dingy yellow cast against the sail locker amid the heaving sway of Saber's groaning hulk. As the stack of sail was stripped down to chest height, one of the French sailors burst out in an excited bout of babble and turned to the group's translator.

"Your friend, monsieur. They have found him. It appears that he has been crushed by the heavy sails. They are unsure if he lives," the translator said in his heavy French accent.

Jack shook his head. "He lives, I just spoke with him. Tell them to hurry."

"Mon ami, he was buried beneath so much. How could he? The weight of those sails would crush him and steal away his breath just as surely as if he were to drown..." the translator's reply trailed away at the sight of Jack's flintlock pistol being pressed toward his nose.

"Dead or alive, we free him, or we all die in the trying," Jack said in a poisonous tone. "That was the bargain that was struck. Tell them to hurry damn it."

More sails were dragged from the locker and Jack pressed his way into the cramped room amid the laborious shuffle of the Frenchmen. The interpreter stood nearby and without averting his stare from Matsumoko, Jack handed the man his lantern. "Hold this," he said before climbing onto the last of the sails and squirming into position to see his friend. He tucked his flintlock pistol back into its place in the broad leather strap and reached out for his friend's hand which lay motionless atop folds of canvas. "Matsumoko?" Jack gave the hand a firm squeeze while tears welled in his eyes. In truth, he had no idea how many friends he had already lost since the sun went down. For all he knew, the rest of his messmates may have already succumbed to the storm, or the opportunistic cutter. He felt Saber's hull shift, and a collective gasp of anxiety and fear rippled through the French sailors surrounding him. But, to Jack it was all periphery. As meaningless as a single drop amid the storm. His every thought centered around Matsumoko. A ragged breath broke through Jack's hearing.

"J-Jack..." Matsumoko rasped.

"He lives!" Jack said in a thunderous shout. He motioned toward the sails that remained in the stack beneath him. "Go on, move these damn things so I can get him free! He is alive, and we must get him up on deck. Hurry!"

With a renewed fury, the crew of Frenchmen flung the last folds of heavy sails to the side while Jack scooped Matsumoko up with an arm under each of his shoulders. Painful groans were all that escaped his friend's lips, and Jack dragged him from the sail locker and out into the companionway. "It is a good thing you aren't very heavy, friend. Yet again." Though he had been freed from the sail locker, Jack knew his friend's condition to be serious. There was a red stain in his mouth that dripped from the corner of his lips. "I'd fetch you to the surgeon if I could, but we have to be for getting off of this ship."

Saber's hull shifted, a deep tremble shuddered through the entire ship. Jack could hear timber cracking and the sound of rushing water. He heaved Matsumoko's weight up onto his shoulders and waved to the crew of French sailors.

"Come on, follow me!"

The deck shifted beneath his feet. His muscles were on fire. He felt the ship heave harder than it had before, it rose with the fury of a wave in a storm and then crashed back down in a sudden jarring halt. The force dropped Jack painfully to the deck. His knees slammed onto the wooden planks beneath him while the ship continued to convulse and tremble in the fury of the storm. With a deep breath, he forced himself back to his feet. Matsumoko grunted in pain.

"We are leaving this ship, friend. You and I, we are getting out of here and this will be another bad memory to be recalled in the small hours of watch for years to come..."

Every step became a battle. Saber's tossing introduced him to the corridor bulkhead in violent fashion, he recoiled from the first impact only to slam into the opposite side. The companionway darkened, but Jack fought onward. It seemed like an eternity, but he reached the ladder well. With one hand he grasped the thick rope handhold while with the other he held his friend's weight steady on his shoulders. Hauling a brace of harpoons seemed like a distant dream from his past, one that paled in comparison with his current struggle. With lunging steps, Jack fought his way to the top of the ladder well before wearing around to tackle the last leg. His legs burned, every muscle protested the strain. He could feel his sails slacking, but from somewhere deep inside he forced himself to keep going. Rain. Rain and the howling wind finally slapped against the flesh of his face. He had made it on deck. A forked bolt of lightning traced the sky and lit the world for the flash of an instant. Jack's blood iced over as he saw Saber's decks in their final state. The bow was gone, nothing but twisted splinters and ragged broken timber. But it was so much worse. Another flash of lightning revealed the state of Saber's crew. They were gone. The longboats had been hoisted outboard. Jack, Matsumoko, and the French sailors had been left to their fate.

Shock overtook him. Saber's deck heaved as a wave struck along her quarter and washed over the deck. He wanted to scream into the howling wind and surrounding darkness. Another bolt of lightning split through the heavens and sent a harrowing brightness through the dark world. Jack saw a huddled mass on the quarterdeck that made his heart drop. He eased Matsumoko off of his shoulders with care and gently lowered his friend to the deck.

"The boats, mon ami. Where are the boats? Saber has four, or had..." the interpreter said through a gust of wind.

Jack shook his head and gestured forward to the destroyed bow. "They left us. The crew took them." He motioned toward Matsumoko. "Stay with him. I have to go look at something."

The interpreter arched his eyebrows in shock before offering only a nod and a dismissive wave. "It was a valiant effort, monsieur. But, we can at least attempt to swim for our lives I suppose. Go, I will wait here with your friend until the very last. The least I can do, I suppose."

Jack clenched his jaw and steeled himself for what he would find. He crossed onto the quarterdeck with a sick feeling welling in the back of his throat. Another flash of lightning confirmed his worst fears. Captain Sifton was huddled against the lee rail, his uniform coat stained by blood.

"Captain?" Jack shouted. He waited for a response while an assault of wind buffeted the ship's stern. Saber lurched again from the force of a wave and he could see movement from the huddled mass of bloody uniform.

"Horner?" came a throaty challenge.

Jack dashed forward for all his legs would allow. He slid onto the deck and grabbed Captain Sifton's stained uniform coat. "Sir? What in blazes? How did this happen?" He searched the captain and found that blood was pouring from a wound just beneath his right shoulder.

"That damned Lieutenant Brusby. After the ship ran aground, he, he gathered a group of hands and they took control of the longboats. They made off for landfall, a small island to the east, or so they believe. I tried to stop them. Brusby shot me with a pistol." The captain's voice was weak. More of a raspy croak than actual speech.

Jack balled part of the captain's coat and pressed on the wound to slow his bleeding. In the intermittent flashes of lightning he tried desperately to find something, anything, to save them. A plank, a barrel, flotsam of any sort. But, the waves had become nothing but rolling dark shadows, omens of a miserable watery struggle before inevitable surrender.

"Horner..." the captain said with a wince of pain. "The jolly boat, off the fantail. Still there..."

Jack felt his heart skip a beat. Of course! The jolly boat was meant to ferry officers and small parties of men between vessels and into port on occasion. It hadn't even crossed his mind until the captain's raspy croak. Together with the French sailors, the small boat would be loaded well beyond capacity, especially with the state of the sea. But, he could find no better alternative.

"Hey there," Jack shouted over his shoulder as the wind drove a fresh wave of seawater across Saber's deck. "Help me to lower away the jolly boat. We will crowd onto her and brave our chances!"

Many in the party of freed French sailors exchanged confused and horrified looks once the interpreter had his chance to recite Jack's words in their native language. But, a handful of men snapped into action.

"They think you are quite mad, mon ami," the translator said. "How are we all to fit in such a small craft. Eh? Or are you planning to lighten the load once we are away from Saber?"

Jack ignored the taunt and stumbled his way across the heaving deck to the fantail. The small boat could comfortably seat eight, in a pinch, he supposed, as many a twelve could fit. But, there were two dozen French sailors, and that did not include him, the captain, or Matsumoko. In the high seas and heavy wind, the small craft would be unwieldy. Overburdened, the little jolly boat would be susceptible to capsizing, or taking on water to the point it could not stay afloat. But a small boat would be better than no boat at all.

A fresh howl blew against Saber's hull and sent another cracking sound splitting from the deck up into the high stretches of her mainmast. Jack looked aloft as a flash of light split the horizon. Her mainmast was slowly giving way under the strained angle of the ship and the counteracting force of the wind. They were out of time. Jack hurried back across the deck to the French interpreter and hoisted Matsumoko up with and arm under his back and one behind his knees.

"We have to get off this hulk, now. When that mast goes, so does she," he said.

The interpreter shook his head and gestured to a group of the French sailors that remained clustered by the aft ladder well. "Some of them have decided to stay with her, until the very end. They may swim once she goes under, but, it is likely they will all perish with the ship."

His mind raced. Jack knew he did not have time to try and talk sense into them. He tried to think of what his friend Bowline Bob would do. "Whatever suits them, I guess." He nodded toward the interpreter. "And, what about you?"

"I go with you, monsieur." The interpreter said with rigid disposition.

"Alright, then. Tell any of them that want to come with us, to get in the jolly boat," he said as he began the fight back to Saber's fantail. "And, someone needs to help the captain."

Jack carried Matsumoko to the precipice of Saber's stern railing and lowered him as gently as he could manage into the jolly boat. He knew his friend's condition was serious, but there was no time to linger on the delicate questions of what was to come. He had to be the man his father had called on him to be.

"Monsieur, your capitan. He refuses to come. He is insisting that he remain aboard his ship," the translator said over Jack's shoulder.

There was no time. Jack could feel Saber breaking up below the waterline. Every second of delay became a greater chance that they would all be dragged below in the rush of sea as the ship finally succumbed to the waves and sunk into the briny depths of crushing silence. The captain had every right to insist on strict adherence to age old maritime traditions. But, the days of captains actually remaining aboard their sinking vessel were long gone but for a few outliers and the odd tall tales shared by sailors in the depths of a long night watch or huddled around their evening grog. There was a viable means of escaping the ship, and Jack meant to see that the man who had given him his step lived to see another day. He crossed the quarterdeck and stood over the huddled mass of Captain Sifton while several French sailors squared themselves away in the Jolly boat.

"Ye mean to go down with yer ship, cap'n?" Jack asked through a torrent of washing seawater sprayed by the wind.

"Go, Horner," the captain said through a spurt of coughs. "I will retain what honor I have left and do my duty."

"Bullocks ter that, cap'n," Jack replied. He bent down and hoisted the captain beneath his arms. "We still need ye, once we get ashore an such." For a fleeting moment, Captain Sifton resisted, but months of working the tops and manning the helm had hardened Jack with exceptional upper body strength. He pulled the fallen captain across Saber's stern and with the aid of a few of the Frenchmen, loaded him into the bow of the jolly boat. Jack climbed in last while two of the sailors unlatched the rigging and lowered the small craft hand over hand down to the tumultuous seas. The oars were locked into place and manned by four men in the middle of the craft. Jack, ever vigilant of his duty, took the tiller in hand and directed their movement. The first few moments were harrowing. Saber's stern presented an immediate threat to the overburdened jolly boat. Rushing waves met them on their beam and threatened to crash them into the sinking ship, but a quick thinking sailor at the oars poled them off the ship at the last moment and allowed the small boat to slip under her lee. They had escaped Saber, and with only fleeting minutes to spare. Jack pulled the tiller close to himself and the jolly boat edged away with waves breaking at the stern and slopping over her transom. The frigate heaved under the force of a wave and every soul aboard the jolly boat bore witness to a horrendous shudder as she slammed against a fixed object beneath the sea surface. Then, with a final groan of surrender, the ship listed full over onto her larboard beam and began finally broke apart.

The sailors at oars in the jolly boat heaved with everything they had. Jack manned the tiller and held their course as close as he could reckon to east, though without a compass, or the hulk of Saber in sight there was no point of reference. Every wave threatened to be their undoing, and there was no good way to take them. Over the side would easily topple the overloaded boat and scatter its handful of survivors into the sea. Taking the waves on the stern was rapidly filling the small craft with seawater that they couldn't bail out fast enough. Jack estimated that if the seas didn't slack, or if they didn't make landfall within an hour, they would be set adrift as a huddle of swimmers. He feared for Matsumoko and Captain Sifton, both men were severely injured and in no shape to swim at all, let alone in foul seas.

Shivers enveloped him. The driving wind and rain in combination with the wash of the sea had stripped away what warmth had remained in his limbs. The tiller fought against his clammy grip while he tried to huddle himself against the onslaught of weather. Darkness filled everything in sight and before he knew it, Jack was completely disoriented. It felt like he had left Saber's wreckage behind him. Or, had he drifted off course northward? He wasn't sure. Everything felt distant to him. The sailors huddled together in the jolly boat, Captain Sifton tucked in between the forward rowers and the bow, Matsumoko huddled in between Jack and the interpreter. The howl of wind and wash of waves became their chief torment. Not a word was uttered while the rowers continued to bend their oars. Waves washed over the transom, and then over the sides. The jolly boat squatted lower into the sea with every stroke at the oars. Their feeble attempt to bail out the invading seawater could not match the ferocity of its assault. Misery set in. Jack's awareness closed around him like a dark curtain. He pulled at the tiller to counteract the motion of the sea, but the realization that he had lost his course set into his mind. He contemplated being adrift in the vastness of the sea for days on end. The thought brought on a terrible thirst. His mouth felt dry and his lips were chapped from the wind and saltwater. A solid clunk against the bow snapped him from his misery.

"Help! Help me!" a voice shouted.

Jack's ears flooded with a rush of warm blood. He squinted against the dark. He hadn't noticed the absence of lightning until then, but the night's impenetrable darkness had not been spoiled since just after the Saber broke apart.

"Help me! Please, dear God Help!" the voice repeated.

"Did ye hear that?" Jack asked the interpreter sitting nearby in the stern of the jolly boat.

Every sailor in the small vessel perked up and looked outboard. Another clunk sounded against the jolly boat's hull.

"Help! Help!" the voice cried out in desperation.

Jack pushed on the tiller to bring the craft to bear toward the sound of the distress call. "Call out, men! Let him know we are coming," Jack said through a titter of confusion that spread through the rowboat.

The interpreter rattled away some angry sounding French and after a heartbeat's hesitation shouts of foreign, throaty sounding French were being heaved outboard for the distressed sailor.

"There is flotsam and wreckage, mon ami. We must be careful not to damage our boat!" the translator pleaded with Jack. "Debris could easily capsize us."

Jack clenched his jaw. An instant passed where he considered heaving the tiller over and steering the boat out of harm's way. It passed. His father's last words returned to him. He wasn't sure if it was the right thing to do, but he knew it was what he would have done.

"We brave the hazard, Frenchman. For our shipmate," Jack said. "Tell them to put their backs into it. I would rather face the risk for a living soul than a body."

More flotsam clattered against the jolly boat's side. The cry for help grew more distinct and more desperate. Jack felt like the croaky growl sounded somewhat familiar.

"Help, fer love of God, someone help!"

Lightning hit Jack's blood. Suddenly, the chill was chased from his limbs. He stood in the stern of the Jolly boat and called out with every bit of breath he could muster. "Bob! Bowline Bob where are ye?"

"Jacky? I knew ye'd come, lad! I'm over here, help me!" Bob's shout sounded through a renewed gust of wind. "I'm holdin' on fer life ter this spar and she's a'goin ter sink me with her!"

Jack sat at the tiller and turned the jolly boat further toward Bob's voice. "Tell 'em to pull for their lives, damn it!" he snapped at the translator.

A stream of vigorous French sent the men at the oars into a fury of heaving. They pulled in time with one another, and soon the jolly boat was surrounded in a stretching field of floating debris. Bob's voice drifted over the water, each shout growing louder than the one before.

"Hold on Bob, we're coming for ye!" Jack shouted over the choppy waves and gusting wind.

The oarsmen pulled and cleared their oar blades from the water, then set the handles forward before heaving back a stroke against the sea. This motion was repeated over and over while waves tossed the small craft mercilessly. Jack scoured the darkness for any sign of Bob and noticed the eastern horizon beginning to show signs of a coming dawn, the faintest glow of amber was beginning to invade a sliver of sky between sea and clouds. Warmth, and light, would soon return to them, and it would be welcomed with grateful hearts.

"Hold on!" Captain Sifton called from the bow of the jolly boat.

Jack had no time to react. The front of the small craft slammed against some form of debris in the water and sent every hand rolling off balance. The dreadful sound of cracking wood pierced into hearing while seawater invaded their only place of safety in the turmoil of waves. Disoriented, Jack released his hold on the tiller and flung himself onto Matsumoko. The sea swallowed them both as the deck of the jolly boat broke apart and scattered. Jack felt as if the world closed around him. The howling of wind and torrent of sloshing waves disappeared and was replaced by a close silence disturbed only by a trickle of bubbles escaping from his ears. He had not been prepared to be submerged. His lungs cried out with an immediate need for air. Jack wrapped one arm around Matsumoko's chest and kicked as if to fight away the depths threatening to swallow them both. With one arm he clung to Matsumoko, and with the other he tore at the sea. He kicked and thrashed, fighting for every inch while his lungs burned for air and his chest began to spasm from the dire need to breathe.

Just as Jack was beginning to lose hope of reaching the surface, his hand broke free from the clutches of the sea. His head and torso rushed upward, he drew in a sweet breath of air just before a wave overtook him and pummeled him and Matsumoko back into the briny water. He struggled again, kicking and clawing his way to find another breath. Panic flooded his veins and the strength of his legs began to fail. His extended night watch at the helm, the storm, the desperate flight to save Matsumoko, it had all caught up to him. Try as he did, his muscles could not summon the strength he needed. He kicked again, but the sensation of being drawn deeper into the sea continued. His kicks slowed. His mind centered on the nearness of death. For an instant, he mourned failing Matsumoko. His mother's eyes gleamed and glossed over, the instant death took her replayed to him again.

His father's words. "You have to be a man now, Jack." Something ignited inside of him. A fire took hold in his chest and burned through his entire body. He summoned strength he hadn't realized he still possessed. His legs kicked, his arm tore through the water and he felt upward momentum. Another heave of effort rewarded him with a breath of air. He pulled Matsumoko upward and bared his friend's face to the open air.

"This isn't our end, not today," he said as he gasped in another breath. A wave washed over them, but Jack fought against it and kicked them back to the surface. As he pulled in another breath, he reached across the water's surface for anything to grab onto. His first attempt yielded nothing but a handful of saltwater which he used to propel himself across the surface. Jack stretched out his arm and kicked his legs with the fury of desperate self-preservation. Another wave rose up and threatened to swallow them beneath the surface, but a few mad strokes and a flurry of kicks kept both him and Matsumoko within inches of open air. His head broke free from the sea and he redoubled his efforts until his head struck into something solid. The impact dazed him and sent a bolt of pain across his scalp. Shocked, Jack reached for the solid object and found that he had run into a rounded section of timber. Hands grasped at his shirt. His disorientation compounded for a moment as the hands pulled at his arms and waistline.

"Up ye go, Jacky," Bob's voice growled. "It's no jolly boat, but she'll keep us on the surface until dawn breaks, I figure."

Jack felt the solid mass of rounded timber beneath him as the hands that had grabbed hold of him dragged his weight from the water. He straddled the mass of Saber's mainsail spar, its buoyancy was barely sufficient to keep them afloat, but with a little effort Jack was able to keep his head above the water. He drew in a breath and savored the sweet crispness of the sea air. Mutterings of French alerted him to the presence of other survivors from the jolly boat.

"Yer rescue attempt floundered, Jacky. But I thank ye fer it all the same," Bob said. "Now, we are all at the mercy of the sea." He slapped Jack on the shoulder and offered a nod and a slight smile. "Right honorable thing ye did, friend. Yer one t' go ter sea with. I knew ye'd not let me flounder by my lonesome out here on the waves."

Jack coughed and wretched as his lungs tried to expel remnants of seawater. "Ye'd do the same likewise, Bob." He sat up on the spar and balanced his weight as a wave slowly broke around them. The seas had calmed, and it seemed that the wind was dying away. To the east, dawn was within minutes of breaking. The sliver of sky was a brilliant band of golden orange that cast its glow along the ceiling of cloud cover. "Is it over?"

Bob grunted and shifted his weight to look in the same direction as Jack. "The storm? Aye, I'd say she has about blown her course. Our ordeal, on the other hand, that is far from over, Jacky. We are in a mess of trouble."

Shipwrecked Men of the Saber
14 July 1770
Exact Position Unknown

Parting clouds let slip golden columns of sunlight that slanted down to the sea surface and radiated the glittering glow off of rippled waves. The wind had died to a fraction of the strength it held through the night and the seas, almost as if to answer the bid of the winds, calmed as well. Jack and his band of survivors clung to the half-submerged mainsail spar. All were beyond tired. The toll of the storm had only been the beginning salvo in their battle against the elements. Wind and wave had bettered them all through the night and into the first waning hours of dawn. Cold crept into their bodies, almost seeming to penetrate through their flesh and into their souls. Teeth chattered. Eyes drooped with the heaviness of long standing fatigue. Hunger gripped their stomachs and stymied their strength. Thirst lingered on each man's mind, though none spoke a word of it to the next. For hours, they bobbed on the slack current that led them ebbing eastward.

"Its perilous, Jacky," Bowline Bob said from his straddle perch at the center of the floating spar. "East lies the Atlantic. If we drift too far…" His voice trailed away, but he didn't need to finish the thought. Every sailor that clung to the spar for their life knew their grim outlook. If they wandered within sight of land, the best they could hope for was a favorable current and hours upon hours of grueling paddling, kicking and swimming to make solid ground. If they drifted far enough eastward without sight of an island or cay, their prospects for survival were naught.

Hours dragged by while the sun climbed behind a screen of broken clouds. The angled beams of light that stretched down like heavenly fingers swayed from an oblique angle to a near vertical pitch before slowly cutting in the opposite direction. Noon had passed, and gray clouds, bright beams of light and hazy bluish sea was all Jack could see. Talk was scarce among the survivors. Even Bowline Bob remained eerily silent in the hours following Jack's approximation of noon. The party was beleaguered beyond idle chatter, even to the point of neglecting their duty of fellowship to the ailing. It concerned Jack, on both counts of his friend Matsumoko and Captain Sifton. Given what little strength he had left, he assumed that they were depleted entirely.

"You saved us from the sinking Saber, mon ami. But, I am afraid, it is as they say, out of the frying pan, into the fire. You know this expression?" the Frenchman who had acted as translator said.

Jack bit his lip for a moment. He scanned the horizon and found nothing that gave him an inkling of hope. "We aren't finished yet. Not while we are still breathing, Frenchman."

The translator shook his head with an exasperated look on his face. "A colonist you are. You live up to the stubborn reputation, monsieur. Massachusetts, no?"

Jack offered a nod. "Boston, to be exact."

"Ah, Boston. The shipyard there is said to be one of the finest in the world, yes?" the translator continued. "I have heard much of Boston, from a dear friend of mine who went in search of work as a whaler. There are many whaling ships that make port there. Unfortunate to say, my friend, he was not successful. But, he found himself passage to France's possessions in the Caribbean. Part of the reason I signed onto the Saber were his stories of the beauty of the Caribbean. The sea, and the women, eh?" He paused for a long moment and studied Jack through narrowed eyes. "I did not mean to offer you insult. It was brave of you, to free us. A very honorable thing you did." He motioned to his chest with a flattened palm. "My name is Pierre, Pierre Dumont."

Jack closed his eyes for a long moment while a beaming column of sunshine broke through the clouds and passed over them. Its heat felt good, but it was a small comfort against their predicament. "My name is Jack Horner, and it is an honor to have met you."

"The honor, is mine, Mr. Horner," Pierre replied. "I should be in entirely different circumstances had we not."

Praise always made Jack slightly uncomfortable. But, given the extraordinary circumstances, it aggrieved him a little less than it normally would have.

"We may still sight land, Pierre," Jack said with another hard glance at the horizon. "We aren't finished yet."

Pierre rubbed a hand over his face and shook his head with a sorrowful look at the water immediately surrounding them. "Like I said, mon ami, you are stubborn as a mule. But, for all of our sakes, I hope you are right."

Every movement was torture. Their fate balanced on a precipice surrounded by the lurking shadows of horrid possibilities. To drown, or to die of thirst? Face a shark attack, or slip off the spar and let the waves take them? The columns of sunlight shifted to a slanted angle as the afternoon wore on into evening. Jack studied his fellow survivors and drew a grim conclusion. If they did not find some means of rest and replenishment, there would be fewer souls precariously balancing themselves aboard the floating spar when dawn found them. He looked at Matsumoko. His skin was pale. He could barely keep himself upright. Jack prayed that he would see out the night. Captain Sifton was in much worse shape. He had long given up on sitting upright and had succumbed to laying along the length of the spar while he straddled the wooden beam with his legs. When a wave washed pup over the top of them, the captain just maintained his half prone position and let the waves cover his face for an instant. If the sea became rough again, Jack feared the captain would be unable to maintain himself and would be washed away like debris. Still, more hours slipped by and the sun dipped ever lower into its final retreat to the west. Jack's heart beat harder as the multitude of grisly fates became ever closer. A sense of panic traced in his blood. They needed to do something, anything, to grab hold of their circumstance and bend it back into their favor. He reached forward and drew back a long sweeping stroke of seawater with one hand. Then, with the other he repeated the movement.

"What're ye doin' Jacky? There be nothin' but sea and skyline," Bob rasped though a parched throat.

"I'm doing something, Bob. We can't just float along to our death," Jack said in between his swim strokes. "Maybe we alter our course, or maybe not. But, I won't just sit here and let this unfold around us without having my say."

Bob winced his face into a deep frown as if he were trying to determine if Jack had gone mad or not. Then, with a slight shrug of his shoulders, he leaned forward and began paddling in the same manner as Jack. It was not long before Pierre joined their effort.

"Paddling to my doom, with the one eyed man from Boston," Pierre snorted with laughter at his own remark.

Jack shriveled his nose and looked toward Pierre. "I still have the eye, Frenchman. Its the vision that I lost. A gift from your captain."

They paddled on in awkward silence while the sun continued to drop westward. One by one, the remaining survivors began to paddle with Jack, Bob and Pierre. When all were joined to the effort, Jack was pleased to note that it seemed they were actually making some sort of headway. There was no point of reference, but the feeling of moving forward kept began to lift his spirit. It wasn't long after that he looked over one shoulder and took in a quick glimpse of the setting sun. The bottom edge of the fiery orb seemed to dance on the watery horizon. Soon, its warmth and light would disappear from the world and again plunge the band of survivors into the thrall of cold and darkness. The thought brought a chill into his spine until he heard Bob's crackled voice.

"Jacky! What's that there? On the horizon, off'n toward the south just a bit. Say three points off'n our bow, er, the end 'o the spar. See it?" he asked.

Jack sat high on the spar and stopped paddling for an extended pause. He narrowed his good eye and scoured the horizon where Bob had pointed. Along the edge of horizon, a sliver of darkness had appeared. He couldn't quite determine what he was looking at. Was it another storm front poised to move in from the east? His vision fixed and finally focused on the low-lying strip of shadow. Then all at once, it hit him.

"Land!" Jack exclaimed. He extended one arm to point out the sighting for the rest of the survivors to take note.

For an instant, the party came alive with excitement. Pierre muttered a string of wild sounding French while his fellow Frenchman shouted excitedly.

"We haven't much daylight left," Bob said. "Better'n we start 'a paddling fer it now, er risk losing it in the dark!" He turned to both ends of the spar. "The current is with us fer now, so we have a chance!"

With a renewed vigor, the beleaguered men aboard the shattered remnant of spar paddled for their lives. It was a race against the sunset. Collectively, they clawed at the sea as the fiery orb began its steady descent below the horizon. Hues of orange and violet striated the western sky. A sight that would normally give Jack great satisfaction and peace had become a torment. To a man, they were racing against the sunset with everything they could summon. Jack shot a look over his shoulder in between frenzied paddle strokes. He knew in his heart that they would not make it before the daylight failed.

"Bob," Jack called as they paddled.

"What ye need, lad?" Bob answered over the din of sloshing seawater.

"We won't make it, Bob," Jack said.

The crew continued paddling, and Jack shot another look over his shoulder. A quarter of the sun's mass had already slipped below the horizon. He gave a quick look ahead. The dark sliver of land seemed a little larger than it had at first, but their progress was too slow. There was no way they would beat the sunset.

"Makes no matter, lad," Bob crowed in between heaving strokes. "If we can keep our course, we will make our destination." He paused in between a set of heaving breaths. "I'm disappointed, Jacky. Haven't ye been listening ter all me old sea yarns? We don't need the sun ter know our course, just the stars!"

Jack paddled again with his right hand and then his left as the realization hit him.

How had he not thought of it? Bob was right. Since he had come aboard the Salem Tide and met Bob, the old sailor had regaled him with tales involving wizened old seafarers who had saved the day with their knowledge of the heavens. He pressed on, eager to take in the age old skill of his friend.

The feel of solid ground beneath his feet brought a wave of relief flooding into Jack's spirit. It had taken all the evening and most of the night, but the band of weary sailors had paddled themselves onto the small island Bob had spotted. Under a scrawling blanket of stars, the sailors collectively staggered ashore, many of them collapsed from extreme exhaustion within steps of the rolling wash of the tide. For hours, all of them laid up in the sand with little strength left to do anything but breathe. Jack stared up into the heavens, thankful for the presence of the island and more than a little shocked that they had reached it. High overhead, the stars shimmered in their glory, a tapestry of brilliance laid out in a sea of never-ending blackness. Bob had picked out the North Star easily enough, later in the evening Orion and Taurus had appeared. Using the constellations, they had been able to keep a rough course until the portion of spar that bore their weight had finally become lodged in the sandy shallows that surrounded their little island. Bob's warning still hung in his mind, their struggles were only just beginning. But, they had survived. Jack knew the perils that lay ahead. Water, food, a means to escape the island and find their way back to civilization, it seemed like an insurmountable wave that threatened to crash over him and wash him back out to sea. But, as he stared up into the heavens, he found a steady peace within himself. He had survived so much already, he knew could press on.

Thank you for reading this installment of

The Patriot Sailor

Be on the lookout for the next titles in the series.

A Leeward Shore

Find my other book series, sign up for newsletter announcements including special releases and giveaways.
Just scan the QR code below.

Follow along on Facebook and Instagram for cover reveals and special announcements.

If you enjoyed this title, please be sure to leave a review on Amazon or Goodreads.

More Nautical Adventures By Cal Clement:

The Patriot Sailor Series

A Bloody Beginning

At the Mast

A Leeward Shore

Treachery & Triumph series

H.M.S Valor

Revenge of the Drowned Maiden

Resurrecting the Maiden

Under the Black Flag

Made in the USA
Las Vegas, NV
06 October 2025